The Ruby Helmet

Michael Paul Howard

ACKNOWLEDGEMENTS

I give thanks to God for giving me the creative ability and opportunity to write and illustrate this book. I would also like to thank my father, Jerry Howard for instilling in me at a young age a love for reading; Wil Sadler for his assistance and guidance; and to my beloved wide Cindy for her infinite patience and support.

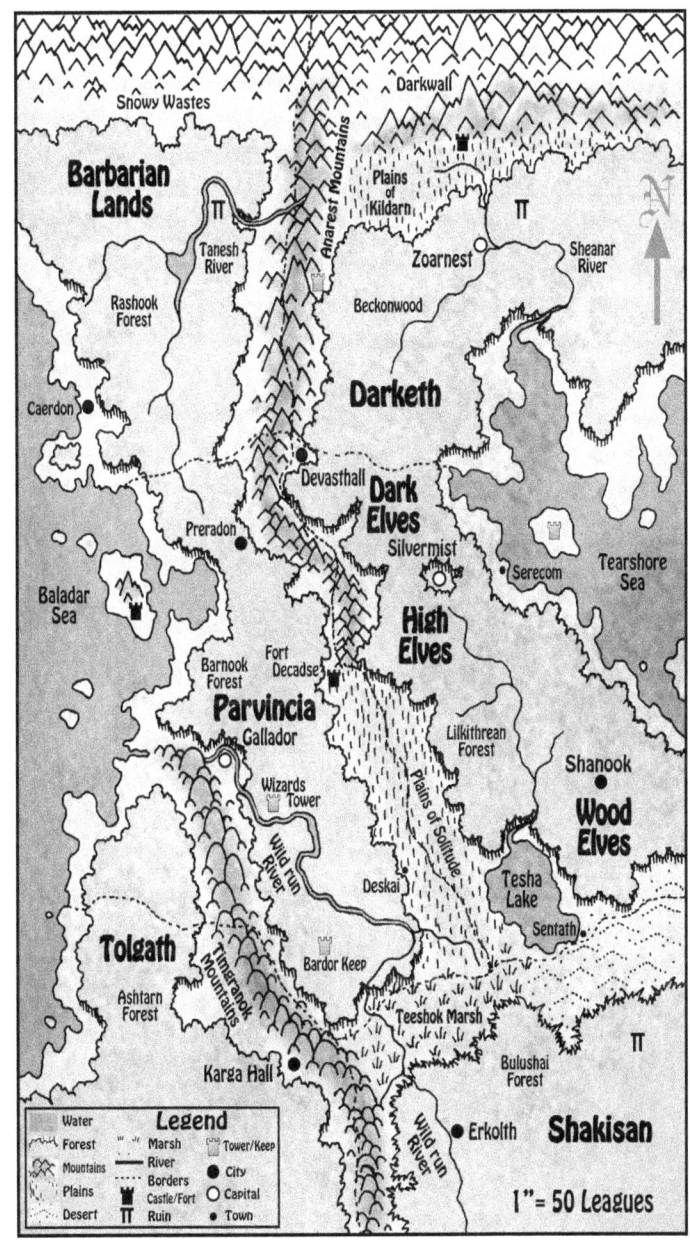

PREFACE

Jair just knew he would be in trouble when he returned to the keep. Kentar would beat him within an inch of his life if he didn't have all of the ingredients that were needed for his latest potion. A concoction Jair knew would end in disaster.

Most of Kentar's magical creations ended that way. They usually exploded, did nothing at all, or produced a bad side effect. That is exactly what had happened with Kentar's last experiment.

Kentar had recently been working on a spell that was supposed to enable goats to grow wool like sheep. He fed his goats a magically brewed grain mixture he had created in his laboratory. The goats ended up hairless, their skin turned purple; and, instead of milk, they produced vinegar. This incident caused them both to do without fresh milk for almost two months, which was how long it took for the spell to wear off.

Besides that, Jair had not finished fixing the roof after Kentar's magical fire starter spell backfired and blew half the roof off. The spell destroyed part of Kentar's laboratory and scorched Jair's hair; and his eyebrows were just now growing back.

All in all, Jair considered Bardor Keep a good place to live when he compare it to the alternatives; which were slavery in the south; or being a bond-servant to Teal the swine herd back in town. He did not care to consider either of those options.

Teal was one of the vilest men in all of Parvincia. The rumor was that small children often disappeared from surrounding farms that were too close to his property. Jair had heard that the missing children were used as food for the swine, and sometimes for Teal himself.

As an orphaned child Jair had been apprehended on the streets of Gallador. Teal was one of the people who had bid on him at auction. Kentar hated Teal. Kentar had easily won the bidding since he had known the auctioneer who owed him a favor. That was when Jair began his servitude, which would bond him to Kentar for the next fifteen years.

Other than his life at the keep, Jair barely remembered growing up on the streets of Gallador. He vaguely remembered stealing, begging and doing whatever he could just to stay alive. Gallador was one of the richest cities in the kingdom of Parvincia, but still had it's share of poverty. The city had everything, including a Merchants Guild. They practically ran all of the commerce this side of the Wild Run River. The city also housed the greatest seat of power in the West, King Ralkath's Diamond Throne. The humans there still had a strong dislike for elves because of the border wars. Since Jair was a half-elf, life had been extremely difficult for him.

As he made his way back to the keep, Jair thought about his past. He did not remember much about his parents, just that his mother was a human from a small family living on the frontier, and his father was an elf. His family had lost everything they owned in a skirmish during the border wars between the humans and elves. That was when his father had disappeared, defending them against a raid on their land. Their home had been destroyed and everything else stolen. No one really knew for sure what had happened to his father. They had assumed he had been killed, but his body was never recovered.

When Jair had been captured in the city, all he had been allowed to keep was a small medallion given to him by his mother. He felt for it beneath his tunic as he walked. He believed it had originally belonged to his father. The medallion looked like a family crest of some kind. It was small, about the size of a walnut; and its outer edges were carved into the likeness of a golden sun with a silver oak tree sprouting in its center. Dangling from a branch at the center of the tree was a small ruby gem on a silver chain. It was not an overly handsome gem, but it had a special glint all its own.

Jair was still amazed that none of the guards had taken it from him. They searched him thoroughly, but took no notice of the medallion. They did not even look at it, passing over it as if it wasn't there. At that time, Jair thought that a silver and gold medallion with a ruby in its center was worth something, but no one ever paid any attention to it. Even Kentar never questioned him about it. Just the same, he kept it hidden.

Jair looked about as he walked through the woods, enjoying the warm afternoon sun on his face. Winter was coming and the warmth would not last long. He thought about the place that had been his home for the last fifteen years. Bardor Keep was a small tower just on the outskirts of Gallador.

It had a two-story tower in which Kentar, a supposed sorcerer, conducted most of his bizarre, ineffective experiments. It had a small main hall that also functioned as the kitchen; and it was there that Jair slept.

Jair's job at the keep was to do all of the cooking, cleaning, general menial tasks, and go out to find whatever disgusting ingredients Kentar needed for his stupid experiments. Jair always had to find things like toadstools, dead animal parts, funguses, and many other things, some too vile to think about. He hated living there.

In return for the work he did, he was allowed his life, food to eat, and a place to sleep, however bug infested and stench filled that it was. Kentar was supposed to teach him a trade so that he would be of some service to the community. So far, all he had taught Jair was how to forage in the woods for things most people would never need; and how to duck and dodge randomly thrown objects, kicks and slaps.

Of course whenever Jair did not move fast enough, or bring back the correct ingredient, he received a strong backhand across the side of his head. Sometimes, for really small errors or when Kentar was in a particularly bad mood, Jair received a good beating at the end of Kentar's heavy oak staff.

As Jair worked his way homeward, he limped a little from the beating Kentar had given him the day before. Every time he took a step and felt pain he thought about Kentar and his resentment toward him grew. Kentar was a weakly skilled magician held in contempt by the rest of the magical community. He was always trying to come up with some new spell or strange gimmick to make a quick gold piece or two. That or he tried to con people out of their money and belongings.

Kentar had learned most of what he knew about magic from a retired old wizard that once lived in the mountains close to Bardor. It was rumored that the old wizard had been a great and honorable member of the Red Robes in the Wizard's Guild in Gallador. Jair thought the old wizard had only taught Kentar because he felt sorry for him and knew he would not be able to do much with his magic.

Kentar had occasionally picked up a few small tricks from the old wizard, but he never learned anything of great value. When the old wizard finally passed away, Kentar stole several of his books of magic before the Wizard's Guild could come to claim them for their libraries. Those books were mainly small spells and cantrips, but they did have a few minor words of power, such as was used in creating change spells or controlling the weather.

Kentar had not quite figured out how to use those words yet, even after having studied them for over twenty years. Jair figured he never would learn them. Kentar just wasn't smart enough to figure them out. Even if he did, something would probably go wrong; and he would end up blowing himself into a million pieces, which would suit Jair just fine.

The smell of putrid burnt chemicals eventually interrupted his reverie. It had reached him long before he came upon the walkway that led up to the pile of small broken stones that were stacked in front of the door of the keep. The door to the keep was battered and charred, barely hanging on to its old rusted brass colored hinges. It looked as if it would fall off at any moment.

The walls of the keep itself were heavily corroded and covered with slime from untold ages of neglect. Nothing seemed to be quite right about the place; in fact, everything seemed wrong about it. Most of the clutter came from Kentar's experimental failures and strange collection of whatnots.

Jair had once heard that the keep was supposed to have been the home of a good knight who had built it for his lady. They were to be married and live out their lives making a happy home near the forest, bearing many children. The woman had run off with a rich merchant's son seeking wealth and quick romance instead of a steady home and honest man.

She left the poor heartbroken knight to dwell alone in the now empty hall. No one really knew what finally happened to the old knight, just that one day he was gone. Kentar moved into the keep sometime after that and had remained there ever since.

It was no wonder the place emanated a sad and lonely air, Jair had thought. That was probably why Kentar had taken it as his home long ago. Kentar was a cruel and twisted person who enjoyed the suffering and misery of others. However, Jair knew he was a coward at heart. He had seen Kentar cower before the Royal City Guards as well as several other people whom he feared.

No one from the surrounding area seemed to like Kentar. He was a short but strong man. He was bent and crooked as if a mule had just reared back and kicked him in his middle for doing something that had offended it.

His face was long and gaunt, with very bony features. He had a large nose that was slender and pointed like a carrot, with small dark thick hairs protruding from it like many small roots. He had a thin, cruel mouth, which remained twisted into an angry snarl most of the time. The only time Jair saw him smile was when he was laughing at someone else's misery, especially Jair's.

Kentar's shoulders were broad and thick with long hairy arms that dangled by his side. His legs were very short and thin, which caused him to waddle when he walked, sort of like a small monkey that hadn't quite gotten the hang of standing upright, but managed it just the same.

There was no mistaking the fact though, Kentar could move surprisingly fast when he wanted to, and he was as strong as a bull. This was repeatedly proven to Jair and attested to by the many lumps and bruises he usually carried on his face and body all the time.

No one really knew where Kentar had come from. It was rumored that he'd come down from the North, out of the Darketh Kingdom. All he'd really brought with him was his cruel ways and hatred of just about everyone and everything. He also harbored hatred and jealousy of anyone he couldn't con or steal something from.

Jair hurried up the cracked, dark gray stone steps and entered through the old rotten door. He tried to look as if he'd been really working hard all morning and had hurried home as fast as he could, to get Kentar his supplies as quickly as possible.

After entering the keep, Jair noticed that Kentar seemed to be in a surprisingly good mood. When he heard Kentar humming to himself, he knew his present potion was probably going as planned; and that this one just might turn out right for a change.

"Jair, is that you boy?" Kentar growled as Jair entered the keep.

"Yes sir." Jair responded quickly, with his head lowered and

6

his eyes to the floor.

"Did you find the ghant root, kile worms, and other ingredients that I need for my new spell?" Kentar asked him.

"Yes sir," Jair replied quickly once again.

"Good, then quit dallying around and bring them to me. I have need of them for the final part of my rain spell. If this goes well, I'll be able to sell this to the local farmers at a high price to pull them all out of this terrible drought we've been having. I should be able to make a tidy profit from all of these imbeciles who call themselves farmers around here," Kentar said, as he cackled lightly to himself.

Jair hurried over to Kentar and placed the contents of his old worn out satchel on the table before his master. He did this quickly so Kentar could inspect them and see if he had brought what was needed.

Kentar gingerly poked one knotted old finger around in the contents from the satchel then raised a hand as if to strike him. Pausing to see if he would get the desired effect of Jair cringing, he then lowered his hand.

Kentar enjoyed getting the expected response from Jair. He mumbled happily to himself since Jair had brought a good haul of ingredients, and he was pleased with himself at keeping Jair in line.

"Yes, yes, these will do very nicely. For once you have done well. As your reward you may clean the main hall, start a fire, and eat. I've left you some gruel and bread on the table. After you've done with that you may go to sleep. I have a great deal of work for you to do on the morrow, so I will need you rested."

Kentar motioned Jair away with a wave of his hand, so Jair quickly turned and left him mumbling to himself, pouring over the contents of the satchel.

The Ruby Helmet

Jair quickly moved over to the table in the kitchen to see what was left for him to eat. Of course, it was a cold, disgusting looking bowl of Kentar's homemade gruel. There was also a stale loaf of bread with a burnt end; but it was better than nothing, so Jair ate it hungrily. He had not eaten since he had left early that morning.

After gulping down the food, he began his work around the main hall. This consisted of picking up all of the junk Kentar had thrown around while looking for things he needed for his spell, sweeping, and doing basic chores.

Several hours later Jair finished up with his work and climbed over a pile of Kentar's junk to reach a shelf on the east wall of the keep. He went there to obtain a magical fire starter stick. The fire starter was one of the few gadgets that Kentar had made that actually worked. Of course, once he made it, he could never make another one and eventually stopped trying. However, this one did work, and worked quite well.

The fire starter was a long cylindrical metal tube that was hollow on one end and looked as if it was made of some type of polished dwarven metal. Jair had no idea where Kentar acquired such a rare, precious metal.

It had a small bone handle which fit snugly in the palm of your hand; and just where your thumb came to rest on the handle was a small shiny silver button. When the button was pressed, the object gave out a small spark that magically lit a small flame at the end of the tube. The size and length of the flame could be adjusted by turning the button to the left, or right, increasing or decreasing the flame's size as needed.

Jair took the fire starter and went over to the fireplace. He felt the evening chill coming on; and he knew a fire's warmth would be welcome. He placed several logs in the fireplace, then used the fire starter to light several small pieces of kindling which he then placed under the logs. After a few minutes the logs took the flame and began to burn brightly.

Night was just falling and at this time of the year, Jair knew it wouldn't take long for it to become cold. The days were still fairly warm after the sun came up, but at night the cold came on quickly. He knew this was just a prelude to the coming winter.

Jair turned back to check the fire and saw that the logs were stacked adequately and the fire was giving off a nice, warm glow. Finishing that, he moved over to his sleeping pallet, pulled off his old worn out boots, and laid down to get some rest.

After a short time, Jair could not sleep so he rose up into a sitting position with his back against the wall. Lighting a small candle, he looked about to make sure that Kentar was not nearby or about to come his way. Kentar was probably too busy working in his laboratory to bother with Jair anyway, which was all right as far as Jair was concerned.

Jair reached over to the wall beside his pallet and quietly worked out a loose stone in the wall. He looked inside to check on his few meager possessions.

The first item inside was a small dagger of fine craftsmanship. It was engraved with many tiny runes and sculpted with little figures. Jair had found the dagger out in the woods one day while searching for some of Kentar's gruesome ingredients. It had been lying next to a human skeleton. Once tested, Jair found that the dagger was extremely light but strong, and could easily cut through most materials such as leather, wood, and even some metals.

There was no doubt in Jair's mind that the dagger was in some way enchanted. If Kentar ever found out he had it, he would beat Jair severely and take it from him. So, Jair kept the dagger hidden, using it only occasionally when he knew Kentar was not around. He usually took it with him when he went on long excursions into the forest.

9

The Ruby Helmet

The second item in the little nook was the medallion that his mother had given him.

The third item was a spell book. It was a small wizard's notebook, which Jair had retrieved several years ago from the old wizard's home up in the mountains.

Jair had followed Kentar into the mountains one day during one of his visits to the old wizard's cave. Upon reaching the old one's home, Kentar had found that he was dead, so he immediately searched the place for whatever he could find. Kentar grew angry when he discovered the old wizard's most powerful items were protected by a powerful spell. Only a high-level wizard could retrieve them. Kentar did find the two books that he now possessed. Jair was glad he did not get his hands on the other books. They could have made him a very dangerous man.

On that day, after Kentar left the cave, Jair went inside to have a look around. The place became increasingly gloomy as the sun went down, but by the light of the small candle Jair had brought with him, he closely examined the room. It was a large cavern carved from solid rock, probably by magic.

To the rear of the chamber was a small partition of tapestry with a scene on it of great battles with monsters and heroes. The partition enclosed the old wizard's sleeping chamber, in which he now lay in an everlasting slumber.

Jair slowly walked up to the old wizard. He looked at him and felt a chill of awe spread across him. The chill was from the look of sadness on the great wizard's face. Jair also thought he saw peace on him, as if a long, hard wait was finally over. The old wizard seemed somehow familiar to Jair, but he could not quite place from where. He guessed that he had probably seen him in the city sometime.

Even in death, the old wizard had a great presence and majesty about him that would not die. Jair gently looked his body over and eventually noticed a small book lying just within the folds of one sleeve of the wizard's frayed robes. He reached over and slowly removed the book, careful not to disturb the ancient figure.

Examining the book, Jair found it was of the finest crafted leather and inlaid with intricate designs. There was no doubt in Jair's mind this was the old wizard's personal notes and was quite possibly his personal spell book. He never thought to wonder why it wasn't protected by a strong spell.

With great excitement, Jair left the cave and headed for the keep. He hurried as fast as he could in order to arrive before Kentar got back. If Kentar found Jair missing, or coming in late, there would surely have been a beating in it for him.

Luckily, Jair made it back just before he arrived. Kentar came in gloating to himself as to how clever he thought himself to be, never letting on as to where he had been or what he had been doing.

Later that night, Jair skimmed over the pages of the old book. Eventually he slipped off into a deep, exhausted sleep, and dreamed of powerful magic and great warriors, intertwining with all of the fantastic stories he had heard as a child from his mother.

Over the next few years, Jair secretly read and studied the small notebook whenever he was able. He practiced his magic and grew more confident in his own abilities. Kentar had taught Jair how to read a few years earlier so he could aid him in his spell making. Jair quickly put this to good use by learning all that he could from the small spell book. However, there was one large section of the book that was written in a language he could not read. He hoped one day he could learn that language as well and unlock the secrets within it.

Jair had found early on that he enjoyed working with magic, even though it was difficult and elusive some of the time. The hardest part was keeping his studies hidden from Kentar. He was afraid to find out how Kentar might react if he discovered that Jair practiced magic on his own.

Within the small book, Jair found many minor spells and several major ones. He had just recently figured out a few of the minor ones and was eager to learn more. His learning was slow due to his heavy workload, and having to hide it from Kentar; but it did not deter him from pursuing it.

It didn't take long for Jair to decide he wanted to be a wizard himself someday. He wanted to be a wizard more powerful than Kentar ever dreamed of being. He also knew sooner or later it would be his time to leave and be on his own. The only problem was that Jair was sure Kentar would not allow him to leave; so he knew he would have to escape.

Obeying the law was never one of Kentar's strong points. With them both living on the outskirts of civilization, there really wasn't anyone who would disagree with him if he chose to keep Jair as a servant.

This was why Jair had made his plans a few months earlier to escape after his time was up. He was nearing the end of his fifteenth year of service, which was only a week away. When the time came, he planned on packing his few belongings and as much food as he could carry; then set off on his own, possibly for the elven nations to the East. He hoped to leave Kentar far behind, forever.

The biggest concern Jair had about escaping was he knew Kentar would come after him. In order to keep him from doing that, Jair was afraid he would have to kill him. All he really wanted was to do was escape with his life and his freedom.

Jair planned to use a sleeping spell from the book to put Kentar to sleep, so he could then slip away quietly. The sleep spell was one of the few spells in the book Jair had learned how to use properly. He had tested the spell on several animals, and also on a lone traveler he had stumbled across while foraging in the forest.

Jair knew he could hide his trail from Kentar. With all the time he had spent in the forest, he'd had a lot of practice hiding from predators. He knew how to track and move through the woods. Kentar's eyesight had also been deteriorating over the last few years so he could not see that well anymore. His age was finally starting to take a toll on him. Sometimes Jair wondered if he aged quicker because he was so mean.

After leaving the keep, Jair had decided he would head east toward the Lower Anar Forest, home of the Wood Elves. It was there he thought he might be accepted and make a place for himself. The borderlands were supposed to be more open to strangers and people of his kind. At least he hoped it was.

Jair wanted to also further his studies in magic and try to make something more of himself than just a lowly servant or street beggar. He'd always had the burning desire to do more than just survive or live a common life. He thought perhaps he had a purpose in life, and someday he was going to find out what it was. Until then, he was determined to carve a decent living out for himself.

Physically Jair was in good shape. He was tall and wiry, with just a few sprigs of beard growth on his face. This was a hint of his human lineage, and proved that he was finally growing up, however slowly.

His hair was a straw yellow and he had dark green eyes. His ears almost came to a point, but not quite. Over the years, Jair had been told that as he grew older he would probably be a little thicker or heavier than most Elves. Given all of the hard work Jair did for Kentar, this seemed to be true because he was fairly strong and tall.

Beside his work at the keep and secret magic studies, whenever possible, he practiced with his dagger and bow. Jair knew fully well that he would have to take care of himself in the future, so he trained diligently. A woodsman who lived nearby in the forest also occasionally taught him a few tricks of the knife and staff. This woodsman's name was Tagor Teel.

Tagor was a veteran mercenary of the Border Wars. He had grown up on the eastern frontier near Gallador. Evidently, it was here he had learned to fight at an early age. Tagor was not very old, for a human. He was probably in his early to mid forties. He had decided to retire from fighting several years ago after getting bored with all of the politics involved. Tagor told Jair he'd grown tired of the wars because of the constant loss of good friends, little pay and high risk involved.

Tagor lived in a small cabin just south of Bardor Keep, next to a small creek, which came down out of the Timgranok Mountains. Tagor made his living by trapping and cutting wood, then selling it to the local farmers. He also had a small outpost, selling basic supplies to other frontiersmen.

He claimed he enjoyed his work now better than when he was killing men on the battlefield. However, Jair always got the impression he really did miss part of the military life. You could tell by the strange look in Tagor's eyes when he talked about it; it was a look of longing for past glory and combat with old comrades on the battlefield.

Jair visited Tagor whenever Kentar would send him down to see him for supplies or firewood. When he was there, Tagor taught him some dagger fighting and sword work. Tagor claimed he never had a more apt or eager pupil. He also said Jair would make a fine warrior some day.

While practicing fighting on his own, Jair lightly danced in and out while feinting, ducking, dodging and slicing, and doing great damage to some imaginary foe. Besides the sword and dagger, Tagor also tried to teach him the use of the staff. Jair found he was quite adept at most forms of combat and was good with many weapons, but not the staff. He never could quite get the hang of it.

The main reason Jair felt Tagor helped him was because Tagor enjoyed his company. It was probably also because of his love of a good story. That's really why Jair thought Tagor let him come around. Tagor loved to tell his stories. Tagor was probably a little lonely too after having lived alone in the wilderness for so long.

Jair put his things away and finally fell asleep while reminiscing. He awoke early the next morning, as usual. Rising quickly, he immediately started in on his daily chores. Placing another couple of logs on the fire, Jair fanned it until some of the smaller limbs caught fire. This quickly warmed away the early morning chill in the cold dark hall. Throughout the following week, Kentar was especially hard on him. He worked Jair extra hard, keeping him very busy. He probably did this because he knew the end of Jair's service time was fast approaching.

By the end of the week, Jair had practically forgotten about it, but, while looking out a cracked windowpane of the keep, he remembered it with both great excitement and dread. Throughout the long, laborious week, Kentar had made no mention of it.

Beginning his chores, Kentar ignored him throughout the day except to hit him whenever he thought Jair was shirking his duties. Kentar also seemed to be in an extremely bad mood because his experiment failed last night.

Watching Kentar carefully throughout the rest of the day, Jair knew in his heart Kentar had no intention of letting him go. So, that evening he decided to put his plan in action.

In order not to raise Kentar's suspicions, Jair intentionally shirked a few of his duties so Kentar would not suspect anything. It cost him a beating.

That night, after Kentar had gone to sleep, Jair quietly packed all of his belongings into the old satchel Kentar had given him. He dressed, collected his spell book and the spell components he thought he would need, and then eased quietly into Kentar's room.

Jair could hear the deep, raspy snores coming from Kentar's pallet. He gently eased toward the terrible sound until he thought he was close enough to cast his spell.

Jair's hands shook with fear as he kneeled upon the cold stone floor of the room. He opened his spell book and laid all of the spell components carefully on the floor before him. Whispering quietly, but not so quiet as to keep the spell from working, he commenced the incantation.

Halfway through the spell, Kentar moaned loudly and turned over on his pallet. Jair held his breath in fear, but Kentar did not waken. He slowly lifted the final spell component, which was a small bag of fine sand, then uttered the final words to the spell while sprinkling the sand upon the floor next to Kentar's bed.

There was a faint whisper of wind and a release of magical energy as the spell was cast. Jair knew he had been successful and his spell had worked.

Jair gathered up his belongings and eased out of the keep. He knew he would have at least half a day's start before Kentar would wake from the spell. Kentar would rise and realize what had been done to him, and probably go into one of his wild fits of rage. Even Kentar's magic would not be able to pick up Jair's trail.

Jair set off quickly. He decided he would first journey southward to visit his old friend Tagor and say a final farewell. Then he planned to move on towards the east and his final destination, the Kingdom of the wood elves.

Chapter 1

The day broke early upon the eastern horizon in a fantastic array of brilliant golds and reds. It was promising to be a great day; and Jair always enjoyed traveling through the forest alone. Searching and exploring as he traveled, there was always something new and fascinating to learn or see in the wild. Jair had always felt a kindred spirit with the woodlands and the creatures therein.

Right after he first came to live with Kentar, Jair found he could easily charm many of the small woodland animals into playing with him. Some would even take breadcrumbs from the palm of his hand.

Once he even befriended a small white hawk he'd named Keerock. The hawk stayed up in the rafters of Bardor Keep, catching mice and other pests and hiding whenever Kentar was nearby. Keerock stayed with Jair whenever Kentar wasn't home.

This friendship went along quite well for some time until one day Kentar discovered the small white hawk up in the rafters. He viciously and brutally ran Keerock off by throwing bottles and rocks at him and by waving his staff wildly. Kentar also threatened to cook the hawk for his midday meal if it ever came back. Jair hoped Keerock was doing well. He wondered if he would ever see him again.

As Jair walked through the forest and by the time mid-morning rolled around, he estimated he'd traveled about ten leagues through the Barnook Forest. He passed many small streams and enjoyed the beauty of the forest and the cool morning air. He thought he could travel quite a ways before Kentar would wake and then try to follow him.

The thought of Kentar awakening and finding him gone, frothing with anger and then coming after him sent a shiver down his spine. However, since the choice was either staying there in slavery or striking out on his own, he chose to be on his own. He would be a free man trying to carve a place for himself in the world without anyone telling him what to do or when to do it. He should have probably left years ago, but the law would have been with Kentar then.

As Jair traveled, he thought about the journey ahead of him. He knew there was many dangers involved when traveling in the forest alone; but he also knew how to avoid most of them. Having grown up in and around the forest, he knew what to look for. He had also acquired a small hunting bow graciously donated to him unknowingly by Kentar. It was the same bow he had used when hunting for their supper.

Continuing on throughout the morning, he stopped briefly once next to a small stream to take a short break and have a bite to eat from his meager rations. His meal consisted of some old bread and dried meat taken from Kentar's provisions. It was better than nothing; and he was sure he could kill some wild game before evening rolled around. He'd worry about that later. For now, he had to be on his way and try to put as much distance as possible between him and Kentar.

Jair set off as soon as he finished his meal. The day and the leagues passed by quickly. He figured that around an hour before sunset he would stop and find a place to make camp for the night. Then he would try to hunt for something to eat. Hopefully, if his luck held, he would make it to his usual camping place not far from Tagor's cabin. That way he would be at Tagor's before late the next morning.

Between Bardor Keep and Tagor's cabin, Jair knew the trails fairly well. So far, he had never met up with any serious trouble. There were natural hazards such as storms, fierce wild animals; and of course, the chance of running into one of the more intelligent and dangerous denizens of the forest such as brownies, dryads, ogres, bandits or trolls.

You could never be too careful these days, especially with all of the rumors of unrest and strange happenings coming down out of the Anarest Mountains. People have sometimes disappeared without a trace. Others would show up horribly maimed and disfigured or completely mad. They would reappear with no recollection of who they were or where they had been, mumbling about the grisly horrors they had seen.

It was rumored that there was dark elf activity up in that part of the world that had significantly increased in the last year or so. There had been many border raids on the upper Lilkithrean forest. Lives had been lost and there had been a lot of looting in small provinces that belonged to the high elves. This caused great distress among the high elves that did not like war. The high elves sought only peace and the study of magic and science.

Somewhat contradictory to their beliefs, the high elves were highly respected as being some of the best warriors in all of the kingdoms. The elves were fabled to be especially good archers and trained their people in the ways of war to protect themselves from their enemies.

The high elves also depended heavily upon their highly developed mastery of magic. They used it to defeat any foe determined enough to attack them. They developed their magic over many generations of study and practice. It dated back for more centuries than anyone could remember. Evidently, they had some of the greatest magic users with the most extensive libraries in the world.

The only major source of magic that could come close to matching the high elves was the Wizards Guild in Gallador. The guild was a combined effort between all of the most powerful magic users from all of the most civilized countries. The Guild had set up three sects in their organization that made up the rules that were used to regulate the use of magic in the known human world. If there were no rules, then there would be many renegade magic users that could run around causing lots of trouble.

From what Kentar had told Jair, in the Guild, one high level wizard is picked from each of the sects, those being good, neutral, and evil. These three wizards oversee the entire Council. The council governed all of the major magic in the area, except clerical magic. The council also makes sure no rogue magic users or unwarranted use of magic took place. The Guild was set up so all magic that was practiced, would be practiced in the right way. This Jair also knew, was set up so no great catastrophe ended up destroying a major city or even the entire world.

The Wizards' Guild was also set up as a major source of study and development for young, untrained mages that wished to become full wizards. At the Guild, they worked on developing new spells and magical devices by doing controlled experiments in their laboratories. It was the sort of work Jair would love to do.

Continuing to walk on briskly for the rest of the day, all the while wandering in his own thoughts, Jair eventually grew tired and decided it was about time to start hunting for some supper. It was only a short distance to where his regular campsite was; and he figured if he could make a small kill on the way to the camp, then he could have his supper when he got there.

Jair stepped off of the trail and started looking for wild game, preferably a small rabbit or squirrel. About twenty minutes after entering the woods he spotted a small hare grazing contentedly in a little clearing not too far from the place he intended to use as his camp. Creeping silently up on the unsuspecting animal, Jair worked his way toward it. Once within range he easily brought his bow into line, sighted down the long wooden shaft, then released the arrow in a single fluid motion. The arrow's course was straight and true to the mark, pinning the rabbit to a nearby tree. Jair quickly ran over and retrieved his prize. He then worked his way to the clearing, which was his usual campsite when traveling to Tagor's place.

Upon reaching the site, Jair noticed someone else had recently passed through there. Many tracks were scattered all about as if a large number of people had passed that way. The type of print that he found was hard to make out because so many had passed through; but they were mostly barefoot with only a few of them wearing shoes. The foot shapes were long and narrow. They were somewhat animal-like but still had a human quality to them. There were also small indentions in the earth at the tips of where their toes were, indicating they had claws.

While pondering over the mystery of who could have passed through, Jair set about cleaning the rabbit. After getting it ready, he built a small fire and then cooked the rabbit. Eating quickly, he washed in a nearby stream, then settled in for a much needed rest.

The night was calm and unusually quiet for out in the middle of the forest. A gentle, cool breeze flowed softly over Jair, causing bright flickering tongues of flame to wave back and forth softly in his fire. This caused an almost hypnotic effect on Jair.

Gradually, Jair's eyes grew heavier while he watched the flickering fire; and finally he nodded off into a deep comfortable sleep. The last few day's events and excitement finally caught up with him. Except for the soft soothing sound of nighttime insects and a few small animals moving about, there was nothing to disturb him.

Shortly after midnight, he was awakened by a sound in the nearby wood. It was the snapping of a twig by someone or something walking nearby. Not taking any chances, Jair rose quietly and slowly made his way over toward the far side of his camp, opposite from where the sound had come from.

Luckily, his fire had burnt down. This helped to hide his camp from anyone close by. The fire had only a few small glowing embers left and a small snake-like trickle of smoke wound its way up into the ebony sky.

The Ruby Helmet

The landscape was faintly lit by the occasional twinkle of distant stars and the glow of two magnificent full moons. The moons and stars peeked out occasionally through slowly moving clouds that had appeared sometime during the night.

Jair worked his way through the dense foliage on the far side of his camp. He moved slowly, careful to not make any sound that would alert whoever or whatever was moving about in the forest nearby. He stopped occasionally to listen and eventually thought he heard the sound of voices coming from up ahead, somewhere to the right of his camp.

Jair eased through the woods, continuing to move silently. He left only a whisper of the wind and an occasional leaf fluttering as he closed in on the speakers. All his years of living in and around the forest, and the lessons Tagor had given him were being put to good use.

He moved closer still and finally spotted a light. It was emanating from a large fire burning in another clearing just up ahead of him. Jair could hear the voices growing louder as he moved closer.

When he finally came to a spot he thought safe enough, Jair stopped and peered through the bushes at the edge of the clearing. Looking around, he saw a large area where a natural depression in the ground had been made from many years of rainwater flowing down off a nearby hill.

The depression made a huge clearing. It was perfectly suited for a large party that wanted to make a camp in an area that could not be easily seen from the nearby trails. Jair was surprised that he had never come across this particular clearing. He did not remember seeing it on any of his trips to Tagor's cabin. On this night, he was glad he had never had found it. Especially after seeing what was using it now.

In the clearing Jair spied on a large band of goblins. They had stopped to make camp in the clearing. He quickly counted fifteen of them, but wasn't sure there weren't more nearby. What they were doing this far south of their homeland, which was normally far to the north, was a complete mystery to Jair. He knew it boded ill for the inhabitants of the surrounding forest and in the nearby villages. A large band of goblins roaming about was definitely trouble.

Jair looked the ugly creatures over with a strange fascination. He had never seen a goblin before, but knew what they were after reading some of Kentar's books that included illustrations. Goblins were a malicious bunch of human-like creatures living mostly in the wilderness. They were shorter than the average human, and were usually thicker and more brawny. This bunch had an ugly brownish green cast to their rough, mottled hide. They sprouted long, dirty, brown-black hair that fell down their thick, knotted shoulders in a wiry unkempt mess.

Some of the ones closer to him had their hair pulled back and tied with greasy leather cords. This revealed more of their gruesome features. Jair was appalled and afraid. If they caught him, they would torture and kill him.

Their facial features were harsh and cruel. Small beady eyes looked out from under thick, knotted brows. They had low, wide foreheads. Poking out just slightly from their matted hair on the sides of their heads were large, pointed ears. This lent evidence to the theory that they were probably akin to gnomes and elves. All of which were considered demi-humans. Elves were considered the higher class, of course.

As Jair listened, he heard the group arguing amongst themselves. Evidently, they were arguing about which direction they should head in the morning. Most of the ones arguing were wearing animal hides, while some of the others wore pieces of old, worn out armor. Jair figured they probably picked the armor off of dead warriors. Several others wore simple cloth tunics.

The Ruby Helmet

The goblins sported a wide array of weapons. This included everything from small jagged short swords to brutal looking cudgels. Jair figured they were perfect for smashing the brains out of some unsuspecting victim. Goblins were notorious in stories for slipping up on defenseless people and killing them when they least expected it. They were also known for abducting people and holding them for ransom.

As Jair watched, there were two goblins that were arguing while the rest watched. The first goblin was taller than the others, and had a nice metal helmet. He wore an odd assortment of mixed pieces of plate mail armor, tied on with old leather rags. He also carried a decent long sword that looked as if it had seen a lot of use.

The goblin opposite him was shorter, but was much thicker through the shoulders. He wore only a few old animal hides and sported a large, wicked looking cudgel. It had several sharpened spikes sticking out of its end. Some of the spikes still had a few scraps of meat and hair stuck to them from his last victim.

The first goblin seemed to be the leader of the group and acted like he was more intelligent than the others. He seemed to be supported by close to half of the goblin band. The other goblin was backed by the other half. The second one was more brutal looking than the first. The goblins that were with him probably supported him more out of fear than any respect or loyalty.

Evidently, the second goblin did not like the idea of their party continuing on with some sort of mission. The first goblin was very eager to get on with it, so it would be over quickly and they could all go home.

Jair could only make out bits and pieces of their broken common tongue. He would have liked to of crept closer to find out more; but he feared leaving his hiding place and being discovered.

He continued to listen, and did make out that the second,

shorter goblin wanted to head for Tagor's cabin and do something to him. The brutish goblin evidently had a grudge against Tagor. Some time in their past they had run into one another and Tagor had gotten the better of him. The goblin kept pointing to a scar that ran across the left side of his face. It went from his forehead to his chin and just barely missed his eye.

During the conversation, many of the other goblins seemed to be in favor of this. They all wanted a break from their long march and from the task they had been sent to do.

Jair remembered something from reading one of Kethok's books about how goblins were notorious quarrelers, especially with one another. When they had gone too long without a fight or committing some heinous act, they usually turned upon one another.

Jair continued to listen and learned that the leader of the goblin band was named was Thuk. Thuk was quick to point out to the other goblin that their mission was more important than any one of their groups' personal revenge. He also pointed out that someone called Telenok would be angry with them if they kept another person named Deshtar, who was somewhere farther south, waiting for the package they were to deliver.

At the mention of Telenok's name, several of the other goblins drew back in fear. This lent weight to Thuk's argument. It also caused the second goblin to become angrier.

As they argued, Jair heard them say that the second goblin's name was Natog. Standing with fierce determination, he proclaimed that he would go no farther on their mission until his personal vendetta with Tagor was settled.

Seeing the determination on Natog's face, and knowing full well that half of his band was going to agree with him, Thuk gave in. Apparently, he hoped the band would be able to get it over with quickly and then continue on with their mission. Jair could tell that

Thuk hoped they would not make too much commotion to alert anyone in the surrounding area of their presence.

Thuk seemed to know that the band had gone a long while without any type of recreation, and this might just be the thing to quiet them down for a while. Keeping them in line without trying to kill one another was the hardest part of being a goblin leader.

Toward the end of the discussion Jair heard Thuk proclaim, "We go smash nasty woodsman, it be good sport then we go on with mission, Dark Lord not be kept waiting long."

After that, the talking ended and the goblin band settled in for the evening. Several of the other goblins sat and talked boldly of how great the sport would be on the morrow, slapping each other on the backs as they discussed about it. The rest went right to sleep, their snores reverberating across the valley.

Jair waited until they all appeared to go to sleep. He could easily hear the long, deep breaths and awful snores they made. By this time, he had already made up his mind as to what course of action to take. He planned on sneaking into the goblin camp, stealing whatever the package was the goblins were supposed to deliver, and then head straight for Tagor's cabin so he could warn him of the impending danger.

After he was sure they were asleep, Jair crept toward their leader. He did not know what it was the goblins were supposed to be delivering, but if it was important enough to be sent with a full squad, then it needed to be taken out of their hands and put into more responsible ones.

Cautiously, Jair worked his way over to where the goblin leader lay. The stench emanating from the band was almost too much for him to bear. He couldn't understand why these creatures didn't take a bath once in a while. He had heard that goblins were afraid of water. It had something to do with the fact they couldn't swim. Jair seemed to remember something about that they sank like rocks when they fell into deep water.

Forcing his concentration back onto the task at hand, Jair quickly determined which package to take. During the argument, some of the other goblins had looked apprehensively at a large satchel that Thuk was carrying after he set it on the ground. Apparently, they were not happy to have it around.

The satchel was sort of like the one Jair had taken from Kentar earlier that day, but this one was in slightly better condition. After slowly easing over to where the goblin leader slept, Jair quietly picked the satchel up. He quickly noticed its weight, and slowly moved away, trying desperately not to waken any of the sleeping goblins.

Jair stopped only once as he made it back to the forest's edge. One of the goblins had rolled over and mumbled in his sleep. He could not believe he had made it in and out of the goblin camp without getting caught. The one thing that had helped him the most was the goblin's snoring. It had covered up any sounds that he might have made during the trip. Quickly and quietly, he then slipped back into the forest, setting off toward his own camp.

At his camp he quickly gathered all of his belongings, kicked some dirt onto the dying fire, grabbed the rest of the cooked rabbit, and headed for Tagor's cabin. He ate while he walked, knowing he might not find time to do so later. The rabbit was cold, but tasted good. He'd not gotten meat very often while living with Kentar.

Kentar had kept most of the good meat for himself. Jair had only occasionally sampled a few scraps here and there as Kentar would allow. Or when he was in the woods scavenging for spell components, he ate what he caught.

Jair traveled through the dark and estimated there were only a few hours until dawn. He hoped by the time the goblins woke, he would be at Tagor's cabin and then both of them could be far away. He knew the goblins would be on their way as soon as the sun came up.

After traveling for the rest of the night, he came to a bend in the trail. He thought he saw smoke rising up into the early morning air. It appeared from just beyond the other side of a small hill. It was a familiar scene as he rounded the bend and looked upon the small crude cabin Tagor had built several years earlier. The cabin was made of oak timbers that had been deftly cut from the surrounding forest. They were cut precise and fitted together with an expert touch that could only have come from someone with many years of practice with an axe. The small cabin was extremely sturdy.

Mud had been mixed with straw; and then packed tightly between the logs forming the walls. The roof was made of wooden shingles, which were hand carved. Pitch was then used to seal a tarp and the shingles over the roof. This gave the roof an almost waterproof resistance that only occasionally leaked on really stormy nights.

Large, round flat stones were gathered and placed before the cabin to make a small walkway. This walkway led up to the large oak door. The door itself was made of thick wooden planks that had been worked by hand until they were very smooth. These planks were then nailed together on similar planks in the back that held them together.

The door hung on large iron hinges. The door was one of Tagor's favorite accomplishments. He made it extra sturdy to be sure no person or wild animal could easily get into his home. He even used a special lacquer to seal it, which he had picked up on one of his trips to Gallador. This sealer made the door waterproof and helped it to last longer.

The Ruby Helmet

Next to the cabin was a large, freshly cut pile of timber. This, of course, was Tagor's main means of earning a living. There was also a small shed to the right of the cabin, which he used as a storeroom for many of his tools, equipment and for the supplies he sold.

Jair quickly made his way up to the small, crude walkway and knocked heavily upon the large wooden door. After pausing for a few moments he knocked again, harder this time; but there was still no answer.

The sun had just risen in the eastern sky right before Jair arrived at the cabin. He had to assume Tagor had already left for his morning excursions. His having already gone could be bad for both of them. Tagor could return to find the band of goblins waiting for him.

He also knew from listening to Natog, that in no way would he let Tagor's death be an easy one. Natog fully intended to make him suffer for a long and horribly painful time.

Searching the area desperately, Jair looked for some clue as to what direction Tagor might have gone. He was just about to give up when he heard someone hail him from behind the cabin on the other side of the clearing.

He quickly saw it was Tagor, carrying a large deer slung across his broad shoulders. He had just killed it; and he was bringing it home to clean and dress.

Jair ran over to meet him as he headed toward the cabin. Tagor easily raised the dead carcass off his shoulders; and laid it gently upon the ground. Happily he extended his hand for a warm handshake and hearty greeting to his young friend he'd not seen for some time.

A warm, friendly smile spread across his Tagor's as he said, "Jair, it is good to see you lad. It's been a long while since the last time you paid me a visit."

Jair smiled at first, happy to see his friend, then quickly grew serious, a scared look replacing his smile.

"I've come to warn you. We have to leave quickly. There is a large band of rogue goblins headed this way; and they intend to murder you. There is one in particular named Natog that seems to really have it in for you. It was over something you did to him a long time ago." Jair told him.

Tagor stopped shaking hands with Jair and looked closely at the surrounding forest. As he scanned the forest, a grim expression came over his face.

"This group of goblins has come a long way for their trouble. It seems to me that a group of goblins this far south bodes ill not just for me but for the surrounding countryside as well." Tagor said.

Looking back at Jair, Tagor noticed the two full satchels he was carrying, so he asked him, "Something else has brought you down this way Jair. I can tell by your look that you've not come all this way just to warn me about goblins. Has something else happened?"

"I've run away from Kentar." Jair told him. "Yesterday was my freedom day, releasing me from his service, but Kentar had no intention of letting me go. I put a sleeping spell on him early yesterday morning and slipped out into the night. I was on my way to visit you first, when I came across the band of goblins camped out in the forest. I overheard their plans and hurried here ahead of them to warn you."

"Ahh, Jair, you are a true friend. I do not think I could have handled a whole band of the monsters by myself. I wonder what else they are doing in these parts? A group of goblins that large isn't just out on a holiday or out for personal revenge. No, there has to be some other motive driving them this far south." Tagor said in contemplation.

"There is!" Jair quickly exclaimed. "While overhearing their plans, I heard them talking about a mission they were on for a dark lord. They were supposed to deliver a package to someone named Deshtar down south, near Erkolth in Shakisan."

"What do you mean were supposed to deliver a package? What has kept them from continuing with their mission?" Tagor asked, eyeing him suspiciously.

"Well, I slipped into their camp this morning and took the package they were supposed to deliver. I thought it might be important or valuable, so I took it." Jair said sheepishly.

"That was foolhardy Jair, you could have gotten yourself killed." Tagor said roughly, pausing for a brief moment to frown at him, emphasizing his displeasure. Tagor's face then split into a mischievous grin. "Foolhardy though it was, a braver act I haven't witnessed in a long time, especially from one so young." He complimented Jair. "Of course, your not quite so young, being part elf and all," He added.

"It is interesting though, whatever it was they were carrying could have boded ill for the people hereabouts and throughout the southern kingdoms. These goblins must be stopped in any case and whatever it was that they were carrying needs to be placed into the right hands." Tagor said to Jair, as he eyed the satchel curiously.

"Bring out this satchel you've pilfered and let's have a look at it. We need to know what's so important to this Dark Lord that he'd send a whole pack of goblins into enemy territory to deliver it to a scoundrel like Deshtar." Tagor said. Jair could tell from what he said that he was familiar with the people mentioned; but he figured Tagor would fill him in later.

Jair lowered the old, worn satchel from his shoulder. He placed it on the ground then reached down and unfastened the small metal buckles that kept the top closed. He opened the flap and reached inside.

When he touched what was inside, a slight electric shock ran up his arm causing him to draw it back quickly. Jair shook off the jolt to his hand and glanced up at Tagor. He then reached back into the satchel.

When he touched the object a second time, Jair still felt a strange tingling sensation in his arm and hand, but it was not painful this time. Sensing the object in some way he could not explain, he felt along its surface. It felt cold and smooth to his touch, as if it were made of metal. That explained the weight Jair noticed while carrying the package.

Jair ran his fingers along its surface. His hand came to an edge that was small and curved. Grasping it, he slowly withdrew what was inside. He pulled the object out into the early morning sunlight and revealed a beautiful elven war helmet. Neither of them had ever seen anything like it. Of course, Jair hadn't seen very many helmets.

Gazing upon the piece of elven armor, the two companions knew right away that the helmet was most unusual. It was definitely not a common piece. It must have belonged to a great warrior or wealthy noble. Made of dwarven steel, the strongest metal known to mankind, the helmet shone brightly in the morning sunlight. They both felt what was almost a presence, or energy, that neither had ever sensed before.

The helmet was of average size, made to fit anyone of human or elf-like proportions. Delicately crafted with many intricate gold and silver designs, it had runes carved all over it and a gold border that framed the wearer's face. This gave it a regal and at the same time ominous appearance. There were two, large metal silvery wings that flowed off the sides of the helmet. Jair could tell they served not just as decorations, but also as a defensive devise that would help to deflect an opponent's weapon during combat.

Jair looked the helmet over and noticed that the most prominent feature was a large, red ruby that had been perfectly cut and shaped; and was embedded into the forehead. It was outlined in a ribbon of gold that set it off splendidly. It sparkled laughingly in the sunlight. The ruby seemed almost familiar to him, like he had seen it somewhere before.

Both men gazed in wonder at the beautiful artifact. There was no doubt in either of their minds that this was something of great importance. Jair looked at Tagor and thought they would definitely have to be very careful who found out they had it. He also knew they were going to have to be very careful with what they chose to do with it.

Chapter 2

Jair quickly placed the helmet back into the leather satchel and slung it over his shoulder again. This was not the time or place to sit and gawk at the artifact, and he said so to Tagor. They still had to deal with the situation at hand. The goblin band was probably getting close to them by now. Jair figured they should do something fast, or they would soon be in a lot of trouble.

The plan of action Tagor came up with was that they should gather some supplies and weapons, and then head for the city of Gallador. Tagor figured they could head west for a couple of leagues in order to avoid the goblin band, then turn north, crossing a small ford that Tagor knew about. The ford was at the Wildrun River.

Tagor figured by traveling this route they would end up close to the city. He hoped they could avoid any trouble. It was a long journey by foot; but they really had no other choice. Someone at the city should know what was going on; and Gallador was the best place to go for higher authority. It was there that something could be done about the goblins.

Once they made it to the city, they could seek an audience with King Ralkath and find out what to do with the helmet. Tagor figured they might learn what all of the activity in the Darketh Kingdom was about, why goblins were this far south, and what purpose the helmet might serve.

Both men went into Tagor's cabin and started putting together traveling packs. Tagor had everything they needed. He tried to keep plenty of supplies on hand since he did a lot of traveling. Besides all of the regular supplies he normally carried, he also chose a length of finely wrought, expensive silk rope. It was thin, but as strong as a steel cable. He also chose an extra cloak made from a strange black material, and a beautifully wrought oaken bow with a quiver of silver tipped arrows, neither of which had Jair seen before.

The Ruby Helmet

The bow was long, thick in the middle, and tapered off delicately at the ends where the string was wound around it many times before it was tied off. All along the sides and the face of the bow were elven markings. Jair knew this from some of his studies with Kentar. Exactly what the markings said, Jair had no idea, so he made a mental note to ask Tagor about them later.

Tagor also chose his regular long sword, a chain mail shirt, and a small round buckler. Since he was expecting trouble along the way, Jair decided to take along a wicked looking short sword and a suit of leather armor that was just a little bit too big for him. All these things Tagor had in his supply room. Over the years its contents had grown, along with quite a bit of other weapons and amour. He had picked most of them up on various campaigns.

After selecting the things he thought he'd need, Jair noticed the great bulk he had accumulated. So, instead of carrying both satchels, Jair emptied most of the contents of his old satchel into the one he had stolen from the goblins. He found that by turning the helmet over he could place most of his things inside the helmet. There were also several smaller pouches on the outside of this satchel. In these he placed his spell components.

While packing their gear, a troubling thought occurred to Jair. He wondered if the king would even agree to see them once they made it to the city. It was quite evident by looking at them that they did not appear to be any sort of nobility. It might be very difficult to get in to see the king. Besides that, Jair was not so sure he was eager to meet a king. He had never been around nobility and was afraid of how he might act. Or that he might say the wrong thing and make a fool of himself.

Jair finally decided to ask Tagor what they would do once they reached the city, and how they would get in to see the king.

"Tagor, what makes you so sure the king will agree to see us? We're not exactly royalty, and a mere woodsman and a half-elf might find it difficult to get in to see him. I'm sure he's very busy and he probably won't want to be disturbed by anyone like us. Why don't we take the helmet to Silvermist and find out what it is ourselves?" Jair asked him.

"I believe the king will be very interested to hear what we have to say. Not to mention the fact that we have the helmet. Besides, the king already knows me." Tagor told him. "I believe that he will agree to see us readily enough, but we'll just have to be careful going about it all the same."

"Well, I hope you're right Tagor." Jair replied doubtfully. His curiosity was piqued as to how Tagor knew the king. Hopefully Tagor would tell him more about it later.

"Once we are inside, what am I supposed to do? I've never met a king before. I don't know how to act, or even what to say," Jair asked him.

"It will be all right Jair. Don't worry about how you act or what you'll say. Just stay quiet; and I'll do most of the talking. If you're asked any questions just watch me. I'll let you know if you're to answer them; and if you do, be short and to the point. There's no need for us to tell anything that doesn't need to be told," Tagor responded.

"We'll have to be very careful, but I trust the king. He's a good man and worthy of his crown; but there are always ears that hear and eyes that see things that aren't supposed to be known, especially in a royal palace," Tagor said, with a grimace on his face.

Tagor gathered his gear and decided to add a small bundle of animal furs that he had trapped earlier for trading. He decided to take them to use as an excuse for them to be in the city. He took one last sad look around his cabin, knowing what the goblins were going to do to it. After that, the pair set off into the forest. Walking at a brisk pace, the two adventurers headed westward, trying to put as much distance between themselves and the band of irate goblins. The goblins were probably furious at having lost their precious package by this time. They had found Jair's trail sometime in the early morning light and then quickly set upon it like a pack of wild dogs eager for the hunt. Jair figured the more distance they could put between themselves and the goblin band; the better their chances would be of making it to the city.

• • •

Not long after Jair and Tagor entered the woods, the goblin band neared Tagor's cabin. Thuk had risen in a bad mood early that morning. Groggily he got up and stretched his long, muscular, hairy arms. Yawning viciously, showing off his sharp yellow teeth, he grumbled to himself as he stood. It had been a long time since he had been at home, fighting amongst his kinsman, raiding nearby settlements, and enjoying regular, brutal goblin life.

Thuk did not like this business of serving a main leader; but he did not have much to say about it. The Dark Lord was the most powerful being to ever bind the goblin nations together and Thuk was afraid of him. He was afraid of what he might do to those who did not serve him obediently. Goblins had always served the Dark Ones whenever they called, that was just the way it was.

Walking about, Thuk yelled and kicked his troops harshly, demanding that the lazy dogs rise and prepare to move out. His men arose stupidly, looking to eat first. They then began arguing amongst themselves. Keeping a pack of goblins in line took cunning, strength and a lot of plain old meanness, all of which Thuk had in abundance. He had become the leader of his tribe after the old leader had failed to watch his back one night during a village feast. It had happened right after a successful raid on a nearby human farm.

Thuk had waited until Jador, their old leader, was very drunk; and then he made his challenge in front of the entire tribe. The battle was short and brutal. Thuk had quickly darted in and caught

Jador with a wicked jab of his dagger just, below the jugular. Jador, being much too drunk, could not move fast enough to avoid the blow. It had all been over before it had really begun, which had been exactly what Thuk had wanted.

The other goblins had heartily congratulated him on a great victory. Most of them only congratulated him because they feared him. The only one who hadn't congratulated him had been Natog, who was the only real threat to him. Thuk knew he would have to watch Natog closely, because Natog would be after his neck very soon. Thuk also knew he would kill Natog whenever the right opportunity presented itself, hopefully sometime in the near future.

Thuk went over to his pack and bent down to get a morsel of dried meat and some water for breakfast. While closing his pack he noticed the satchel they were supposed to be delivering was missing from its resting place next to where he had lain down to rest for the night.

Howling in anger he immediately started storming through the camp demanding that whoever had stolen the satchel give it back or die by his hands.

A quick and thorough search of the camp revealed the package was missing. Upon closer inspection, one of Thuk's scouts found a set of small human-like tracks that lead off into the forest.

Frothing with anger, knocking heads together, and causing the smaller goblins to scuttle out of his way, Thuk immediately broke the camp up and then the gang moved out to try and catch whoever it was that had done this to them.

It was not only that he had so easily been robbed, but it was also the fact that there was a lot of fear, way down in the bottom of his cold gray heart. This fear was of the terrible consequences of losing one of the Dark Lord's prized possessions, and for failing to carry out his mission.

The Ruby Helmet

A while later the goblin band stumbled into the clearing in front of Tagor's home. The band immediately charged the front door of the cabin only to be buffeted from the hard, smooth wood. Thuk had them bring one of the large logs that were stacked next to Tagor's cabin. Using it as a battering ram, the goblins eventually smashed their way in through the door, twisting the lock as if it were paper. The goblins charged in with their weapons drawn. They sought only to do murder and mayhem. Once inside, they were dumbfounded and angered by the empty cabin. No one was there for the goblins to vent their rage upon.

Thuk's band was too late. Whoever had stolen their package had already been to Tagor's home and warned him. His scouts soon found their trail a little ways off from the cabin. One thing they did notice that whoever the thief was, he was now traveling with Tagor. Taking whatever useful items they could find, including the deer Tagor had slain, they smashed everything else and then headed west.

While they marched, Thuk seethed with anger and trembled with fear all at the same time. He had to retrieve the magic helmet, because if it fell into their enemies' hands and they discovered what the helmet was, it could mean a devastating blow to the Dark Lords' scheme of conquest. All of the Dark Lord's plans for surprise and the secret downfall of the other kingdoms would have been for naught.

• • •

Meanwhile, in another part of the forest, Jair and Tagor traveled on ahead of the goblins. They spent part of the first day heading west, trying to avoid Thuk's band that they knew would soon be on their trail.

They then headed north, hoping that they were going far enough out of the way so that they would not run into the goblins. They aimed for the Wildrun River, which they would then follow until they came to the ford Tagor had talked about. From there it would only be about another day or so of traveling until they came to Gallador.

The first day was rather uneventful and they made good time. They had an informative conversation as they walked through the forest. Sunlight filtered gently down between the leaves of the thick, tall trees of the Barnook forest. Jair filled Tagor in on what had happened to him since they had last seen one another, and on his way to Tagor's cabin after leaving Kentar. In return, Tagor told him of what he had been hearing, of the rumors of a Dark Lord in the north, someone named Telenok. He also had a few suspicions as to the nature of the helmet and where it might have come from.

As they walked, Tagor started telling Jair what he knew and had heard over the last few years, "It seems that this Telenok person is some sort of powerful evil wizard and is supposed to have found two ancient hidden artifacts."

"These artifacts were supposed to be very powerful magic items that were created by the first members of the Wizard's Guild, right after the first great holocaust," Tagor explained.

"One item was created by each of the three guilds in order to give none of them an advantage over the other. This was also to help prevent another unbridled release of foreign magic like in the holocaust. The top wizard of each of the three sects secretly created an artifact. Each artifact was immensely powerful, and of entirely different properties. The only thing that allowed all three artifacts to be used together in a time of great need was a powerful spell cast over the third item by the most powerful of the wizards. He was an elf who was the leader of the red robe guild," Tagor said.

"Of these artifacts, the first was a sword of wondrous crafting with a blade that had been made from a strange new metal. It was a long blade with a bluish tint, and it had been engraved with many runes and designs of magic. The hilt was in the form of a silvery dragon with wings extended out to form the crosspiece. A scaly hide ran down the handle forming the body, and its elegant tail spiraled around and around to make the pommel. In the center of the dragon's wings its head extended out toward the blade and it had a large diamond in its forehead."

"The sword was called Stalendar, which was a dwarven name that meant 'Life Seeker.' The high wizard of the white robes is the one that made Stalendar. He was a dwarf. Its magic is mostly unknown, but is fabled to dance in the wielders hands, giving its holder almost invincible abilities on the battlefield. It also supposedly lent the wielder's forces or allies great morale and aided them in their fighting," Tagor said.

"The second item was a staff of power; and its name was Kethelnard which meant 'Death Giver.' It was a long black staff made of an unidentifiable wood that was as black as pitch and had been smoothed down to a shine that reflected light like a black mirror. Upon its head was a small golden skull crafted so well that it looked like a real skull, only smaller. This skull had many magical runes of some old forgotten language written upon its smooth, shiny surface. Embedded in its forehead was a cold, black onyx stone that burned with an eerie fire when gazed upon.

"The high wizard of the black robes created this artifact, putting all of his skill and knowledge into it. He was supposed to have been a great evil human wizard that was widely feared among the people back then. This staff he created gave the owner great magic casting abilities, raising them up to the highest of magic user levels," Tagor continued.

"The third and final artifact was a great and beautiful silver helmet. Its name was Estolorn, which meant 'The Challenger.' Made of dwarven steel, the helmet was fabled to be a wonder to behold. It was supposedly crafted with many intricate designs of gold and silver and it had many runes carved into it, kind of like the helmet in your pack," Tagor said, while pointing toward Jair's satchel, "Flowing off of the sides of the helmet were two large silvery wings

42

and embedded into the forehead was a large ruby. This helmet had been made by a very old, and wizened elven wizard that had been the master of the red robes. He had sought a way to bring neutrality between the other two artifacts, and to bind them together. This helmet he had made was of the strongest magic. Crafted many years ago, this wizard had supposedly made the helmet underneath the elven city of Silvermist."

"When the wearer went forth with this helmet upon his brow, no sword could cut him and no spell could be weaved against him. The only drawback to this was that the wearer could not cast any spells either, but he could bear weapons. It was a way to cancel out the other two artifacts and keep them in check," Tagor said, with a serious look on his face.

"The wearer was supposed to be able to use the helmet to neutralize the other two artifacts and then channel their magical energy so it could be used against some outside foe or unknown force that was not born of the normal flow of magic. It sort of created a null zone of normal magic, but that doesn't take into account other powers and forces not known to most of us. I suppose it somehow gathered the other two item's powers; and united them in a new way that fought against unknown magic."

"It was also rumored that the powers of the staff; and sword combined could be used to open up gates into other worlds and only the power of the helmet could be used to stop them. The leader of the black robes had done this to the staff so that one day his guild might rule the world."

At this point in the story, Jair interrupted Tagor and asked him, "Tagor, do you suppose that Telenok is trying to claim all three of the artifacts in order to use them for his own evil purposes, to try to take over all of the kingdoms?"

In response, Tagor replied, "I don't know, but I doubt he would try to use them against the kingdoms directly, at least not until he'd gathered a large enough force to back him up. The three wizards had created these artifacts because of some terrible force that had almost destroyed the world. This thing happened many centuries ago, so long ago in fact, most people today think it is all just a made up story. I figure he was sending the helmet to be destroyed. If he could destroy it, then he could use the other two artifacts to conquer and destroy."

"It must have been a terrible creature that had come from another distant plane of existence, according to the stories. It was probably brought into our world; and worshipped as a god. From the stories I have heard, this creature supposedly entered into our world only to drain the life force from everyone and everything in it, good and evil alike," Tagor said.

"Tagor, it could be that Telenok is trying to use the other two artifacts to raise some such monstrosity, hoping to gain total power through it," Jair added.

"That's true; anything is possible with a power hungry madman holding such weapons. The balance maintained by the Wizard's Guild makes it almost impossible for any one person to gain that much power normally." Tagor replied.

"The first two artifacts were hidden in a temple where only the strongest and most powerful or the most cunning would be able to get them in a time of great need. Telenok is supposed to have the staff. Where he got it is anyone's guess. He probably stole it from someone else, or just got lucky. No one knows where the sword is. Whoever had it would be a great foe indeed."

Jair soaked in all of this information. He had never heard this tale before and he really didn't know anything about the Wizard's Guild. Also, something about this tale made him uneasy. He thought about it as they traveled.

While they talked, the pair continued to travel for the rest of the first day, stopping only briefly for a short rest and to get something to eat out of their packs. They traveled until it became too dark for Tagor to see where they were going, so they decided to make camp.

Tagor found a small clearing just as dusk was setting in. It would serve them well as a campsite, so they stopped for the night. They opted not to make a fire. Both of them ate dried meat and bread, which was standard rations for traveling.

Throughout the night they took two watches. Tagor took the first one and shortly after midnight, he woke Jair to take the second. When Tagor awoke early the next morning he found Jair sound asleep, still sitting where he had left him.

Tagor quickly picked up his belongings, and walked over to where Jair was sitting slumped on the ground. Shaking him roughly, Tagor finally woke him up. Jair jerked violently from some dream that had disturbed him, even as he awoke.

Tagor looked at him, wistfully shaking his head with a saddened, doubtful look on his face, but with a humorous gleam in his eyes as he said, "You fell asleep during your watch. If you're to be a warrior some day you're going to have to learn to sit your watch without falling asleep. What if the goblin band had found us? They would have been upon us and slit our throats before we even knew what was happening."

Jair turned sleepily to look at Tagor, an apologetic look on his face, "I'm sorry Tagor. I didn't mean to fall asleep, I just did. I guess with all of the excitement over the last few days I was more tired than I thought. It won't happen again," Jair promised.

"Well, see that it doesn't," Tagor said to him seriously, then smiled, "We'll need to be on our way so gather your things. We can eat as we walk. The more distance we put between us and the goblins, the happier I'll be."

The Ruby Helmet

The two companions packed up their belongings and had a quick meal of rations as they started toward the river. The day was warming up a little, but it did not promise to be as nice a day as the last few had been. Fall was here and Jair knew winter would be on them soon. There was a slight cloud cover that hung limply in the morning sky. Only occasionally did it allow the sun to peek through, as if it were playing hide and seek with the travelers far down below it.

Tagor estimated they should reach the Wildrun by mid afternoon, and from there they would be able to follow it almost to Gallador. The city itself had been built close to the edge of the Timgranok Mountains, which were nestled snugly at the edge of the Barnook Forest.

The forest used to grow right up into the side of the mountains. Over the last few centuries, the expansion of the city and growth in population had slowly eaten away at parts of the surrounding woodland. The people had to make room for farmland and homesteads.

As they walked, Jair asked Tagor how the city had been formed and where it had gotten its beginnings. So Tagor told him, "Gallador was a very old city, supposedly founded by a very powerful and ancient shaman of a mysterious barbaric tribe of humans that had come down out of what is now the barbarian lands in the north. This shaman led his people to the base of the Timgranok Mountains where they settled. They started out building crude huts and by surviving off of the land. These people were a hardy stock of hunters, born and bred to the wilderness. They knew how to survive."

"The journey was a long and dangerous one for these people. Along the way, they had to face many dangers, both natural and unnatural. This was not many centuries after the time of making, the time of the beginning for all of the races. Men were just developing as a race and were still crude and uncivilized."

"The dwarves were formed from a group of humans that had left; and went off to live in the mountains. Digging into the rock itself, they made their homes. Living deep in the ground, it is believed earth magic caused their bodies to become short and thick. Living there also taught them how to work and use the metals they found there."

"It is believed that the elves were humans once also. They went off to live in the woodlands and made their homes in the trees. They became great students of magic. It is thought that their study in the arcane arts is what changed them into what they are now. They were the first true magic users." Tagor said.

"It is thought that all of the other human-like races developed from these three races, the halflings, orcs, goblins, giants, pixies, etc. All were branches off of the three main races, and all of those originally from humans. Each of these peoples had moved off to form their own communities. Some were just changed by time and or by strange magical forces."

"Anyway", Tagor continued, while trying to get back to the main story, "This shaman led his people to this area because of a great flow of magic he had felt coming out of the land. It is believed he was a prophet and that he could see the future. In his dreams it was revealed to him and he saw this land with its great magic; and abundance of wild game and that it would be a good place for his people to live."

"After the tribe settled in, it prospered and grew. The wild game was plentiful, and the old shaman studied the magic of this land, in turn teaching it to his people. His was a more natural magic, more like a druid or cleric. Later, due to the village's growing size, the settlement was moved further east of the mountains, where Gallador now rests. This was also supposed to be the central apex of the flow of magical energies that the old shaman had felt," Tagor explained to Jair.

"The settlement continued to grow, advancing in its knowledge and wisdom of all things like weaponry, carpentry, hunting, farming, and in magic."

"Over the next several centuries these people prospered, building what is now the city of Gallador. Back then it was called Cerenok, 'The City of Dancing Light.' This was a name derived from the flow and movement of magic in the land that the old shaman had originally described to his people upon first arriving there. Only someone with true magic ability is said to be able to see it."

"Later the shaman found out that the magic came not from the earth, but from a being called Anu, one of the earliest entities worshipped as a god that had helped form the world. This being visited the shaman in dreams and taught him and the people the ways of priestly magic and healing. For many years they prospered under the guidance of their shaman and their god."

"Later many of the people fell away from the worship of Anu and turned to other, newer gods. This caused the city to go through a time of great tribulation and wars that lasted for years. They were kept busy fighting off wild bands of goblins and orcs that came down out of the north, and they also had to deal with raids from the elven people, who were still fairly barbaric also."

"The city was almost completely destroyed in one fierce battle. The people of Cerenok had a leader who had also been a priest. He was a direct descendant of the original shaman. This young priest led the people in a battled against an evil ogre wizard that had become the leader of a large band of ogres, goblins and orcs. Half of the city was destroyed, but the people overcame the oppressors and sent them scuttling back into the forests and mountains, confused and leaderless."

"It was this evil ogre wizard who had been the first to try to bring an entity from another world into ours. He tried to use its power to rule all the land. He failed to do so because he could not control it. He also failed because the good cleric and leader of the people of Cerenok found a powerful good magic that had come from their god and from the land itself. They used this magic to defeat the entity and send it back to its own world," Tagor said.

"Was it this young priest that helped to reestablish the temple of Anu?" Jair interrupted.

"Yes." Tagor answered him, "It was also through his help that the towers of sorcery were established in order to control and regulate magic in all of the kingdoms. That is also when the name of the city was changed to Gallador."

"Gallador has several colleges, and one great library housing a great collection of magical information. Even the elves come there to study and take their test of power. Only Silvermist has a collection as great."

Tagor finished his story then walked in silence. Jair now had a better understanding of the city's origin as well as the surrounding kingdoms. Kentar had never bothered to teach him any local history; so he had really known very little about it.

Jair contemplated all of this as they traveled. His feet also began to hurt. Eventually they broke through a small gap in the tree line near a ridge. It opened up to a magnificent view of the Wildrun River.

The Wildrun was fairly broad and it made a large cut through the land. It formed a silvery-blue trail that continually glittered and danced as the sun peeked through the billowy clouds overhead. The water was clear and cold as it cascaded over its rocky bottom.

Jair stopped and looked about when he reached the steep bank of the river. He scanned the broad horizon and could see the movement of large fish swimming in the river. He also saw several small animals scurrying along the bank, scavenging for food.

The Ruby Helmet

As he looked at the river, the spectacle of it amazed him. He had never seen a river this large before. When Kentar had bought him to the city they had not passed this way. Tagor saw the look of awe upon Jair's face and chuckled softly to himself, knowing that the Wildrun was a fantastic sight to a young man that had never been more than a few leagues from his home.

"It's quite a sight isn't it?" Tagor said to Jair.

"Its amazing Tagor. I've never seen anything like it. Even the old pictures in some of Kentar's books don't compare to this. How are we ever going to get across it?" Jair asked.

"We'll travel on upriver for a couple of leagues. We should be able to find a ford in the river where the water is shallow enough for us to make a crossing. We'll have to be careful though, the river seems to be up a bit and that current is pretty strong, but I think we can make it across all right. If we're lucky, we might find a barge or riverboat to take us across. I don't particularly relish the idea of getting wet in this cool fall air," Tagor told him.

They traveled for about another league and a half up river and came to a spot that looked as if it had been crossed before. They stopped to take a look around and Jair noticed something moving on the other side of the river.

Pointing this out to Tagor, the pair watched silently as something moved across the water toward their side of the river. After a few moments the object came nearer and was easier to make out.

It was a large wooden barge that was being pulled across by a large, gray skinned man. The figure was pulling on a thick, knotted rope that had been strung across the river and run through large metal hooks set into thick posts of wood that were attached to the sides of the barge. The rope had been hidden from view at first due to an overgrowth of plants and shrubs next to a stone block that it was attached to.

The stone block was set in the ground next to the riverbank and was made of a large, black stone that had been smoothed down until it was shiny. It also had several distinct carvings upon its surface.

As the barge moved closer, Jair could tell that it was no ordinary man that pulled the barge across the river. Upon closer inspection he saw that it was a manlike creature who was extremely lean, muscular, and of immense proportions. He had a grayish, mottled skin that looked to be as thick as tree bark. His head was hairless and he had small ears.

The clothing the creature wore was mostly animal skins and furs that had been tied together with old yellow leather cords. He wore old faded brown trousers that were ripped and torn in many places and had large, dirty bare feet.

The features of the creature were somewhat brutish looking. It had a low forehead and thick eye ridges that ran all the way across its face. Yellowish-green eyes peered out from deep-set eye sockets, and it had a mouth that was wide with thick lips. Altogether the creature had a fearsome appearance. Tagor was taken aback by it, so he cautiously drew his sword.

Easing over next to Tagor, Jair asked him, "Tagor, what manner of creature is that?"

"It's a hill giant." Tagor replied. "And a particularly large one at that. I've never seen one this far south before, and I've never known of one to use a barge. Giants generally stay away from water because they sink."

As they watched, the giant drew the barge up to the landing and then hooked a rope over the wooden post to hold it in place. After doing this, the giant just stood there staring blankly at the two travelers.

Not knowing what else to do Tagor slowly walked over toward the giant, stopping just out of reach of its long muscular arms. He kept himself between it and Jair. Trying to not show any fear, he calmly asked the creature, "Who are you, and what are you doing on this barge?"

In response the creature held up one giant paw and extended two fingers, then made a fist and did a sweeping motion towards the river, then he dropped his hand.

"Tagor, what does it want?" Jair asked.

"It seems to want two silver pieces to take us to the other side."

Tagor glanced down and noticed a large manacle that was attached securely to the giant's right leg. The other end was attached to the barge. There was also a small pouch hanging from a rope belt at its waist.

"It would seem that someone has set up a means of making money from weary travelers who are trying to cross the river. It looks like this big fellow has been captured and set upon this barge to demand money from any who would cross here."

Tagor looked at Jair and added, "Our large friend here was probably captured by a wizard. You know manacles wouldn't normally hold someone like him so they must be enchanted."

Hearing this, the giant sadly shook his head in affirmation, pointing to a large tower that could just barely be seen above the treetops on the other side of the river. It was only a short ways into the forest. Jair also noticed that the giant had a large club leaning against the rail behind him, probably to enforce or defend against anyone trying to cross without paying.

Sheathing his sword, Tagor reached into his belt pouch and

retrieved two silver pieces. Flipping them to the giant, who deftly caught them and put them into his pouch, the two companions stepped upon the barge. It lurched forward after the giant removed the rope anchor and began pulling on the rope in the runway.

It didn't take long before they were close to the other side of the river. The giant's size and strength proved to be immense. His silent presence slightly disturbed Jair, but also intrigued him. It was his first experience at meeting a real giant, and this one didn't meet any of his expectations. It was nothing like what he had read and heard stories about. As far as its physical presence though, Jair was impressed. He just wasn't what Jair had expected in a giant. Most of the stories made them seem even larger, and fiercer.

Jair moved over to stand next to Tagor and leaned slightly forward on the rail. He looked cautiously at the giant. He then asked Tagor, "How come he doesn't say anything? I thought that giants could speak."

"They can speak", Tagor replied. "I don't know why he doesn't, must be a mute."

At this, the giant shook his head in affirmation, and then pointed again to the tower on the other side of the river. It embarrassed Jair slightly at the ease with which the giant had overheard their conversation.

"That must be where the wizard that captured him lives," exclaimed Jair, "He must be a powerful wizard to have captured a giant like him."

At this a fierce, angry expression came over the giants face. It was a look of intense hatred. Looking at Tagor, the giant stopped pulling the rope and began to make a series of hand movements. After several minutes of this, Tagor replied with like hand signs. This continued on for several moments, after which Tagor finally stopped and turned back to Jair. The giant went back to pulling the rope.

"It seems our large friend here was an outcast from his home village. Because of his muteness and small size, compared to other hill giants, the others ran him off. I believe they were afraid of him. It had something to do with his resemblance to an ancient spirit out of giant folklore," Tagor said.

"He's been traveling the kingdoms, living off the land and hiring out to do odd jobs. He's done whatever he can to find people that aren't too afraid of him to provide work to help feed and shelter him."

"Somewhere down the line he found an old hermit that took him in and taught him the sign language of the rangers. It's similar to what the border patrols used to communicate in silence during the border wars. Evidently, the old hermit taught him a lot about the rest of the world. He seems to be a very bright fellow."

At this, the giant looked over at Tagor and nodded his head in acknowledgment of the compliment. He never stopped his rhythm or momentum while pulling the barge across the river.

"The wizard captured him after he had been wounded in a fight with a hippogryph. He killed the hippogryph, but fell unconscious from the loss of blood. The wizard found him, bandaged up his wounds, then set him to work on the barge. The wizard magically bound him to his service by the collar he wears. The wizard feeds him daily and allows him to sleep in a small shack out back of his tower. The wizard also beats and tortures him whenever it suits him. From what the giant says, this wizard is very evil. He says he has killed many people and preys upon anyone he believes he is stronger than," Tagor told Jair.

"The wizard brings him down here and chains him to the barge every morning, and then comes and gets him just after dusk every night. The giant would really like to get his hands around the wizard's neck. I think he would do just about anything to win his freedom."

Just as Tagor was finishing the tale, they arrived at the other bank. They docked with a slight jolt. The giant placed the rope over another wooden post on that side of the river. He then stood silently by while they stepped off the barge onto the bank.

Jair looked at the giant standing there quietly as they walked away. He felt sorry for him. Not being too sure that his story was true, he turned to Tagor and asked him, "Tagor, do you believe his story. Do you think he is telling the truth?"

Tagor turned to look at the giant again and replied, "Yes, I think he is. For some reason, I believe him. He could be extremely dangerous though," He said to Jair while nodding toward the giant.

"I've seen them wade through a half a dozen heavily armed men as if they were no more than stalks of grain in a field. They are devious fighters too, surprisingly quick for their size."

"Well, I think we should help him," Jair said, as they walked further down the path that led away from the river.

"What? Are you crazy?" Tagor responded in shock, "Go up against a wizard just to free a renegade giant that would probably turn on us and cave our skulls in the first chance he got?"

"My instincts tell me he would not harm us," Jair responded, "Especially if we help to free him. Besides, if we help him, he may travel with us to Gallador. We could use his strength if those goblins catch up with us, or anything else for that matter. This wizard sounds like a menace to the area. We'd be doing a service to the surrounding community. Plus a wizard is bound to have plenty of treasure and we might be able to pick up a few things that we could use. I also may have some magic of my own that we can use against him."

"I don't know about this Jair. I've been on a lot of campaigns and adventures, but this seems a little too risky. An old warrior, a boy wizard, and a mute giant do not sound like a great team. This goes against all of my instincts," Tagor said, while shaking his head negatively.

He pondered the situation for a moment while standing in silence in the road. He looked Jair in the eyes. Slowly his dour expression changed to one of reluctant acceptance. His sense of adventure had taken over.

"Well, I suppose you're right. We could use his help if the goblins catch up with us." Tagor responded.

"It's settled then. Will you talk to him and see if he will agree to join us if we free him?" Jair asked him.

Tagor nodded his head in affirmation. Jair then said, "Ok, if we can get a closer look at the tower I think we can come up with a plan to break into it tonight."

Tagor grumbled to himself, shaking his head as he walked back down to the rivers edge where the giant was silently waiting for another customer. After a few moments of excited hand signals, Tagor walked back up the bank to where Jair was waiting for him.

"Well, what did he say?" Jair asked.

"He agrees to go with us if we can free him. We are to meet him in the small shack where the wizard keeps him shackled at night. He thinks he may know of a secret entrance into the tower. It's one he's seen the wizard use before," Tagor said.

"Oh, and by the way, he says his name is Kethok, of the hill tribe of the Benar. It is one of the largest and most feared bands of giants in the Anarest Mountains. He must have been really feared or weak for them to of run him off. Only the strongest hill giants can survive in that clan. Even though he is a little smaller than most I've seen, he doesn't seem to be all that weak," Tagor noted as they set off.

Tagor and Jair turned toward the woods and made their way toward the lonely tower that jutted out of the top of the dense forest canopy just ahead of them. It was going to be an interesting night, and they needed to get some rest before entering the dark tower.

Chapter 3

Everywhere upon the cold stone floor of the cave were piles of human bones. A large, dark figure slowly picked its way over the grisly remains. It moved silently, searching for the beast that lived there. The beast had wrought terrible devastation and brought great loss to the surrounding area.

A foul, putrid stench of death and decay emanated from deep within the dark, dank catacombs in which the figure now transverse. The smell caused the figure to reel with disgust. Knowing the awful power of its enemy however, the figure shook its head to try and clear it so it could continue on. This caused its long dark hair to shimmer slightly in the dim light. Reflections flickered across the silvery, well-worn ornamental helmet it wore.

The figure's upper body was covered in plate mail armor. It glittered faintly from the few thin beams of light that filtered down into the mouth of the cavern. The figure's dark leather breaches and soft, high riding leather boots barely made a sound as it softly padded its way toward the ominous entrance to another, larger cavern.

In the figure's strong muscular hands it held a large, heavy, double bladed battleaxe. The axe was made of the finest steel crafted by dwarven blacksmiths in the Timgranok Mountains. The axe shone with a faint, slightly visible silver glow. This gave it an eerie appearance in the darkness.

The figure's presence in the cavern was not a natural one. Rats scurried before it as it worked its way toward the next room. The beast within the cavern was waiting, knowing full well that a victim had entered its lair. It waited hungrily for its enemy in the comfort of its own home, confident that it would be feasting well this night.

Rakkon knew full well the extent of the situation that he had gotten himself into. He moved forward cautiously, listening strenuously for any sign of the beast he knew to be lying in wait.

While traveling south to join King Tredebould's growing mercenary army in the ongoing war of the Creahaul, Rakkon had been talked in to ridding a small town named Caerloon of a vicious reptilian killer that had been preying upon the town's inhabitants. The creature crashed its way into homes late at night and dragged its victims off into the nearby mountains. It had left many bloody trails and screaming on many a night. Rakkon had agreed to do the dangerous task, for a small fee of course. He was always glad to help others in a time of need, especially if there was a profit to be made.

Rakkon was a warrior, born and bred. He grew up in the Anarest Mountains in the barbarian warrior clans of the Teargor people. He was first among his clan in battle prowess and in war knowledge. He had decided to leave his people when he had become bored. Most of the people back home were at peace, so the only fighting was between his kin. Rakkon had set out for the kingdoms of the South, seeking adventure and wealth.

He continued to move forward slowly, listening for any sound that might give the creature away, or give him some kind of advantage over it. He had trailed the beast from where it had made its last kill. It had taken a small farm family in a house just outside of the town. The trail of blood and entrails was not too difficult to follow, especially in the bright moonlight. It had led right up to the mouth of the cave that served as its lair.

Rakkon moved to the left of the large cavern entrance and stopped suddenly, standing very still. There was a faint rasping noise like sandpaper being rubbed over rough wood. The sound was coming from directly ahead and to the right of the chamber. He strained his eyes and could just make out the moonlight faintly reflecting off of hardened, leathery scales.

Rakkon edged his way forward, and prepared himself. He reached deep within himself for the place of the warrior, bringing forth the inner being that one sought when entering into combat. It was the part that showed no mercy, and knew only the power and surge of battle. He reached down into his muscles, sinew and bones. Power flowed out of him into the cold, hard steel that he held in his hand.

Rakkon reached down into a pouch that hung from his thick, black sword belt. He withdrew a small round object. It was smooth and spherical, about the size of a dove's egg. The object was pale white in color.

He turned his head away from the direction of the beast, then drew his arm back and threw the small sphere toward it. The sphere spun toward the large reptile and exploded upon impact. It released a powerful blast that produced a large ball of bright, white light that seemed to cling to the face of the reptile.

Rakkon quickly attacked what he could now see was a large pseudo-dragon. Pseudo-dragons were winged beasts made of pure hatred. An evil created out of total darkness. They came from a time when evil ran rampant over the world, many centuries ago. Evidently, many of these creatures still survived, plaguing all of the humanoid races, good and evil alike.

Pseudo-dragons were one of the toughest of the smaller dragon types to kill. This one was about fifteen feet long from snout to tail tip. It had two wickedly curved feet with sharp talons, a set of small leathery wings, and a poison tipped tail that was razor sharp. It bared sharp, ivory teeth that could rip a man's head off in one bite. Upon seeing the deadly creature, Rakkon knew he faced an extremely dangerous foe.

He took full advantage of the dragon's momentary blindness, and dove in on its right side, seeking a vulnerable spot on the underside of its soft underbelly. Rakkon knew that attacking the monster's rough scaly outer hide would have taken too long, even with his enchanted blade. He would not be able to avoid the deadly spiked tail for very long.

He came in fast, quicker than most would have believed for a man of his size. He ducked under one of the dragon's flailing wings and came in with a vicious cut to the beast's upper chest. Rakkon attacked as it reared up while trying to fight off the light that had momentarily blinded it.

Fortunately his attack was true to its mark. It opened up a terrible wound in the monster's chest. This caused it to bellow with a loud roar of pain and fury. It had never been so easily thwarted. The cut itself gushed out a thick, warm, green ooze. The ooze stung and burned Rakkon's skin wherever it touched him.

The reptile swung around toward the source of its agony and lashed out with one of its large talons. Its attack cut a vicious arc in the air right in front of Rakkon's face. It caught him with a glancing blow to the side of his helmet. The attack left a large gash in it. The blow sent Rakkon reeling back, toward the cave wall. He stumbled on a stalactite and lost his balance, toppling to the cave floor.

Rakkon barely noticed the follow-up attack of the beast's deadly tail. It had come around, just missing pinning him to the wall. It would have ended his short, adventurous career. His fall had inadvertently saved his life.

He quickly rolled to one side and came up swinging. He aimed a powerful uppercut to the beast's exposed neck. The monster had closed in on him, hoping to finish off the vile human that had so painfully wounded it. It had expected Rakkon to be knocked unconscious from the crushing blow it had landed on his helmet.

With almost superhuman speed, Rakkon sliced the monster's neck from ear to scaly ear. In finishing through with its bull like charge, the dragon bowled Rakkon over even as he was ending its life. It threw him into the cave wall once again.

The beast thrashed about and crashed onto the floor of the cavern. It went through its final throes, dying just as violently as it had lived.

A short while later, Rakkon eased back into consciousness, eventually clearing his head from the blow the dragon had dealt him. He sat up slowly and felt a sharp pain in his abdomen. Evidently the dragon's little love tap had cracked a few of his ribs and left a knot the size of a marble on his head. It had also slit his armor. The tear was from where the dragon's poisoned tail had barely missed him. All of this testified as to how deadly pseudo-dragons really were.

Resting for a short while, Rakkon managed to get to his feet and then worked his way out to the main cavern near the entrance. Before leaving he took the head of the dead beast as proof of his deed. He would need it so he could collect the money the townspeople owed him.

While he passed through the outermost chamber of the cavern, a small glint to the left of the room caught his eye. He limped over to investigate it and discovered a small pile of treasure. It seemed that even small dragons still had the age-old desire to hoard treasure, even if it was mostly garbage and farmers' tools.

He pilfering through the pile of rubble and found a few gold and silver pieces that he placed into one of his pouches. Continuing his search, he also found some old rags that looked like they had been someone's clothing, a couple pairs of boots, a belt, a couple of knives, an old rusty sword, and set of bracers.

Rakkon looked everything over and picked up the bracers. He rubbed some of the grime off of them. When cleaned, the bracers shone brightly and looked to be made out of polished silver with gold inlay. The patterns on it formed intricate and delicate designs of a nature Rakkon had never seen before.

Admiring them a little, Rakkon placed them on his forearms. He didn't notice the little surge of energy that came from the bracers as he placed them on his wrists. He then left the cave and headed toward town. He thought that he might be able to sell the bracers after he collected his money.

A few days later, as dawn was slowly breaking over the eastern horizon, Rakkon crested a small hill somewhere close to the southernmost tip of the Anarest Mountains. He rode a new warhorse and was carrying a new shield he had purchased while at the city of Preredon. He rode high in the saddle. He felt proud and strong and completely full of himself.

The people of Caerloon had been reluctant to reward Rakkon for the heroic deed he had performed in their stead. When he had walked into town and asked for his money, they had denied it. They gave him several excuses, which only angered him. One citizen even threatened him, until Rakkon glowered at him. It was evident they had never really intended to pay him, or thought he could kill the monster.

Rakkon had immediately stormed into the town's council hall. Covered in dried dragon's blood and stinking of death, he approached the city council members who were in session along with the mayor. He revealed the dragon's head by maliciously throwing it onto the center of the council's large oaken table, making the council members scatter in fear and loathing. He then pulled out his great axe and demanded the payment that had been promised him. He then threatened to stay in town until they paid him. They gave in when he mentioned calling on the mayor's daughter, marrying her and settling down there permanently.

They must have really wanted Rakkon out of their town. They were afraid of what damage or mischief he might have caused while staying there. They knew that none of them, even their best men-at-arms, could have easily overpowered or defeated the huge warrior. They were too cowardly to band together.

It was a sad little town as far as Rakkon was concerned after dealing with their reactions. It was definitely better to move on and continue his journey.

He rode on for the following week and entered the Barnook Forest. He only stopped at a few small towns and villages for supplies and rest. He took his time as he went. He wanted to enjoy his journey and his life. He also wanted to let the wounds he had received from the pseudo-dragon heal properly.

Sometime after he had fully healed, Rakkon thought he would go ahead and join Lord Tredebould's army in the west. He figured he would head for the capitol city of Gallador, pick up some supplies, and then try to find out the latest gossip on what was happening in this part of the country, including how Lord Creahaul's war was going.

It was a land dispute between two minor nobles, Lord Tredebould, who owned land in northern Parvincia, and Lord Creahaul, who owned land just south of Tredebould's. How the dispute actually got started only the gods really knew.

It was believed to have something to do with one of Tredebould's boisterous ancestors who had supposedly taken a large hunting party and entered into the woods in the northernmost tip of what the Creahaul family claimed as their territory. Someone had killed someone else and before everyone knew it, the two families were at war.

Neither lord was very powerful by himself. Both owned small provinces within Parvincia and boasted at having more than a thousand trained knights and warriors on hand at all times. After hearing most of the rumors, it seemed to Rakkon that Lord Tredebould paid the better wages, so that's who Rakkon had decided to join up with.

Both nobles owed allegiance to King Ralkath, who was

supreme ruler of Parvincia, by birthright and by might. Ralkath was famed to be a great warrior. Trained by his father, King Galdath, and his personal bodyguard, the Red Dragons, Ralkath grew up fighting for his father on the eastern frontier. The frontier was quite unstable back then and very much a stationary battle line.

Ralkath had been a better diplomat than his father. He had worked out a way to make peace with the elves. When he took over the kingdom after his father died he brought about the Treaty of Deskai, which he and the High Elf king at that time, Stelenost te Aranesh, both signed. It brought peace to both kingdoms and allowed trade to open up between the two peoples. This treaty allowed prosperity and growth on both sides.

Rakkon mulled this over as he continued down the road. He only came across a few minor settlements and towns that were scattered along the way as he rode on toward Gallador. According to some of the local people he had stopped and asked directions from, the road wound slightly south of the city before turning back north and then west. He did not know what adventure lay ahead, but he was eager to find out.

Chapter 4

Dark, eerie shadows fell upon the black, stone wall of the old wizard's keep. Jair and Tagor arrived at the edge of the clearing just after sunset. They quietly worked their way to the edge of the woods next to the tower. From there they observed the wizard's tower and its surrounding grounds. As they looked it over, Tagor worked on a plan for them to break in and free Kethok.

Jair had made camp about a quarter of a league from the tower. Before taking on the wizard, Tagor decided to visit a small village not too far from where they were and gather more information. What he had discovered there had not been good. The wizard had been victimizing the locals for many years. Evidently he had inflicted a lot of terrible things on them. Most lived in fear and many had left the area or were thinking about leaving. The stories they told Tagor were horrible and made him feel better about doing something about the evil wizard.

When he returned to their camp he told Jair what he had found out. The pair then ate a small meal from their supplies and rested a while before the sun went down.

Dusk had quickly turned into night as the two of them had set off in the direction of the tower. They had just reached it as the sun sank gracefully into the western sky.

Jair focused his attention on the tower and noticed that it was shorter than it had looked from the river. It was built of large, black stones that were probably hewn from the nearby Timgranok Mountains. Polished to a smooth, illustrious finish, the stone made it nearly impossible to scale from the outside. It was the same type of stone they had seen at the barge. The tower was approximately forty feet high, about twenty-five feet in diameter at the base and it tapered slightly as it rose. It was about twenty feet in diameter at the top.

Jair checked the base of the tower and could only see one

visible entrance. It was a large metal door made of a dark rusted iron. It looked to be in good working condition. It was either oiled regularly or had magic preservation cast upon it.

A large stone arch framed the doorway. The arch had been carved from one solid piece of the black stone. The door itself was a solid sheet of metal with large iron bands bolted into it in two places, giving it support. No hinges were visible from this side. It looked to fit snugly inside the stone frame. There was a small keyhole to one side. It did not look like something that would be easy to break into or pick.

As they were looking the tower over, Jair noticed something odd. It was as if there was a strange shimmer in the air just in front of it, like when heat rises up off the ground on a hot summer day. Jair realized that any attempt to try a forced entry through that portal would probably meet with disaster. He guessed the door was magically protected and he told Tagor what he saw.

The small shack Kethok had described to them was leaning next to the eastern wall. It was actually a supply shed and small stable used for keeping the wizard's horse and any other beasts in his service. The shed was built from old rotting beams and had a sunken roof that was badly in need of repair.

Jair and Tagor silently watched and observed the tower as the moon slowly rose into the partly cloudy evening sky. It was just nearing the midnight hour when they decided to head over to the shack and try to find Kethok.

Tagor motioned for Jair to follow him and they worked their way along the edge of the woods and then quickly moved across the clearing to the back of the shed. Once there they moved around to the front and halted just inside the entrance.

They allowed their eyes to adjust to the dark interior before entering. Tagor made out the shape of the giant, lying on some old, moldy straw in one of the stalls in the middle of the building. They moved over to him and were slightly startled as the giant quickly came to his feet. Kethok motioned for them to follow him and then moved toward the back of the building. He had to walk a little hunched over due to the low ceiling. He picked up his chains as he went so they would not make any sound. His chain just barely allowed him to reach the far side of the back of the shed where there was another door.

Kethok made several hand signals and opened the door. This revealed a small storage room right next to the base of the tower. Tagor leaned over to Jair and whispered to him what Kethok had signed.

"Kethok says there is a secret entrance here at the base of the wall. The wizard does not know that Kethok has seen him use it. It is through this entrance we can enter into the tower, but after that we are on our own."

Kethok leaned forward toward the back of the wall. He placed one of his large hands on a small stone. He pushed in on it and a section of the wall that was lined with shelves slid silently inward. It revealed a small passageway. Jair moved forward to lead the way since he could see in the dark. He looked back to see the hopeful look on the giant's face. He had glanced down before entering the passage to get a good look at the giant's chains. He saw where the chains had scarred him. He also discerned that the bonds were magically bound to him. The only way to release him would be to get the wizard to do it voluntarily, find the special key, or kill the wizard.

Jair moved inside and found that the passageway wound about halfway around the outer edge of the tower. It stopped somewhere close to the back of the tower where the passage came to a flight of stairs. Jair cautiously started climbing the narrow stone steps. Their passage stirred a small cloud of dust with each step. Evidently, this passage hadn't been used for quite some time.

Upon reaching the top of the stairway they came to a blank wall. Jair looked around and finally made out a small lever to one side of the wall. He listened for any sounds on the other side and prepared himself to enter through the hidden door. He brought the words of hold person and silence spells to the forefront of his mind. He had memorized them both the day before from his spell book. Before entering, he glanced back at Tagor for reassurance. They both looked for traps, but didn't see anything.

Tagor eased up behind Jair and whispered, "Kethok said that this should open up to a large room which is the wizard's study and bedchamber. To the left of the door there should be a small bed, and to the right there should be a large table and some bookshelves.

"He also said that the magic keys to his manacles hang from a small peg driven into the wall beside the table. Hopefully we can sneak in, grab the keys and a few valuables and be off before the wizard ever wakes up."

Jair nodded silently, then reached up and gently pulled down on the lever. The wall slid quietly backward and to the right side, allowing them access into the room. Jair looked through the opening and scanned the contents. He was glad the door had not made a sound. Just as Kethok had told them, there was a large oak table on the right, upon which stood many books, scrolls, magical implements and spell ingredients. Behind the table were two large bookcases that were also filled with books and scrolls. To the left of the room was a small bed upon which the wizard was soundly sleeping. The rest of the room was filled with odds and ends, most of which seemed to be junk.

Jair quickly got out his spell components then began whispering his spell of silence. Once the spell was finished, everything became deathly quiet. They could no longer hear the wizard snoring, insects chirping or even their own breathing. His spell had worked.

Jair went toward the table, spotting the small peg from which dangled the keys to Kethok's manacles. Meanwhile, Tagor eased over to a large trunk that was set against the far wall. It was next to the door that led from the room at the top of the tower.

Jair reached the keys and removed them from the peg. He'd had a lot of practice at sneaking around while living with Kentar. He then placed the keys into one of his belt pouches. He looked around the room and then scanned some of the scrolls that were lying upon the table. He realized that several of the scrolls contained very useful spells, so he rolled them up and tied a piece of string around them he'd found lying on the table.

Tagor went over to the chest and quickly examined the front of it, looking for traps. He then gently pulled up the latch and started raising the lid, stepped to one side as he did so. As he lifted it, the moonlight chose that moment to shine in through the small window on the other side of the table. It illuminated the room and filled Tagor's eyes with reflected moonlight that came off the gold, silver, gems and many other items that were in the chest. One item in particular caught Tagor's eye right away. It was a jeweled long sword that was lying on top.

Tagor turned his attention to the sword after glancing quickly over at the prone figure still lying on the bed to make sure he was still asleep. Upon closer examination, Tagor decided it was a good weapon. It had obviously been finely crafted and covered with gold and diamonds. It was a little flashy, but that was ok with him. The blade was straight, shining softly in the moonlight, which made its beauty stand out even more. Tagor was just about to reach in and take the weapon with his left hand when the lid closed shut with a loud clump. It caught his hand inside and caused him to let out a loud yell. Evidently there had been a trap spell on it. Also, from all the noise, they both knew that Jair's spell had worn off.

Jair had made his way over to the exit and was turning to motion for Tagor to hurry up when the lid closed on his hand. The noise made by the lid and by Tagor's yell brought the wizard to an upright sitting position. His eyes were still cloudy from sleep, but the expression Jair saw on his face in the gloomy moonlit room was not a pleasant one.

The wizard wore a silky black robe that was covered with many various designs and symbols. His face was fairly young, but harsh looking. He was darkly tanned with a thin mustache that drooped down on each side of thin, cruel lips. Straight black hair hung down to his shoulders and was tied back with a leather strip. Upon his brow was a circlet of silver in the middle of which was a large diamond.

"Who goes there?" The wizard shouted, "Thieves in the night. I'll skin you both alive and feed you to the creatures of the forest. Before I'm done, you'll both beg for mercy. No one disturbs my rest and enters my home unbidden without paying for it with their lives."

Jair immediately started mouthing the words to the hold person spell that he had been practicing earlier. Reaching down to his belt he withdrew the spell components from one of his pouches and held them out.

At the same time, the wizard rose from his bed and raised both of his hands high above his head. He began the mumblings of some dreadful spell as he stepped toward Tagor, who was closer to him. The anger and hatred was clearly on the wizard's face in moonlight.

With great effort, Tagor pulled the lid to the chest back open. He quickly reached back in with his other hand and pulled out the shiny sword. His left hand throbbed from the impact where the lid had closed on it. It felt like he had a few broken bones. A small trickle of blood ran down the back of his hand where the lid had cut him. He brought the shiny sword around to bear in front of him, hoping to have a small chance at taking a swing at the wizard before he cast his spell.

As he did this, the sword came up with a sharp jerk all its own.

Its weight was surprisingly light in his grasp. It almost felt like it was leading him. Tagor followed the sword's lead and quickly charged at the wizard. He swung the sword in a viscous arc toward the mage's head, all the while yelling a battle cry.

Meanwhile, Jair finished saying the final words to his spell and felt the surge of power as it flowed out of him and formed the spell he had just cast. He looked over to see what was going on and found he had been quicker in casting his spell than the wizard had been on casting his. This caused the mage's aim to be off with his spell.

At the moment Jair's spell took hold, freezing him in place, the mage released a bolt of lightning from one of his fingers. It just missed Tagor, arching over him toward the far wall where the wizard's table and spell components were.

It struck the table and exploded into a giant ball of fire. The bolt's concussion threw everyone to the floor. The ensuing explosion blew out a whole section of the tower's wall and caused part of the flooring to give way.

Tagor was the first of them to regain his feet and senses. He Lunged forward and pointed the tip of the sword at the now frozen mage's chest. A look of horror formed upon the mage's face as he looked upon the sword Tagor was thrusting at him.

The wizard was unable to break Jair's spell in time to move out of the sword's path. The sword's tip penetrated his chest, just to the right of center. It slid in with ease, all the way to the hilt. The mage let forth a terrible scream of pain and rage that ended in a low, bubbling gurgle. His eyes rolled up into his skull, and then he slumped to the floor, sliding off Tagor's shiny new blade. Blood pooled beside his now lifeless body.

Jair made it to his feet and looked up in time to see the wooden floor between him and Tagor give way. Flames caused by the explosion of the mage's powerful spell had started eating away at the right side of the tower.

Tagor yelled at Jair from across the opening in the floor, and over the roar of the fire and falling debris, "Jair, I'll take the inside stairs and meet you outside." Tagar pointed out the other door.

Jair nodded in agreement, looked over longingly at the wizards burning spell books and magical items, then headed down the stairs of the secret passageway. He took them two and three at a time. The walls to the passageway were already growing hot and smoke seeped in through cracks in the mortar.

Jair finally reached the bottom of the stairs and pushed down on the lever to open the outside door. Nothing happened! There was no response, even after pushing and pulling on the handle several times. Trying not to panic, Jair pounded on the secret door and yelled for help, hoping that Kethok was still outside.

Shortly thereafter, there was a loud boom and the wall fell crashing in from the outside, barely missing Jair. Outside stood the looming figure of the mute giant. Smoke clouded his ominous figure in the waning moonlight. Jair rushed out, grabbed Kethok's chain and unlocked it with the key he'd taken. The spell was gone, but the lock was still functioning. Kethok might have been able to break it, but the key was quicker. The two of them then ran for the edge of the forest.

Meanwhile, within the burning tower, Tagor rushed through the other door in the upper room and ran down the main stairway. The burning tower had fallen through in several places and had sent the rest of the building up in flames. The heat was almost too great to bear.

Ripping a large tapestry off the wall as he ran, Tagor covered himself in it and dashed through a large wall of fire that was blocking his way to the outside door. He couldn't believe how quickly the fire had spread. Reaching the door, he dropped the tapestry that was now in flames. He then cut off a small piece of the material with his sword. He used the piece of material to grasp the bolt on the door and slide it back. Smoke emanated from the cloth in his hand. It burned from the heat on the metal door handle.

Tagor threw back the bolt, jerked the door open and rushed out of the tower. He ran for the eastern edge of the forest, where they had waited earlier for night to fall.

Upon reaching the edge of the forest, Tagor stopped when he spotted Jair and Kethok. He walked over to them breathing hard and began coughing from the intake of smoke.

"See Tagor, that wasn't so bad," Jair exclaimed, after Tagor had caught his breath, "We did alright."

At that moment the wizard's magic supplies that were still in the tower exploded. A large fireball rose into the night sky, lighting everything up for several leagues. The blast from the tower knocked the three companions to the ground and showered them with small splinters of wood and chips of stone. When they looked up they saw that one whole side of the tower was completely gone.

Tagor looked once menacingly over at Jair, who only smiled slightly and shrugged his shoulders, trying to look innocent.

They picked themselves up off the ground and headed back to their earlier camping place, which was only a short distance away. There they collected their things and decided to put some distance between themselves and the burning tower. They also wrapped up Tagor's wounded hand. As they set off, Jair figured there was no telling who or what would come out of the woods to see what had caused the fire. If the goblins were nearby, it would definitely bring them running.

They traveled on toward Gallador for several hours. Walking through the forest in the dark wasn't easy, so Jair led the way. When there were only a few hours left until dawn, they stopped to rest, dropping to the ground. Jair quickly fell asleep, exhausted.

• • •

Elsewhere in the forest, only a short distance away, Thuk watched as the ball of fire reached up into the night sky. The band of goblins had been traveling hard; trying to catch up to pair that had robbed them.

The loss of the Dark Lord's prize and the fact that the woodsman had escaped them had put the band into an exceptionally foul mood. It was causing a lot of quarreling amongst them. Only through Thuk's threats and by beating several of the band members had he kept them together.

The ball of fire had drawn the goblins' attention, causing them to stare in wonder. Some of them looked about in fear, not knowing what it was that could cause such an explosion. Many of the goblins believed it could only be magic.

The explosion also drew the attention of many other dwellers of the forest. Thuk shouted orders at his troops to break camp and head for the disturbance before anyone or anything else could get there. He hoped that it might be a lead as to the whereabouts of the two they were following.

The goblins had lost the tracks of the companions the day before. They had lost them after crossing a small rocky knoll. Not knowing what else to do, the goblin band decided to go on toward the river. Thuk had hoped to pick the trail back up there.

The band picked up their equipment and moved off at a brisk pace. Most of them grumbled and moaned about not getting to rest and that Thuk was pushing them too hard. Goblins were lazy by nature and never overextended themselves unless they were forced to.

Thuk knew the consequences would be very dire if they did not retrieve the helmet. He told his troops this, and by so doing, kept them moving. Fear of the Dark Lord was enough to keep them all moving. The troops feared the Dark Lord even more than they did Thuk; and everyone feared Thuk except Natog. Natog feared very little. Probably because he wasn't smart enough to be afraid.

Upon reaching the river, the band came to the barge crossing. It was still on the other side of the river. Thuk picked out two volunteers and ordered the young goblins to cross the river to bring back the barge. Both goblins protested loudly because goblins disliked water, but they obeyed and entered the shallows, wading across while holding onto the thick rope.

A short time later the goblin band arrived on the other bank. They barely fit on the barge. Thuk led the way as they went back into the forest toward the burning tower. It's light had begun to diminish as the fire burned down.

After reaching the clearing and doing a thorough search, one of Thuk's scouts found the tracks of the two they were following. To their dismay, they also found another set of large tracks belonging to a giant.

A howl of pleasure escaped several of the goblins' throats as they began the hunt once again. Before leaving, a grim thought went through Thuk's mind as he studied the carnage of the tower. He wondered what had happened at the tower and he was curious why a giant would join with the two they had been following.

Two humans were one thing, but he did not want to face a giant. It also looked like one of them was a magic user. Thuk knew that he would have to be very careful. Not that he was afraid of losing any of his troops. It was just that he didn't want to take a chance on losing the helmet. Battling a human fighter, hill giant, and a wizard were not high on his list of things to do. He would have to plan this carefully.

• • •

Jab, jab, something sharp poked into Jair's chest rousing him from his slumber. He woke slowly and was surprised to find the tip of a crude stone spear being poked into his chest. He looked up and saw the spears' owner. It was a goblin scout grinning evilly down at him in the early morning light.

Glancing around their makeshift camp, Jair saw that Tagor was in a similar position and not able to move or defend himself. Jair quickly looked around, but saw no sign of the giant. He had a sinking feeling in his stomach as he looked up at his goblin captor. Fear crept up his spine. It was a feeling that he didn't particularly care for.

All of the years of living with Kentar had conditioned him to constant beatings and punishment, but that was completely different from being tortured to death at the hands of goblins.

Earlier that morning, Jair and Kethok had not had any trouble working their way through the forest. They used their infravision, which allowed them to see the heat given off by all of the living things around them. This allowed them to move around confidently in the dark. Tagor had no such luck. After a few hours of stumbling around, he could not continue on so they had decided to stop until the sun came up.

Once they had finally stopped, Kethok had kept the first watch, signing to them that he was not that tired. He and Tagor looked around, but did not know what had become of him.

Tagor glanced over at Jair. It was obvious that Tagor thought Kethok had abandoned them during the night. "Good for nothing giant," Tagor muttering under his breath. Evidently he felt the giant had left them to be slaughtered by the goblins.

As they lay there waiting, a loud guttural shout came from the other side of the clearing. The rest of the goblin band came out of the woods with Thuk in the lead. A wide, evil grin spread across the ugly goblin leader's face as he emerged from the forest. He walked smugly over until he stood before the two captives, grunting out orders in the harsh, guttural goblin language as he approached.

His orders were immediately carried out by the other goblins. Jair and Tagor were stripped of their weapons and packs and their hands were tightly bound behind their backs.

Thuk moved over and stood before the pile of their belongings. He bent down and retrieved the old, worn leather satchel that contained the magic helmet. He opened the pack and examined the helmet, then dumped the rest of Jair's belongings on the ground. Thuk grinned from ear to ear due to the fact that the Dark Lord's prize was once again secure.

The goblin leader closed the satchel and slung it across one of his dirty green shoulders. He then turned back to face the two weary travelers. Another cruel smile played across his face as he spoke in a crude form of the common tongue.

"You give Thuk good chase, make Thuk very mad. Take Dark Lord's prize. Now Thuk punish ugly human and half-elfling. Make hurt very long, be good sport for warriors".

He turned toward Tagor and grinned even more. He then turned toward the rest of the goblin band and motioned for one of them to come forward. Jair noticed that the new goblin was shorter than the leader, but with a thicker build. The new goblin's face was heavily scarred. This gave him an even more fearsome look than the rest of the gang. Jair recognized him as the one that had a personal grudge against Tagor.

Thuk looked at the other goblin and started spouting off grunted words in their own language. He then pointed toward Tagor. The other goblin looked at Tagor and gave him a look of pure hatred. He then responded to Thuk.

Jair leaned over toward Tagor while the goblins were conversing and whispered, "What are we going to do? That's the one I heard talking about you the first time I came across them in the forest. He's the one that really hates you."

Tagor took a long hard look at the shorter goblin and replied, "I remember him from a few years back. He was part of a raid on a small village. A large goblin band, just on the other side of Caerdon, had been raiding villages. I was a mercenary then. The goblins attacked the village that my squadron was staying in. We slaughtered most of them. I thought I had left him for dead. It would seem I was mistaken."

"He remembers you well enough. He hated you enough to find out where you lived. He volunteered to go on a dangerous mission into hostile territory just to have a chance at getting back at you," Jair said.

Tagor thought about their situation for a moment and remembered a goblin custom. "We might be able to work this to our advantage," Tagor said.

"What do you mean?" Jair asked him.

"If I can get the short one mad enough at me and challenge him to a duel, the commotion might give you a chance to get free, and hopefully get to your belongings. Do you think you might have a spell in that book of yours that will help get us out of this?" Tagor asked him.

"Yes, I think I might have something that will do the trick. What if you get killed before I get free?" Jair replied.

"Then you're on your own," Tagor said flatly as he turned back to watch the discussion still going on between the two goblins.

The goblins finally finished their talk and turned toward their prisoners. Thuk went over to where Jair was standing. He looked him up and down then said, "Elf-man steal helmet. Cause Thuk lose much honor. You die first, make great sport. We cut you long time."

Tagor heard this, looked over at Jair, then turned toward Natog and said, "I remember you rat face. You're the one I left for dead at that village in the north years ago. Goblins are cowards, but you are worse than most. I was surprised you were even there. I should have..."

That was as far as Tagor got before Natog burst into a bellowing rage and charged toward him. The only thing that stopped him was a quick shout made by Thuk for some of the other goblins to grab him. Seeing his chance to possibly rid himself of both of them, an idea sprang into Thuk's mind.

Thuk spewed out a few more sentences in goblin. He called Natog forward, reminding him of their customs. What the plan consisted of was a fight between Natog and Tagor. It would be a fight to the death for honor. It would allow Natog to defend his honor and provide sport for the other goblins.

Natog jumped at the opportunity to kill the human ranger while improving his status among the goblins. Natog thought his defeating the human in mortal combat would also make his chances of becoming leader better. He hoped the other goblins would turn and follow him.

Thuk ordered Tagor to be cut loose and his sword handed to him. The rest of the goblins formed a large circle in the clearing. All of them kept their weapons out in case Tagor tried something foolish. Several had bows at the ready.

Thuk walked over to Tagor, and said to him, "You fight Natog, to the death." Tagor replied and asked him, "If I fight and win what do I get in return?"

Grinning mirthlessly with his jagged yellow teeth showing, Thuk replied to him, "You get quick death." Then he turned back to face the circle of goblins.

Tagor shook his head slightly, feeling that they didn't have any other options. He turned and looked at Jair who nodded his head slightly to say he was ready.

The goblins were all howling and shouting out their encouragement to Natog. They were all hoping to see Natog crush and splatter the puny human for their sport and entertainment. Natog picked up his large club and advanced into the middle of the circle. There he waited for Tagor to enter the circle.

Tagor tightened his grip on his sword. He felt how light it was and drew strength from it. The sword seemed to pulse and throb in his hand, but he thought it might just be his own heart beating nervously as he entered the ring. A goblin guard shoved him roughly before he stepped through the circle. This caused him to stumble slightly and brought a roar of laughter and jeers from the surrounding goblins.

Natog immediately charged him. He wanted to end the fight quickly and not give the human warrior a chance to defend himself. Natog knew the human was very skilled and had been through many campaigns, but he also knew he was getting old. Natog's brute strength and speed would be the determining factor in his favor. His anger at the memory of his defeat by Tagor years earlier also helped.

Natog swung his heavily studded club in a viscous arc toward Tagor's head. Tagor was barely able to dodge out of the way in time. Surprised by his own quickness, Tagor found his sword coming up in a slicing parry, stopping the goblin's attack with a loud clang.

Natog jumped back with disbelief showing on his face at the

speed with which the human had parried. Natog knew now he would have to be more careful for the remainder of the fight. It was not going to be as easy as he thought.

Thuk stood silently off to the side grinning to himself at his own cleverness. This human might just have a chance to defeat Natog. That would be so much the better as far as he was concerned. It would allow him to finally be rid of his competitor. His position as leader would be more secure and then they would kill the human and half-elf and carry on with the rest of their mission. Thuk thought to himself that it would bring him favor with the Dark Lord.

Meanwhile, over at the edge of the camp, Jair was trying to slip his bonds. The goblins were so intent on watching the fight that they had forgotten about their other captive. He slowly edged his way toward his things that were scattered on the ground. While he was doing this, he worked on his bonds. He almost had them by the time he arrived at the pile. He tried not to draw the attention of any of the goblins.

The ropes on his wrists had been fairly tight, but he finally succeeded in removing them. He then slowly reached down to retrieve his belongings. He then eased back toward the edge of the clearing and slipped into the woods. He had his spell book and some of the scrolls he had taken the night before from the wizard's tower. He could not believe his luck, so he was extra cautious as he moved around the edge of the camp.

Jair sorted through the scrolls and came across a spell he thought might work. It was a fireball spell, one of the big ones. He hoped he had the proper spell components and skill to use them. Digging through his pouches, he found what he needed and let out a sigh of relief. He then looked up and around to make sure no one had spotted him and then began the spell.

By this time Tagor and Natog were in heated battle in the

center of the goblin ring. They were shouting and hollering, placing bets and enjoying the spectacle.

Tagor had a large bruise forming on his upper left arm where Natog had caught him with a crushing blow from his club. His arm hung limply at his side and looked to be broken, along with his hand. Natog also sorely injured. Tagor had cut him in several places, none of which were fatal, but together were draining the goblin of his blood and energy.

The battle continued and the combatants circled one another warily looking for an opening. Both of them knew they were going to have to finish the fight soon. If they did not, Thuk would decide it for them.

A short way off in the woods, Jair had almost completed memorizing the spell and was saying the last few words, preparing to release it on the goblin band.

Suddenly, from across the far side of the clearing came a large, hurtling mass that burst from out of the forest. It smashed into the foremost goblin warriors scattering them like rag dolls. With a force that was unbelievable, something had attacked the goblins, taking them completely by surprise.

Jair looked up from his spell and saw that the goblin's attacker was Kethok. He charged into the thick of the goblin band and smashed away with a giant club he had cut from a tree in the forest.

The club was huge. It was a little over five feet long, six inches at the base and tapered to almost a foot in diameter at its tip. The giant swung away repeatedly at the surrounding goblins that swarmed and milled about in a mass of confusion. Several were lying still on the ground.

Tagor chose that moment to make his final attack, as Natog was momentarily distracted. He charged forward and came in low with a powerful uppercut toward Natog's throat. The goblin barely saw the attack coming and tried to bring his club up to block it. This turned out to be futile.

Tagor's aim was on target. His blade clove cleanly through the goblin's thickly banded neck muscles, completely severing them. The goblin stood for a moment in shocked disbelief, then toppled to the ground with his head rolling a few feet off to one side.

At the same time, Jair finished uttering the last few phrases to his spell and felt the surge of power as it was released from within him. The spell components vanished from his hand and were replaced by a small ball of flame that floated just above his palm. The small ball started to grow, swirling and churning in mid-air.

As the ball grew to about three feet in diameter, it set nearby limbs on fire. Jair struggled to keep his control over the spell. He looked around at the milling, confused goblins and found a group advancing toward him. After the initial shock of Kethok's attack had worn off, some of them had spotted him. He pointed his finger at them and released the magical ball of flame. It swirled toward the oncoming goblins, growing in size as it went.

Flames roared over the goblin warriors, burning them into ash and cinders almost instantaneously. How many goblins were actually caught in the fiery ball of death Jair wasn't sure, but there were several charred masses lying on the ground. Several other goblins had been knocked to the ground by the fireball's passing.

Meanwhile, a large pile of broken bodies had formed around Kethok. He had slain two or three more of the ugly creatures while the rest were warily trying to surround him for a final charge.

Tagor had cut down several other goblins while weaving a deadly pattern before him with his sword. None of the goblins dared to face him alone. At the same time as he was trying to hold some of the goblins off, he tried to work his way toward Kethok. If he could get closer to him, they could work together.

Thuk looked around at the chaos and decided things were not going well. He realized this after the half-elf had released the fireball, decimating a third of his troops.

Because the odds were no longer in his favor, Thuk decided to leave while he had the chance, so he took off into the nearby forest. He knew there would be no mercy at the hands of his group if he were caught by whoever was left. Even if he lived, it would be even worse for him if the Dark Lord caught him.

On the other side of the clearing as the fireball dissipated, Jair saw that his friends were still in trouble. He laid down his spell book and ran over and picked up his bow, which was still lying on the ground nearby.

He drew out an arrow from the quiver and carefully took aim at one of the goblins that was in the back of the group. He then let the arrow fly. It split the goblin's head, dropping him to the ground. Jair thought that if he picked off the ones in the rear, the rest of them might not know he was firing at them until it was too late.

Jair drew a bead on another goblin and released another arrow with a small twang. This arrow flew at the goblin, piercing it just below and between the shoulder blades. This one also fell to the ground.

Meanwhile, Tagor made his way over to Kethok who silently nodded his head in acknowledgment. They teamed up, back to back, in order to take the oncoming final rush of the last of the goblin band.

Tagor turned to face their opponents and saw one of them drop from behind. He spotted Jair kneeling by the edge of the clearing, bow in hand, knocking another arrow to let fly.

Another goblin fell leaving only four more to attack them.

They came in fast and together, hoping to overcome them.

Kethok caught the first one to his right with a crushing blow to its skull. He whipped his giant club around in a devastating arc and caught the other in its midsection. This surprised both goblins at the speed with which he had responded. The blow impaled the second goblin on one of the small limbs that was still protruding from the freshly cut club.

Tagor met the other two goblins in a fierce display of swordsmanship. He caught one's sword and blocked it while severing the tip of the other's spear at the haft. It stepped back drawing a dagger. Tagor then whipped his sword around and hammered several more blows down on the first goblin's sword. This forced the first goblin into a position between Tagor and the other goblin that had stepped back.

Tagor caught the goblin's sword as it came back in and easily beat the crude weapon aside. He then lunged forward impaling it on his sword. Seeing his companion fall, the second goblin turned to flee only to find a feathered shaft protruding from his chest. He quickly dropped to the ground, eyes glazing over as he fell.

Tagor lowered his blade, wiped it on one of the dead goblin's tunics, and then sheathed it. He took a quick look around at the carnage before him and made sure there were no other enemies about. He walked over to Kethok and placed his good hand on the giant's arm, giving him a nod of acknowledgment and thanks. He then turned his attention to Jair and said, "Where's Thuk?"

Jair turned and pointed in the direction where he had seen Thuk run into the woods and said, "He ran that way, right after I cast the fireball."

A frown crossed Tagor's face as he replied, "We'll need to gather our things and set out after him quickly. He does not need to get away with the helmet."

The Ruby Helmet

Jair glanced down at Tagor's arm, concern showing on his face. "It's broken now as well as my hand. I'll need a healer to mend it. There's not much we can do about it at the moment," Tagar said.

The other two nodded their heads in agreement and gathered their belongings. Jair only stopped long enough to bandage Tagor's cuts with a few strips of cloth torn from one of the dead goblin's clothes. He then made a crude splint for his broken arm.

While they were doing this, Kethok went over the dead goblin's bodies searching them for valuables. He found a few coppers and some silver, but that was all. After that, the trio set off into the woods to try to stop Thuk from escaping with the helmet. The helmet was something that did not need to stay in the wrong hands. They hoped they could catch up with him in time to stop him.

Chapter 5

Thuk ran recklessly through the woods. He knew he had to put as much distance as possible between the battle and himself. It didn't really matter which side won, he was dead either way if any of them caught him. The human and half-elf would not let him get away after all that had happened, especially since Thuk now had the helmet. It was just his luck they would have to run into a half-elf that was a magic user and a thief.

The elfling must have been able to see past the ring of aversion the Dark Lord had given him. If it had not been for that, the elfling would have never noticed them and come snooping around. Of course, the Dark Lord had not expected them to run into any elves in these parts, and the dark elves had given them safe passage underground until they were past the high elves' domain.

During the entire trip, Thuk knew he and the other goblins had to deliver the helmet to its final destination or the wrath of the Dark Lord would most definitely be upon them. His fellow goblins did not know the Dark Lord had placed a spell upon them. If they did not complete their quest, all of them would die a terrible death.

Thuk had seen the spell worked upon some of the Dark Lord's other servants who had failed in their missions. The servants used whatever was nearby and killed themselves. One death he had witnessed was when a servant had failed her mission she had thrown herself from a window high up in a tower. Another slit his own wrists, and another leapt into fire.

The thought of what the Dark Lord could do sent a shiver down Thuk's hairy spine. This spurred him on to an even greater speed. He only had a couple of days to complete his mission and it would probably take him that long to do it. Deshtar would not wait much longer before contacting the Dark Lord and asking the whereabouts of the magic helmet.

The Ruby Helmet

Thuk ran on through the woods and suddenly came out onto an old dirt road. There were many wagon, hoof and boot tracks that ran up and down it, but it had not been used for some time. Plants had begun to grow over it.

He had just stopped for a moment to ponder which direction to take when the clopping of hooves sounded from around a bend in the road. He looked up as a mounted warrior came into view. The warrior sat upon a huge black stallion and was fully armed.

The warrior let out a curse as his horse reared up from the goblin standing in the middle of the road. He drew a huge battleaxe that was slung off the stallion's saddle. He quickly gained control of his steed and then spurred his horse into a gallop. The warrior charged Thuk, who stood in shocked amazement.

Thuk came to his senses, dropped the satchel and then drew his long, wicked scimitar. He had faced mounted warriors before and he knew how to deal with this one. It was common for humans to attack goblins on sight. The enmity between the two races was long standing.

Thuk looked at the charging human and knew he needed to dispose of him quickly so he could continue with his mission. If he didn't, the others would soon catch up to him. As he waited in the middle of the road, the mounted warrior charged toward him. He swung his battleaxe toward Thuk's chest. Just before he reached him, he swerved a little to the left, trying to avoid the goblin's scimitar and protect his mount.

Thuk, being smarter than the warrior had anticipated, ducked at the last minute and slashed with his scimitar to sever the horse's front left foreleg. The horse to topple forward and threw its rider from his saddle. Clods of dirt, grass and dust flew into the air as they crashed.

The human warrior hit the ground and rolled. Somehow he

had miraculously retained his grasp upon his weapon as he came to his feet. He turned to face his opponent, knowing he was not dealing with an ordinary goblin. This one was smarter than most and had obviously been in many battles.

The two combatants quickly faced off and began circling one another warily. Both of them were looking for any weakness or opening. The human warrior was the larger of the two, but the goblin's thick, wiry muscles told of a primordial strength and speed. He had a strength that had been developed in the wilderness and from many years of hard living among his violent goblin brethren.

Thuk wanted to finish the warrior off quickly, so he charged in with his scimitar flailing. The warrior deftly parried and dodged the goblin's swift attacks, manipulating the heavy axe as if it were made of straw.

Thuk could not believe the speed and strength with which the human warrior blocked his attacks. This infuriated him; and also caused fear to enter into his cold, cruel heart.

The fight raged on for what seemed an eternity but was actually only a few minutes. Both of them hacked and slashed, ducked and dodged with neither giving way.

Just as Thuk was going to charge in for a final attempt at defeating the warrior, three figures emerged from the forest's edge just south and to the left of the combatants. It was close to where Thuk had left the woods just a few moments earlier.

The three figures that had emerged were the human, the half-elf and the giant. Thuk saw caught them out of the corner of his eye. They had defeated his men quicker than he thought possible.

Overwhelming fear sprang into his dark, cold heart at the sight of the new arrivals. Thuk made a final, desperate charge at the human warrior. He slashed viciously at the human's head, chipping a piece off one of the horns that protruded from his worn helmet. The blow momentarily stunned the human. Thuk's only chance was to finish him off quickly and escape before the other three could get to them.

Thuk tried to think of something that would get him out of his predicament. His attack had left the human warrior slightly dazed, which gave him enough time to lunge over and grab the fallen satchel. He threw open the cover on the satchel then reached in and pulled out the helmet. He took a quick look around at the approaching trio and recovering warrior, then placed the helmet on his head. It was a last desperate act.

Thuk had heard about the fabled powers of the helmet and knew what they were supposed to be. In the present situation, he decided it was his only hope. Once the helmet was on his head it did not seem to do anything. Jair, Tagor, and Kethok approached Thuk warily with their weapons drawn. They came to a halt just a few paces away from him. The large barbarian warrior also regained his feet and stood over to one side, cautiously watching the goblin and the newcomers at the same time.

As everyone watched one another, the magical helmet began to glow an ominous blue. Thuk grinned evilly as he felt the power of the helmet flow over him. He wasn't sure what it could do, but believed he now had the power to destroy his enemies. He could not understand why the Dark Lord would want to destroy such a marvelous weapon. With the power that washed over him, he felt he could destroy the Dark Lord himself!

A few seconds passed, then the helmet began emitting a low humming sound. Thuk turned to face the trio when a wave of severe and intense pain overcame him. Smoke started pouring from out of the eye and nose slits as a terrible and growing heat washed over his skull.

The others watched in horror, stepping back as the helmet

began to glow brighter, eventually turning a molten red. Thuk let out an ear-piercing scream as the helmet began to cook his skull from the inside of the helmet. After struggling for a few moments, the goblin stiffened, and then fell to the ground. The helmet fell loose and rolled off his blackened skull to lie at one side. It rocked back and forth a little before sitting still.

The charred remains of the goblin leader lay upon the ground as the companions moved closer to investigate. The human warrior also walked over, reaching the body first. He squatted for a moment to examine the grisly remains. The helmet's handy work impressed him and at the same time made him a little nervous.

The warrior rose and looked to see the three companions cautiously moving toward him. He lifted his battleaxe and moved into a defensive position. The warrior backed up a few steps to give himself some room to fight, if the need arose. He wasn't too concerned about the other human and what seemed to be a young half-elf, but the giant was enough to make him take two steps back.

Jair, Tagor, and Kethok kept their eyes on the barbarian as they cautiously stepped forward. Jair reached down and retrieved the large satchel, and then walked over to pick up the helmet. The helmet's surface was cool to the touch and had no trace of the magical fire that had just enveloped it. There wasn't a mark on it. Jair put the helmet back into the satchel then turned toward the barbarian warrior.

Tagor stepped forward to face the young barbarian. He could tell that their appearance alarmed him. He was very careful with his actions.

The young warrior quickly examined the three newcomers. The human seemed to be an older warrior, perhaps a ranger. His face was bruised and scarred and several fresh cuts marked his features. A sling was on one arm, and on his hip hung a magnificent long sword. He also carried a small round buckler that was strapped to his back. His face was kind, but weary; and he looked as if he had been on a long journey. He also had a beard shaped so it came to a sharp point with a mustache that curled slightly on the ends.

The half-elf looked young, but not quite a grown man. He noticed that he carried a pack, two longbows, two quivers of arrows, and a short sword strapped to his side. He also wore old leather armor that was slightly too big for him and he had a belt with many pouches. This told the young barbarian that the half-elf might also be a magic-user.

The young barbarian looked nervously at the giant. A human and half-elf he could handle, but a giant was something else entirely. He was a huge brute of a beast and wore old ragged animal skins that had been roughly stitched together.

In his left hand, he carried a large wooden club recently cut from a small tree. There was fresh blood still smeared upon its tip. The giant's face was not altogether ugly for one of its kind, but its sheer physical presence was ominous.

Tagor glanced over at his companions, and then looked at the young warrior. "I am Tagor, the woodsman. This is Jair, (he said nodding to the half-elf), and Kethok, (he said motioning to the giant)."

"We appreciate your help in stopping this goblin," Tagor said to the young man. "He and his band set upon us in the woods early this morning, capturing us. Were it not for the help of our large friend here, we would have been killed," he added while motioning toward Kethok with his thumb.

"This fellow was their leader. When he saw we were defeating his comrades, he ran off. We'd been chasing him for the past half hour and were about to give up due to our wounds when we stumbled onto this road and saw you engaging him. We are deeply grateful," Tagor said.

The young warrior lowered his axe and leaned upon its haft. He relaxed slightly, but was still wary for any tricks. He responded in a slow, deep voice.

"I am Rakkon, a mercenary and adventurer. I was headed for the city of Gallador when I came across this goblin standing in the road," Rakkon said, as he looked down upon the charred goblin remains.

He then scowled and said, "I hate goblins. Never could stand them after I saw what they did to a neighboring village close to where I grew up. I kill them whenever I get the chance."

"We were headed to Gallador ourselves. You are welcome to join us," Tagor responded.

Rakkon nodded his head in agreement and replied that he would join the companions as far as Gallador; but after they arrived there they would part company. He then mentioned to them his plans to join lord Tredebould's army in the ongoing war in the west. He glanced once curiously at Jair as he shouldered the satchel with the helmet, but decided it wasn't any of his business.

Rakkon walked over to his wounded mount and regretfully put the beast out of its misery with his axe. He knew the horse was dying and that just leaving it there would be cruel. It had been a faithful beast and had carried him well.

He gathered his equipment, slipping it over one of his broad shoulders. After checking to make sure everything was still in place, he turned and let the others know he was ready to leave.

They set off at an easy pace as they marched toward Gallador. They followed the small dirt road that headed in the direction they wanted to go. It was an old road that had seen many travelers going to and from Gallador. It had probably started out as a small hunting trail many years ago. As the city had grown, so had the road as more people passed that way. Eventually another road had been built farther north, so this one wasn't being used as much.

The companions chatted a little as they traveled. Jair talked the most because he was curious about his two new friends. He started out by questioning Rakkon, asking him where he was from and what adventures he had been on. Rakkon was reluctant to talk at first, because he did not know these people, but after Jair's persistence, he finally obliged with a few small tales. As he talked, he really gave out very little information about himself.

Jair told Rakkon and Kethok about his escape from Kentar's keep and his longstanding friendship with Tagor. He also told them where he had been heading after leaving Kentar.

Jair left out the part of taking the magic helmet from the goblins. After what they had just witnessed with the death of the goblin leader, Jair knew that the helmet was very powerful. It was possibly even the helmet Estolorn. His omitting the part about the helmet brought a nod of approval from Tagor, who walked along in silence. Tagor wanted Jair to keep the helmet a secret because they did not know if they could trust the young warrior, the giant, or anyone else.

Jair also told Rakkon that he had decided to travel with Tagor to Gallador, who was going to do some trading of furs he had trapped earlier in the year. He then told Rakkon of how they had met and rescued Kethok from the evil wizard, and how Kethok had saved them from the goblins that morning.

Rakkon noticed Jair neglected to mention anything about the mysterious helmet; but he didn't say anything. It might have been the helmet that had killed the goblin, or it may have been a spell Jair had cast on him. Rakkon didn't understand or like magic so he kept his thoughts to himself.

Jair also asked Kethok a few questions about his life. Rakkon was relieved that the focus had turned from him to the giant. Kethok, on the other hand did not seem to mind being asked a lot of questions. The fact that he could not speak made little difference as Kethok shook his head a lot and gave hand signs to Tagor who translated. Tagor later told Jair that Kethok was easy going compared to the other giants he had met. He also seemed to like humans better than the rest of his kin.

The companions traveled throughout the day and finally decided to find a place to camp for the night. The day had been young when they had started for the city. As they settled in to rest, Jair noticed that the air was still warm, but hinted at the coming of winter by cool breezes that played gently through the turning trees.

They moved off the main road for a short distance. Jair found a spot he thought they could use for a campsite. He found it just before the sun fell below the horizon. Working quickly, he built a small fire pit while Kethok went into the forest to find some wood. Rakkon decided to try his luck at hunting before it got too dark, so he borrowed one of Jair's bows. Tagor found himself a good spot next to a large tree where he sat down to rest. His arm hurt terribly from both of the wounds he had received. The day's events and his injuries had taken their toll and he was at the end of his endurance.

While gathering stones to place around the fire, Jair decided to ask Tagor some questions that had come to him while they had been walking. Speaking as he placed the stones into a circle, Jair asked him, "Tagor, do you think we can trust Rakkon? I mean about the helmet and the Dark Lord and everything."

"I don't know, Jair," Tagor responded. "We've just met him and we don't really know that much about him. I think it best that we keep it to ourselves for now. The fewer people that know about it, the less danger and trouble it will cause. Besides, after we reach Gallador we will be splitting up; and Rakkon will be setting off to join Tredebould's army." Tagor concluded.

Jair paused in his work, looked up at Tagor and asked, "What about Kethok? What will he do once we reach the city?"

Tagor replied, "He'll probably have to stay outside of the city and wait for us, or just go his own way. I doubt the people of Gallador would relish the idea of a giant waltzing around their fair city. We only asked him to go as far as Gallador with us. After that, he can go wherever he wishes. Since he saved us from the goblins this morning, I figure that makes us even."

That being said, Jair finished making his fire pit. He gathered a few small twigs and branches and began working with his flint and steel in order to spark the kindling.

Tagor grimaced slightly as he eased himself up into a better sitting position. He rested against a small tree at the edge of the clearing. He thought about what had happened over the last few days and the things he had been hearing over the last few months. Strange things had been happening in the lower kingdoms. Goblins roaming about in the Barnook Forest were not a common occurrence. Many strange travelers had also been seen on the road of late. Rumors of this Dark Lord had been floating around at some of the local inns and villages. And now there was the appearance of what seemed to be the fabled magic helmet Estolorn.

Tagor pondered the situation as he sat quietly and waited for the other two to return. Jair decided to go get some water, so he gathered up all of their water skins and went to look for the stream he could hear nearby. Shortly thereafter, Kethok emerged from the forest bearing a large armful of logs. He also had a string with several fish dangling from it, both of which he promptly dropped on the ground beside the small fire Jair had started.

Kethok then kneeled down beside the fire and started breaking up some of the larger limbs. He placed them on the fire. Jair came back and saw the fish, so he went over to the woodpile and retrieved several long sticks. He took out his knife and began scraping off the bark, shaping it into a spit to cook the fish with. After that, he set about cleaning them.

Night settled in over them while Tagor sat idly by, resting against his tree. He was almost asleep when Rakkon appeared out of the forest bearing two young rabbits. He brought them over and then he and Jair cleaned them. They then set them over the fire.

A short while later, after they had finished cooking everything, they ate quietly. Kethok ate everything he was given, including the bones. After having Jair check his bandages, Tagor used one of the packs as a pillow and covered himself with one of the small blankets he and Jair had brought along. He fell asleep immediately. Jair worried about what kind of shape Tagor was in. He did not seem to be doing very well.

Jair commented to Rakkon about Tagor's condition as they walked down to the small stream to throw out their scraps. They then washed up, scrubbing their faces and hands in the cold water. Jair was surprised by the amount of dirt and grime that came off of him. As they walked back to camp, Rakkon told Jair he wasn't sure about Tagor, but thought he would be ok.

Kethok merely raised a hairless eye ridge as the two emerged from the forest. He had already found himself a good spot for the night and had lain down. Rakkon decided to take the first watch, so Jair settled in for the night, pulling in close the satchel that contained the helmet. Rakkon was to waken Kethok next, who would then wake Jair a short while before dawn. They had decided to let Tagor sleep all night because of his injuries. They knew he needed the rest more than they did.

The others quickly fell asleep, leaving Rakkon to sit and ponder the current situation. It seemed to him that there was more going on here than his new companions were telling him. Jair clung too tightly to the satchel with the helmet he'd taken from the dead goblin; and Tagor acted edgy whenever he'd tried to talk about the incident.

The Ruby Helmet

Rakkon knew it was too early into the season for them to be going to market to try and sell or trade furs. They were only carrying a small bundle. He felt there was something else going on. What it was he just didn't know. As far as people go, Rakkon liked all three of the companions well enough; but he was still a little leery of the giant. It just didn't seem right for normal people to go traveling around with a giant. Kethok held more secrets than he let on too, but Jair and Tagor seemed to trust him well enough.

Rakkon had heard many of the rumors coming down out of the Darketh Kingdom while he had been traveling. Evidently there was a lot of movement in the countryside, and there had been large bands of goblins and giants moving about. This was unusual because goblins did not get along well enough with each other to travel in large bands, and giants were usually solitary creatures. Occasionally giants banded together in larger communities, but most lived in small groups.

He had also heard there was a lot of activity up near the dark elf kingdom. There had not been any reports of dark elf sightings in many years. The dark elves were the cousins to the high and wood elves. Several thousand years ago, they had been forced to leave the lands of their cousins. This was after they had started using black magic. The high and wood elves had reached a point where they could no longer tolerate the cruel and evil behavior of their darker brethren. They eventually had to drive them from their lands.

The dark elves had traveled to the Anarest Mountains, where they had found an opening to underground caverns. They journeyed down into the earth where they made their homes and practiced the dark arts.

The way things were shaping up, Rakkon thought that something big was going to happen soon. He planned to be a part of it. He hoped to make a lot of money by being a mercenary. With this Dark Lord gathering troops, and all of the activity abroad, it could only mean war eventually. All the signs pointed to it.

It had been over five hundred years since anyone had tried to overthrow the southern kingdoms and Shanoal; the Oppressor had almost done it. Shanoal had been a powerful half-orc lord who had united the orc clans into a formidable army. His organizing of the orcs, plus recruiting a lot of human mercenaries and goblins from out of the north had almost brought the southern kingdoms down.

Rakkon knew about it after hearing stories around the family fire as he was growing up in his homeland. He remembered hearing about Shanoal, who had his stronghold in the Kingdom of Cilentia, just north of the Tanesh River and west of the Anarest Mountains. Many orc bands had been scattered throughout the Anarest Mountains back then, and Shanoal had brought them all together. Shanoal had been an adventurer who had come across a treasure of some kind. This treasure had given him the means to buy equipment and supply his army. He had built his army in secret over a period of several years.

Shanoal had supposedly also found an ancient magical weapon that had allowed him to control the orcs and keep them unified. No one else had been able to do that before, at least not as successfully. Gathering his troops until they were of sufficient size, Shanoal had marched southward into the Kingdom of Parvincia, and then east invading the elven kingdoms. He had tried to destroy whatever he could not conquer.

It was only through a united effort that the other nations were able to defeat him and destroy the evil artifact that he had possessed. They had sent his horde running back to their lairs. The humans that had taken part during the war lived in shame for several generations after that.

During all of this, the dark elves had stayed underground. They had not wanted to get in the middle of a fight they didn't care anything about. The dark elves looked down upon all of the other races. They especially looked down on the orcs and their kin and it would have been beneath them to follow a half-orc leader.

Rannon's watch passed uneventfully. At the appointed hour, he cautiously woke Kethok to take his turn. Kethok rose silently and nodded to Rakkon, who silently lay down and went to sleep.

Kethok moved over to one side of the fire that had been burning low and placed a few more logs on it. That helped to chase off the chill that had crept into the air. He leaned his club beside him, and silently watched over his new companions.

He had never had friends before. These humans had treated him better than any of his kin. They definitely treated him better than the mage that had captured him a few months ago after his battle with the hippogryph. Kethok decided he would stay with them, at least for a while. He had nothing better to do and there was something about the half-elf that intrigued him.

Chapter 6

A cold wind blowing in from the north woke them in the morning. The cool air warned of the coming winter. Dark, ominous clouds blanketed the sky as the companions rose. Jair woke and saw Kethok sitting by the fire. The giant had placed the last of the logs on the diminishing embers, trying to give them a little warmth while they slept.

The cold wind didn't really bother Kethok. He was use to it, having been raised in the icy peaks of the northern Anarest Mountains. Giants were thick-skinned and very tough by their very nature.

Sometime early that morning, Kethok had managed to slip away long enough to catch a small animal that he had cleaned and spitted over the open fire. Jair couldn't tell exactly what it was, but it looked like a large bird. He was grateful for the opportunity to eat another meal. Over the last few days, he and Tagor had only eaten a little of their meager rations. Their last two meals had been very welcome.

Jair rose and put away his blanket. He then removed a heavy wool cloak from his pack. He was thankful that Tagor had told him to bring it along. Jair placed the cloak around his shoulders and fastened it in the front. He then picked up his satchel and went over to where Kethok sat tending to the small animal as it cooked over the open flames.

Kethok nodded to Jair as he sat down. He tore a piece of meat off of the bird and handed it to Jair. Kethok also took one for himself. Jair accepted the meat thankfully and tore into it. Rakkon and Tagor also rose and put away their blankets. They then came over and joined the other two by the fire.

Everyone ate quickly and in silence, washing the bird down with fresh water from the nearby stream. After eating, they decided it was time to leave so they picked up their belongings, put out the fire by covering it with dirt, then walked through the forest toward the road. Once there, they resumed their journey to Gallador, setting a moderate pace.

Jair didn't think the day was going to get any warmer while they walked. His two human companions brought out their heavy cloaks to help ward off the chill. He had to help Tagor put his cloak on, due to his injured arm. He could tell the coming winter was going to be a rough one. It had started growing cold much earlier than usual.

As the morning wore on, Tagor started looking worse. His face was very pale and his breathing came in long, labored gasps as he walked along the road.

Evidently, the fight with the goblins had taken a more of a toll on him than he had let on. He had lost a lot of blood from all of the minor cuts he had sustained during the battle. None of the wounds had seemed fatal, but together they had drained him enough to weaken him greatly. He also complained that his ribs hurt. Jair figured some of them were broken.

Jair kept an eye on him as they traveled throughout the day. He wondered what they were going to do once they arrived at the city. He thought that Tagor needed serious medical attention, as soon as possible.

A short time past noon, Jair spotted something off in the distance. As they came around a bend in the road, they sighted a tall gray spire that reached up into the cloudy sky. It had a golden pennant that bore the crest of Gallador, fluttering in the wind just above it.

As they approached the city, Jair was not sure he wanted to see the place where he had been enslaved as a child. It brought back a wave of scattered memories and emotions. They were especially sad ones of his mother. He also remembered the hunger and fear from living on the streets.

The trail before them eventually opened up, leading to a well-paved road. Once on the paved road, the forest gave way around them to large, open fields. Workers and farmers were in these fields, trying to get in the last of their crops before the winter settled in. The coming winter would probably destroy what little they had grown if they did not gather it in time.

As they passed by Jair noticed that the people were mostly peasants. According to Tagor, they made up the majority of the areas population. They seemed to be strong and hearty workers. Tagor also mentioned that Gallador's king protected them.

The road cut through the fields and lead up to the massive iron gates that formed the entrance to the city. Jair guessed that the gates were magically reinforced, due to the city's magical history, its powerful inhabitants, and the runes that covered them.

Surrounding the gate was a massive gateway built of large, square, dark stones. The stones were smoothly cut and had been placed upon one another evenly. Jair thought they had probably been cut out of the rock in the nearby Timgranok Mountains and had been hauled down to the city below by slaves. The thought of slavery disgusted him. He did not understand why a place so advanced in some ways was so backward in others.

Thick walls flowed out from behind the gateway. These walls stood more than forty feet high and were built out of the same cold, dark stones. Battlements were placed evenly along the walls with closely placed merlons in between them. These allowed archers to shoot down at attackers, yet gave them cover from attack. The walls were heavily manned. Jair could see guards that were pacing back and forth along the rim, their spears and pikes sticking up above the walls.

The city spanned out before them as they drew closer, reaching back for over a full league. It stopped at the edge of the Wildrun River. Gallador was supposed to be the largest city in the southern kingdoms. Silvermist was the only other city close to it in size. Gallador supported more than fifty thousand people, half of which were probably troops and military families.

As they traveled toward the city, several slaves in the fields stopped to stare at them. Jair finally realize they were staring at Kethok. He quickly motioned the others to stop for a moment to assess their situation.

Jair looked at Kethok then stepped over next to Tagor. He looked at him and asked quietly, "Tagor, do you think this might be a good time to have a talk with Kethok?"

Tagor looked around at the workers in the fields who were still staring at them. He silently shook his head in agreement and stepped over to Kethok.

They spoke quietly with sign language for several moments. When they had finished, Kethok turned and started walking back down the road. He paused for a moment and turned to nod and wave good-by to Jair and Rakkon, then continued on his way. Jair waved back, then watched his large friend lumber slowly back into the forest.

Jair turned back around to face Tagor with a sad expression on his face. "What did you tell him? Is he going to wait for us?" Jair asked.

"I told him I thought it best if he were to stay in the forest. I told him the people of the city might not like him walking freely about in their midst. He agreed. Most people fear what they do not understand. I put it as gently as I could. He seemed to understand and acted as if it was ok." Tagor replied.

Tagor watched the giant until he disappeared into the forest then said, "He said he would wait for us for four days and would meet us on the morning of the fifth at our last camp site. If we do not return by then, he is going to head off on his own."

Jair nodded his relief, evident by the expression on his face. Rakkon shrugged then started walking toward the city once again. The other two followed in behind him.

When they finally arrived at the gate, two sentries halted their progress by crossing long, wicked looking halberds held firmly in gauntleted hands. From up above them, on top of the battlement overlooking the gate, came a voice that called down to them, "Who goes there? State your names and what business you have in Gallador!"

Rakkon stepped forward, somewhat annoyed at the guard's attitude, then replied, "I am Rakkon, a mercenary. I have come to your city for supplies and rest. I am on my way to serve in Lord Tredebould's army in the west. This is Tagor and Jair, here to trade furs. Tagor is wounded and in need of healing. We were set upon by goblins in the forest."

There was a short pause, and then a stocky looking man with a thick beard and wearing a shiny silver helmet peered out over the wall to look down at them. Presently, there were several orders given and then the two guards raised their halberds allowing them to pass.

Once through the gate, the short man with the beard and helmet met them just inside the gatehouse. He had come down a stone stairway inside the gatehouse. Several tough looking guardsmen followed him. The man strode forward and stopped in front of Rakkon. He looked the three of them over, carefully.

"I am Captain Buckner and am required by law to ask everyone that enters our city who they are and what business they have here. You must sign a register, state where you will be staying and how long you will be here." The captain said.

The Ruby Helmet

He turned around and headed for a small door that was off to the left of the gatehouse. As he went through the door into a small room, he motioned for the others to follow.

Once inside, Jair could see that the chamber was an office with an old desk, several chairs, and a small cabinet in each corner. A full weapons rack leaned against the far wall, right next to another door that was on the right.

The captain pulled off his helmet and set it upon the desk. He reached over the desk and picked up a large book that he opened and thumbed through until he found the page that he wanted. He then turned to face the trio and eased around to the back side of the desk, where he promptly seated himself in an old oak chair that looked as if it had seen better days. It creaked loudly as it took his armored weight.

He placed the open book on the front of the desk and motioned Rakkon forward, grinning up at him. He then pointed to the book and said, "Sign in here. State you name, your purpose for entering the city, and where you'll be staying."

Rakkon glanced over at his two companions, then bent down and started scribbling into the book. Finishing his writing, he looked back over at the captain and smiled back at him smugly. Evidently, the captain had not thought he could write, and Rakkon knew it.

"Can you recommend a good inn? Never having been to your fair city, I am not familiar with the available accommodations." Rakkon asked, in a cool, deep voice.

The captain glanced down at the register to see that Rakkon had left off where they would be staying; he then looked up and responded in his own gruff voice, "Talbard's place. It's called the Raging Minotaur. It's not one of the best inns in town, but he has good rates and the foods not bad. Tell him that Captain Buckner sent you."

"Where is this Raging Minotaur?" Rakkon asked him.

The captain looked back up from the register after writing in the name of the inn, and replied. "Go down the main street until you hit Strip's Crossing, go right for about four blocks and it's on the corner. You can't miss it."

The captain then held the quill out for the other two to sign in. Jair signed in first, and then Tagor stepped forward to sign in. He teetered a little as he did so. Tagor dropped the quill back on the desk when he finished, splattering a few drops of ink on the pristine white pages.

"Is that all captain, or will there be anything else?" Tagor asked as the captain frowned up at him. His face was pale.

"There's one other thing," the captain replied sternly. "We do not tolerate troublemakers in our city. We've had enough problems just dealing with the regular riff raff. If there's any trouble out of you three, we won't hesitate to use force to put you in your place. Do you understand?"

Tagor only glared at the captain in response. He then turned sharply and walked back out the door, trying to forget the pain he was in. He went out through the back of the gatehouse and entered onto the main street.

Tagor slumped slightly once they were out of sight of the gatehouse. Jair trotted up to catch him as he collapsed. He leaned heavily onto Jair's shoulder to keep from falling to the ground. Jair gave him a worried look and suggested they hurry and find a healer.

Rakkon led the way as the trio worked their way through the crowded city streets. His ominous size and demeanor helped clear a path. No one wanted to be in the way of the barbarian as he moved up the street.

All kinds of merchants and shopkeepers lined the thoroughfare and some of the smaller side streets. Many called out loudly toward each passerby, proclaiming what their wares were and that each of them had the best prices and products in the market.

Rakkon gently lead them, pushing their way through the throng of milling people. He finally led them to an intersection that was somewhat clear. Jair looked around for some indication as to exactly where they were. He finally located a small street sign on the other side from where they stood. The sign was six feet up in the air on a decorative wood pole. It was about a foot and a half long. Carved and painted into the face of the wood sign were black, bold letters that said Strip's Crossing.

Jair pointed across the street toward the road sign. He told Rakkon and Tagor that this was the street they were looking for. Rakkon immediately set off down the street to their right. Jair and Tagor followed as quickly as they could. Tagor did not seem to really be aware of where he was. There were fewer people passing down this street, so they were able to make better progress.

They followed the captain's instructions and four blocks later found themselves standing in front of a large, wood, two story building. Protruding from the face of the old building, just above the wide double doors, was a large wooden sign hanging from a long metal pole. The sign was a big, flat piece of wood that had been cut into the shape of a bull's head. It was painted blood red and had large golden letters just above its face that read, "The Raging Minotaur."

Rakkon looked over at the other two, and then stepped boldly through the double swinging doors that formed the entrance to the inn. Jair led Tagor through the opening right behind Rakkon. Once inside, a flurry of strange sights, smells, and sounds assaulted Jair's senses all at once. This surprised and intrigued him. He had never been to an inn before. On the few trips he had made to the city, Kentar had made him stay in a stable.

Jair looked around and could barely make out some of the figures that were seated or standing around in the dark, smoky room. The room was fairly large, with many tables and chairs scattered all around it. To the left side, against the far wall, was a series of six small booths. He knew that these were for people who were looking for a little privacy.

To the far end of the room, straight ahead, was a long wooden counter that had many stools all along it. To their right was a large, open fireplace that was built into the wall.

Rakkon led them as they worked their way across the room. He went directly toward the counter. They passed several tables along the way. Jair could see there were quite a few people already at the inn, even though it was still early in the day. At one table there sat three large, armored warriors who fairly bristled with weapons. They sat talking and laughing amongst themselves.

At another table were two women. One was a large, dark hared human warrior who was covered in chain mail and carried a broadsword. The other was a tall, thin, blond elf maiden. She wore leather armor and carried a small arsenal of daggers that were tightly strapped about her slim, muscular body.

As Jair passed by them, the elf maiden gave him a long stare. He didn't know what to make of it. The other woman looked up and smiled at Rakkon, who quickly smiled back; and then he continued on his way toward the counter.

Jair couldn't make out many of the other patrons as they passed by. This was due in part to a thick, black smoke emanating from many small oil lamps that were scattered throughout the room along the walls.

Rakkon made it to the counter, leaned upon its smooth wooden surface, then cleared his throat loudly to get the owner's attention. The innkeeper turned around to face them, then walked over to stand in front of him. As he over, he kept on cleaning a mug with a rag. Jair and Tagor moved up to stand beside Rakkon. Jair carefully began scanning the room, looking the other occupants over. He tried not to look conspicuous.

The innkeeper looked them over and then asked, "What can I do for you?"

Rakkon removed his battered helmet and set it on the counter. He then answered and said, "Captain Buckner of the city guard sent us. He said you would have rooms available."

The innkeeper smiled broadly and set the glass he had been cleaning onto a shelf under the counter. He then leaned on the top of the counter. "Buckner sent ya, huh?" he said. "Well, you must be all right then. He hasn't steered me wrong yet."

The innkeeper sized them up with a glance. He then continued speaking and said, "Rooms will run a silver piece per night. One gold if yer gonna stay a week. Two meals per day are included with the price of the room."

Rakkon looked over at the other two to see if it was all right with them. Tagor silently nodded, then reached down into one of his pouches to retrieve two gold pieces that he laid on the bar. Rakkon did likewise.

The innkeeper motioned for them to follow him, then turned and walked toward the left side of the counter. Before moving out from behind the counter, he retrieved a large metal ring upon which were fastened a group of iron keys. He then headed up a flight of wooden stairs that were just around the corner on the left side of the room.

Once they came to the top of the stairs, the innkeeper led them down a long hallway along which were many doors. The trio followed him to the last three doors on the left, where he removed three keys from his ring. Using each in turn, he opened the last three doors at the end of the hall. Each door opened into a small room that was furnished with a bed, a little wooden table, a mirror hanging on the wall, and a small pitcher for water and a bowl for washing.

The innkeeper turned to face them with his large meaty hands upon his thick wide hips and said, "Fresh linens and water will be furnished in the mornin. Breakfast is served first thing after sunrise, dinner promptly after dark. If you need anything, all you need do is call for me. My name is Talbard."

"Check out is by noon on the last day of the week that you paid for. If you wish to stay longer, you can pay me then." He then handed a key to each of them and turned to leave.

Before he left, Jair quickly spoke up and asked, "Sir, where might we find a healer? Our friend was injured on our way to the city and is in need of healing?"

The innkeeper responded, "You can find a healer down on Temple Street. Go back down to the main street, turn right for about five blocks. You should be able to find someone to help you there."

Jair thanked Talbard, who then the lumbered off down the hallway and headed back down the stairs. He turned to Tagor who was looking worse. His injuries looked as if they were just about to do him in and he seemed as if he were about to pass out. He was sweating. Jair thought he had a fever. He looked up at Rakkon and said; "I think I should get him to a healer now."

Rakkon nodded in agreement, and then said, "I'll wait for you both here at the inn and meet you in the common room downstairs."

Rakkon went into his room to store his gear while Jair and Tagor did likewise. Jair opted not to leave the helmet. He then helped Tagor back to his feet and led him down the stairs and out of the inn to the street below. Following the innkeeper's instructions, Jair led Tagor down several streets to the right. They eventually came to the road they were looking for, Temple Street.

They turned right on it and Jair started looking for a temple that might have a healer. Tagor moaned and grumbled along the way, looking around himself once or twice to try to get his bearings. His fever seemed to be making him somewhat delirious.

In a moment of clarity, Tagor reached down inside of his tunic and took out a small gold medallion, which he then handed to Jair. Upon the face of the medallion was the beautifully engraved image of a sun that was partially blocked by a cloud. Tagor then mumbled a few words in a raspy, shallow breath, "Find the temple of Anu using this sign." He said to Jair while pointing to the amulet, "It is there that we'll find a healer."

Jair took the medallion and continued leading Tagor down the street. Upon reaching a wide intersection, Jair spotted a temple that had the same emblem as the amulet. It was on the far street corner to their left.

The temple was quite large and seemed to have a lot of worshippers and patrons going in and out of its two massive, wooden doors. Above the temple doors was a detailed carven image, just like the one on the amulet.

Jair secured a better hold on Tagor, who was starting to slump. He then headed across the intersection toward the temple. Upon reaching the temple's front doors, Jair noticed two armored clerics who were standing guard. One was on each side of the doors. Jair led Tagor as best he could up the large stone steps. They stopped upon reaching the doors and Jair turned to address one of the clerics.

The temple's guards were both tall humans. Each wore full plate mail armor that was brightly decorated in silver and gold and had medallions similar to the one Tagor had given him. Both wore large war hammers that were slung from leather straps at their hips. Both of the men looked very capable of using them.

Jair assumed that the guards were placed outside to keep troublemakers out and to prevent thievery. As far as he could tell they had not stopped any of the other people that had gone in; so Jair wondered if they would allow them to pass.

Addressing the guard on the right, Jair asked him, "Sir, my friend here is seriously wounded. He asked that I bring him to this temple."

Jair lifted the medallion that Tagor had given him so that the temple guard could see it. The guard eyed the amulet briefly, then told Jair and Tagor to remain where they were. He then turned and went inside the temple.

Several moments passed as Jair held on to Tagor. He was barely conscious. His weight was getting to be too much for Jair to bear, but he held on to him anyway, trying not to let him fall to the ground.

After what seemed an eternity, the guard re-emerged from the temple with three more clerics right behind him. Two of the clerics wore white robes. They came over and took Tagor from Jair and led him inside. The other cleric wore a blue robe. He told Jair to follow him, then turned and entered the temple. The guard had gone back to his former position beside the open temple door, offering no explanation. Jair quickly stepped inside behind the blue robed cleric, wondering what was going to happen.

Chapter 7

Upon entering the temple, Jair was astounded by what he saw. They walked through a small antechamber that led into a large vaulted sanctuary. In passing, Jair noticed that the antechamber also served as a guardhouse and weaponry. Cabinets filled with weapons and equipment lined the antechamber's walls.

The sanctuary was about a hundred feet across and three hundred feet long with huge wooden beams that rose up to form a vaulted ceiling. Gazing up at it, Jair thought it could almost reach the sky. Rows upon rows of long wooden benches lined each side of the hall. The benches left three narrow isles, one in the center and one down each side. The aisles were heavily carpeted and led up to a large platform at the far end that had an altar.

Above and behind the altar was a dark, wooden pedestal. Behind it, upon the wall, were several large decorated tapestries. Each tapestry was a beautifully detailed depiction of ancient and powerful clerics of the church, doing great and heroic deeds for their god. Between the tapestries rested a large golden disc of about six feet in diameter. The disc was carved into the shape of a large golden sun that was partially covered by a small cloud.

Jair gazed in wonder as he hurriedly followed along behind the blue robed cleric. As they walked down the middle aisle between the many rows of benches, Jair saw that the sanctuary also had golden colored glass windows. These windows were placed high up on the walls and were spaced out about every ten feet. It was these windows that allowed shimmering shafts of golden sunlight to filter down into the great chamber. This brightened it wonderfully due to the early morning sun.

Besides the windows on the walls, there were highly polished metal plates that were about two feet around. They had small metal torch holders on them that had unlit torches attached to their bases. The plates were very smooth and shiny in their centers, and had small, delicately carved designs along their outer edge.

Jair knew that the metal plates were used for reflection to help illuminate the chamber at night. He also noticed that the torch holders were very clean. They had little or no soot on them from the torches. This told him that the clerics must be meticulous in their cleaning.

He followed the blue robed cleric up to the front of the chamber. The cleric turned to the left, after reaching the front of the sanctuary, and then headed out through a small door that Jair could now see had been hidden by one of the tapestries. The cleric paused long enough for him to catch up, then passed on through the door. The cleric pulled the door closed after Jair passed by, then continued on down a small, narrow passageway.

The walls of the temple were made out of large stone blocks that Jair could not identify. He followed the cleric through a series of winding and twisting corridors, up several flights of stairs and past many other doors and hallways, until he knew he was lost and was completely confused as to their current location.

They finally came to another small wooden door at the end of a long corridor. The blue robed cleric opened this door with a large golden key he removed from somewhere within his robes. Jair followed him into the room that turned out to be a library and study.

This room was also quite large. To the right side of it there were two large, wood and glass doors that led out onto a small balcony. The walls were lined with many bookshelves that were filled with hundreds of books. A large desk sat on the far side of the chamber, and to the left was a table with many chairs around it. The table was between the door and the desk.

Where the shelves didn't cover the walls, there were several very expensive looking tapestries and paintings. Shields with ancient clerical coats of arms also decorated the walls, and a large, very comfortable looking cushioned chair, sat next to the balcony.

The blue-robed cleric moved over to the other side of the large desk and pulled out a delicately carved oak chair. He then casually sat down. He motioned for Jair to have a seat in one of the other chairs, and then cleared his throat to speak.

"Your friend will be well taken care of. His wounds were serious, but if tended too properly, should not be fatal. It was good that you brought him here when you did. If you had waited much longer he might have died. The teeth and claws of goblins are known for disease and can cause infection from their unclean living conditions," He told Jair.

As the cleric spoke, Jair listened carefully to what the he said, but also tried to examine the room around him. The rows and rows of books upon the heavy wooden shelves reminded him of his home back at Kentar's keep. A slight shudder ran down Jair's spine at the thought of Kentar, so he quickly brought his full attention back to the blue robed cleric.

Jair started to speak, but the cleric interrupted him with a knowing look. It was as if he could read Jair's thoughts.

"My name is Darnok. I am the High Cleric of the temple of Anu. Tagor's father was a high level cleric in our order and my friend. His name was Ganor. He was a very powerful cleric who was slain while attempting to rescue a group of settlers in the northern wilderness. They had been attacked a by a group of raiding dark elves. Tagor's father slew many of the elves, but was himself overcome by their overwhelming numbers."

"The elves were a part of the many rogues that had been marauding at that time during the border wars. We knew it was Tagor with you because of the medallion you presented at the door. It had belonged to his father."

"Tagor was quite young when his father was killed. He had been close to what your equivalent human age would be now when it happened." Darnok said.

"Tagor was in training to become a cleric himself when his father died. It was very difficult for him. They had been very close. Anger at his father's death caused him to abandon his training with us and to join the king's army that was headed for the border. He went on to become a great warrior and quite skilled as a scout in the king's service. I had heard that he finally got his fill of killing in the border wars. We have not seen him until today."

Jair pondered over what Darnok was telling him. He could not comprehend the meaning of having lost a father because he had not known his own father. No one had played the part of a father to Jair either, except for Kentar, who did not even come close. Jair did wonder from time to time who his father had been and what it would have been like growing up with him.

Darnok paused for a moment to let Jair think about what he was telling him. He knew that the half-elf boy seemed to be very young, but was probably much older due to his elven lineage.

"Jair," Darnok said. "Tagor spoke very highly of you before he fell asleep. He said that you were on a very important mission and it had something to do with seeing the king. He would not tell me what this mission was. Would you care to enlighten me as to what this is all about?"

Jair held his pack tighter and his mind raced. He could think of no way around the conversation, or of a plausible explanation. He also did not know if he could really trust Darnok and the clerics from this temple.

Jair looked at Darnok's expectant face and decided to be straightforward and tell him as much as he could. He didn't know why, but a sense of wellbeing and peace passed over him and all of a sudden he felt that he could trust the older man with most of their story, but not all of it.

"Well sir," Jair said nervously. "We have been on a hard, long journey and came across something on our way to the city. Tagor believes it to be something critical to the safety of all the free kingdoms." From there, Jair proceeded to tell the Darnok some of what had happened to them. He kept the part about the helmet to himself.

"I am sorry, but until Tagor says that it is ok, I will not reveal what we found. I hope you can understand that?" Jair said.

Darnok smiled warmly back at Jair and then slowly rose from his chair. Placing his hands behind his back, he started pacing about the room casually, looking over some of the many books that lined his shelves.

"I respect your faithfulness to Tagor and will honor you in this matter, whatever it may be. I will personally send a message to the king telling him of your arrival and that Tagor wishes to speak with him privately about an important matter. I believe the king will see him. He is also a son of Anu and our church is highly favored by him. Tagor is also known to the king." Darnok said.

"Tagor's father and the king's father grew up together. Ganor had served as an advisor to the king. Because of that Tagor and the king had also known each other as children and had been friends for many years. The king had honored Tagor's wishes to enter the army in the border wars after his father's death." Darnok said while he paced.

"Tagor was an apprentice cleric in the ministry at that time and would have probably made a fine cleric for our blessed Anu. The loss of his father and chaotic political times caused him to turn from following in his father's footsteps to become a ranger. I believe that Tagor still has a part of the clergy in him. From talking to him a while ago, I believe he still has a strong belief in our God. This belief still lends to him some inner strength and comfort, but for the most part, Tagor is his own man."

As Darnok finished speaking, he came to a stop in front of his desk. Jair was slightly surprised at the mention of Tagor having been a holy man. He realized that over the years he had known Tagor, it was true that he seemed to stand by a strict code of honor and ethics, somewhat like a cleric.

"You are welcome to stay with us if you wish," Darnok told Jair. "A room will be made ready for you and food can be brought if you wish it. At the first sign of his recovery I will personally notify you and the king."

Jair rose from his comfortable chair and stood before him. Not knowing really how to act before a high cleric, he politely declined the offer to stay, even though he wanted to be there for Tagor.

"I thank you for your hospitality, but we have another friend that awaits me at the Raging Minotaur. He has already acquired rooms for us and I think I will stay there until Tagor is well enough to see us. Then we can decide what to do," Jair told him.

Darnok turned toward a small rope that was hanging from the ceiling and reached up to pull lightly on it. He then returned to his seat behind the desk.

"I know the inn of which you speak. At the first sign of Tagor's recovery I will summon you so you may see him." Darnok told him.

Presently the door to the room opened and a young, white robed, male cleric entered the room. Darnok turned to face the young man and told him, "Senok, please escort our young friend out of the sanctuary."

He turned back toward Jair and said. "Until we meet again Jair,

I bid you good day and may Anu bless you."

Jair nodded once toward Darnok, then turned and followed the white robed cleric out of the study. He followed the young cleric quietly, keeping his thoughts to himself.

It was not too long before Jair found himself once again in the large inner sanctuary that led to the outer doors of the temple. He followed the young white robed cleric back through the hall, which was now occupied by several worshippers.

By the looks of them, Jair guessed they came from all walks of life. There seemed to be a mix of people that were scattered throughout the temple. Jair noted everyone from carpenters and merchants to warriors and peasants as they each filed slowly in and out. He remembered from some of his studies with Kentar, and from a fleeting memory as a child, that some people came daily to worship while others only came occasionally. It all depended on how devoted you were.

Jair exited from the temple and noticed that the sun had already passed its zenith. It was starting to dip down into the west. He had been in the temple a lot longer that he had at first thought. A large part of that time had been spent traveling through its maze of corridors.

He walked tiredly down the temple steps and slowly made his way back through the busy city streets. Business was just now winding down toward the end of the day.

He thought about the last week's events as he made his way back to the inn. He wondered what was going to happen to him and his companions. Jair came out of his reverie as he found himself facing the ugly visage of the roughly painted bull's head on the sign just outside the Raging Minotaur.

He entered through the swinging double doors that led inside and paused for a moment to let his eyes adjust to the dark, smoke filled room. He quickly spotted Rakkon seated at a table over to the far right side of the room. It looked like he was eating something and drinking from a large pitcher that had been placed on the thick, old wooden table in front of him.

Jair worked his way through the inn's crowded main room over to where Rakkon was seated. He pulled up a chair and seated himself across from him. Rakkon looked up once from his meal, nodded to acknowledge Jair's presence, then resumed eating.

Jair eyed Rakkon's plate of food hungrily before speaking. "I left Tagor at the Temple of Anu. The head cleric said he would be all right, but he needs a lot of rest and care. They promised to notify us at the first sign of his coming around."

Rakkon grunted his acknowledgment around a mouthful of food. He stopped every so often to reach for his cup and take a great gulping drink. He would then resume eating. He stopped once and looked up at Jair who was just sitting and watching him while he ate. "Are you hungry?" he asked Jair, who nodded eagerly.

Motioning for one of the severing girls, who promptly came over to them, Rakkon said, "Another plate of stew, a half loaf of bread and another cup for my friend." The serving girl nodded, then turned and headed back toward the kitchen.

Rakkon looked at Jair who thanked him. Rakkon only grunted once again as he finished off the last of his stew. He sopped up the remainder with a piece of bread.

As Rakkon finished eating, Jair asked him. "Rakkon, do you plan to leave for Tredebould's army right away?"

Rakkon picked up his cup and leaned back in his chair before answering. "Well, I guess there's no great hurry, but I will probably leave in the next few days. I would like to join up with his mercenaries before anything major starts happening."

Jair nodded in reply. Relief passed through him since he now had someone he sort of knew in the city, at least for a couple of days.

His food arrived and he set to devouring it hungrily. Rakkon tipped the girl with a few coins from his money pouch. Jair had not realized how hungry he was until the serving girl had placed the steaming plate of stew and bread in front of him. Setting to it with a hearty gusto, it did not take long for him to finish it all off.

He slid his plate over to the side of the table for the serving girl to pick up, and took a small drink from his cup that Rakkon had filled from the pitcher on the table. He sat back, fully satisfied from his meal. Jair looked over at Rakkon who was silently leaning back against the wall with his chair, casually scanning the other occupants of the room.

As they both sat and rested from their long journey and the days' events, Jair eased into a quiet conversation with Rakkon. He told Rakkon what had lead up to his being there, carefully leaving out any mention of the helmet or their trying to see the king. A look of respect showed on Rakkon's face as Jair told him about what they had done for Kethok before they had met Rakkon on the road.

Rakkon in return, told Jair a few more of his adventures and of when he had struck out on his own and headed south. Jair was enthralled by Rakkon's stories. He listened eagerly as Rakkon narrated them in his slow, deep voice.

Rakkon seemed a quiet person, keeping mostly to himself, but as he spoke of his adventures his tongue moved swiftly with entrancing words, describing every deed in graphic detail, leaving out nothing. The story that caught Jair's attention the most was when Rakkon told how he saved a whole village from a wyvern.

Dragons were almost unheard of, and wyverns were just as

scarce. If Rakkon were telling the truth, then he was a great warrior indeed, Jair thought as he listened to the story.

The evening wore on as the two young men got to know each other better. Jair felt as if he had known Rakkon for many years, even though it had only been a few days. Traveling and adventure seemed to lend to quick friendship, but Jair was glad he had met the young warrior from the north.

A lull in their conversation allowed Jair to look about the inn. It had grown late and many of the other occupants had left for the night. Rakkon noticed a tired yawn from Jair. Standing and stretching, Rakkon rose and moved out from behind the table, picking up his weapon before leaving.

"It's growing late." Rakkon stated. "I do not know about you, but I am weary from the road and would take my leave to rest, so I bid you a good night, and I will see you on the morrow." Rakkon said. He then turned and headed toward the stairs.

Jair paused for a moment then picked up his belongings and followed him. Upon reaching his room, he felt the tug of exhaustion pulling on him and he quickly shut and bolted the door behind him.

He turned to look about the room and decided to place his belongings under the bed instead of in the chest at its foot. He was not going to make it easy for anyone to rob him during the night. The chest would probably be the first place they'd look, and under the bed the second.

He then went over to the windowsill and checked the lock on it. Jair did not know why, but he did not feel very safe as he looked out the window and over the city. It was that and the fact he was still carrying the helmet that made him decide to take an extra precaution for the night.

He searched through his belongings and located his spell book.

Flipping through the crinkled yellow pages, he finally settled on a page with a spell he though he could use. He then set about memorizing the short spell after pausing to gather the components that it required.

The spell was a fairly simple one. It was a spell of alarm. It only required a piece of string and the carcass of a dead firefly, but when triggered, would light up the entire room. Jair hoped this would alert him to any danger while he slept.

He went over the spell several times and quit when he thought he had it firmly memorized. He closed his spell book and laid it on the bed beside him. He relaxed and concentrated on casting the spell. He took a deep breath and started uttering the first few phrases of the spell. As he said the words, it grew increasingly difficult to speak, but he continued to say the words flawlessly, drawing on his willpower and training.

As he came to the end of the spell, Jair held out the components in the palm of his hand. He spoke the final words with a strained gasp and the spell components disappeared. He took a deep breath and opened his eyes to survey the room. He looked closely at the floor under the window and saw a faint glittering line that was like a thin spider's web. The line ran all the way around the room's perimeter, just a few feet above the floor.

Jair let out his breath that he had been holding and was relieved that the spell had worked. Anyone trying to enter his room by the door or window would trigger the trap, immediately alerting him and momentarily blinding them, hopefully giving him enough time to escape.

Jair replaced his book into the satchel, washed his face and hands in the basin that had been provided, then lay down to sleep. In only a few moments he was asleep, the last few days events finally taking their toll. All thoughts on what had happened to him drifted away into dreams as he fell asleep.

Chapter 8

Night crept in over the city of Gallador. The moon rose slowly as dusk settled into full darkness. The moon cast eerie shadows all across the city. The creeping darkness fell listlessly upon the cold cobblestone streets. Dark shadows danced merrily from the street lamps that had been lit by the night watch. They failed to adequately lend any semblance of security to the city at night.

As the regular inhabitants lay down for the evening, its darker, seamier side awoke. It was a dark side that most cities have, but never want to admit to.

Along with the city's other evening dwellers, two black clad shadows worked their way up the side of a building. They hid in the murky blackness while they used a small, finely crafted rope and grappling hook to scale its heights. The hook had been thrown quietly up to the roof where it had easily grabbed a ledge. The two figures expertly went up the thin cord. They stopped just below the roof, right in front of a closed window.

They paused briefly in front of the window. The first figure pulled out a small, curious looking metal tool from the back of a sash that was tied about its waist. The figure reached up to the window and slid the tool into the gap between the window's two doors, easing it gently upward. The latch came up off its catch, and then gently swung the window open with only a faint click.

The first figure carefully eased the window open and then dropped, cat-like, down onto the wooden floor of the small room. The figure made no sound as it moved very slowly to the right side of the window, making room for its companion to enter.

As the first figure turned and moved to the right of the window, it felt something brush lightly against its ankle. Suddenly there was a loud crack and a burst of brilliant white light. The first figure cried out and was blinded. The second figure, still perched on the windowsill, drew back as the light exploded right in front of them. The bright flash caused the figure to lose its grip on the sill and rope, falling backward into the night. The figure only let out a small gasp as it fell.

The sound and sudden light woke Jair with a start. He turned and quickly rolled off the bed, kneeling beside it. He looked around to see what had set off the alarm. As the light faded, Jair saw that he was not alone. He paused long enough to grab his dagger and the satchel, and then backed toward the door.

The black clad figure shook its head to clear its vision, but heard Jair moving toward the door. The figure quickly pulled out a wicked looking short sword that had been strapped to it's back. The intruder waved the sword menacingly in Jair's direction. Jair noticed the intruder's hesitation and concluded that it was still partially blinded from the spell.

Jair drew back his arm and threw the satchel at the intruder. He followed the satchel by lunging toward the intruder with his dagger. The satchel caught the intruder in the chest, making a loud thud as it hit. This caused the intruder to drop his sword, which gave Jair the opportunity to come in low with his dagger. He did this in the hope that he could take the intruder down before he had time to recover.

Jair thrust forward with his dagger. It felt as if his weapon had a life of its own, guiding his hand toward his opponent. He caught the intruder in the lower abdomen, sinking his blade it in to the hilt. His successful attack caused the intruder to let out a loud grunt, but didn't immediately stop him. Jair grappled with the figure for several moments, twisting his blade until the intruder finally relaxed its grip. He slowly slid off the blade, falling limply to the floor.

Jair stepped back from the intruder and stared down at the bloody dagger that was in his hand. The intruder's warm blood covered his hand and forearm, glistening wetly in the waning moonlight that filtered in through the open window. He moved over to the bed and sat down heavily, breathing deeply and letting his adrenaline and heart rate go down.

As Jair sat there, the door to his room burst open with flying splinters of wood. Rakkon came in through the opening with his axe in his hand. He glanced toward Jair, a wild look in his eyes then shouted, "DUCK!" Before Jair could say a word or even respond, Rakkon flew past him toward the open window. As Jair turned his head to follow his actions, he caught a glimpse of movement out of the corner of his eye. It was enough to cause him to duck as a dagger flew by his head.

The other black clad figure that had fallen back out the window had re-entered the room and had been creeping up on Jair. Evidently he had caught the dangling rope outside the window and stopped his fall to the cobblestones below. The figure had almost snuck up on Jair, when Rakkon had crashed in through the door.

Rakkon charged toward the figure, slashing with his axe. Dodging and ducking the blazing arcs and cuts, the other intruder jumped back toward the window, defending himself as best as he could with a scimitar.

The intruder made a final jab at Rakkon with his sword, then leapt out the window and grabbed the rope. He swung outward and quickly pulled himself up toward the roof. Rakkon took another swing at the intruder as he headed for the roof, taking a chunk out of the window frame.

Rakkon reached out for the rope and stepped up onto the sill. He then started out as if to climb up after the intruder. He hesitated for only a moment, but it was long enough to leave him grasping for the window frame as the rope came tumbling down beside him. He paused to catch his breath and look up for any sign of the intruder. He then re-entered the room and looked down at the body of the intruder Jair had slain. He shook his head slowly in anger and bewilderment.

Rakkon walked over to the body, stooped and then began searching it. After several minutes he looked up in disgust, coming away with only a few thieves' tools and the dead man's sword. He then removed the dead man's hooded mask to reveal a dark face.

The man had dark olive skin with unusual features. He had a wide, flat nose, long wavy black hair, and thick, broad lips. His eyes were small and very round and he had high cheekbones.

Rakkon looked him over then grunted, "He looks to be Erkolthian, probably from down in the southern regions. Erkolthian's are known for their assassins and thieves. From the looks of it, he was one of them. Erkolthian's do not work cheap nor do they steal without a good reason. You are very lucky to be alive." Rakkon said to Jair with a grim look on his face.

Rakkon looked at Jair with a questioning glance. Jair walked over to the corner of the room where his satchel lay and picked it up. He stooped to wipe the blood off his dagger on the dead man's clothes and then turned to respond to Rakkon.

"I was nervous about staying here so I cast a ward spell before I went to sleep. The spell set off a bright flash of dancing lights and a noise when the intruders tripped it. It blinded them momentarily and woke me." Jair said.

"It gave me enough time to grab my dagger and defend myself. I threw my satchel at this one to distract him and followed in with my dagger. I guess the other attacker was still outside the window. I didn't see him." Jair said to Rakkon.

"If not for you the other one would have killed me. Thank

you," Jair said in a serious voice.

As Rakkon was about to respond, the inn's owner came bustling in through the shattered remnants of the door.

"What's goin on up here? Who do you two think ya'll are? Who's going to pay for the damage? Wrecking one of my best rooms, destroying my property and waking up my guests, I'm callin tha guard!" The innkeeper exclaimed.

"Calm down innkeeper." Rakkon growled at him between the innkeeper's blustery remarks. "There was a break-in. Two thieves broke into this room and tried to murder my friend. As you can see, one of them is still lying on the floor. The other one escaped to the roof before we could stop him." Rakkon stated.

As he spoke, Rakkon held up his axe in a menacing way, shaking it back and forth as he spoke. His knuckles turned white from the angry grip he had on its shaft.

The innkeeper stepped back from the irate young warrior's threatening demeanor. It dawned on him that the young man seemed to know quite well how to use the large weapon he was waving about in the innkeeper's chubby face.

Jair stepped forward and got in between Rakkon and the innkeeper. "We are truly sorry for all of the noise, and we will be more than happy to pay for any damages, but it is true what my friend has said. Two thieves broke into my room and tried to murder and rob me in my sleep. Were it not for my friend, I would be dead and the reputation of your inn would be greatly diminished."

At this, the innkeeper's eyes became very wide and an expression of fear came across his large, sweaty face. A small crowd of the inn's other patrons had formed just outside the door and they were trying to get a peek to find out what all the commotion was about.

The innkeeper looked at Jair and started wringing his hands. "What do ya mean that tha reputation of my inn would be damaged?" He stuttered.

Jair looked at the innkeeper and said, "Would you have everyone in the city think that your inn is unsafe and that anyone who stayed here might be subject to an attack by thieves and cutthroats in the dead of the night? Were it not for your faulty locks and bad security, this might have never happened." Jair said this so the crowd could hear. A murmur of dissent arose from the onlookers as they heard his words.

The innkeeper became angry at Jair's words. He started to make a snide remark about the ignorance of a low life half-elf, but thought better of it as the crowd outside the door craned their necks to hear what was being said. The innkeeper heard several of the other patrons murmur assent to Jair's words and decided that he had better change tactics quickly if he were to keep most of his customers.

He turned so the other customers could hear him and said, "I know that this seems ta be bad, but I assure ya'll that my inn is one 'o the safest in tha city, please go back to yer rooms and forget all about this."

The innkeeper turned back to Jair and smiled gently while holding his hands out wide with the palms turned up. "Don't worry bout payin for any damages. I'll take care of all the repairs and see to yer needs. My apologies for any inconvenience this may have caused ya young sir."

Before anything else could be said, several city guards came in through the crowd and entered the room. Several more guards stayed outside and started questioning them. After a few minutes they dispersed the crowd. Jair and Rakkon stepped aside as the guards began searching the room and examining the body. A young captain came up to Jair and Rakkon and started questioning them about what had happened.

After Jair and Rakkon finishing telling the guards what had happened, the guards called for two men who came into the room and removed the body. The young captain turned to Jair and said, "We will try to make an identification of the body, but I can give no guarantees. In a city this size it has become difficult to weed out all of the scum, but I assure you that we will investigate this incident. Do you have any idea why they picked your room?" The captain asked suspiciously.

"We are strangers to your fair city captain. I suspect they thought I might be an easy target." Jair replied, trying to steer the captain clear of other questioning.

"Well, see that you stay out of trouble and are where we can find you if we have any more questions." He responded.

The captain spun about and exited through the splintered doorway. A couple of cleaning boys entered the room per the innkeeper's instructions, and they started cleaning up the mess that had been made.

Rakkon motioned toward Jair and they both headed out the door and down the hall toward Rakkon's room. Jair went in first, with Rakkon following right behind him. Rakkon turned to face Jair and then motioned for him to have a seat on the bed as he closed the door. His demeanor said the he was seriously concerned about what had just happened.

"Jair, I think there is a lot more going on here than you and Tagor have told me. Two assassins like the ones that just tried to kill you don't randomly break into a room and try to kill someone. They were here for a reason. I know we don't really know one another, but you might ought to explain what you've gotten me into. Now that they have seen me with you, I could be a target as well." Rakkon said.

Jair sat back on the bed and thought for a moment. Coming to a decision, he reached down to his satchel that was resting on the floor next to him, and placed it on his lap. He reached down to the front of it and undid the two straps that held the flap down and opened it.

He reached inside the satchel and fished around for a few seconds. He then pulled the helmet out of the satchel.

Rakkon watched curiously as the dim light from the candle he had just lit played across the helmet's shiny metallic surface.

Rakkon's eyes grew wide as he gazed upon the finely crafted piece of armor. He stepped over and stood in front of Jair and reach out to grab the helmet, but looked up at Jair for approval before doing so. Jair nodded and handed it to him.

He had only glimpsed the helmet when the goblin leader had put it on the day before. He had not been paying that much attention to it at the time. The smoke and fire that had emanated from it had obscured his view, and after that Jair had retrieved it quickly and put it back in the satchel. Rakkon had assumed that it had been a spell, and not the helmet that had killed the goblin.

"Jair, this helmet is like no other that I have ever seen." Rakkon stated. "It's magnificent. Where did you get it?"

Jair then proceeded to tell him the full tale. Trying not to leave anything out, he explained to Rakkon where he had gotten the helmet and what he and Tagor thought it was. The full consequences of their find and the importance of it settled on Rakkon rather quickly.

As Jair finished telling his story, Rakkon set the helmet down upon the small wooden table that sat in the corner of the room. He brought the candle over next to it and slowly examined the mystical artifact as he leaned on the table.

135

The Ruby Helmet

In the dim candlelight, the helmet seemed to give off an eerie mystical glow. Flames cast from the flickering candle played gently across the shiny metallic surface of the helmet. This lent to the magical feel, and added to Jair's story.

After looking at the helmet, Rakkon turned back to Jair and then seated himself on the small wooden chair next to the table. "Jair, we know that not just anyone can wear the helmet of legend. That goblin's quick, fiery death attests to that. Whom do you think the helmet is meant for?" Rakkon asked him.

A blank look came across Jair's face and he shrugged his shoulders in ignorance. "I don't know for sure. Tagor believes only a very powerful wizard can use it. We planned on taking it to the king here in Gallador and letting him decide what to do with it. Something like this is too important for the likes of me to decide." Jair said.

As Jair spoke, a cold chill ran down his spine from a thought that occurred to him. Putting his thoughts into words Jair said, "the legends say that the helmet was a protection against physical and magical attacks. I do not remember anything about people dying from putting it on. It's a good thing that none of us has tried it on. We could have died like the goblin leader."

Rakkon glanced back over at the helmet, then noticed Jair's shaken look. "I'm not so sure Jair." He said. "There could be a lot of reasons the helmet didn't work for the goblin. Reasons we just don't know about. The helmet obviously does not work for just anyone. It probably takes someone special to operate it. If it was crafted by an elf, maybe only elves can use it."

Rakkon walked back over to the bed. He reached down and removed a blanket from his pack at the foot of the bed and then threw it to Jair. "You can stay here for tonight. There's no use worrying about everything else until tomorrow." He told Jair.

"Tomorrow we'll get you another room and hopefully get a few answers from the king. I don't like it when people are attacked for no apparent reason in the middle of the night. Especially by professional assassins."

Jair nodded his head in agreement, then laid the blanket down on the floor and replaced the helmet in his satchel. Using his satchel for a pillow, he used his own blanket as a cover, and then lay down to get some sleep.

Rakkon had already lain down and was seemingly fast asleep by the time Jair got settled in. Jair stayed awake for a little while and contemplated what had happened, and what might still happen.

He was positive the helmet had magical properties, based on what he'd heard from the dead goblin leader. Jair just hoped the king could help them find out what the helmet was and where it belongs. He wanted to be rid of it so he could get on with his search for his father's family, and to pursue his studies in magic.

The only big problem he had was that even though he wanted to be rid of the helmet, he was getting an odd sense of attachment to it. He really wanted to know what the helmet was, what it might do, where it came from, and who could wear it. It was by far the most dangerous and exciting thing that he had ever come across.

Jair had a feeling that the helmet was the same one as in the ancient stories. There was something about it, nothing that he could put his finger on, just a feeling he had.

Chapter 9

Jair woke the next morning feeling slightly stiff and a little sore from the past few day's events. Rakkon was already up and donning the rest of his armor as Jair rose.

He put away their blankets then splashed some cold water on his face from a bowl and pitcher that had been placed on the one table in the room. He ran his fingers through his hair and tried to make himself more presentable for the king.

Rakkon looked over at Jair as he readied himself for the day and wondered about the previous days events. "Good morning," he said to Jair as he strapped on his shoulder plate.

"Good morning," Jair replied. He picked up his spell components, satchel, and then placed his dagger and short sword on his belt.

"I am going downstairs to get something to eat. Do you want to come with me?" Rakkon asked Jair. "Sure," Jair responded. "I'm ready," he said. Together they left the room and headed down the stairs.

Upon reaching the inn's main room, Rakkon led Jair over to the same table they had shared the previous evening. Before seating himself, he motioned to one of the serving girls who were already busy getting things ready for breakfast.

Jair looked around and noticed that the inn was still quite empty. He figured it was because it was still early. There were only a few of the inn's patrons in the main room. Jair remembered a couple of their faces from the crowd that had formed in the hallway outside of his room during the commotion during the night.

Rakkon ordered them both some breakfast, then leaned back in his chair. The sun was just rising up out of the east with its fiery tendrils of light peeking in through the inn's now opened shutters.

The sunlight barely pierced the inn's dirty glass windows.

The sounds of the waking city could be heard from without and a chill hung in the early morning air as Jair and Rakkon waited for their breakfast. A fire had been lit in the hearth in the center of the room, giving it a cheery glow. Jair stood and walked over to the fire, then placed another log on it, trying to shake the early morning cold.

He returned to his seat and the two of them sat in silence, enjoying the early morning stillness, thinking about the day ahead. A short while later the serving girl brought them their breakfast and they ate from a plate that consisted of a freshly baked loaf of bread, a slab of cheese, some dried meats and several pieces of fruit.

They finished their meal in silence and sat back and relaxed with their stomachs full. Jair was about to say something to Rakkon when the door to the inn was thrust open, allowing a cold breeze to flutter in.

Sunlight spilled into the dark interior of the inn. Through the open doorway several figures entered. Their features were unidentifiable in the sunlight that filled the door. Jair had to squint when he looked their way. As the figures came into the room and shut the door behind them, Jair's eyes quickly adjusted back to the dim interior. As he looked closer he could see that they were four city guardsmen. The guards looked around the room and spotted Jair and Rakkon on the far side. They then headed in their direction.

Rakkon eased his hand down beside him to rest upon the handle of his axe as the guards came toward them. Jair just sat silently and watched them, not knowing how to react as the four guards worked their way across the room to where they sat.

They stopped when they reached their table. The lead guard stepped forward in an official manner and spoke to Jair. "Are you Jair and is this your companion Rakkon?" The guardsman asked.

Jair looked at Rakkon, and then responded. "Yes, I am Jair, and this is Rakkon."

"We were sent to escort you to the temple. Your friend is awake and you are both to be escorted to him. Please follow me," the guard said as he stepped back and motioned with his hand for them to follow.

Jair glanced at Rakkon who only shrugged then stood up. Rakkon towered over all of the guards as he picked up his axe and stepped out from behind the table.

They stepped back as Rakkon moved around the table and brought his large axe up, cradling it in one arm. The guards looked at one another nervously, but stood their ground. They were not eager for trouble.

Jair stood and picked up his satchel. He slung it over one shoulder, then moved forward in front of Rakkon. "Lead the way." He said to the guard. He then stepped into line between them. Rakkon grunted slightly once and followed Jair's lead. It had occurred to Jair that Rakkon did not care for city guardsmen.

The four guards spread out around Jair and Rakkon. They marched in a stiff, formal manner. Their small group left the inn with not a few questioning looks from other patrons. They marched down the street at a brisk pace, straight for the temple.

As they walked, Jair could see that many of the city's store owners and shopkeepers were already up and about for the day. They were getting their stands ready and opening their shops for the coming day's business.

It did not take long for them to reach the broad, gray steps of the temple. The city guards easily cleared their way. Jair and Rakkon were led up the steps to the wide double doors of the temple. Once they had arrived at the top of the stairs, the lead guard reached up and banged heavily upon the ancient wooden door.

After a few moments, a small window opened up and Jair could just make out the features of one of the temple's clergymen gazing out at them. The city guard whispered something to him, and then stepped back. The large wooden door swung inward and the cleric stepped aside to allow Jair and Rakkon inside. The four guards turned and headed back down the steps, their mission complete. Relief was evident on their faces as they turned to leave.

Once inside the temple, the cleric quickly shut and bolted the temple door behind them, then motioned for Jair and Rakkon to follow him. It was still early in the day and many of the temple's followers would not begin showing up for several hours yet.

The cleric led them through the temple's twisting and winding inner sanctum. Jair was once again awed by the temple's magnificence and beauty. Rakkon gazed about quietly but said nothing as the cleric led them along.

After a while, they arrived at Sir Darnok's private chamber. Jair was once again utterly confused as to their whereabouts. The young cleric opened the door and ushered them into the room, then closed the door behind them.

As Jair entered the room he was glad to see that Tagor was there as well as Darnok and two other men. Tagor was seated in the large, comfortable chair over to the right of the chamber. Bandages were swathed about his wounds. He looked up as Jair and Rakkon entered the room and a broad smile spread across his face as he waved at them.

Darnok was behind his desk where he sat quietly, with a serious look on his face. Jair had never seen the other two men that were in the room. The first was a large, domineering man that was seated in a wooden chair beside Darnok's desk. He sat with his legs crossed and one elbow on the chair's armrest. His chin rested on his fist.

He wore a richly decorated shirt, soft purple pants, dark leather boots, and a magnificent red cloak that hung about his shoulders. A large jewel encrusted sword hung from his hip. However decorative, the sword looked as if it had been well used. His features were strong but tired, as if the weight of the world were upon his shoulders. He had a large, rounded nose, dark, deep-set brown eyes and a full, gray streaked beard.

The other man was slightly shorter but thicker in build. He stood to the first man's right, leaning next to one of Darnok's bookcases. This man wore full upper body plate mail armor and his lower body was covered in chain mail. He carried an old, plain, heavy looking broadsword at his side and his features were somewhat sharper than the first man's.

Thick black hair hung down to the nape of this man's neck where it was cut sharply. He sported a thick, black mustache that drooped down on each side of his mouth and his eyes were a sparkling blue.

Jair and Rakkon entered the room and Jair quickly walked over to greet Tagor, shaking his good hand. Darnok stood and moved around to the other side of his desk to greet them.

Darnok spoke and said, "Young Master Jair and Master Rakkon I presume." He said nodding toward Jair for affirmation as to Rakkon's identity. Jair nodded in affirmation.

Darnok turned toward the other two men and said, "May I present to you his majesty King Galdath and General Calith Bital."

"Your majesty," Darnok said as he turned toward at the king, "This is young Master Jair and Master Rakkon."

Jair froze at the announcement of the king. He had never been before royalty, especially a king, so he didn't know what to do. He paused for a moment, and then snapped out of his fear. He managed a clumsy bow and uttered out a few words.

"I'm very pleased to meet you your majesty," Jair said nervously as he looked at the king.

Rakkon merely nodded his head toward the king. The king nodded his head back at Jair and Rakkon then stood and walked over to stand beside Darnok.

"I understand that you have something to show me. Something you and Tagor believe might be of great value and importance to my kingdom." The king said as he looked over at the two young men. As the king spoke, Jair noticed the familiar tone the king used when mentioning Tagor's name. He spoke as if Tagor were someone with whom he was familiar.

Tagor looked at Jair and nodded for him to proceed. Jair walked over to Darnok's desk and set his satchel upon it. Undoing the straps and opening the flap, Jair reached inside and pulled out the helmet.

He set it on the desk and stepped back to let the others take a look at it. The king stepped forward and picked the helmet up, examining it closely. After looking at it for a few moments he handed it to Darnok who went back around to the other side of his desk so that he could sit down and examine it more closely.

The king looked at Jair curiously as he went back to his chair and sat down. He motioned for Jair and Rakkon to also take a seat.

"Tagor has filled us in on your journey. It sounds as if you have had quite an adventure." The king said.

Jair nodded in agreement while the others sat in silence. A grave look came over the king's face as he contemplated his words before he spoke further.

"As Tagor has feared, our scouts have uncovered a lot of

movement near Zoarnest in the north. It looks as if Telenok is amassing troops and is planning something big."

"Over the last two years a lot of the raiding parties and trouble along the border has diminished. At first we thought it just a temporary lull in northern activity, but we now know it is because the goblin and giant tribes have been united and are on the move. There are even rumors of orcs and trolls traveling with them." The king said with grim emphasis.

"Dark elf activity has also increased according to our emissaries in Silvermist. Many Dark elves have been spotted moving along the Anarest Mountain's. Many of them are in large groups." The king continued.

Before the king could say anything more, General Bital stepped forward and interrupted him. In a deep gruff voice the he said, "Our contacts have confirmed most of this. Scouts have reported a lot of the dark elf movement in these areas."

The king then continued, "Trade and commerce have also picked up over the last year or so with the Darketh kingdom. Even though this is good for our city's commerce, we believe they are stocking up on supplies for a major incursion."

Tagor looked over at Jair who was trying to take everything in. "Jair, the king and his council believe Telenok is planning an invasion of the southern kingdoms. The only thing they're not sure of is how or when it is going to happen. We don't really know what type of resources Telenok has at his disposal. It is almost impossible to get information from that part of the country."

Nodding in agreement with Tagor, the king continued, "There have also been reports from scouts out of Erkolth about a warrior rebel prince named Deshtar. He seems to be causing some kind of uprising among the Tubitai Clans in the south."

At hearing the name Deshtar, Jair said, "My lord, the goblins that I took the helmet from said they were delivering it to a man named Deshtar in the south. Is this the same person that is in league with Telenok?"

The king paused for a moment to think, looking questioningly at his general. "What do you think Bital?" He asked him.

"I do not know my lord, but it does bear investigating. I will put the word out to our network and see if they can come up with a connection."

Nodding satisfactorily the king continued, "The Tubitai are one of the largest bands of fierce, jungle tribes living in Shakisan. They tend to run things down in Erkolth. Their leaders stem from royal families much as our royalty does, but that changes often due to the fact that royalty is established through combat and challenge. They are a proud people."

"Anyone strong enough and backed by enough reigning nobles can challenge another noble. If the challenger defeats the reigning noble in mortal combat, he and his family become royalty. It is really a lot more complicated than that, but you get the gist of it."

"Deshtar's uncle was the reigning king. Many of the tribes followed him, but not all. He died last year very mysteriously from some unknown ailment and left no heir. Deshtar has a terrible reputation among his own people. There are those that suspect him of poisoning his uncle. If he became king, many of the tribes would still follow him, even to war with us. There has been a lot of chaos and intrigue in Shakisan since the king's death. Deshtar is the most likely of the candidates, but several of the other, stronger tribes, have given him serious competition. They are all trying to place one of their own upon the throne."

"After the king's death it was decided by all of the tribes that at the end of one year all of the strongest tribal candidates would enter a tournament. This goes back to ancient rites used for centuries by their people. It is to be an elimination contest. The last one standing will be king. It is usually a brutal and bloody way of selecting a leader, but to the Shakisan it is the most fitting and honorable way."

"We are hoping a leader from one of the other tribes will succeed. Right now we are on good terms with many of the Shakisan peoples and would not welcome trouble from there as well as from the north."

"Their people are fierce fighters. They are used to moving about on foot so they can march for long distances and they have great endurance. By our standards they are very barbaric but their methods and styles of fighting are something to be reckoned with."

While the king paused general Bital added, "If there is a connection between Deshtar and Telenok, it could mean trouble for the middle kingdoms. The Shakisan tribes would be a formidable force to deal with, even for our experienced soldiers."

The king nodded his head in agreement then added, "The High Elves are currently remaining neutral. I do not believe however that they are capable of resisting Telenok's forces should we fall. Their long standing conflict with their dark skinned brethren as well as the other evil races massing hopefully will encourage them to join us. Whether or not we will actually get them to align with us remains to be seen."

"As for the dwarves of Karga Hall, our ambassadors have given us favorable reports, but that is only if things do come down to all out war. The dwarves would be formidable allies, but they are also reluctant to commit themselves at this point. They have always been reclusive and also tend to stay neutral in these types of matters, except when directly threatened." The king said.

The general turned to Rakkon and asked him, "We have not had many dealings with the barbarian tribes of the North. Nor have we had many reports as to how they will stand if there is war. Do you think they will stay out of the fray or to join with us against Telenok?"

Rakkon pondered the question for a moment before answering. "I do not know about the other clans, but the Teargor Clan will not join with a sorcerer. Most of the clans do not like sorcery and magic. They distrust sorcerers altogether, but if Telenok were to promise the other clans great wealth or power, he might be able to sway them into joining him."

Getting the answer he expected, general Bital stepped back, leaned against the bookcase and crossed his arms over his broad metal covered chest. From behind the large antique desk Darnok spoke up after having closely examined the helmet.

"This helmet is very ancient and powerful. I can sense a great aura emanating from it, but cannot discover its secrets. The markings are definitely elven, but it is beyond my power reveal what it can do."

"I recommend taking it to the elven city of Silvermist. It is only there that the exact nature can be revealed," the cleric stated.

The king looked at him then reached out to take the helmet. Darnok handed it to him, and the king examined it for a moment. He then stood and walked across the room to where Jair sat. He placed the helmet into Jair's hands.

"Jair," the king said. "I can think of no one better suited to carry the helmet to Silvermist than the one who has carried it thus far. It would seem that your destiny and the helmet's are one."

"You and your companions will be less conspicuous on the road than a company of soldiers. I am asking that you do this for my kingdom and for all of the good people in this land. I would not ask this of you if I did not think it of great importance." He said to Jair.

Then he said, "One day I would also like to meet this giant friend of yours."

Jair was taken aback by this revelation. He did not know that Tagor was going to tell them about Kethok.

The king was about to turn back toward his chair when he noticed Jair's amulet. His eyes narrowed briefly as if with recognition and he started to say something, and then stopped himself. Jair noticed the look on the king's face, but didn't say anything. Jair wondered why the king could see the amulet when most others could not.

He also wondered what it was that the king had seen that had so surprised him. Jair thought it better not to question the king. Hopefully he would have the opportunity to ask the king about the amulet in private.

As the king returned to his chair, he looked toward Darnok and general Bital for further counseling.

Neither of them said anything else so Tagor spoke up, "Your grace if it pleases you, I will accompany Jair on his journey." Protests quickly erupted from the group.

Tagor held up a hand to silence them and said, "I know that I am wounded, but the clerics have done a fine job of healing me. A few more days of rest and I will be as good as new. Besides, I have come this far with Jair, I might as well go the rest of the way and see how this plays out."

The others could only nod their heads in agreement. The king could think of no one better suited than Tagor to go with Jair and he said so. With his many years of woodcraft and battle experience he was a formidable fighter and skilled tracker. The king also said, "So be it. Tagor will also accompany Jair."

Rakkon stepped forward and said, "I will also accompany them, if they would have me." He looked questioningly toward Jair as he spoke. "It would seem that I am entwined in this somehow. Besides, if there is going to be war, I would assume that Lord Tredebould's army will probably be needed elsewhere, so there should be plenty of mercenary work for me here in Gallador."

Jair felt somewhat trapped and looked around the room at the men that were gathered with him. Expectant looks showed on all of their faces. Jair had yet to say whether or not he was willing to go on the mission. He mulled it over and thought about all that he had been through.

From the time he had left Bardor Keep until now, he had been going non-stop and hadn't had time to think about his original plans or what he really wanted to do.

He had intended to seek out the High Elves, so that he might find out who his father was. He knew there was a slim chance to find him, but it was all he had to go on.

He had come a long way and made new friends. Things were happening fast, but Jair knew inside himself that he would go on the journey for not just his friends, but also for all of the many lives that were now in jeopardy. It was something he knew he had to do. Finding his father would have to wait.

Jair made his decision and looked at the king, who was waiting expectantly. "I will carry the helmet to the elven city. If my friends, a king, a high cleric and a general think it's that important, it must be." Jair replied.

"I don't understand why you chose me for this task. I am not important. I have no special skills or training. I am no one." Jair said while shaking his head slowly, not really understanding the king's decision.

The king smiled at Jair and said, "You are more important than you know." He then looked back at Darnok and asked, "How long before Tagor will be fit enough to ride?"

"A couple of days at least. He needs a week, but I do not think we have the time to spare," the high cleric replied.

"Well then, we have plans to make." The king said as he stood. Everyone else stood with him.

"Darnok, will you see that our friends are made comfortable here in the temple?" The king asked the old cleric.

Darnok responded with a nod, then looked at Jair and Rakkon, who began to protest. "By the way, we heard about the incident at the inn last night. We believe the Erkolthian assassins are tied to the helmet somehow. The helmet will be safer here in the temple."

The king used a very authoritative tone, brooking no resistance. He gave each of the companions a hard look, and then said, "You will stay at the palace or at the temple. You are not going back to the inn."

The king crossed the room toward the door. He turned one last time to face the group. General Bital was right behind him. "Tagor, I will try to see you before you leave. We still have a few things to discuss," the king said. He looked at Jair and said, "Jair, I wish you and your companions good speed and safe passage. We will see that you are fully supplied and armed for the trip." The king and the general then turned and left the chamber.

Tagor looked at Jair and smiled slightly. "Well lad, it seems that our little adventure continues for a while longer." He nodded toward Rakkon and said, "I'm glad that you are accompanying us Rakkon. Your skill with the axe will come in handy if there is trouble along the way."

Rakkon nodded back at Tagor, acknowledging the compliment. Darnok then rose from his chair. He walked around to the other side of his desk and leaned against it, then spoke.

"There are still a lot of unanswered questions about all that is going on. I hope that many of them will be answered in Silvermist; the others probably will be in time. We will continue our research here to see what we may find. I fear that there are still unknown elements at work."

"I will have rooms prepared for you and have your belongings sent for from the inn. In the meantime, you three can visit while I see to the arrangements."

Darnok exited the room, leaving the trio alone. Jair got up and walked over to sit in the chair next to Tagor. Rakkon stood and went over to a cabinet that contained beverages. Once there he poured a cup.

"How do you feel?" Jair asked Tagor.

"Well enough after all that we've been through," he replied. "The clerics did a fine job on patching me up. Most of my wounds are healed. It is the big one that will take a while to get over." He said while holding up his bandaged arm.

"Tagor, why didn't you tell me who your father was and how you really knew the king?" Jair asked him.

Tagor looked off into space for a moment before replying. A painful expression was on his face. "I didn't think it all that important I guess. I don't like thinking about my father's death. It still pains me to do so, even after all these years." Tagor said.

Jair nodded in understanding. He knew how it was to feel the loss of a parent, even though his was a long time ago.

"Tagor, do you think this is going to be that dangerous of a journey?" Jair asked him.

"I get the feeling the king was not telling us everything he knew. That and the fact that someone tried to kill you last night seems to make things a lot more complex. Whoever sent those assassins will be trying to stop us from reaching Silvermist. So yes, I think that we will be in a lot of danger." Tagor replied.

Jair pondered that for a few moments as Rakkon walked back over to join them. The three sat and discussed their plans for the next few days. They also discussed the long journey that lay ahead of them, until Darnok returned to show them to their rooms.

Jair remained anxious. Something nagged at the back of his mind as they discussed the events of the last few days and of the days ahead of them. The look the king had given him when he had seen his medallion still bothered him. It left him wondering what it was all about.

Chapter 10

The night sky was clear and cold. The stars glittered brightly above the treetops. A thunder of hooves pounded the earth and echoed through the dark forest as ten dark figures raced through the woods on large black mares.

Pushed to exhaustion, the rider's mounts were covered in sweat. Foamy lather dripped from their mouths as their breaths came out in long, labored gasps.

At first glance, any passerby might have mistaken the riders for human, but on closer inspection they would have found them to be something far from it.

The lead rider was a tall, hulking figure. If seen standing, he would have probably measured almost eight feet in height. As for the rest of his companions, they were a variety of sizes and shapes, none of which measured up to the size of the first.

The riders were clad in glossy black plate, dark chain mail, or dull brown leather armor. The styles were mixed and varied. None of them were garbed alike, but all of them were of the same race and had the same dark demeanor. They were all also heavily equipped and armed. Each carried a small arsenal.

Traveling only at night, the riders had been escorted close to the southern tip of the Anarest Mountains. They had been led there by a small band of dark elves that were in league with their Lord.

From there, they had headed into the elven forests following the western edge, close to the Plains of Solitude. Their destination was unknown by any save the Dark Lord, and their purpose was grim.

Meanwhile, a hundred and fifty leagues to the southwest near Gallador, Tagor led the way as the four companions rode down a small, well-used trail. Two full weeks had passed since they had met and spoken with the king, and Tagor was now mostly recovered from their battle with the goblin band.

During Tagor's recovery, Rakkon and Jair had left the city and gone to visit Kethok. He had been waiting for them in the forest, not far from where they had left him. After explaining to him what had happened in the city and where they were planning to go, Kethok declared that he was going to join them on their journey. He wanted to go to Silvermist so he could protect them.

Jair still had a hard time at first trying to understand Kethok's sign language. He and Rakkon practiced with Tagor and Kethok as they traveled and eventually began to catch on. He was surprised at how complex and diverse the system was.

Jair fidgeted in his saddle as they rode. He tried to get comfortable, which seemed impossible to him while sitting in the hard saddle. During their two weeks in Gallador, Rakkon had also given Jair some quick riding lessons at the royal stables. The king had furnished each of them with one of his best warhorses. Jair had been quick to learn, but could not seem to get used to being in the saddle. It made him uncomfortable and sore, especially from the last two days of riding.

The four companions had set out at dusk the day before and had picked up Kethok as they'd reached the forest, just outside the city. Jair laughed to himself at the sight of the giant when he had tried to climb onto the horse that they had selected for him from the king's stable.

Kethok had balked at first, never haven ridden a horse, but at the others insistence, he had given it a try. The whole situation had been funny until Kethok became so frustrated he finally stormed off into the woods. Jair went after him and eventually talked him into rejoining them. The only way he would get back on and try again was after everyone promised not to laugh.

The horse they had found for him was some sort of crossbreed that the king's retainers had bought from a trader somewhere up in the northern lands. They had bought it as a novelty for the king. The horse had supposedly been reared and broken in by a stone giant. The giant had then traded the horse to one of the barbarian clans for food and weapons.

The horse seemed to be good-natured. It was a lot stronger than other horses. The king's men said the large horses' stamina was almost inexhaustible. Kethok still looked awkward astride it.

After they had set out, Jair found that Kethok did not have the same problems he did with soreness. The giant's thick, tough hide protected him from chafing. This was his only advantage however, because the giant had a lot of trouble balancing from atop a horse. It took Kethok several days of practice while riding through the forest to even stay up on the giant beast's back. It took several more days for him to figure out how to control the animal.

Besides the gift of the horses, the king had also been generous in equipping them for the journey. Jair was given a new set of leather armor and leather boots. He was also given a thick, fur lined riding cloak. He was especially proud of the new long sword. He'd never seen such a fine weapon. They had also allowed him to go to the wizard's guild to apply for an apprenticeship.

When he had entered the guild, Jair had been quite nervous. He was ushered in to see the guild's magistrate, who was named Gargaro. The magistrate was a human male of the white robe caste and was supposed to be the most powerful wizard in Gallador.

Upon meeting with Gargaro and the rest of the wizard council, Jair was heavily questioned by them. After they were done, the council met alone to decide if Jair knew enough magic or was skilled enough to take the test of passage to enter the guild.

Gargaro came out of the meeting and smiled at Jair, betraying the outcome. He came out and announced that the council was in favor of allowing Jair to take the test. Gargaro seemed to like Jair right away, but several of the other council members showed a complete dislike and prejudice at having a half-elf amongst their number.

When Jair took the test a few days later, he found it was long, arduous, and by no means easy. He had not been fully prepared for what he'd had to endure. Gargaro had briefed him a little on what was expected, but he did not tell Jair what would actually happen during the test.

The test itself had consisted of a series of conflicts and problems, each of which presented a different situation in which Jair had to use his wits and his magic to solve them or escape.

Jair passed the test, but just barely. Studying up on all of his spells, he had prepared himself as best he could. The little bit of magic he had learned from Kentar and from studying on his own had proved to be just enough to get him through it.

Upon entering the guild after being accepted, Jair had to make his choice of the three guild alignments. After giving it some careful thought and seeking out his own feelings on the three sects, Jair decided to join the white robes. Even though he did not fully understand what each of the classes represented, Jair felt that the white robed wizards held values that were closest to his own.

During their last week in the city, Gargaro had placed Jair under the tutelage of some of the other, younger wizards that were in the guild. These wizards laid out the differences between the alignments for Jair, and taught him many basics for controlling magic. These basics were things that he had never learned from Kentar.

Besides his training and the gathering of equipment, his companions were also fully outfitted and equipped for their part in the journey. Each of them had what they thought they would need.

Tagor and Rakkon had taken heavy riding cloaks in addition to some other gear. Kethok on the other hand only requested a new, fur lined vest and leather pants. His tough exterior and having been brought up in the wilderness gave him adequate protection from most of the elements.

Tagor and Jair each had taken along bows with a quiver full of arrows, and Tagor had chosen to bring along the sword he had taken from the wizard's tower where they had freed Kethok.

Tagor believed the sword had magical properties and that it was a fine addition to their party's weaponry. He also opted to wear a shirt of chain mail that Darnok had given him. He had declined using one of the heavy helmets worn by the cleric's militia. He preferred his old leather cap.

Rakkon decided to carry his usual array of weapons and armor. The king's smith had made a few repairs for him, so his armor looked new. His huge battleaxe was hung securely from his saddle. New black leather boots rode high upon his calves and a new shield was strapped onto his pack. Rakkon was quiet as they rode. Only occasionally did he make comments.

Kethok had been especially proud of a large, metal, spike tipped mace that had replaced his crude cudgel. A huge gapped-toothed grin split his face when he had hefted the brutal looking weapon. It had been found in the king's armory. Swinging it through the air a few times, the giant quickly threw away his old weapon in favor of the new one.

At the guild, Jair had also been given several new spells to add to his book. Gargaro had been reluctant to give him any spells above what he thought he was capable of handling, but the king had insisted that they be given additional magical assistance.

In addition to a few lower level spells, Gargaro had given Jair a powerful wand. The wand was of magic missiles. Gargaro had shown Jair how to invoke it and was quite pleased with how quickly Jair had brought the weapon under his control. The wand was now fully charged, which Gargaro said numbered in twenty. Jair had felt confident that he could use the wand if there was a need, but hoped there would not be.

As they rode, Jair shivered slightly from the cold that had finally settled in over the city. Tagor had mused that he thought they might even get snow any day.

Winters in the middle kingdoms were never usually that harsh, but it was known to occasionally blizzard, which made travel practically impossible during the deep winter months.

Their first day on the road passed without incident. They traveled through the forest, and passed many small villages and settlements. The only real problem they ran into was from local people running and screaming in fear, or becoming angry and violent at the sight of Kethok. That and many of the humans that lived thereabouts seemed to still have a strong dislike for elves.

After a few minor incidents with local villagers, Tagor decided to lead the party down some less traveled paths. These paths were old, but at one time had been well used. It was evident Tagor knew the business of rangering, and knew it well. Jair knew that he would have become lost very quickly trying to find these old paths.

In his early years, Tagor had traveled many of the roads between Gallador and the Plains of Solitude, especially during the Border Wars. His time of service back then proved useful to them now as they skirted the many small villages and homesteads scattered along the main road. The further they traveled from the city, the fewer people they saw. Eventually they saw no one at all.

Besides all of the other things that had happened over the last two weeks, Jair had come to realize he did not know Tagor as well as he had first thought. Tagor had spent most of his time in Gallador at the temple or with Darnok and the other clergy. In a short time a noticeable change had come over him. Jair had observed that Tagor seemed to be getting closer to his religion. He also spent time getting reacquainted with some of his old friends.

Jair wasn't comfortable with church and religion. He had never been to a church nor had he met many religious people. Most of the ones he had met were not of much interest to him. But, there was something to be said for the work they did, or at least what he had heard the good ones did. Some seemed to really try and help people that were in need. The few he had met also seemed to be honest and sincere in what they believed. They did not try to force their beliefs on him. He had head of religions that were oppressive. They tried to force people believe in and serve their gods.

The thought of a supreme being that controlled the universe did intrigue him. Trying to pick one, or figuring out which of the many gods was the right one, seemed too complicated to him. Some day, he thought he might look into it further and see if there was really any merit to what any of them taught.

As he tried to shrug off the cold, Jair's thoughts wandered back to the look the king had given him when he had seen the amulet. It was curious that a king might recognize an old elven family symbol. Jair wondered what it might mean.

As Jair mused over this and the others rode along beside him, the day passed quickly and uneventfully. There was no doubt the air had grown colder, and a thin cloud cover now hung over them. Jair shivered in his saddle as the cold seeped in through his new leather armor.

Tagor saw Jair shiver. He also had a lot on his mind, especially since their departure from Gallador. Tagor getting re-acquainted with the church had forced him to search his heart. He had found that his belief in Anu was still there. The only thing that he was still unsure of was what he wanted to do about it. He had spent many hours talking with Darnok. Darnok had reminded him of his obligation to his god and for all of the many blessings Anu had given him in this life. He had also been reminded of the great rewards that awaited him in the next life, if he was faithful in his service to Anu. It had given him much to think about. He had spent too many years living in the wilderness away from people. People he knew cared about him.

When his father had died, his anger had steered him into entering the king's army and becoming a ranger. He still believed very strongly in Anu, but whether or not he was meant to be a cleric like Darnok wanted him to be, still remained to be seen. He would see how he felt once their mission was over.

Tagor was a lot older now. His years of being a rash, young, vibrant officer in the king's military was well past him. Living as a ranger in the southern part of the Barnook forest had given him a lot of time to think about everything that had happened over the years. His love of his god and his desire to do something meaningful with his life had never dissipated. There had always been the dilemma over what it was exactly that he wanted to do with his life, especially since his father's died many years ago. He just never could quite find the direction he wanted to go in.

The two weeks he had spent in the temple had strengthened his resolve to re-enter the clergy, even at so late a time in his life. He felt that it had strengthened his spiritual determination. He had always thought that teaching the will of Anu was very important and that many lives could be improved by it. No, it was not just improving lives, but saving the souls of the lost. He still believed that only through service to his god could one be saved. And not just to any god. There were many false gods in the world. Only the teachings of Anu proved to be true. From his many years of study, he had no doubt that the writings of the book of Anu were the true words of god.

Anu was merciful, but firm. According to his word he

punished those that disobeyed him and rewarded those that followed and served him well. But more importantly, through service and obedience to him, there was eternal life. Tagor knew better than most that no one lives forever. He had seen his share of death.

Tagor continued to ponder this as they rode along and finally came to a decision. Pending the outcome of their journey, he would re-enter the clergy and the church for good. This mission was of great importance to the middle kingdoms as well as to the world at large, but afterward there was still a lot he could do for his god and for the people of this land. Perhaps he would even find himself a woman and marry. Contrary to many of the popular religions in the world, Anu permitted his servants to marry.

Tagor felt as if a great burden had been lifted off of him once he had made his decision. As he rode down the small winding trail ahead of his companions, Tagor thought the medallion of Anu that hung about his neck warmed him a little.

Tagor then concentrated on the task before them. Their priority was to get Jair and the helmet to Silvermist. Once there, they would decide what needed to be done. Of course, that was pending what they found out about the helmet, if they could even get into the city, and if the elves would even be willing to help them.

Before they had left the city, the king had received reports on additional movement and activity that spotted around the city of Zoarnest and in the Beckon Woods. The king's scouts reported large numbers of goblins, giants, trolls, human mercenaries and Dark Elves traveling together and converging near the city.

Also according to the scouts, it appeared that Telenok was preparing to do something soon. As a precautionary measure, the king sent a thousand troops to Fort Decadse, located on the eastern border of the elven kingdoms, north of the Plains of Solitude.

This fort was built two hundred years ago, right after the last

Great War. It was constructed with the intention of being a buffer between the elven nations, the barbarians of the northwest, and Parvincia. The fort's walls had never been breached, and it had served its country well. It also served as a trading post between the elves and the humans.

It was for the fort that the companions were now headed. From there they would receive a guide who was to lead them to Silvermist. Tagor had been to many parts of Parvincia, Tolgath and some of the western edges of the elven forests, but he had never made it to Silvermist. As they road along they discussed what they knew about Silvermist, which was very little.

Thoughts of seeing Silvermist cheered Jair. Their discussion helped to pass the time. The sun eventually peeked out from an opening in the clouds. This warmed everyone a little as they rode.

Visiting Silvermist was more than Jair had ever hoped for. He also hoped he would be able to find out something about his father after they learned whatever they could about the helmet. Perhaps they would be able to accomplish both while there.

Jair urged his horse forward until he was beside Tagor. He asked him to continue teaching him sign language while they rode. Tagor agreed and began showing him new words. It wasn't easy to do while riding, but Tagor managed as best he could while holding his reigns in one hand.

The companions continued traveling for the rest of the day. They maintained a steady pace. As the sun eventually got ready to set, Tagor told them they should be about another half a days ride from the fort. He estimated that they would reach it sometime after noon the following day.

Rakkon rode ahead to find a place for them to make camp for the night. He returned shortly before dusk and led them to an area he had chosen that was near a small stream. By the time they got there, darkness had fallen.

They used their night vision, an ability that elves and giants shared. Jair and Kethok went out and gathered fallen limbs with which to build a small fire. As it grew colder out and they had the long day's ride behind them, they felt extra warmth for the night would be beneficial. They thought they could take the chance of anyone seeing them.

The group sat around the small fire, gathering warmth from its glowing embers as they shared a small meal from their provisions. They were all tired and a little sore from being in the saddle all day, especially Kethok. Even though he didn't chafe, his joints ached. No one spoke while they ate. They were each lost in their own thoughts.

As they relaxed for the evening, Kethok started making hand motions at Tagor. His hands moved skillfully in the unspoken language. Jair couldn't keep up with what was being said. He could only make out a few words here and there. After a few moments, Tagor's expression changed to concerned. He turned toward the others and said, "Kethok says he thought he saw something following us later this afternoon. It looked like a large black bird, flying far enough behind us so that it could barely be seen. He also said it looked bigger than any bird he's ever seen."

Jair and Rakkon looked at Kethok as Tagor spoke for him. Kethok nodded his head acknowledging what Tagor was saying, and urging him to continue. Tagor then said, "He said he first spotted the bird shortly after noon and then continued to see it throughout the remainder of the day. He's pretty sure it has been following us."

Tagor tried to read the expressions on Jair and Rakkon's faces in the flickering firelight. They all knew the chance they were taking on making this journey, especially with what it was they were carrying. The odds were good that they could be followed or attacked along the way by some of the Dark Lord's minions. If someone found out what they were carrying, then there would be powerful and dangerous people coming after it.

Rakkon spoke up and said, "On the morrow I think we should all watch for this bird. If the chance presents itself, it might be best if Tagor and Jair put their bows to use. At the worst, it will let our enemies know we are not unaware nor helpless, and perhaps it will blind them to our whereabouts for a while."

The others nodded in agreement and decided to get some sleep so they could get an early start in the morning. Kethok took the first watch as the rest of them unrolled their bedrolls and settled in for the night. It didn't take long before Tagor and Rakkon were asleep. Tagor's snoring was loud enough to wake the entire forest.

Jair stayed up for a while so he could study his spells. He also worked on mastering some of the techniques in controlling magic he had learned at the Wizard's Guild. He covered some of the new material he had been given, then quietly put his things away and laid down.

Kethok watched Jair in silence as he slowly drifted off to sleep. Memories of his own childhood came to mind as he looked upon Jair. His mind worked slowly, as only a giant's could, but very purposefully and with determination.

Kethok would follow the young half-elf anywhere, even unto the ends of the earth. Not only because he and Tagor had saved him from the evil wizard, but also because he had recognized Jair's amulet when they had first met on the barge at the Wildrun River. He had seen that mark before.

When he'd been a child living in the hills with his people, there had been a story drawn in the dirt around their campfires. An old story passed down for generations. It was a prophesy about a man who was not a man and an elf that was not an elf who was supposed to help free his people from the Dark Lord. The Dark Lord who had subjugated his people for many generations, binding them to him with trickery and deceit. Kethok thought Jair might be the one prophesied from the stories. Even if he wasn't, he might lead Kethok to the one who was. He was loyal to his people, even though they had rejected him. He would still help free them if he could.

He remembered the story well and could still see the sign as it had been drawn time and again. A golden sun shone behind an old oak tree. The tree had an eye glinting out from its center. It was the same sign as the one on the amulet Jair wore. To the giants it was called "Grithmalkin".

Chapter 11

The sun rose slowly behind a thick veil of clouds. A cold winter wind cut sharply through the companions' thick, fur lined cloaks as the sun tried to penetrate the gray sky above them.

Jair awoke to the smell of meat cooking and sounds of a crackling fire. He rolled over to take a look and saw Rakkon squatting next to a rekindled fire where he was roasting several small hares.

Jair sat up and stretched. An unwelcome feeling of gloom and melancholy spread over him as he searched the sky for any sign of the bird from the day before. The day was going to be dark and depressing and it looked as if it could snow any time.

Jair looked for Tagor and saw he had already put away his gear and re-saddled his horse. Kethok was up and waiting silently for the meat to finish cooking. He had a hungry look on his face. He smiled at Jair.

As Jair rose, Rakkon grunted a good morning to him. He replied in kind then set about putting away his bedroll. He gathered his things and secured them on his horse, then returned to where the others were now eating.

Jair quickly devoured his portion of rabbit. After eating they washed at the stream, then climbed upon their mounts and set off. Jair and Kethok had a better time controlling their horses, but were both still really sore from the previous days riding.

Shortly after mid-morning Kethok urged his mount up past Jair and Rakkon until he was next to Tagor. He made several hand gestures, and then looked at Rakkon. Tagor nodded his head once forward then back, toward Jair. Rakkon understood what Tagor wanted so he dropped back until he was next to Jair.

Rakkon spoke softly to Jair. "Kethok has spotted our flying

friend not far behind us. Don't look up at it or let it know that we've spotted it." Rakkon said quickly as Jair started to look back.

Rakkon continued speaking quietly. "We are going to continue riding as if nothing is happening, but at the first opportunity, Tagor is going to slip off into the woods and get a closer look."

Jair nodded slowly to let Rakkon know he understood. He nudged his horse forward again. Rakkon then resumed his place in line.

Jair looked around and noticed a slight change in the terrain. The forest had begun to thin out. It had given way to a more open, flat expanse. The trees were becoming sparser and smaller. The ground itself seemed to be getting harder and rockier.

Sometime close to noon, Tagor said they should stop to take a break. They had come close to the edge of the forest, which would soon give way to the large open expanse of dark grassy plains. The wide, flat, rolling landscape that Jair could see off in the distance, could be no other than the Plains of Solitude.

Jair had heard stories about the Plains of Solitude. He had heard about the many wondrous and dangerous animals and peoples that roamed it.

Jair looked around and tried to remember the king's map that showed the plains stretching from the lower tip of the Anarest Mountains, southward to the Teeshok Marsh. From there it stretched along the eastern edge of the Barnook Forest and to the western edge of the Lilkithrean Forest.

As far as Jair could see, the plains stretched on like a rolling sea of grass. It made him think of other stories he had heard. In these tales there were large bands of nomadic herdsmen who traveled on horseback and lived in wagons and tents.

These tribes were supposed to be fierce warriors. They also

herded domestic animals. Occasionally they traveled close to the outlying forts or small villages along the edge of the plains for trading. Other than that Jair had heard that they were very reclusive and didn't like outsiders.

When they came to a spot Tagor deemed suitable, Jair dismounted and then looked back out onto the plains. Tagor disappeared into the forest, and Rakkon and Kethok stretched their legs, drinking a little water from their skins.

Jair gazed into the distance and thought he could just barely make out the faint outline of mountains in the north. He looked at Rakkon, pointed and asked, "Rakkon, are those the Anarest Mountains?"

Rakkon turned and shaded his eyes with one hand looking in the direction Jair indicated. He nodded his head affirmatively and said, "Yes, that's them all right. I traveled along their western edge on my way south from Caerdon. It was in the Anarests that I killed the wyvern." Rakkon said.

The two men stood and stared out across the grassy plain. While they did so, Kethok walked over to stand next to them. Jair looked up at his friend and saw a strange look on his face while he gazed at the distant mountains. It was a look of longing and loneliness.

"Kethok, you were born and raised in those mountains weren't you?" Jair asked him.

Kethok shook his large head affirmatively. Seeing the hurt expression in his eyes, Jair thought that he'd better change the subject.

Jair went over to his horse, removed his water skin and took a small drink. He then handed it to Rakkon who also took a swallow, then started to hand it to Kethok who only shook his head no and walked off.

Rakkon shrugged, capped the water skin and handed it back to Jair who replaced it on his saddle. Jair looked around, and became alarmed when he noticed that Tagor was not with them.

"Rakkon, where is Tagor?" Jair asked him.

"He has gone to get a closer look at our spy." Rakkon replied in a low tone.

Jair turned and looked about the edge of the forest for Tagor. He then scanned the sky for any sign of the bird, but did not see anything. He gave up and went over to check on his horse and pack animal. After taking care of them he found a spot to sit and relax. While he did that, Rakkon began sharpening his axe and Kethok practiced fighting with his new mace. There was nothing else they could do until Tagor returned.

After a short while, Jair decided that if Tagor didn't show up soon, they would have to look for him.

Meanwhile, as the others waited, Tagor slipped into the forest. He tried to stay under cover as much as possible while he worked his way back through the thinning woods and quickly blended in with the natural surrounding.

The only sound that could be heard by his passing was a whispering of the wind. He moved cautiously, leaving a trail that even the most skilled of trackers would have had a hard time finding.

As he worked his way further back into the forest, he kept an eye on the dark, cloudy sky. He paused every few moments and scanned the horizon. He looked for the small black speck that would betray the presence of the bird that had been following them since the previous day.

Eventually he spotted something moving slowly across the sky.

Gliding gently across the treetops and spiraling down every so often, the large black bird flew closer to where the companions had stopped to rest.

Tagor watched the bird as it neared their position and was amazed at its size. The bird's body was as large as a sheep. It's wingspan was more than eight feet across, and the dark, blue-black coloring of its feathers seemed to absorb what little light fell upon it. He knew that it was not a normal bird.

As the raven closed in on them, Tagor removed his bow from across his back. He drew out one of the silver tipped arrows from his quiver and notched it to his bowstring. He took careful aim at the growing black target and pulled back on his bow until his right thumb brushed his cheek.

He waited until the bird's body was angled just right, held his breath and then released his hold on the string. With a small twang the bow snapped and released its deadly shaft. Following its lightning arc across they sky, Tagor watched as the silver tipped missile flew toward the giant bird.

Time seemed to slow down for a moment as the arrow streaked across the sky toward its target. It was like watching something in slow motion but Tagor knew it was actually happening very quickly. His arrow was a silver streak in the cold gray sky.

With a shriek, the arrow embedded itself into the chest of the giant black bird. The force of the blow knocked the bird backwards several feet before it began tumbling toward the ground. In a writhing mass of kicking clawed feet and flailing wings, the giant bird plummeted to the ground. There were several loud cracks as it passed through a tree, snapping off limbs as it fell. Then there was an audible thump as it hit the ground.

Tagor dashed from his hiding place. He laid aside his bow and drew out his sword as he ran. He leaped through the underbrush and quickly made it to where he had saw the bird fall. Upon reaching the place, Tagor was appalled by what he found.

Where there should have been a giant black bird lying on the ground, there was now a dark skinned elven woman. The woman was small and thin, about five feet tall. Her skin was a dark gray with high arching brows and long, pointed ears. There was no mistaking it. This was a female dark elf.

Tagor cautiously walked over to get a better look at the wounded elf. He kept his sword extended in front of him as he neared the figure that lay upon the ground.

As he did so, he could see his arrow protruding from the chest of the dark skinned woman. Blood covered her chest and body from where the arrow had pierced her heart. Her body lay broken and twisted from the fall.

Tagor bent down to take a closer look and noticed a small ring on one of the dark elf's fingers. He checked for a heartbeat, but could find no sign of life. He was sure that the elf was dead. He reached down he gently pulled the ring from off her finger.

He then stepped back to examine the ring. He could see that it was fashioned into the likeness of a small raven. Its wings were wrapped around in a circle, with their tips barely touching at the top. The head was in the center and was turned to one side. The claws extended below it, as if it were about to grab some prey. In its center there was a small diamond set into the bird's eye. A gem that glinted evilly as Tagor examined it.

A snapping noise of a breaking twig from the forest behind him brought Tagor about. He moved from the noise, dropped the ring and rapidly brought his sword up into a defensive position.

The noises grew louder as the sounds of moving figures came toward him. As Tagor prepared himself for whatever it was that was headed his way, Jair, Rakkon and Kethok emerged from the forest.

Tagor let out a grateful sigh of relief and waved them over to where he was standing. He then began looking around for the ring he had just held. Upon reaching Tagor, the others quickly saw the prone figure of the dark elf. Jair walked over and gazed down in repulsive wonder. He had never seen a woman that looked like that, especially one with an arrow sticking out of her chest.

"What happened Tagor?" Jair asked him.

Tagor replied, "I slipped into the forest and waited for our flying friend to come in for a better look. When the bird came within range, I took aim and fired on it hoping to rid us of it. This is what I found where the bird fell. All she had on her was a strange ring. I dropped it when you three made all that noise getting here. It should be around here somewhere." Tagor said as he pointed to where he had been standing when they arrived.

They all took a few moments to look around, but none of them could find the small ring he had just dropped. They gave up after a thorough search, and went back to examining the body.

"Tagor, you said that she was a dark elf. Where did she come from? Who do you think sent her?" Jair asked.

"She's a dark elf all right." Tagor responded. "I've battled enough of the vile creatures to know one when I see one. As to where she's from, there's only one place, Devasthall, the kingdom of the dark elves." Tagor said with a sour look on his face.

Tagor paused to let that information sink in, then continued. "The only one who could have sent her is Telenok himself. He's the one that probably gave her the ring that allowed her to transform into a bird and to stay out in the daylight. Everyone knows that dark elves can't stand daylight. It burns their skin and eyes and weakens their magic."

Tagor then suggested, "I think we should bury her so no one can find her and be on our way. There's no telling what other surprises Telenok has out here waiting for us. He may not know for sure if we have the helmet, but will now know that we are aware of his meddling.

The companions agreed and quickly buried the dark elf's body. They then made their way back to their horses where they mounted up and set off across the plain.

They headed straight toward the base of the Anarest Mountains, where Fort Decadse lay. It was here they were supposed to find someone to guide them to Silvermist and obtain additional supplies.

Once they were out on the grassy plain, a dreadful feeling came over Jair. It was a feeling of being exposed. Having grown up in the forest, being out on the plain was a very unnerving experience.

Jair was not the only one to feel that way. Tagor and Kethok also disliked the flat openness that lay around them. Tagor had also grown up near the forests and Kethok was used to living in the mountains.

Rakkon however, did not seem as disturbed by it. When Jair asked him, Rakkon only shrugged and said that one place was as good as another to die and as long as he had his weapons he was content no matter where he was. Upon hearing that, Jair figured it was a barbarian thing. It did however make him feel a little better.

Late into the afternoon, Rakkon finally spotted the fort. It was lying far off into the distance at the base of the mountains. The Anarest rose ominously up before them in the cold, dark sky.

Upon seeing the mountains, Jair gazed wonderingly at them. He had never seen mountains before. He had only seen small hills and mounds in the forest. This trip was proving to be increasingly wondrous to him. All his years at Kentar's keep had surely kept him from seeing anything of the world, and there was so much of it to see. He wished the circumstances were better so that he could really enjoy it.

As they rode toward the fort, Kethok started motioning vigorously to Tagor. Tagor pulled his horse to a stop and spun around in his saddle to see what Kethok was motioning about.

Tagor saw that there was a large cloud of dust in the distance that was moving toward them. A large group of riders were thundering their way. Tagor scanned the riders, then turned his horse around toward the fort and spurred it into a full gallop, all the while yelling at the others, "Make for the fort or we're done for!"

Heeding Tagor's words, they all spurred their mounts on, charging toward the fort at full speed. As they closed in on it, Jair could barely make out some of the figures standing on top of the large, stone walls. He assumed that they were garrison soldiers. Hoping for the best, he sped along with his heart racing as fast as his horse's hooves pounded the earth below him.

Jair glanced back and got a better look at the riders that were gaining on them. The riders were clad in dark colored, loose fitting robes. Their bodies were covered from head to toe. They had tightly wound turbans covering their heads and faces, and soft, knee high leather boots on their feet. Being able to see them that clearly alarmed him even more.

Most of the riders were brandishing sharp, wicked looking scimitars. Several also had short, thick bows. They held the bows in their hands and notched arrows as they rode, controlling their mounts with their knees.

Jair urged his horse to even greater speed. As the four companions drew nearer to the fort, Jair thought he saw some commotion on top of the outermost wall. The few guards he had spotted earlier had grown into several dozen, and all of them were now armed with longbows and crossbows. Jair wasn't sure whom they were aiming at though. He hoped it wasn't at him and his friends.

As an arrow zipped past Jair's head from behind, he hunkered down lower in his saddle. Several more whizzed passed with one sticking into the back of Rakkon's saddle. The riders were almost upon them as Tagor's horse thundered across the lowered drawbridge, leading them into the fort.

Jair, Rakkon and Kethok were quick to follow as Tagor led the way through the fort's gate. With only seconds to spare, a large iron gate fell into place behind them, cutting off the pursuit of the dark robed riders.

Amidst the clattering of hooves and shouts of men, the four companions pulled their horses to a stop just inside the courtyard. Jair turned and could see the milling riders just outside the gate as two large wooden doors were pushed shut by the guardsmen.

The soldiers on top of the wall fired randomly down into the milling mass of riders outside. The riders in return shot back a few random arrows that didn't hit anyone inside the fort. After a few moments of this, the riders finally decided there was nothing else they could do so they turned their mounts and fled back out into the open plain, leaving behind their fallen comrades.

Jair took a deep breath and sighed with relief. He thought that he would collapse from the excitement. That was one of the most harrowing experiences he had ever had. He also wondered who the riders had been and why had they had chased them?

Chapter 12

As they dismounted, Jair's heart started slowing down. The commotion outside the gate had ceased so the soldiers returned to their regular posts, looking on curiously as to who their guests might be.

Sweat and dust covered the companions, even in the cold, brisk winter air. Calming down a bit, Jair looked over at his companions to see if anyone was injured. Luckily, no one seemed to be. Rakkon had come the closest. He reached up to the back of his saddle and removed the arrow that had lodged itself there during their mad dash to the fort. He held the arrow up so that the others could see it. As he did so, a loud voice rang out from behind them.

"Thee and thine companions werest surely lucky this day. Tis not many that canst escape Ilshadizar Raiders. Once they hast a target, one is usually quite dead."

The group faced a middle age man covered in full plate armor. He was striding quickly toward them as he spoke, clanking as he walked. Jair saw that he had short, brown hair that hung down to the nape of his neck and he sported a long, flowing mustache that Jair thought to be a custom among officers and knights in the Parvincian army.

As he approached them, the officer barked out several orders to the other men in the courtyard and then sent for a stable boy to take their horses.

The man arrived to where Jair and his companions were standing. He stopped and then presented himself in formal military fashion. He stood at attention with his plumed helmet tucked under one arm and had a serious expression on his face. He saluted them and after Tagor returned the salute, he spoke.

"I am lieutenant commander Mengistu Selassie of King

Galdath's fifth regiment of the imperial army. If thou and thy companions wouldst be so kind, please followest me."

The commander turned and marched off toward the main part of the fort. Jair removed his satchel from his horse before falling in with the others. He hung it on his shoulder and followed the commander and his friends across the courtyard.

Jair looked the fort over as they approached the main complex. He could see it was more of a heavily fortified castle than a fort. The walls were over twenty feet high and seemed to be several feet thick. They'd had many years to work on it to get it to its present state. It was in good condition. It may have started out as a fort, but was now a major fortification.

The castle was embedded partially in the mountainside, which rose up steeply behind it. Jair could tell that no army would be successful in attacking the fort from the mountainside. The only way was to attack it was from the front, by air, or by magic.

Jair looked the fort over as they walked. He realized it was quite a bit larger than he thought it was going to be. He had not been given a good description of the fort while in the city. It definitely looked like it was built to play an important role in keeping peace between Parvincia and the elven nations.

As they followed the commander, Jair could see that there was a lot of activity going on all about the fort. The outer walls were heavily guarded and were being closely watched by seasoned, veteran soldiers.

Within the compound itself, other soldiers were practicing their skills. Some practiced archery and swordplay while others practiced military drills and maneuvers. Jair had never seen a well-trained military garrison before, and the spectacle it provided fascinated him. Upon reaching the building, Jair thought that he even saw several wizards among them.

They followed the commander through a large wooden door that led into the castle. They passed down a long corridor and up a short flight of winding steps. They eventually came to another door.

The commander opened the door then stepped aside and ushered everyone into the room. It was a medium sized chamber, approximately twenty feet wide and thirty feet long. The room appeared to be a meeting hall, or an officer's dining room. It was plainly decorated, but had a long, expensive looking table with matching chairs.

The commander motioned them all to take a seat. He waited until they all had done so before seating himself. Everyone sat except for Kethok, who was too large for the chairs. Kethok moved over to one side of the room to be out of the way, but still be able to hear what was going on.

The commander laid his helmet on the table, glanced nervously Kethok's way, then cleared his throat before speaking.

"I presumest that thou art Tagor the woodsman and that these art thine erstwhile companions that the king wrote me about?"

Tagor paused for a moment before answering. He nodded his head in agreement to the commander's question. It had been several years since Tagor had dealt with imperial officers and he knew it would take him a few moments to get used to their heavy accent.

The commander relaxed a little after getting the answer he had expected, then continued, "I am truly glad that thee and thine companions hast made it safely to the fort. We haveth been expecting thee for several days now, since the arrival of the king's imperial messenger."

"From the descriptions that the king hath given us, I take it that this is Sir Rakkon," he said nodding toward Rakkon, who nodded back. "And that this is young master Jair the apprentice wizard," He said looking at Jair.

Jair quickly shook his head yes. He was at a loss as how to deal with the imperial commander. He knew that he was going to have to leave this to Tagor.

Tagor leaned back in is chair and spoke to the commander. "I see that the king was quite thorough in informing you of our mission commander. I hope we are not inconveniencing you in any way, but I must tell you we are passing through here on a very important mission, for the good of all the southern kingdoms."

"Aye sir," the commander responded. "I knoweth that our king spoketh well of thee and thine friends in his letter, and that I and my men were to extend to thee every courtesy to aideth thee on thine quest."

"We hath arranged a guide to lead thee to Silvermist. Once thy mission is complete thy guide is to bring thee back here, where thou willst be escorted back to our capital and unto the king."

"As to the nature of thine quest I willst not ask. His royal majesty hath not disclosed the nature of it to me, only that it be kept as quiet as possible." The commander said.

The commander spoke in an official manner. Jair could tell he was a man that took his job seriously. Concluding the matter of their mission, the commander changed the subject.

"Rooms hath been made ready for thee. Thy horses and equipment shall be looked after and a place for thee to cleanse thyselves shall be made ready. If thee and thine companions wouldst care to join me this evening, we wouldst enjoy thine company for supper." The commander asked them.

Tagor graciously accepted the invitation and thanked him for his hospitality. Tagor then asked the commander a question before he left.

The Ruby Helmet

"Commander, I was wondering if you could tell me who those men were that were chasing us and what they might have wanted?"

The commander looked at Tagor as he stood up, and replied.

"Ahh, the Ilshadizar Raiders. They art a large band of fierce, rogue bandits that hast been roaming these plains for many years. Thee and thine companions were truly lucky to have escaped them."

"The Ilshadizar art made up mostly of outcasts from nomad tribes. They art criminals and troublemakers that hath banded together for their own nefarious ends."

"They must hath truly desired thy heads to have ridden up to our very gates. They usually remain out upon the plains, raiding small villages and unwary travelers. It twould seem that these rogues have become braver and more dangerous as of late, but methinks that mine troops would surely make quick work of them shouldst they try again."

The commander then donned his helmet, saluted, and headed for the door. He turned back toward them before he exited the room and said, "Someone wilst come and showest thee to thy rooms. There thou canst wash off the dust from the road and warmst thyselves by a fire. I shall send for thee when dinner is served, until then, good day gentlemen."

After the commander left, Jair and the others relaxed until the servant arrived to show them to their rooms. Following the servant's lead, Jair and the others were led back downstairs, and along several corridors.

They were each ushered into a room of their own where a bath and clean clothes awaited them. Jair tiredly removed his dirty clothes and eased himself down into the steaming tub of hot water. He soaked his tired muscles for a short while and then vigorously scrubbed the grime of the road off.

Jair dried himself off after he got out of the tub. He shivered slightly from the cold winter air that filled the room. He put on a new tunic and breeches that had been laid out for him. He found that they fit him comfortably, but were a little big for him.

It was going to be a while before dinner would be served, so Jair decided to walk down to Tagor's room and wait with him. He left his room and strode down the hall. Upon reaching Tagor's room, Jair rapped lightly several times upon the door, then waited for a response.

Jair heard footsteps coming toward the door from the other side. Tagor opened the door, saw that it was Jair, then stepped aside and motioned for him to enter. Jair went inside. Upon entering he saw that Kethok and Rakkon were also there. They were sitting in chairs on the other side of the room. The chair Kethok sat in strained under his immense weight.

Jair moved across the room to a table that sat under a shuttered window where he pulled up another chair. Rakkon and Kethok both nodded to Jair as he took his seat next to them. He noted that Kethok looked somewhat damp and disheveled.

"I see that everyone is somewhat refreshed from our recent excursion," Tagor said with a smile as he strode over to where the others were seated. Upon reaching the other side of the room he casually leaned against one wall.

"I for one feel a lot better having bathed and donned clean clothes," Jair said. "Several days on the road and in a saddle help you appreciate the streams back home, even in the winter."

At the mention of bathing, Kethok looked at Jair with a strange expression on his face. Tagor saw the look and explained, "Giants do not make it a regular habit to bathe. It was a new experience for him."

Kethok shook his head in acknowledgment to Tagor's words and had a sour look on his face. Jair smiled slightly as he thought of the giant trying to fit into one of the small tubs humans used for bathing. It must have been a terrible ordeal.

Jair looked back at Tagor and asked, "How long are we going to stay at the fort?"

Tagor thought about it for a moment and then replied, "That really depends on the weather and when our guide arrives. I would like for us to be back on the road by early tomorrow morning, but if our guide does not show up, we will have to wait until he gets here. If he doesn't show before too long, we will set off without him."

Jair turned toward Rakkon, a worried look on his face. He thought that setting out to look for Silvermist without a guide would be disastrous. None of the four companions had ever been there, nor had they ever been to the Lilkithrean forest. It would be dangerous and the chance for error would be great if they had to do it on their own. That and the fact the Dark Lord knew about them made it even more dangerous.

Rakkon noticed the look on Jair's face and spoke up. He supported Tagor's words and tried to ease Jair's fears as he said, "I agree with Tagor. If the guide does not show by tomorrow morning, we should set off on our own. Somewhere between here and the Lilkithrean forest we should be able to pick up a guide that will take us on to Silvermist."

Rakkon spoke with a determined confidence. Having been on many travels, he was more self sure than Jair. Kethok only nodded in agreement, a stern look on his brutish face. Jair looked at his three companions and his fears lessened. Surely with three stout and skilled companions such as these they could find the city.

Jair relaxed after that and they fell into idle conversation. Tagor interpreted for Kethok when he occasionally interjected something, using hand signs. As they were discussing their plans, a knock came at the door. When Tagor opened it, a servant was waiting to tell them that dinner was ready and they were to follow him.

Jair and the others were once again led through the winding stone corridors. After a short time they were ushered in to the large dining hall.

The chamber was quite large and made of the same dark gray stone as the rest of the fort. At its center was a large fire pit that was open on all four sides. Above the pit was a large, metal, funnel shaped cylinder that led upward to a smaller pipe that ran up out of the ceiling. The fire was roaring gleefully as a servant placed more logs upon it. Tongues of flame moved about the pit as another servant turned a spit with a large boar roasting over it.

As they entered the room, a hush fell over the soldiers that were gathered together there. The soldiers curiously examined the newcomers, and several partially drew out their swords at the sight of Kethok.

Jair saw that there were quite a few soldiers and knights already seated along the long wooden tables that filled the room. As they filed into the chamber, the servant led them to a large table at the far end of the room. Commander Mengistu was seated at the center of the table. To his left were four empty seats, which Jair and his companions were ushered to.

The commander greeted them courteously once they took their seats. "I am truly glad that thee and thine companions have joined us. As thou canst see, I generally dine with my men. Tis customary here in the borderlands for it lends to a good rapport with mine men."

As the commander spoke, the tension that had filled the room eased. Most of the men returned to idle conversations and eating.

Meanwhile, Tagor shook his head in agreement to the commander's words. "Commander, the officers did likewise when I was fighting in the border wars. It always made the men feel better about their commanders and gave them strength in combat when given orders by officers they felt they knew and could trust."

As Tagor spoke, the commander's interest was peaked. As they spoke they found they shared common interests and a background in military life. This led to a deep discussion, which later led to mutual respect.

Jair sat and watched the other men in the dining hall as he ate his meal. The men were served common enough fare, but it was good food, so he fell to it. Kethok and Rakkon set to their meals as well, with Kethok consuming three times as much as everyone else.

After the meal, they sat and talked casually. Tagor and the commander continued speaking about old campaigns, and a few of the other officers joined them. The rest of the men were in smaller groups and were occupied by their own conversations.

At first, many of the men in the hall were reluctant to be around Jair and Kethok. His elven heritage was evident enough in his features that they did not seem to want to be around him. Jair could tell that the humans still did not trust elves or even half-elves. Fear kept them away from Kethok. This hurt Jair at first, as it always did. Rakkon struck up a conversation with some of the men. In the process of telling them about himself, he went over some of what they had all been through. After that, they seemed to respect him and Kethok. Jair noted that he left out any mention of the helmet.

Curiosity eventually helped the soldiers overcome their fear of Kethok. Their interest was also peaked by Rakkon's story. As they talked, several other soldiers came over to listen to the tale and to get a better look at the giant. Most of them had never seen a giant up close before.

Eventually one of the soldiers actually spoke to Jair. As he did so, Jair found that as a whole, most of them were very patriotic and determined to serve the cause of their king and country. It seemed that every one of them was willingly serving in the king's army and would happily give their lives in order to defend their home.

Such a vigorous and honest love for their homeland and service in it's military made Jair somewhat envious of them. Each of them was a part of something important. Each one had a purpose and a cause. None of them seemed to think much about the future, only that they were doing what was needed.

Jair sat and wondered about his cause and what his purpose in life was. What was it that he truly wanted to do with his life? After their mission was over, what then? These were serious questions that Jair did not have the answers for, at least not yet. Questions he had never really thought that much about before. Everything depended on what they could find out about the helmet when they reached Silvermist. He also felt it might help if he knew more about his history and where he came from.

More than ever Jair felt he needed to know whom his father was. It was a sense of finding one's self through family. He had never had a real family and he had barely known his mother before she had died.

Jair hoped he would find answers at Silvermist. Maybe there he would find what he was looking for.

Chapter 13

It was still dark outside when Jair was roughly shaken awake. He struggled for a moment until he came out of the deep sleep he had been in. He looked up and saw Rakkon standing over him. He was dressed and looked ready to leave.

Jair wiped the sleep from his eyes and sat up. "What's going on, what's happening?" He asked.

Rakkon picked up Jair's clothes and threw them to him. He replied. "Hurry and get dressed. Our guide has arrived. It's time for us to leave."

Jair nodded his head in acknowledgment. He quickly rose and donned his clothing. As he dressed, he noted that his old riding clothes had been neatly cleaned and pressed, probably by one of the commander's servants. He buckled his sword belt around his waist, and then splashed some cold water on his face. He then hurried to follow Rakkon out of the keep, grabbing his satchel as he went.

They eventually exited through a small door. Jair found himself just outside of the stables. He followed Rakkon inside the stable and stumbled slightly over something in the darkness. The sun had not yet risen and his eyes had not adjusted to the early morning gloom.

When his eyes did adjust, Jair noted that Kethok and Tagor were already checking their horses and pack animals. He went over to his own horse and found that his animals had already been taken care of. He went ahead and checked them anyway.

He placed his satchel securely behind his saddle then turned to see what was going on. He came around to the other side of his horse and saw that someone else had entered the stable. They were talking quietly to Tagor. Jair quietly walked over to stand beside Rakkon to see who it was.

The other figure that was standing next to Tagor was a very tall, thinly built man. He wore green and brown woodsmen's clothing. He wore tall boots made of soft, dark brown leather that came almost to his knees. Most of the rest of his attire seemed to be made out of tanned animal hides and finely woven fabric. Underneath his dark green tunic at the neckline, Jair caught the glint of a finely crafted shirt of mail. He leaned on an extremely tall longbow.

Tagor finished speaking to the man and turned toward the rest of them. Jair caught his first glimpse of the stranger's features as he turned into the dim morning light. His features were chiseled as if from marble. He had a thin, angular nose, high arching eyebrows, dark tan skin and slanting eyes. The most distinguishing features though were a set of sharply pointed ears that poked out from under his long, dark brown hair. The man was a wood elf.

Jair gawked for a moment at the first full-blooded elf that he had ever seen. He noticed the similarities in the features of the elf and of his own. He also noticed some of the differences. Differences brought about by his human blood.

Tagor addressed them after finishing his conversation with the elf. "Gentlemen, I would like you to meet "Rhys Huon". He will be our guide through the Lilkithrean forest and on to Silvermist."

They each introduced themselves, Jair being the last. He was a little reluctant to meet the wood elf. If humans didn't like him, what would an elf think? For a moment Rhys had a disgusted look on his face when he saw Jair, but grunted out a civil hello. He then turned away toward his horse. Jair shrugged off the somewhat rude greeting and went back to his horse. It seemed that elves disliked mixed breeds as well as humans. It was something Jair was getting used to but still didn't like.

Taking their horses by the reigns, Tagor led them out of the stable and into the main courtyard. When they neared the gate, everyone mounted and prepared to leave.

Jair heard a faint clanking sound over to their right as he settled into his saddle. No one other than the sentries that were marching along the parapets were about at that time of the morning. Jair looked up and wondered whom it was. He saw Commander Mengistu striding toward them from across the courtyard.

He stopped just before Tagor's horse and patted his mount's head. The commander looked up at Tagor and then over at the others. "Doest thee and thy companions have everything that thou wilst need for thy journey?" He asked.

"Aye sir. I believe we have everything we need to see us through." Tagor replied. "You have been a most gracious host commander. We thank you for your hospitality."

Tagor reached down and clasped forearms with the commander. "I hope that thee and thy companions art successful on thy quest. I wish thee well and good journey." He replied. The commander released Tagor's arm and stepped back. He motioned for the two guards in the gatehouse to open the gate.

Jair heard the sound of moving gears and the clanking of a chain being let out as the drawbridge was slowly lowered and the gates were opened. Rhys led them out. Jair and the others urged their mounts forward. He looked back and waved once at the commander who waved back solemnly. A grim expression played across his face in the waning moonlight.

Rhys led the way, heading North and East across the rolling plains along the southern edge of the mountains. About an hour after leaving the fort the sun began to rise behind more gray clouds. It was another overcast day with a cold wind biting through their thick winter cloaks.

Jair rode quietly through the first part of the morning, just like everyone else. Every so often he would glance nervously over his shoulder. He wondered if the same band of raiders that had pursued them the day before might be out on the plains, waiting for them.

After a short while he decided they were not going to be attacked, so he turned his attention back to Rhys Huon. He fascinated Jair because he had never been around another elf. He remembered seeing a few visiting the city when he was a boy, but he never had an opportunity to speak with any of them. It had been so long ago that he really didn't remember anything about them. Most of what he knew about elves was from the stories told to him by others.

Jair eventually urged his horse up until it was next to Rhys's. His curiosity overcame any apprehension that he had. The elf glared at him, but didn't say anything. Jair then asked him, "Rhys, where exactly do you hail from?"

He glanced at Jair with a somewhat bothered look on his face, and then responded dryly. "I grew up in the central Lilkithrean forest. My parents were both foresters close to the northern tip of the Serecom River."

"How did you end up as our guide?" Jair asked him.

"I owed the commander a favor." Rhys replied. "He was leading one of his patrols close to the forest where me and a couple of friends were attacked by an owlbear. The commander and his men helped us slay the beast. If not for them, I would not be here right now."

Jair shuddered at the thought of facing an owlbear. He had heard they were supposed to be fierce creatures that looked like a cross between an owl and a bear, hence the name. They stand upright; around ten feet tall and supposedly have yellowish brown fur, a small pointed tail, and a yellowish beak instead of a snout. Mean tempered and always hungry, owlbears reportedly attacked anything living on sight and were very hard to kill.

Rhys continued speaking and said, "Over the last couple of years I occasionally help the commander when he needs a scout for patrols in the nearby forest. In return I am well paid and am allowed to move about freely in this part of the country."

"Have you been to Silvermist before?" Jair asked him.

Rhys nodded his head yes, but offered no further comments. Jair pulled back on the reigns slightly and dropping back a few paces so that he was riding next to Rakkon. Jair looked at Rakkon. He smiled and shook his head from side to side. It was obvious to everyone from the elf's tone that he really didn't want much to do with Jair.

"He does not seem to be very friendly, does he?" Rakkon commented to Jair.

"No, he does not." Jair replied.

"Do you think all elves are like that?" Jair asked him.

Rakkon looked at him and responded. "I have only met a few in my travels. Most were vagabonds or thieves, but they all kept to themselves. Elves seem to be a very secretive lot."

"They don't like people prying into their business. It makes them uncomfortable. I guess it's from all those centuries of being secluded." Rakkon said.

He ended their conversation with a shrugging of his massive shoulders. The day passed on and finally, late in the afternoon, Jair noticed something up ahead of them. He could see that not very far in the distance there was a large expanse of trees that stretched from the North to South, as far as the eye could see.

They had arrived at the edge of the Lilkithrean forest. As near as Jair could tell, it was close to mid-afternoon. It was hard to say for sure though. The sun was still hidden behind a thick layer of clouds.

Jair rode up next to Tagor and asked him to help him work on his sign language skills. He and Tagor signed back and forth with Tagor correcting and making suggestions every so often. It didn't seem like much had time had passed before the forest was looming right before them.

They stopped for a moment at the forest's edge, then Rhys turned and headed northward following the forest's perimeter. Jair noticed that there was not a gradual decline in the woodlands as there had been when they had left the Barnook forest. This forest ran right up to the plains and then stopped.

Jair noticed that this forest was unlike the one in which he had grown up. The trees were much larger, huge in fact. They reached way up into the sky for many hundreds of feet. They were much taller and thicker than the ones back home. They also had a dark feel to them.

The surrounding vegetation was also very thick. If not for the cold chill that carried on the early winter wind, Jair thought the forest could be almost tropical. Even with its fall colors it had a jungle look.

The companions followed their guide as he led them along the edge of the forest. Jair studied the forest carefully as they passed along its edge.

They rode on for a while and Rhys finally turned off onto what looked like a small trail that went into the woods. They continued to follow his lead and stayed in single file as they entered the forest.

Animals had probably originally created the trail. Then later on began being used by men and elves. It was a small and slightly overgrown trail that looked like it had been there a long time.

As they left the plain, Jair was glad for the surrounding plant life. The giant trees and plants helped to cut down on the wind and chill. Jair felt as if he had been out in the cold for weeks instead of for just a few days. He also didn't feel as exposed as he had out on the plain.

Besides the bone chilling cold and his tired, aching muscles, there was something that nagged at the back of Jair's mind. It was almost a sixth sense telling him there was something not quite right as they rode along the trail.

Rhys finally called a halt in a small clearing he had found. They all climbed down from their mounts, glad to be able to stretch their legs after the long day's ride.

Kethok signed toward Tagor who relayed to the rest of the party that even he was getting tired of the many hours they'd spent in the saddle. He walked slightly bow legged, which looked very strange for a giant.

Jair stretched then removed some food from one of his packs. They let the horse's mill around, picking through the waning grass. Jair went over to a fallen log where Rakkon and Kethok had already retreated. He found himself a place to sit and eat.

Rhys walked over and whispered something to Tagor, then slipped into the forest. Tagor retrieved some of his rations and joined the rest of the group.

As soon as he found a place to sit, he quickly began eating. Their iron rations consisted of dried meats, bread, cheese, nuts and a few other assorted goods, all of which were somewhat bland but nonetheless filling.

While they rested and ate, Jair asked, "Tagor, where has Rhys gone off to?"

Tagor replied between mouthfuls of food. "He has gone into the forest to take a look around. He said that for this time of day it is unusually quiet in the forest. He wanted to go out alone so he could

192

move swiftly and quietly to see if anything strange was happening."

For the rest of their break and while waiting for Rhys to return, Tagor and Rakkon had sword practice with Jair. Kethok sat and watched in his usual stoic silence as the two men instructed the young half-elf.

Jair had filled out some over the last few months with all the exercise and good food. He had not eaten that well while back at the old keep. A light beard had also begun to show along his jaw line. Most elves were thinner and did not have beards.

While resting for a moment in between lessons, Jair was startled. Rhys appeared right next to him from out of the forest. As quiet as the wind, Jair never heard a sound as the wood elf silently slipped up behind him. He suspected the elf did it on purpose.

He went over to the rest of the group and motioned for them all to come closer. "Something strange has entered the forest. I cannot tell what it is, but the regular forest creatures have cleared out. I have a bad feeling about it. I think we should move on. There is a small elven outpost a few hours ride from here and I think we should try to reach it before the sun goes down."

Everyone agreed, checked their equipment, watered their horses and then climbed back up into their saddles. Rhys set a brisk pace and led the companions quickly down the old path. They were each aware of the ominous feeling of something unnatural in the forest.

Jair looked around as they rode. The others also kept a wary eye on the surrounding woods. An unknown element following them as they traveled into a foreign country was very unsettling.

Jair knew that his earlier feeling of uneasiness, right after entering the forest, was not unfounded. It was unsettling not knowing who might be out there.

Chapter 14

Tendrils of thick, black smoke rose steadily from the slowly burning embers of what remained of the small eleven outpost. It was nestled in the top of one of the forest's giant trees. Rhys reined in his horse, drew his sword and dismounted to take a look around.

He quickly ran up a long, rope and wood walkway that started at the base of one of the tree's thick roots and wound itself partway up around the trunk before stopping at a large platform. Once at the top he searched through the remains of the two, small wooden buildings that had served as a home and outpost. Inside the main building he found the bodies of the proprietor and his two young sons.

While Rhys inspected the buildings the others drew their weapons and dismounted, spreading out to search the area. The main building and a large part of the tree had been burned. The small storage building was still intact. Inside of it they found that anything of value that had not been taken had been destroyed.

After checking the perimeter, Tagor motioned for the others to re-join him along with Rhys at the top of the platform. Anger and disgust clearly played across Rhys's face at what had been done to the proprietor and his sons. He had dragged their bodies out onto the landing and partially covered them with a blanket he had salvaged.

After the quick search, each of them told what they had found. Rhys motioned toward what he had found inside the charred remains of the building. He shook with anger as he spoke.

"This was the proprietor and his sons." Rhys stated. "Their bodies have been burned. I believe one of the boys was still alive at the time. The father had been run through with a sword and the eldest son was almost torn in half."

"Evidently one of the boys had been captured and tied to the

194

building's center beam. It was then set on fire after being ransacked. Fortunately the other two were gone before the fire was set. The father and oldest boy must have put up a fight." Rhys said.

A stern look came across his face as he continued. "It bodes ill for the forest folk hereabouts when raiders such as these enter our woods. Tielgrun, the proprietor, was a good man as were his sons." Rhys told them.

Seeing the bodies caused a wave of nausea to pass over Jair. He tried to keep from becoming sick. He stepped away as if to look around and took several deep breaths of fresh air.

Tagor gave Rhys a sympathetic look and placed a hand on his shoulder. "There are many sets of hooves and boot prints all around the compound." He explained. "I estimate at least eight to ten riders. The boot prints varied from several very small, childlike ones to a few that were much larger than a normal man's."

"It would seem that after ransacking and setting fire to the buildings, they set off in a northerly direction." Rakkon added. "They were very thorough in their work and they left in a hurry."

Kethok interjected quickly with several hand signals that there was an unusual stench lingering in the air that he had never smelled before. Being raised in the wilderness, his sense of smell was quite acute.

After compiling their findings, the companions helped Rhys to bury the remains of the elven proprietor and his sons. They covered the rest of the burning embers of the outpost with what dirt and water they could carry up to the platform from a nearby stream. They then mounted up and set off once again for Silvermist.

Rhys estimated that if they kept up their earlier pace they should reach the elven city by the day after tomorrow. Jair felt that the sooner they reached the city the better.

Rhys led the group at the same rapid pace for the rest of the day. They traveled east for several hours, then turned northward to reach the elven city from the south. They did this so that they might not run into whoever it was that had destroyed the outpost. They followed several small trails and Jair was totally lost by the time Rhys decided to stop for the night.

Rhys finally had everyone stop after locating a suitable clearing. Jair and the others dismounted, trying not to force their aching muscles to do more than they had too.

Following Rhys's example, each of them saw to the needs of their horses. Before leaving the fort, Tagor had decided to leave their pack animals behind. He felt they would be able to move quicker without them. Their mission had seemed to become more urgent.

After seeing to their horses, Jair and the others quickly ate a meal from their rations. The group opted not to build a fire, even though Jair thought they could have benefited from the warmth. Rhys warned them against having a fire. He did not want to draw attention to them. Tagor and Rakkon were quick to support this.

The watch was set with each of them taking turns, divided equally throughout the night. Jair went first, in order to study a few of his spells and unwind after the long day.

He picked himself out a spot next to a tree and settled in to study his spells. The sun set quickly behind another thick wall of clouds as the rest of Jair's companions fell asleep. The cold crept in around him as he got still, so he pulled his blanket tighter around him to try and keep warm. Every so often he would look around, carefully scanning the forest while listening for any strange sounds.

He scanned the pages of his spell book until the light faded and he could no longer see. He then worked on his spell casting, running through them in his mind and practicing hand gestures. Several hours passed until Jair decided it was time for Rakkon to take his turn at watch. He replaced his spell book in his satchel and went and gently woke Rakkon.

Rakkon rose quietly. It only took a light touch on his shoulder to wake him. This startled Jair. Evidently he was a light sleeper.

Jair went back over to his own blanket and settled down for a cold, uncomfortable nap. He slowly drifted off into a disturbed, fitful slumber that lasted throughout the early part of the night. Jair tossed and turned as his dreams were filled with terrible images and threats from dark, evil beings. He slept but did not get much rest.

Early the next morning Jair woke to find all of the others except for Rhys still asleep. His had been the last watch. The sun had not quite risen as Jair wiped the sleep from his eyes. He lay under his blanket and tried to remember what it was he had been dreaming about. His head throbbed slightly as he tried to remember, but nothing came readily to mind.

Jair rose and saw to repacking his things and putting his saddle on his horse. Rhys only looked at him as he moved about in the early morning gloom. He removed some of his rations from his pack and ate quietly. He then walked over to where Rhys squatted down at the edge of the clearing. He was staring solemnly out into the forest.

"What is it you look for?" Jair asked Rhys quietly as he approached him. He looked over his shoulder at Jair and shrugged once before returning his attention to the surrounding forest.

"I watch and listen to the forest itself. I listen to see what it tells me. I watch to see what is happening out there." Rhys said as he pointed into the woods.

Jair peered into the forest, searching for some sign of what it was that Rhys was looking for. He gave up after not being able to see anything out of the ordinary. Jair squatted down next to Rhys.

"What can you learn by listening and looking into the forest?" Jair asked him.

"Sometimes you can learn what the forest is thinking and how it feels. By listening to the sounds of the forest you can tell many things, and by looking into its heart you can see another world." Rhys responded with a far away look on his face.

Jair stared once more into the woods. He listened carefully. The silence was only broken occasionally by the sound of the wind rustling through the trees. For a moment he thought he could hear something. He closed his eyes to concentrate. It was like something was reaching out to him. He realized that it was the forest itself. He could feel that it was angry and afraid.

Then the feeling passed and he could sense no more. Jair listened for a few moments more but couldn't feel or hear anything else. He stood as he heard the others moving about behind him. He turned around and walked back over to the camp and helped the others to gather their things and saddle their horses.

Nothing much was said as everyone got ready for the long days ride. The others ate a quick meal and washed up using a small, icy stream Rhys had found nearby. After mounting up they set off once again through the forest. The sun was just beginning to rise behind the slow moving clouds.

The same chill hung in the air that had been with them for the last few days. Today however, Jair felt there was something else amiss. The gloomy mood that had been with them was definitely still there, but now it felt like something else was adding to it, making it worse. He guessed that maybe it had something to do with the weather.

He pulled his cloak a little tighter about his shoulders and held loosely onto his reigns as they rode. Knowing there might be trouble ahead of them, he reached back into his pack to remove the wand the

High Wizard at Gallador had given him. He thrust it through his belt, next to his dagger.

The added comfort of knowing the wand was within easy reach made him feel a little better, but did not completely remove the gloom that had spread over all of them. He mentioned it to Tagor who agreed there was something in the air, but told him they didn't need to dwell on it.

They rode on for the rest of the morning. Rhys only called a small rest to see to the horses and to eat something before urging them all onward once again. The pace was grueling.

The day wore on relentlessly, never seeming to end as league upon league of thickly wooded scenery passed them by. The day warmed up slightly during the afternoon, but cooled quickly as it waned toward evening. It was the first fair day they had seen in almost a week.

Jair pulled up beside Tagor and rode beside him as they slowed their pace. Rhys was trying to decide which way to go next. As the forest shadows grew black with nightfall, Rhys rode up ahead to try to find a decent place to make a camp for the night. The others trotted along slowly behind.

"Tagor, when do you think we will reach Silvermist?" Jair asked him.

"Rhys says we should be there by sometime tomorrow morning." Tagor answered. "We've been making pretty good time even though we had to work our way through the forest. It is a lot slower passing through this forest than riding out on the open plains. I think tomorrow will see us there."

Jair looked at Tagor and said, "I can't shake the feeling I've had since entering the forest. It feels like something bad is going to happen."

Tagor nodded his head in agreement and responded, "I know what you mean. I've felt it too. There's definitely something out there waiting for us. I just wish I knew what it was. It's the not knowing that's the worst." Tagor said.

Tagor smiled slightly at Jair and said, "It's also something that will do us no good dwelling on it. Keep your mind on good thoughts. Think of things that make you happy. If we dwell on these bad feelings they will overcome us."

Tagor's words helped Jair feel better. What Tagor said made sense, but doing it was much harder than just talking about it. As Jair was about to say something else, Rhys rode back toward them and announced that he had found a suitable place to make camp for the night. They turned their attention toward him and followed as he passed down another small trail.

Jair cast a searching glance into the forest and tried to find the source of his uneasy feeling, but still couldn't pinpoint it. Rhys rode silently up in front as he led the way through the growing darkness.

As they rode, Jair realized just how tired he was when he almost fell from his saddle. He glanced at Tagor who was riding beside him. Even in the dark, he could tell his face was mask of seriousness.

As they turned a bend in the trail, dark figures dropped from the trees and burst forth from the thick brush. With great screams, two of the figures leaped on Jair and his horse before he knew what was happening.

Meanwhile, Tagor had two of the figures coming at him from each side of his horse. From behind, Jair could tell that Rakkon and Kethok were also being set upon, as was Rhys up in front.

Reacting more out of fear than out of skill, Jair whipped his wand out of his belt and held it up, pointing it at one of his assailants. He immediately yelled out the incantation that activated it. A bright burst of white light erupted from the tip of the wand, streaking toward the closest attacker.

Jair was horrified by what he saw during the brief flash of light from the magic missile. The figure was almost gnome-like in its appearance, but horribly distorted. His features were coarse and bloated. He had a scraggy beard and mustache that hung limply from his face.

As the missile struck the horrible little man full in the chest, Jair could see that the figure was wearing black metal armor. The magical bolt threw him backward for several feet, leaving him sprawling in the grass with a smoking hole in his chest.

The second attacker saw what had happened to the first so he quickly tried to move around behind Jair's horse. This was so Jair might not be able to get another shot off at him.

Jair spun about in his saddle, and tried to turn his horse and aim his wand at the same time. He uttered the incantation just as the second figure leapt up at him from atop a large fallen tree. A burst of light once again briefly lit the scene as another magic missile shot out of the wand. This missile only glanced off the other assailant's shoulder, allowing him to continue with his attack. The impact had thrown off his aim however. The gnome like man slashed viciously at Jair as he came down on him and his horse.

Dodging as well as he could from his saddle, Jair barely escaped the deadly cut. It bounced off the rump of Jair's horse, where his pack was nestled. The small figure dropped lightly to the ground, rolling as it went. Smoke rose from its shoulder where Jair's missile had struck it. The missile had done some damage, but not enough to stop him.

Jair urged his horse forward as the little man came to his feet. He charged in with the thunder of hooves, bearing down on his assailant. He reached the little man before he could fully recover and attack again. With a crushing impact, Jair's horse trampled the small man into the earth.

He reigned in abruptly and turned to see what was happening around him. He searched about in the dark and could barely make out what was going on from the shouts and grunts of fighting all around him. His infravision wasn't working in the twilight of sunset.

He reached down into his belt pouch and removed the ingredients for a spell. He brought the spell's words to mind as he quickly uttered the incantation while holding out the components.

Saying the last word the components disappeared and a bright ball of blue light formed in the palm of his hand. He held it up into the air so he could see what was happening. The glow from the magic light fully illuminated the area.

The first thing Jair saw was Rakkon down on the ground with two of the small figures hacking and slashing at him from both sides. As he rolled back and forth trying to avoid their attacks, Jair could see blood running down the back of his armor. Rakkon was struggling to bring his axe up to defend himself.

Kethok had taken down one of their opponents and was struggling with another over to the right. This attacker was a giant version of the other assailants. He was even taller than Kethok. They were now entangled, punching and trying to get a better hold on one another. Kethok's mace lay on the ground not far from where his horse had wandered, and his opponent's sword lay broken on the ground.

Jair saw that Tagor had felled one of his attackers but was now struggling with another, another giant one. Being on horseback gave Tagor some added height and maneuverability. As for Rhys, he was nowhere to be seen.

Jair decided to help Rakkon and raised his wand and incanted. The flashing missile quickly struck one of the small men in the back, knocking him to the ground.

Rakkon took advantage of the momentary distraction. He swung his heavy axe with both hands, bringing it around so swiftly that it whistled through the air. The blade sank into the middle of the other attacker's waist, cutting him almost in half. The body fell to the ground with a sickening thump.

Seeing Rakkon's attackers down, Jair turned his attention to the others. Kethok seemed to be holding his own against his giant gnome. His own size and strength seemed an even match.

On the other hand, Tagor wasn't doing well at all. The other giant had cut a terrible gash into his leg, which was bleeding freely. The loss of blood and the day's exhaustion caused Tagor to sway in the saddle as he tried to better position his horse for another charge.

Jair brought his wand up once again and aimed it at the giant that was attacking Tagor. Before he could utter the incantation, the giant saw what he was about to do and spoke a few quick words of his own while pointing a finger at Jair. Jair's wand exploded in a burst of white light, burning Jair's hand and blinding him in a shower of sparks and small splinters.

Jair covered his eyes with his other hand and paused for a moment until his vision returned. With the giant's attention turned toward Jair, Tagor charged in swinging his sword. He cut deeply into the giant's thick neck, dropping him to his knees while grasping for his throat.

Tagor turned his horse around and brought his sword back for another swing. He completely removed the giant's head with the second stroke. He then backed his horse away from the body as it toppled to the ground.

Jair turned his attention back on the others and saw Kethok just as he was grabbing the other giant by the throat. Jair and Tagor rode toward the pair. He drew his sword from its scabbard. Pain shot through his burned hand, but Jair tried to prepare himself to attack the giant and help Kethok anyway. Before he could get close enough to attack, Jair heard a loud snapping noise and saw Kethok release his hold on the giant gnome.

The giant slumped to the ground before him, his head grotesquely twisted around. They all scanned the area but did not find any more attackers.

Jair glanced at the dead bodies, and the others stared in wonder as the giant ones slowly began to shimmer and shrink. Several moments passed until the giants were the same size as the other attackers. They were all around four to four and a half feet tall.

Jair climbed down and ran over to Rakkon, who was kneeling on the ground. His face was very pale. Jair barely caught him as he toppled.

Jair laid him gently on the ground. Tagor limped over to see what was going on. He had wrapped a quick bandaged around his wounded leg. They rolled Rakkon gently over and Tagor raised the back of his chain mail shirt, revealing two terrible gashes. There was a gash on each side of his broad back. They looked to have been made by daggers. One of the attackers had used them while dropping on him from a tree.

Jair could see that the wounds were pretty bad, and was amazed Rakkon had stayed on his feet as long as he had. He glanced worriedly over at Tagor and asked him, "Tagor, he's lost a lot of blood and these wounds look pretty bad. What are we going to do?"

Tagor moved closer and then pushed Jair gently aside. Jair held his magical light out so Tagor could see. Tagor then placed his palms together over Rakkon and began uttering a prayer. His hands began to glow with a faint illumination as he placed them over the gaping wounds on either side of Rakkon's back.

Intrigued by what he saw, Jair watched intently as the wounds slowly stopped bleeding then sealed up leaving only a small, pink scar where the open wounds had just been.

Rakkon's breathing eased up and his color returned, but he did not waken. Jair looked at Tagor in wonder and amazement that he could do such a thing. He dropped back on his heels and let out a small sigh of relief. It was then that Jair noticed the still bleeding wound on Tagor's leg, so he moved over to see about it.

"Tagor, you're wound?" Jair said to him.

"Humph, its only a scratch. I've had worse." Tagor said gruffly, but quickly changed his tune as Jair probed it. "But, I guess there's no need to let it go." Tagor said with concern and pain on his face.

Kethok quickly removed some bandages from a kit in one of their saddlebags. He handed them to Jair who in return handed Kethok the glowing light sphere he'd cast. Being careful with his burned hand, Jair tried to stop the bleeding.

"Tagor, can you not heal yourself like you did Rakkon?" Jair asked him as he opened Tagor's pant leg to get a better look.

Shaking his head no, Tagor responded. "No, my god only allows me to do it once per day, for now. It has been a long time since I have uttered a healing prayer from Anu. I was afraid he would not listen."

Kethok watched in silence, a distasteful look on his face at having to hold the magical light. Wrapping the strips of cloth around a patch, Jair carefully placed pressure on it to try to stop the bleeding.

The wound was not a terrible one, but bad enough to elicit concern.

"Tagor, what were those things that attacked us?" Jair asked shakily as he worked on the wound.

"Well, from stories I've heard, I would guess they were spriggans. I never thought to see one of the vile creatures though. They are an evil form of gnome, only meaner and viler." Tagor said.

"They travel in small bands like the one that attacked us. Besides being viscous fighters they are supposed to be thieves and even have some magical abilities. Looks like you found that out the hard way." Tagor said through gritted teeth as Jair tied the bandages.

"That would explain what the big one you were fighting did. He cast a spell at me causing my wand to shatter. That wand was a great loss." Jair said remorsefully while also grimacing in pain from the burn on his hand.

"It might also explain how two of them became giants and how they snuck up on us like they did." A voice said from behind them.

Whirling around and reaching for his sword, Jair saw it was Rhys who was leading his horse back toward them. Blood covered most of his body as he walked into the glowing light. He was a grisly sight.

Jair grew concerned for a moment at all the blood, but Rhys assured everyone he was all right. "When we were attacked my horse bolted into the forest. We drug our attackers along for a bit before I knocked them off. Once I finally got my horse under control I turned and attacked them."

"As we fought, I was knocked from my horse. One of them landed on my sword as we fell. It is mostly his blood that covers me." Rhys said with a grim look.

"The second one came in more cautiously and we fought for a

while. He was a pretty good swordsman, but I was better. I believe these were the ones that attacked the outpost. I hope the old elf and his sons can rest in peace now that they have been avenged." Rhys said emotionally.

Jair asked Tagor, "Do you think these were the ones responsible for what happened back there?"

Kethok made some hand signals, and then Tagor said, "Yes, according to Kethok, the spriggans have the same scent that was at the outpost. All of the other signs point to them."

Rhys nodded his head in agreement and suggested they make a litter for Rakkon and put some distance between themselves and the battle scene.

As they were preparing the litter Rhys said, "I don't know why you are heading to Silvermist or what it is you plan to do when you get there. I usually don't involve myself in the affairs of others, but there is something dangerous about the four of you."

"I do not believe these spriggans were waiting here for us by chance. They were sent here for a purpose and knew we were coming. Someone wants you all dead. Because of you, three good people are gone. When we reach Silvermist, my commitment to you is over. After that you will have to find another guide to lead you back to the fort." Rhys said. He then turned and went to see to his horse.

Jair looked questioningly at Tagor who only shrugged at Rhys's words. Trying to rise, then getting a little help from Jair, Tagor insisted on searching all of the bodies before they left.

He went through all of the Spriggan's belongings. The only thing they found of interest was a small, golden ring in the form of a raven. It was just like the one Tagor had seen on the dark elf woman they had encountered.

Jair looked it over, but could discern no distinguishable markings and he could not detect any magic on it. He placed it in a pouch on his satchel for further study.

Tagor got Jair to help him up onto his horse. Kethok pulled Rakkon behind him. They followed Rhys once again as he led the way. Jair brought up the rear just as his light spell faded. This threw them all in into darkness. Fortunately Rhys could see pretty well in the dark now, that night had fully fallen.

They traveled in the dark for a while until Rhys found the spot he had originally intended for them to make camp. Jair dropped off his horse and went over and helped Tagor to dismount and unsaddle his horse. He then helped Kethok untie Rakkon from the litter. They placed Rakkon on the ground and carefully covered him with his blanket. Jair then went and removed his own things from his horse.

Tagor gave Jair a salve for his hand. It had been with their first aid supplies. Jair dropped to a spot on the ground close to the horses and applied the salve, covering it with a bandage. As he worked, he wondered about what would happen when they reached Silvermist in the morning. Thoughts of finding out about his family, the true nature of the helmet, and what part the Dark Lord played in everything danced through his head. Groggily, just before dozing off, he thought he saw Kethok move over to sit nearby, staring somewhat intently at him in the dark. Tomorrow would surely be a better day he thought as he drifted off to sleep.

Chapter 15

Jair rose slowly to find Rhys sitting next to a fire. He stretched to work out some of the cramps and soreness, then stood and rolled up his blanket.

A large portion of a deer hung spitted over the crackling flames as Rhys tended to it. Jair could smell the meat as it roasted. It made his mouth water.

He moved closer to the fire to warm himself, and squatted down across from where Rhys was seated. As he scanned their encampment, Jair saw that Rakkon was also up and about, taking care of feeding and watering the horses and acting as if nothing had happened the night before. Only an occasional wince on his face showed that he had even been injured.

Jair wondered at Rakkon's miraculous healing by Tagor, but decided not to say anything more about it. Broaching that subject seemed to make Tagor edgy and Jair didn't want to add any more stress than was necessary. He thought it must be something really personal that Tagor's was dealing with. He was sitting on the ground next to his saddle, checking his wound. Kethok was nowhere to be seen.

Jair was concerned, now more than ever, as to what might befall them on their journey. The Dark Lord really wanted the helmet and it looked like he would go to great lengths to get it. He not only knew who they all were, but were all the time. This really worried him as he contemplated what they might do about it.

Rhys reached up with a dagger and began cutting off small portions of the cooked meat. He reached over and placed a portion on a plate along with some of their bread rations and handed it to Jair. He took it eagerly. Rhys motioned for the others towards the fire so they could all eat, since the meat was finished cooking.

"Rhys, where did the deer come from and why the fire?" Jair asked as he ate.

"I borrowed Tagor's bow and shot it earlier this morning. Since we killed the Spriggans, I figured it wouldn't hurt to have the fire and get a hot meal." Rhys replied.

Jair looked at him, wondering why he had borrowed Tagor's bow when he had one of his own. He saw Jair's questioning look and explained, "I must have lost my bow during the fight. When I arose earlier, it was not on my saddle."

As Rhys spoke, Jair noticed a strange look on his face as he looked at Tagor's bow. It was a look Jair had seen on Kentar's face many times before. It was a look of longing. It was a look of wanting something that belonged to someone else.

Jair nodded his head as if accepting Rhys' explanation and then finished his meal. He rose after washing down the rest of his food with some water from one of their skins.

"Tagor, where is Kethok? Jair asked him as he stood. He had cut a crude walking stick and was using it to lean on. He grunted slightly from the effort and the pain of his sore muscles, then stood and hobbled over next to the fire.

"He went off into the woods just before you woke. He didn't say where he was going. He only signed to me that he would be back shortly."

Tagor accepted his portion of the food from Rhys's. Rakkon had already joined them and was eating.

Besides the few short words he had spoken that morning, Rhys was solemnly silent. It was evident that he was not happy with his situation and was eager to be rid of them.

As the other three sat around the fire and ate, Jair had a cold chill run over him. Since he was finished eating he went over to his horse to check on his gear. It was all tied securely to his saddle. The satchel containing the helmet was still there. He let out a small sigh of relief as he closed the outer flap on the satchel and glanced mistrustfully at Rhys.

During all of the excitement of the previous night and from his exhaustion, he had all but forgotten about the safety of the helmet. Jair chastised himself and vowed from now on that he would take better care of the package. If it were lost or stolen, their whole journey would have been for nothing.

They all finished their meals so they rose and saw to saddling their horses. As they were doing so, Kethok came strolling back into the camp with his mace across one shoulder.

Seeing him re-enter their camp, Jair asked him, "Where have you been? We are ready to leave."

He placed his mace on his saddle horn, turned to face Jair, and then signed, "I went back to where the fight was. I had to get my iron club where I had dropped it last night."

Kethok's statement was short. Jair smiled and nodded his approval and understanding. He was starting to understand the sign language better, even though Tagor had only been teaching it to him a short time. He only had to ask Tagor a few of the words Kethok had signed. The rest had come to him, but he knew he still had a lot to learn.

Jair turned back around and got up on his horse. Everyone else did likewise. Once again they followed Rhys's lead as they headed back into the forest. The pace was fast once again.

They continued traveling throughout the morning, drawing ever nearer to their destination. Jair noticed as they rode that they seemed to be steadily gaining altitude. The ground was rising.

They came around a small bend in the trail and the forest began to open up. Jair gazed ahead, through the thinning forest and spotted something shimmering in the distance. He looked closer as they neared an opening in the trees. As the trail widened, Jair could see the city as they entered a clearing.

They came to a stop on top of a small ridge. A giant, fertile valley opened up before them. It looked as if it spanned several leagues.

The city appeared to cover a large portion of the valley's center. Silvermist glittered brightly in the afternoon sun that had just started peeking out through the clouds. Dazzling rays of light flickered off of the city's many towers and battlements.

Jair sucked in his breath and held it for a moment as he looked upon the ancient elven city. Magnificent silver and gold trimmed spires jutted forth from among the many buildings and homes that lay within the city's huge, white stone walls.

A pair of massive wooden gates lay open before a large, well-fortified gatehouse. From where they sat, Jair could see many people moving in and out of the entrance. Most looked to be merchants and farmers from the surrounding community, but several were nobles and warriors. The people came and went along a well-paved area that only went out a short way from the city.

"It's more magnificent than I ever could have imagined!" Jair exclaimed to everyone while letting out the breath he had been holding.

"Hmm, it's very impressive." Tagor commented.

Rakkon and Kethok only sat and stared, keeping their thoughts to themselves. Rhys allowed them to look at the city for a few moments more, and then urged them on. They worked their way down the small road that led off of the ridge that overlooked the city.

"There is not a main road that leads to the city." Rhys said while they worked their way down the ridge. "Most of the people that live here know the way through the forest. People from outside the city usually have to hire a guide to lead them here. Guides are being needed less and less though as more people from outside the elven realm learn the way."

"Foreign trade has been increasing, especially since the border wars. The king feels that trade will help the city and elven people to prosper. So far it has been profitable, but many of the high councilors and citizens object to it. They are concerned about the long term effects of opening the city to foreigners and what it might do to their way of life." Rhys said.

As Rhys was telling them this, Jair looked around. Rhys led them down off the ridge and onto another trail. This trail led them into the valley and ended up merging with a larger dirt road. As they followed this road, Jair could see there had been many people that had passed this way.

They worked their way along the road and entering into the valley. Jair saw large fields that now lay barren for the winter. Small farms and houses dotted the valley where elves had built their homes. Many of the homes and farms were finely crafted out of stone, brick and wood.

Other than the few travelers that were on the road, Jair only saw an occasional farmer or local villager who lived outside of the city's secure walls. Most of the people he saw were doing their chores or herding small animals to the city market.

They finally arrived at the main gate where Rhys called a halt. Two guards stopped them and asked some basic questions. The guards looked dubiously at Kethok. Their group had gotten use to his presence, so they tended to forget how others saw him.

Rhys spoke quietly to the guards for a few moments. The

guards then motioned for Jair and his companions to continue on inside the city.

Once they had passed through the gate and entered the city itself, they found it was more beautiful on the inside. Almost all of the buildings were exotically decorated. Most were delicately carved from a smooth, white stone.

Trees and plants grew beside almost every home and small gardens were commonplace. Most of the people they saw were elven, but occasionally Jair saw a human, dwarf and even a few halflings scattered amongst the traffic.

Kethok drew many stares, looks and exclamations of surprise as they rode past, but no one bothered them. The fact that a giant was walking about in their fair city did not seem to excessively upset anyone. Jair could feel tension in the air as they passed by however.

They followed the main avenue and Rhys led the way through the busy city streets. Compared to the few people they'd seen on the outskirts of the city, the inside was a busy metropolis. Vendors of all kinds lined the streets. There were even more vendors at the central market square they passed through toward the center of the city.

Just like in Gallador, the merchants and vendors plied their wares and tried to sell you something as you passed by. Jair could tell there was a difference between how the elven people acted and the humans in Gallador though.

Whereas humans were more aggressive in selling their wares, the elves seemed to be more conservative and reserved. Only occasionally did someone shout anything, usually over the haggling of a price. Most of the conversations were quiet and low key. The shops and stalls were also a lot nicer than what he had seen in Gallador. Jair also noticed that a lot of the vendors were human, dwarf or halfling.

The Ruby Helmet

Rhys eventually led them to a small inn that looked to be in a nice part of the merchant section of town. They brought their horses around to the back where there was a stable. Rhys dismounted and handed his reigns to an attendant.

The others followed his lead. Jair and his friends dismounted and then handed their reins to the attendant. Before leaving his horse though, Jair quickly untied the satchel from his saddle and slung it over one shoulder. He then followed the others inside the inn.

They entered through a back door. Jair followed in behind Kethok. They entered through another door that lead them down a short hallway. Once at the end of the hall it opened up into a large common room that was lavishly decorated. It had comfortable looking, padded chairs and beautifully handcrafted tables. Compared to the inn they had stayed in at Gallador, this one was a palace.

Jair looked around at the few patrons that were there. He listened to Rhys as he conversed with the owner who was standing behind the counter. He was very tall, even for an elf. He was also one of the first elderly looking elves Jair had ever seen. He must have been very old by human standards. He had snow white hair that fell down to his shoulders and was nicely dressed with elegant breaches and a finely embroidered tunic. He politely welcomed them to his inn and recognized Rhys, who had evidently been there before.

"Good day Rhys. It has been a while since you have graced my humble establishment. What has kept you away from our fair city for so long?" He asked.

Rhys placed his foot on a rest under the counter and said, "I've been doing a little scouting for Mengistu up in the forest next to the Anarest."

He jerked a thumb in Jair and his friend's direction and said, "Mengistu hired me to deliver them to the city as a favor to King

Galdath. We just arrived and are in need of rooms." Rhys told him.

The innkeeper eyed Kethok suspiciously, and then asked Rhys, "How long are you planning to stay?"

"I will only be here for a few days," Rhys responded, looking questioningly at Tagor.

Taking that as a cue, Tagor said, "We will probably be here for a week, possibly a little longer."

The innkeeper nodded his head then said, "My name is Stelon. I am the owner of the Golden Circle Inn. Rooms are a silver piece per week or four coppers per day. Meals are served at noon and sunset each day in the common room and they are not included with the price of the rooms."

The innkeeper scrunched up his nose a little and said, "There is a bath house around the back and it's free with the rooms, I suggest you take advantage of it."

Grudgingly, Tagor reached into his pouch and removed four silver coins. He placed them into the palm of Stelon's hand, paying for a full week's lodgings for each of them. "If we need to stay any longer I'll pay you for it then." Tagor said as he shouldered his pack.

Stelon nodded went to a rack on the wall behind him. He removed several keys from their pegs and motioned for them to follow him through another back door.

They went down a small walkway and entered an adjacent building that opened to another hall. This hallway had a series of doors all along it. Each door had a different number on it. He handed them each a key. Jair saw that the key dangled from a small metal ring that also had a flat, wooden disc hanging from it. Carved onto each disc was a different number.

Jair noticed that all of their keys had numbers that

corresponded with the numbers on the doors along the hallway.

The innkeeper left them in the hallway and returned to his counter. After placing their belongings in their rooms, Tagor suggested they go to the baths. Jair shouldered his satchel that contained the helmet and followed Tagor.

After everyone had bathed and changed into clean clothes, Jair suggested they get something to eat. He had checked Tagor's leg wound to make sure it wasn't getting infected. He also told Tagor that he probably needed to get a healer to look at it. Tagor ignored him and went on about their business.

As they came out of the bathhouse and walked across the inn's courtyard, a few small flakes of snow brushed across Jair's face. Clouds had covered the sky once again and were now threatening to begin a heavy snowfall.

Tagor also noticed the small flakes that were gently falling as he limped back to the inn. "The first snow of the winter," He commented. "It's still early for a first snow. Probably means it is going to be a rough winter."

After they entered the common room they ordered food and relaxed at one of the large, decorative tables until it arrived. They all found the food to be quite excellent and hardly spoke a word while they ate. After they finished eating, Tagor moved his chair over beside one of two, large open fireplaces in order to warm himself. The other joined him.

There were only a few other patrons in the room, talking quietly amongst themselves. They glanced curiously at Jair and his companions, but no one said anything to them.

As Jair relaxed, their traveling began to weigh heavily on him. He was starting to doze off when a cold breeze washed over him. The door to the inn had been thrown open and the strong winter wind came billowing in.

Several cloaked figures entered with the wind and now heavy snow. They quickly shut the door behind them. The first figure was smaller than the other two. They walked over to an empty table on the other side of the room and seated themselves. They pulled off their cloaks and laid them on a chair.

The two larger figures were both heavily armed elven warriors. They were garbed identically. Both carried a long sword, dagger and wore expensive chain mail armor. They both also wore an imperial emblem embroidered on their tunics. Jair thought they looked very tough and capable.

The third figure captured Jair's attention as she removed her hood. He was enraptured as he saw a golden shower of blond hair fall from about the shoulders of a beautiful, young elven woman.

The young elven woman wore a beautiful white dress, which was delicately embroidered with intricate little silver designs. Soft white, fur lined leather boots rode midway up her calves and she had matching gloves that graced her delicate hands. From her small pointed ears glittered emerald earrings set in a stunning silver design that matched the pattern on her dress. From about her neck dangled a small, silver pendant that was in the form of a dove.

As the young elven woman and her two companions seated themselves, Stelon hurriedly waited on them personally, giving them all of his attention. Several of the other patrons politely said hello to the young woman. They all seemed to know who she and her companions were. From their response to her entering the inn, Jair could tell she was very well respected.

Almost everyone in the inn stared openly at the young elven woman while she dined with her guards. Jair wondered who they all were. The two guards continually scanned the room, giving disapproving looks toward anyone that stared for too long. One of them gave Jair an especially hard look when he noticed Jair was looking at them. Jair knew the look. He'd seen it many times before. He could tell they did not approve of him being a half-elf.

Tagor nudged Jair with the tip of his boot under the table. Then he quietly cautioned him, "It is not polite to stare, especially while someone is eating. We are here to find out what we need too and then leave, nothing more. It will not help matters if you get us into trouble by gawking at some elven woman." Tagor said.

Jair nodded his understanding along with his embarrassment. He tried to get back into the conversation that was going on at his own table. Occasionally he chanced a quick glance over at the young lady. Whenever he did, his heart pounded quicker within his chest and he hoped to some day meet her.

After finishing her meal, the young woman was handed a leather case that one of the guards had been carrying. She pulled back her chair a little and opened the case. She then brought forth a small golden harp. She laid the case upon their table then gently set the instrument upon her lap.

As everyone in the room looked on, she began strumming it softly and checking its tune. Several of the patrons moved closer. Finally, after she had it adjusted to her liking, the young woman began to hum a tune. She found the chord she wanted, then began to sing and play. As Jair listened, he believed it was the most beautiful thing he had ever heard.

The music the singers and musicians at the festivals back home played was nothing compared to what he was hearing now. It was a sad love ballad he had never heard before. It was about a prince that had met a woman and fallen in love with her, only to loose her in a terrible tragedy.

Most of the words drifted by him as he and the other patrons listened. The melody and gentle rhythm of the girl's voice kept them mesmerized.

The tone of the song was sad and several of the patrons openly wept as she came to the end. A roar of cheers fell over the crowd that had formed, followed quickly by applause as the girl finished and lowered her hands from the harp. Even the inn's staff had come out to listen. Several patrons quickly piped up and asked for another song. Some asked for specific titles or favorites, none of which Jair had ever heard of.

Appeasing the crowd with her guards glowering dangerously about, the girl quickly began another song. This one was a joyful tune that all of the patrons quickly started clapping and stomping their feet to. The mood quickly changed from sadness to one of gaiety and cheer.

She played a few more songs and finally grew tired and put away her harp. A disappointed sigh washed across the room as she did so, but several patrons generously thanked her for performing.

The evening was getting late so Tagor rose to his feet. He looked over at the other, stretched and said, "It's getting late. If we are going to get anything done on the morrow we should be off to bed."

The others murmured agreement, rose and started toward the exit. As they moved across the room, the young woman and her guards also rose to leave. Jair passed near to where the woman was seated. He took one last look at her as he passed by.

The young lady looked over, saw Jair, smiled at him and said, "Good evening." All Jair could do was blush hotly and stutter, "Good evening to you milady." The fact she had even spoken to him at all stunned him.

Jair worked his way toward the exit. He tried to watch her out of the corner of his eye as he neared the back door. He barely saw her don her cloak and follow her guards out of the inn as he exited the room. He wondered who she was and why she had been there. Jair eventually made it to his room, somewhat in a daze.

Once inside his room, he dropped his satchel at the foot of his bed, pulled off his boots and quickly slid beneath the heavy blankets. He was so deep in thought, he didn't even take time to wash or take off his clothes.

It was not long before he slipped off into a deep sleep. He dreamed of the beautiful elf maiden and her wonderful voice. For the first time in a long while, he slept peacefully, without any dreams of the Dark Lord.

Chapter 16

Jair awoke refreshed and fairly rested the next morning. He rose early, changed his clothes, strapped on his sword, washed up, and slung the satchel containing the magic helmet across his shoulder. He left his room and made his way down the hall and to the common room.

Tagor and Kethok were already there eating breakfast as he made it to their table and pulled up a cushioned chair. He looked around for Rakkon and said, "Good morning."

Tagor responded through a mouthful of food and Kethok signed his greeting. Jair motioned for one of the serving girls and placed an order for food.

"Where is Rakkon?" He asked his friends.

Tagor took a sip of water, and then answered him. "He left after eating to go and check on the horses. He said he was going to find a blacksmith after that. He chipped his axe the other night and he wanted to have it sharpened."

Jair nodded and relaxed while he waited for his food. Before long it was delivered and he took his time eating. By the time he was finished, Tagor and Kethok were ready to go.

There had been no sign of Rhys since he had left them the day before. Jair figured he had other business to attend to. That or he really didn't want anything else to do with them. Jair figured it was more of the latter. Rhys had a bad attitude toward them after what had happened on the way to the city. Jair felt guilty about the family that had been killed, but didn't know what to do about it. They had killed the ones responsible. Evidently Rhys still held their deaths against them.

Jair wiped his mouth on a napkin, then followed Tagor and Kethok out the front door. Once outside, Jair's feet crunched in the snow that now covered the ground. It had snowed steadily during the night and a thick blanket now covered the entire city. The effects of the snow and ice were beautiful on the already majestic city, but the thick layer of clouds overhead still made it feel somewhat gloomy.

They only had to stop once to ask for directions. Tagor led the way, limping along as they walked through the busy city streets. Rakkon had checked Tagor's wound that morning before leaving and had said it looked like it was healing fine. Jair still felt that Tagor should have seen a healer.

Merchants, travelers and businessmen were already busy about their work. The main streets were covered with slush and ice from wagons and pedestrians that had already passed by.

Their destination was the ancient elven library Illikaren, which was rumored to hold books and scrolls dating back for thousands of years. Jair hoped they could find one that would tell them something about the helmet or help them to at least identify it. There was no doubt in Jair's mind that it had magic powers. Just what all those powers were he did not know and was somewhat reluctant to find out. Especially after seeing what it had done to the goblin leader.

During their journey, Jair felt that the longer he carried the helmet, the more he needed to find out about it. Fear kept him from trying it on. The fate of the goblin leader was enough to keep him from putting it on. Curiosity was beginning to outweigh his fear however. It was as if the helmet was calling out to him. He had felt it pull at him several times since he had obtained it. He had ignored the feeling as best he could and tried to concentrate on the task at hand.

They stopped to ask directions once, then arrived at the library. Jair glanced up at the giant stone building as they drew near. The front of the library had large, gray marble steps that lead up to wide double doors. The library was several stories high, with several large, round, marble columns that supported an overhanging facade.

They passed the marble columns after climbing the front steps. A platform led them up to one of the double doors. Tagor went first, turning a small silver doorknob then pushing open one of the large doors. It opened easily, allowing them inside. Once there they found themselves in a large, open room.

They could see there were many other doors and chambers that lead off of the larger one. The main chamber was had many rows of tightly packed bookshelves. There were also several tables and chairs scattered about so that people could sit and read or study.

The shelves were almost three stories high. Where one shelf stopped and another one started there was a small, wooden walkway that went all the way around the room. Winding wooden stairways led up to each level and Jair could see there were several people who were looking for books. There were several other people in the room already, doing research.

They looked about the library. None of them knew where to begin. Just as Tagor was about to suggest they start looking in a section over on their left, a scholarly looking older elf came through one of the doorways and walked up to them.

"Hello, may I be of service?" He said as he approached, looking at them curiously. Tagor spoke up, remembering to tell the story that they had come up with earlier, about why they were looking for information about the helmet.

"Yes," Tagor responded. "We were wondering if we might be able to find information that would tell us something about the magical helmet Estolorn. My friend is a student in Gallador and is doing research for a professor there."

He raised fuzzy white eyebrows at the odd request. The old elf placed one hand on his elbow and started tapping a finger from his other hand on his chin.

"Hmmm, let me see," he said as he continued to tap his finger. I think I may be able to help you. If you will follow me, I believe we have some older tomes that might contain information that would be useful to you." He then turned and headed off deeper into the library.

Tagor, Jair and Kethok followed him out of the main room and down several long corridors. "No one has asked about the helmet in hundreds of years." The old elf said as they followed him.

"As I recall, it was crafted by a wizard of the red robes several thousand years ago here in Silvermist. The exact nature of the helmet is really unknown, but rumors of its power still linger with us today." The old man told them as he led the way.

They entered into another chamber after descending a small flight of stairs. The old elf brought them to a chamber in what looked to be the basement. The books and scrolls in this room looked very ancient and were covered with a thick layer of dust. The old elf searched through the tomes for several minutes. He finally reached up to a middle shelf and pulled out a large, thick, leather bound book.

He placed it on a table with a thud. He blew off a layer of dust and gently pried open its cover, and then started thumbing through its yellowed pages. Several minutes passed as the old elf mumbled to himself, and continued to flip pages.

He quickly scanned the pages with practiced ease. His long, bony fingers were used to mark his place as he read. He finally looked up from his search.

"I think you will find what you need here. This book and several others in this room deal with the topic of ancient artifacts and magical items like the one you are looking for." He told them.

The Ruby Helmet

"If you need anything else just ask one of the attendants for Master Xenosea, that's me. I am the libraries' chief magistrate and am an expert on ancient lore," he said as he turned and left the room.

Tagor thanked the old man for his help and pulled out a bench from under the table. He and Jair took a seat and began reading through the book.

As they enveloped themselves in their research, Kethok moved around the room, looking at the binders on some of the other books. He also searched the headings on some of the scrolls.

They skimmed down the page that Master Xenosea had found for them. Jair and Tagor read the old handwritten script that was on the book's ancient pages. The book was a history and theology on the creation, use and disappearance of ancient magical artifacts.

The chapter they were reading dealt with three powerful ancient artifacts that were all linked together. From what they read in the book, it looked like their helmet was one of the three. As they looked over the pages, Jair quickly spotted the part where the helmet Estolorn was mentioned. The article read:

• • •

"The magical helmet called Estolorn was the last of three great artifacts crafted by the founders of the original wizard guilds. The name Estolorn means "The Challenger". Seeking a way to bring neutrality and control over two other artifacts, it was created by the leader of the red robes. It is believed that the high wizard of the red robes crafted the magical helmet in a forge deep within the elven forest. This place was supposedly close to where the ancient elven city of Silvermist began.

In creating the helmet, the high wizard used dwarven steel mined from a small dwarven city in the Timgranok Mountains, near Karga Hall. It was the same batch of ore as had been used to make the other two artifacts.

Upon the forehead of the helmet he mounted a giant, magic ruby. There had been rumors that it had been formed by one of the elven gods, as a present to an earthly elven maiden, (See Vol. IX, Gods & Goddesses of Silvermist).

The final act in the creation of the helmet was a binding spell. This spell was used in order to make the helmet powerful enough to force the magic sword and staff to come under the control of the wearer of the helmet, neutralizing them. In order for the spell to work, the high level wizard had to bind the helmet directly to the other two items. The helmet had to be in close proximity in order for the spell to be bound to all three. They had to of either have been in his possession, or close by. This binding spell also had to include the lifeblood of a willing person.

Choosing from one of the oldest bloodlines of the elven people, the red wizard cast a powerful spell. The elf that volunteered cut his arm at just the right moment, spilling his blood into the molten metal as the helmet was cast. The spell worked and the helmet was created, but it was at the cost of the elf's life. The spell drained more from him than had been expected. The wizard had not known this would happen, nor did he know the full extent of the helmet's powers. Later it was reported that the helmet worked and was used by the forces of good to defeat evil users of the other sword and staff. (See Vol. XIV, The First Great Cataclysm).

After creating the helmet, the wizard also discovered that only someone of the same bloodline as the sacrificial elf could use the helmet and invoke it powers. This was an unforeseen element that later became an asset in keeping the helmet out of the hands of the other wizards.

In binding the helmet to a family bloodline, the magic of the helmet limited who could wear and use it. This differed from the sword and the staff, which could be used by anyone of the proper alignments for which they were made.

In order to protect the helmet's bloodline thereafter, and to insure a potential wearer down the line, the wizard trained the family's descendants as wizards and warriors. This helped to protect them and preserve their lineage.

Several generations came and went and the helmet was passed down among them. The descendants grew in power and number. Eventually they became the major ruling class over the elven nation. Due to the second and third great holocausts, the elven nation was split and many of the original family's bloodline died out or were lost. During this time the high wizard of the red robes mysteriously disappeared. No one knows for sure what happened to him.

This is when the high elves, wood elves and dark elves were formed, creating the three separate elven nations. During the turmoil, some of the remaining family members of the helmet's bloodline decided to hide the helmet until a time came when it would be needed again.

They hid it from the world. Later, it was prophesied that the helmet would once again be discovered when there was a great threat to all of the nations. It was also prophesied that one of the descendants of the helmet would appear to wear it and defeat whatever evil threatened the world."

• • •

After they finished reading the last paragraph, Jair sat back in his chair and stretched his neck. It had become stiff from bending over the book. He glanced over at Tagor, who was sitting as if in deep thought. Jair also sat and considered what they had just read.

"Tagor," Jair said as he looked at him. "This is going to be impossible. How are we supposed to find one of the last descendants of this special elven bloodline?"

Tagor paused patiently, then answered. "This library and Master Xenosea are probably as good a place to start as any. He was quick in finding us information about the helmet. Maybe he can help us find something on this elven lineage mentioned here. In a library and city as ancient as this one, there is bound to be some record somewhere of who these people were. The thing that strikes me as odd though is why this author did not mention the name of the family."

Jair nodded in agreement, then rose and started searching the rows of books along the left side of the chamber. He searched, hoping to find a book on elven lineage from this same timeline. Tagor also rose and started working his way across them room in the opposite direction.

As Jair and Tagor quietly began their search, Kethok also slowly continued moving about the library. Having worked his way into a smaller, adjacent chamber, he scanned across the many rows of books and scrolls piled upon the shelves. He stopped when he came to one in particular that caught his eye. He picked up a small candle that was on a table in the room, lit it and returned to the shelf to examine more closely the book he had found.

Kethok looked around the room and noticed that this chamber was much older than the rest of the library. It looked as if there had not been anyone in it for many years. He reached up and pulled out the book that he was interested in. It was a book on hill giants. It was one that had quickly sparked his curiosity, even if he couldn't read it very well.

As he pulled the book out, Kethok heard a tiny click. He stepped back quickly when he noticed movement in front of him. He also heard a mild grating sound. He was astonished as he saw the bookshelf in front of him slowly swing back, revealing a set of old stone steps that lead down into a dark, narrow passage.

He glanced curiously into the passage, and then replaced the book on the shelf where he had found it. He then stepped back once again as the bookcase swung shut.

Jair was getting slightly frustrated by this time at not being able to find anything about what they were looking for. He was about to suggest that they search for Master Xenosea to ask for help when Kethok entered the chamber again. He began motioning excitedly for Jair to follow him.

It took Jair a few moments to get Kethok to slow down his hand signing before he understood that Kethok had found something and wanted Jair and Tagor to come and see what it was.

Jair couldn't tell exactly what it was Kethok was telling him, so he told Kethok to wait until he went and found Tagor. Tagor was in another room wandering amongst a selection of books covering spells and spell components. Making a mental note to try to return to this part of the library, Jair quickly told Tagor that Kethok wanted to show them something.

They returned to the chamber where Jair had left Kethok. They then followed him back into the other chamber where Kethok had been. Kethok reached up to one of the shelves. Jair and Tagor looked on curiously as Kethok removed one of the books, then stepped back.

As the trio stood there, Jair and Tagor expectantly waited to see what it was that had so excited Kethok. The bookcase before them swung open, revealing the dark stairway and passage beyond.

A dank, musty smell wafted up from the once hidden opening. Jair looked over at Tagor, a questioning look on his face. All of them were intrigued as to where the passage might lead and why it had been put there.

Chapter 17

Jair asked Tagor, "Where do you suppose it goes?"

"I don't know, down probably." Tagor responded sarcastically. Jair thought his sense of humor must be returning since he was feeling better.

"As ancient as the city of Silvermist is and being in this part of the library, there's not much telling where it might go. Kethok only stumbled across it by accident. I'm sure whoever built it had never planned on a giant entering the city of Silvermist, much less to come into the library itself." Tagor said with a smile, looking over at Kethok and scanning the title of the book he had removed.

Jair stepped over to the edge of the opening and glanced down the shadowy staircase. He couldn't hear anything, but sensed something strange that he couldn't quite explain. He had a really bad feeling about it.

He glanced back over at Tagor and asked. "What do you think we should do?"

Tagor shook his head. "I don't know. Following it could be dangerous. Hidden passageways and tunnels are sometimes trapped. Not to mention the fact there could be all kinds of dangerous monsters living down there. But, you never know what we might find. Treasure perhaps."

Jair glanced once more down the dark passageway before stepping back away from it. His imagination let him hear the sound of heavy breathing as if from something large and evil that was waiting just beyond the reach of their flickering candles.

"We might better wait until we have more help with us." Jair said as he backed away from the opening.

As Kethok reached up to replace the book on the shelf, Tagor stopped him as he noticed something on the wall right inside the passageway. He stepped over to the opening, picked up a candle and held it high so he could see what it was.

He brought the light to bear and revealed several small inscriptions on the wall. Jair stepped next to him so he could also see what it said. Jair read the inscription out loud.

"Behold the secret chambers of the red moon,"

"The follower of the way."

"Traveler of the secret past, preserver of today."

"Enter here this passage, enter he that dares."

"Enter here the one that seeks the emptiness,"

"The one to end despair."

Jair read the words with a sense of foreboding. The words were strange and twisting, but very meaningful in an eerie way. Tagor stepped back and motioned for Jair to do the same. Kethok placed the book back on the shelf as they stood quietly aside. The bookcase swung shut once again, leaving them all in contemplation.

"What do you think we should do about this Tagor?" Jair asked him.

"I think we should go back to the inn and wait for Rakkon. From there we will gather together some supplies and return here before dark. It would be best if we waited until later before entering the passageway, so no one will notice." Tagor said.

They turned to exit the chamber with Tagor leading the way.

They worked their way out of the inner sanctum of the library, and eventually exited through the main double doors.

They quickly made their way back across the city to the inn. They stopped only once, at Jair's insistence, to get a healer to look at Tagor's leg. It was getting infected. For a small donation the healer cast a spell on it. Jair decided to get his burned hand looked at as well. By the time they arrived at the inn, Tagor was walking a lot better.

As they entered the inn, they noticed that a small group of people had gathered in the main room and were quietly talking among themselves.

Jair looked around the room, searching for Rakkon. He found him at a small table over to the right. Jair started to make his way over to him, but stopped as Tagor caught his arm.

Tagor quietly signed to Jair that he and Kethok were going on to their rooms to gather supplies and weapons and that Jair should fill Rakkon in on what they had found. Jair shook his head that he understood, then continued on over to Rakkon.

Jair came to the table where Rakkon was seated, and quietly informed him of their find and what they were going to do. Rakkon agreed to go with them and quickly rose to follow Jair to their rooms.

Once they arrived there, Jair and Rakkon gathered what supplies they thought they might need and headed over to Tagor's room. When they got there, Kethok and Tagor were already waiting for them.

Tagor had his bow, a small backpack with rope, and his sword. Kethok stood waiting silently, leaning on his mace. Rakkon chose to take only his armor and his axe while Jair carried his satchel containing his spell components, the helmet, and his long sword and dagger. He also took out a small water skin and put it inside the helmet.

They sat around a table that was in Tagor's room, and quickly made their plans. They waited until only an hour remained before dusk and then set off in the direction of the library. They stopped to pick up a few torches from a small merchant along the way. Then they stopped and at a well where Jair filled his water skin. They then made their way back across the city's slushy streets to the library.

Once at the library, Tagor led them through the twisting rooms and corridors until they reached the chamber where the secret passage was hidden. The few remaining patrons that were still in the library gave them wary looks as they passed by, but no one said anything to them.

Tagor entered the chamber, then waited until the others came in behind him. He shut the door, then walked over to the bookcase and selected the book that Kethok had found earlier.

He reached up and pulled the book out from the shelf and stood back expectantly as the bookcase once again slid back. He gazed down the dark passageway and motioned for the others to follow him as he stepped toward the opening.

Jair held up one of the torches they had purchased and removed something from one of his pouches. Uttering a few words, he sprinkled the contents over the torch he was holding. A small flame sparked, igniting the torch, spreading flames across its pitch-covered tip. He then touched it to all the other torches, igniting them.

Jair handed one of the torches to Tagor and the other to Rakkon. Even though Kethok and Jair could use their ability to see in the dark, the two humans would have to rely on the light from the torches to make their way.

Tagor checked to make sure that everyone was ready, then set off down the dark, dust covered stairway that led beneath the library.

The four companions descended the cold stone steps for what seemed an eternity. Jair was amazed at the length of their descent and the depth to which the stairway was leading them. As they finally came to the bottom he noticed that the walls and flooring had become somewhat damp, and that the air was actually a little warmer.

Tagor paused briefly at the bottom of the stairs and turned to face the others. "From here on out, we will have to be extra careful. We don't know what's down here so we are going to have to be very cautious. Make no unnecessary noise and try not to slip on the wet stone."

He turned once again and moved down the small corridor that led away from the stairwell. He reached up to the wall as they entered the large passageway and made an arrow on the wall with a piece of white chalk he had pulled out of a pouch. The arrow pointed in the direction they had just come, marking their way just in case they got lost. He also added a number one.

As they walked along, Jair noticed that the passage itself was made of large, carved stones that had been neatly fitted together to form the large tunnel. The ceiling was almost a head taller than Kethok and curved as it went up, forming an archway.

At first, Jair had been afraid of bringing Kethok due to his size, but his fears quickly abated when he saw the height of the passage. It was well above his head.

As they explored, Jair noticed an odd fungus that was growing all over the walls of the tunnel. He had never seen anything quite like it before.

The stones of the floor were covered with moisture, making their footing precarious. So far there had been no signs of life other than the fact that someone had built this tunnel in the first place.

They traveled at a brisk pace with Tagor still in the lead. The tunnel led on and slightly downward as the four of them walked in silence. Finally, after Jair was about to give up on finding anything interesting, the tunnel opened up into a small chamber that had three more tunnels that branched off of it.

They scanned the chamber and did not find anything out of the ordinary, so Tagor continued to lead them by choosing the tunnel on the right. He marked it with his chalk before entering, then cautiously stepped through the archway holding his torch out in front of him.

This tunnel led them on for another hour, twisting and winding as it went. Jair thought the ground was still sloping downward as they followed the passage deeper into the earth.

He also noticed that the stones in the walls seemed to be getting older and smaller the deeper they went. As they came to a bend in the tunnel, Tagor gasped loudly as he went around it.

The other followed right behind him, and then spread out as they came around the corner and saw what had startled him.

A massive creature lay before them, blocking the tunnel. Its body was dark gray and looked to be about twenty feet long. It was almost three feet in diameter and it had many yellow, legged segments all along its body. At one end the creature had a bulbous head and large, many faceted red eyes that glittered in the flickering torchlight.

Several small, yellow antennae waved about from above the eyes and it turned its head quickly away from the sudden light of their torches, as if the light caused it pain.

Fearful to take a breath, Jair watched silently as the creature slowly moved along the tunnel and casually started walking up the left wall. Tagor motioned for them all to start slowly backing up as he tried to keep an eye on the creature. It moved toward them along the wall and ceiling. It was not afraid of them and continued moving toward them.

Jair looked closely at the creature and saw that its feet were like little clamps with suctions on their ends, allowing it to easily grasp the smooth, wet walls. The creature also had a set of large, fierce looking mandibles that slowly opened and closed in front of a gaping, tooth filled maw.

They eased their way back around the corridor and down the tunnel with Tagor pushing them more quickly as the creature followed. Jair saw that the creature was speeding up, so he broke into a run and led them back down the passage.

Tagor glanced back occasionally to see if the creature was still following them. After a few moments he called a halt, telling them he could no longer see it.

Breathing heavily and being quite shaken, Jair stopped and leaned against one damp wall to catch his breath. "What do you think that thing was?" He asked no one in particular.

"It was a form of giant centipede." Rakkon answered while trying to catch his breath. "They live in caves and underground dwellings and like to devour dead flesh. They don't mind live flesh when they can catch it. That one was a lot bigger than any I've ever heard of. The smaller ones are fairly common in the caves back home."

"Well, I think it's gone now." Tagor said as the others rested. "We'll wait a few minutes and try the tunnel again. I don't think we want to tangle with that thing unless we have too. Hopefully there is another branch that it will take, leading it away from us."

While they were resting, Jair looked about at the part of the tunnel in which they now stood. It was a wider section that looked almost like a large room. The ceiling rose much higher than the other parts of the tunnel they had been in. It was almost farther than what their torches would light at the top.

The stone walls here were very ancient, but better made than many of the other sections of the tunnel they had been in. Jair thought he saw movement out of the corner of one eye. As he turned toward it, a large blur went by him, moving toward Rakkon. It knocked him to the floor of the tunnel.

Rakkon's torch flew out of his hand and spun wildly across the stone floor. He was then picked back up and hurtled into the nearest wall. Jair heard a loud hiss as he turned to see what it was that was causing all of the commotion. He was surprised to find the hulking figure of the carrion crawler now moving amongst them.

Its large, jagged mandibles opened and closed noisily as it turned its attention back on the rest of the group. Evidently the creature had followed them, crawling along the ceiling where they could not see it. It had silently snuck into the chamber while they were resting.

It had dropped from the ceiling when they were least expecting it. The creature had seen its chance and taken it. The crawler quickly selected its next victim and darted forward with its many small feet propelling it faster than anyone would have thought possible.

Jair lunged to one side, barely avoiding the mandibles. He felt a searing pain in his left hand as one of its antennae brushed him. In his hurry, he dropped his satchel to the floor and rolled to one side. Tagor was somewhat quicker than the others and had his sword drawn as the beast came at him.

He cut viciously at its head as it passed by but didn't do any damage. Not being able to gauge the creatures' speed, he ended up only giving it a minor gash upon its back. Meanwhile, Kethok raised his massive club and brought it whistling down on the hind portion of the crawler that was closest to him.

His attack smashed the creature's rear end to the floor with a loud scrunching and snapping noise. His blow had crippled the last quarter of the beast. It continued on without pause however. The rest of the creature spun about and made for another pass, dragging its back end.

Jair glanced over at Rakkon, who was still lying on the cavern floor, before removing his short sword from its scabbard. He turned back to face the creature and sprung forward, swinging his sword with all his might.

Tagor and Kethok both engaged it from the front while Jair attacked it from behind. He cut savagely at the creature's segmented body. His attack went completely though the creatures body, severing it neatly in the middle through one of its segments. Jair watched in wonder as the rest of the creature kept on moving.

It was clear that the creature could be severed at its segments and keep right on going. The rest of the body thrashed about on the cave floor, spewing slime everywhere. Jair realized their jeopardy and yelled over at the others, who were having a hard time defending themselves from the crawler's flailing antennae and clasping mandibles. He also had to watch out not to be crushed by the flailing body he had cut off.

"In order to kill it, I think we'll have to cut off its head. Cutting the body doesn't do any good." Jair yelled while dodging the body. Tagor nodded his head in agreement, then moved forward to attack again when he saw an opening.

Jair also launched himself at the creature. He thought he might be able to distract it long enough for Tagor or Kethok to deliver a killing blow.

He hacked at the body and not the divisions between them this time. He had made several deep cuts until the creature whipped violently at him with its remaining end. Its body smashed into Jair, throwing him to one side of the tunnel. Tagor received a serious cut over his right eye from one of the mandibles and Kethok's left arm dangled limply at his side from a wound one of its antennae had given him. Kethok moved in and swung his massive weapon with one hand, cracking the creature's head a little. It's hard outer shell had still protected it from any major damage.

Tagor took advantage of the creature's momentary disorientation from Kethok's attack and drove in with his magic sword. He drove the point in between the creatures glistening red eyes where the small crack was, and pushed with all of his might until the blade forced its way in through the crawler's thick exterior. His sword slid in through its thick shell and finally into its brain. Tagor leapt back out of the way and watched as the crawler thrashed about violently a few times on the tunnel floor, then finally lay still.

Jair let out the breath he had been holding and ran over to see about Rakkon. He picked up his fallen satchel as he went. He quickly made it to him and then helped him into a sitting position. After a few minutes, he saw that Rakkon's senses were coming back to him. He reached around to his pack and grabbed his water skin, then held it up for Rakkon to have a drink.

Rakkon pulled on it strongly, and then handed it back to Jair who also took a drink. He then handed the water to Tagor and Kethok who had joined them. Rakkon seemed to be all right from the fall, but was still a little shaken and bruised.

Tagor and Kethok both seemed to be fine too. Tagor's cut was minor and Kethok's feeling was coming back into his arm while he stretched and moved it slowly about.

Rakkon looked over at the dead carcass of the crawler and said, "Humph, I must be getting soft to let a crawler get the best of me."

"Anyone can be caught off guard Rakkon." Tagor said.

"Even Jair didn't hear the creature's approach and he has good ears. We are lucky to be alive. If the creature hadn't missed some of us in its initial attack, we would probably all be dead right now." Tagor said.

Jair pulled Rakkon to his feet, and then saw to fixing Tagor's cut using a small strip of cloth to stop the bleeding. He then went over to examine the creature. He pulled out his dagger and removed part of an antennae and eye, placing them into one of his sealed pouches.

Tagor looked at him questioningly and asked, "What are you doing that for?"

"I read somewhere that a crawler's antennae and eyes can be used in the casting of some good spells. They might be worth keeping or selling later." Jair replied.

Tagor shrugged his shoulders and picked up the torch he had dropped during the fight. Rakkon also reclaimed his torch, then followed in behind Jair as Tagor led them on down the tunnel.

Jair's left hand throbbed painfully from where the crawler's antennae had touched him. So much so he couldn't concentrate on much else. The creature had exuded a poisonous substance that could be absorbed through the skin, causing whatever it touched to become numb and useless. He could not feel anything at all except pain. Evidently the poison was not as toxic to giants as it was to elves and humans. Kethok didn't really seem to mind his wound even though his arm still hung limp by his side and was a funny color.

Jair looked to Tagor for assistance and asked, "Tagor, is there anything you can do for my hand? The crawler's poison has left it useless."

The Ruby Helmet

Tagor stepped over and took a look at Jair's hand under the torchlight. He then removed a small vial from his pack. He opened the vial, removed a small dab of a creamy substance and then smeared it on Jair's hand, where the crawler had touched him.

Jair's hand stopped throbbing and started to feel better immediately. Seeing that his salve was going to do the trick, Tagor then turned to look at Kethok's arm.

He spread some of the slave on the spot where the crawler's antenna had touched Kethok's arm, then replaced the vial in his pack.

"Tagor, what was in that stuff?" Jair asked him.

"It is a healing salve the clerics in Gallador gave me before we left. It is primarily used for small wounds, rashes and things on the skin." Tagor replied.

Jair stretched out his hand and flexed it slightly. He could feel most of his movement returning. He looked at Kethok and could see the giant was also recovering from the contact poison.

"Well, whatever it was, it did the trick." Jair said in relief.

Seeing that they were all ok, they continued on down the tunnel for a short distance. The tunnel narrowed and then finally came to a large, old wooden door. There had been several, small tunnels that had branched off, but Tagor had chosen to stay in the main tunnel. He held up his torch, examined the door carefully, and then began to try the latch.

Jair caught his hand right before he touched it. He stepped forward, pointing up at the door facing. There he pointed out several small runes that were faintly carved into the wood.

"I think this door is spelled with a trap." He said to Tagor.

He took out his spell book and flipped through it until he found what he was looking for. He set it down on the floor and then squatted down and sat behind it.

Jair raised his hands before him and uttered strange words. As he spoke the spell's words, the door facing began to glow and hum faintly. It seemed to vibrate.

He continued to speak while holding his hands out, waving them slowly back and forth. There was a loud clap that rang all of their ears, and then the humming ceased.

Jair looked at the others, and then touched the door handle. He tried to open it, but it would not open. Even though there was no longer a spell on it, it was still locked.

Tagor handed his torch to Jair, and then removed a small bundle from his backpack. He placed the bundle on the floor, and then unwrapped it, revealing a small set of tools. He selected one of the tools and turned toward the door.

Tagor reached up toward the door handle and fiddled with the lock for several moments. They all heard a small click, then a twang and a thunk as Tagor triggered something inside the door.

Kethok had been standing next to Tagor as he worked on the door. There was now a small needle protruding from the side of his club. He began to pull it out but Tagor yelled, "No, don't touch it!" This startled Jair.

Tagor smiled apologetically and took a small piece of cloth to remove the dart. He held it up to the torchlight so they could all see it. The dart had a dark, wet, oily substance covering it.

"Poison." Tagor said as he threw the dart away. He then returned to the door and worked on the inside of the latch with his tools for a few minutes more. He eventually grunted in satisfaction and swung the door open.

Tagor took his torch back from Jair and held it out, revealing a large room on the other side of the door. They stepped cautiously through the opening, entering the room.

Once inside they found that the room was some sort of old laboratory. Several large wooden tables filled the center of the room. They were covered with an assortment of strange bottles, mechanical devises, books and chests.

Several large bookcases rested against the walls. They were filled with a wide assortment of books and scrolls. Many of them looked to be a lot older than the books they had seen up in the library. Tagor motioned for the others to spread out, then went over to a chest by the far wall. Once he was there he lit several old torches that were on that wall.

Cobwebs and thick layers of dust covered everything in the room. There was no telling how many hundreds or thousands of years it had all been down there.

Jair immediately went to the bookshelves and began scanning the labels on the assorted books and scrolls. Kethok walked about somewhat stupefied as he examined the contents that were on the tables. Rakkon walked over to an old forge that was on the left side of the chamber.

Jair found that many of the books were in a language that he could not read. Whoever had lived there had been very literate, but had probably been from another country, with a different language. The more he looked them over however, the more he decided they were not a foreign language, but were a language so ancient that it was no longer spoken or written. Even though he could not read many of them, there were a few that he could decipher. There were also several books on magic and magic lore.

"Let's see," Jair said to himself as he scanned the books. "Basics Fundamentals of Sorcery, Bats & Their Many Uses,

Understanding Witchcraft, ahh, what's this?" he said as he pulled out an old tome. Something about it had drawn his attention. The cover had strange glyphs and carvings all over it that seemed somehow familiar to him.

"A History of the Elven People," Jair read on the cover of the ancient book. The text had been difficult to make out at first. He blew on the cover, removing a layer of thick dust. He then ran his hand across it, wiping away the rest. He slowly opened its cracked leather cover, revealing old, yellowed pages. He carefully started skimming through its pages. What he read there, in bits and pieces, seemed more like a journal than a regular book. He searched until he found something that was of interest.

"From the creation of the helmet I have found the only users of its power are the elves from the family Est Stolorn. It was one of their sons that volunteered to help me to bind the helmet's magic to our earthly plane of existence. He gave his life for this cause. We were successful in thwarting the use of the other two artifacts and have hidden them. Our enemies now search for the artifacts and have tried to kill all of those that might use it against them. It is because of this that I have hidden several of their children to make sure that at least one might survive in order to one day wield the helmet when it is most needed again. I have not been able to devise a plan to destroy the other two artifacts and my time grows short. Hopefully a son or daughter of the family Est Stolorn will one day accomplish this task. The artifacts are much too powerful for any one person to wield. They could mean the destruction of our world."

Directly below the paragraph Jair saw a drawing of an insignia. His eyes grew wide when he saw it. He immediately recognized it. He had known it his entire life.

He reached down inside his cloak and pulled out the pendant that his mother had given him. He turned it over shakily in his hands and laid the pendant down next to the drawing in the book.

Comparing the insignia on his pendant to the one in the book, Jair found that they were identical.

Shock passed through Jair as comprehension of what he had just found set in. Wonder and fear also passed through him as he contemplated what he had just discovered. Or at least what he thought he had discovered. Denial then set in. He simply could not believe it was true.

The evidence had led him to believe that he was a descendant of the family Est Stolorn. The pendant Jair's mother had given him as a child had come from his father. She had only told Jair that it was a family heirloom. His father must have been a descendant of the original family.

Jair paused for a moment, then turned toward the others. "Tagor," he said shakily while he walked across the chamber to where Tagor was picking through the contents of one of the chests.

"Yes Jair, what is it," Tagor replied. "Have you found something?"

"Have a look at this and tell me what you think." Jair told him as he went to the other side of the room. He placed the book on another table close to where Tagor was searching.

Tagor held up his torch so could read the book. Jair laid his pendant on the open page next to the sketch.

Tagor took a few moments to read the passages Jair indicated. Then he closely examined the pendant.

"Where did you get this?" Tagor asked him holding the pendant up. "I don't recall ever having seen it before."

"My mother gave it to me when I was a child." Jair replied. "I think it has a charm on it so no one notices the wearer having it on. It belonged to my father. He gave it to her right after they were wed.

He disappeared not long after I was born. I didn't think much about it until recently. I have wondered about my father, who he was and what happened to him. My mother did not tell me much about him."

Tagor absorbed what Jair was telling him. Understanding dawned on his face as he realized what the evidence was leading them to. Rakkon and Kethok had moved over to listen, so Tagor handed Rakkon the book, indicating where he should read what they were talking about. Kethok looked over his shoulder, and then they both examined the pendant.

"If what this book says is true and your father was one of the descendents of Est Stolorn, then you should be able to wear the helmet and might even be able to invoke its powers. If you are the one that can wield the helmet, then our search is over." Tagor said.

Kethok kept looking at the pendant with big eyes as Rakkon finished reading the passage out loud. He closed the book and handed it back to Jair. A serious look was on his face as his mind pondered the information.

"If you are the heir to the magic of the helmet, there's only one way for us to find out. You need to put the helmet on and try to invoke its powers. That's the only way we'll know for sure. How confident are you that your father didn't just find or steal that necklace?" Rakkon asked him.

Anger played across Jair's face for just a moment. He realized that Rakkon wasn't trying to be mean to him about it. He just wanted Jair to be sure. His life would be at stake. Jair looked at Tagor and Kethok, who only looked back at him with blank expressions on their faces. This was a decision Jair was going to have to make on his own. No one else could help him with it. It all came down to how much trust he had in his mother and who he thought his father was.

Chapter 18

Jair's pendant glittered in the torchlight when Kethock handed it back to him. While his companions watched expectantly, Jair slipped it back over his head and walked over to the nearest table. He cleared a space by sliding some of the contents of the table over to one side. He then removed his satchel and placed it on the table.

He undid the latch, lifted up the flap, then reached inside and carefully lifted out the helmet. Warm torchlight flickered across the helmet's shiny surface, reflecting off of its many, ornate details. A strange glow seemed to emanate from the helmet as Jair lifted it up and stepped back from the table.

He glanced one last time at his companions, who only looked at one another uncertainly. He lifted the helmet up over his head and gently lowered it down.

At first, Jair felt nothing, so he began to relax. He then began to feel warm all over. Then a feeling of electric energy ran through him like a huge jolt, jarring him. Panic and fear gripped him as the strange sensation grew. He imagined his skull being burned to a crisp, just like the goblin leader when he had tried to use it.

The vision lasted for only a moment, and then Jair grew determined and tried to focus all of his concentration on the helmet. He tried to harness the power that was now flowing through him. As he did so, the helmet rebelled against him. It seemed to have a mind of it's own. Only by using all of the training he had gained over the last few months was he able to let his senses expand to envelope the magical energy as it pulsed out from the helmet. He also realized that part of the struggle came from somewhere within him.

Jair let his senses surround the magical energy of the helmet. He grabbed it with his mind and focused on capturing the flowing strands as they came out from the helmet. His concentration tightened and wrapped his mind around the raw magical power.

Sweat beaded up on Jair's forehead and ran down his face while his friends stared in wonder. His entire body glowed with a bright, reddish-orange light.

The others could see that there was a terrible struggle happening between Jair and the helmet, but none of them knew of anything that they could do to help.

Time passed as the struggle wore on. Jair felt his concentration start to waver once, and the power of the helmet almost overcame him. He quickly recovered and was able to bring it back under his control.

With a final surge of his own willpower, Jair thrust out with his mind in a final effort to gain control of the helmet. His mind fully enveloped the flowing energy as it coursed within him and the helmet finally began to yield to him. As the wave of battling energy receded, Jair could now feel all of the helmets power that was now at his disposal. It was unlike anything he had ever felt before. It was almost more than he could bear. It was a different kind of magic. Once he was comfortable with his control, he released his hold on it and shut the helmet down.

Jair let out a final gasp and dropped to his knees on the cold, stone floor. He now had full control over the power of the helmet and had an idea of what it might be able to do. Once control had been established, it was only a matter of time and practice before the wearer would be able to fully use it. He felt that now that he had control, the helmet had accepted him and was now guiding him with how to use it.

Tagor rushed over and helped Jair back to his feet when he saw that the glow had faded. Rakkon brought over an old wooden chair. Jair seated himself, then reached up and removed the helmet. He set it down on the table.

Kethok stared at Jair with a quiet awe. Rakkon kept his face mostly impassive. Jair could tell they were all slightly shaken from what they had just witnessed. He also thought he saw a little bit of fear on all of their faces.

Sweat covered his face and dampened his hair. He looked as if he had just been in a heavy downpour. He took in a few long, deep breaths. Jair looked at his friends and gave them a little smile to let them know that he was all right. He pulled out his water and took a long drink.

"What happened," Tagor asked him with a look of concern.

Jair shook his head to clear it a little. He thought about what had just happened and how to try and explain it to his friends.

"When I put the helmet on there was a surge of power. In order to keep it from burning me up like it did the goblin, I had to force it to bend to my will. It was the most difficult thing I have ever had to do." Jair told them.

Tagor leaned back against the table and spoke while Jair rested. "Well, we know now who can wield the helmet so our quest here is done. Now all we have to do is find out what the Dark Lord is going to do and what we can do to stop him." He said.

Jair nodded his head in agreement, but still harbored some doubts as to what they could do against the Dark Lord. Even with the awesome power of Estolorn, the Dark Lord was a force to be reckoned with.

Jair rose slowly and replaced the helmet in his satchel along with the book he had found. He securely tightened the flap. His hands shook a little. Tagor looked at him questioningly, but Jair assured him that he was all right.

"Well, now that we've gotten that all settled I guess we can return to the city. Or we can stay down here and explore a little more." Tagor said with a small gleam in his eye.

Jair smiled at Tagor and nodded his head that they should keep exploring. He now knew that the room had belonged to the wizard of the red robes that had created the helmet. They spread back out and starting looking through the room's contents.

Jair walked about the chamber, picking through the old materials and wizards' artifacts that were still strewn about. He picked up an occasional spell component that he thought he might use, but didn't see anything that was very interesting. Most of the stuff that was left in the room was useless. He was wondering why that one book had been left behind when he realized it was connected to his pendant. Only someone with his bloodline and wearing the pendant could have found that book. It had a spell on it. He knew that now.

He looked back through the many scrolls and books that were on the shelves. He finally picked up another one that seemed interesting. As he touched the ancient pages, they crumbled into dust and fell to the floor.

Upon further examination, most of the other books and parchments were in similar condition, and probably of no use. He looked for just a few moments more, then spotted several more scrolls that were in a glass case. They had been partially hidden by other books.

Jair removed them from the shelf and peered through the dusty glass to try and read them. He tried to make out some of the wording and found that he could not read any of it. He determined that it was written in the other language, the one that he did not know. He decided that he could try and translate them later, so he stuffed them into his bag.

Kethok followed silently behind Jair while Rakkon and Tagor both went to the far side of the chamber. They went to examine the rest of the chests and the forge.

They poked through the remnants of the room. Rakkon flipped open the lid to one of the chests, using the toe of his boot. Inside the chest there were a variety of items. Most of the contents seemed to have been clothing, but were now just rotten and moldy rags.

Tagor reached in with a gloved hand and pulled out the remnants of clothing to see what lay beneath. He searched the bottom of the chest and thought he noticed something strange about the way the chest looked and had been made. He thumped the bottom, and he and Rakkon heard what sounded like another chamber in the bottom.

Rakkon pulled out his dagger and ran it along the bottom inside edge of the chest. He slid it down and gently pried up the bottom, revealing a hidden section beneath.

Within the section were several items. There was a golden wand, a coil of thin, silvery rope, and a small gray statue of a serpent that was coiled as if about to strike.

Tagor looked at the objects for a moment, and then motioned for Jair to come take a look at them. He told Jair he thought they might be magical items and hoped he could identify them.

Jair walked over and glanced into the chest. He reached in and carefully removed the wand and the rope. He left the serpentine figurine where it was.

He took the two objects over near a torch and closely examined them. No one noticed the slight shimmering of movement from within the chest. Rakkon and Tagor had turned their backs on the chest and had followed Jair over to the light.

Jair placed the objects on a table and removed several spell components. He then concentrated on a spell. He uttered the magical words and held out the spell components. A light glow emanated from the two objects.

After the glow from the spell faded, Jair lowered his hands then retrieved the objects. He held up the wand and said, "I cast an identifying magic spell on them. The wand is of fireballs and still has several charges in it."

He then dropped the rope to the floor while still holding the other end. He uttered a word and threw it into the air. To the amazement of the others, the rope hung in the air and started to rise until Jair told it to stop.

Jair glanced over at the others and smiled broadly. "This is a rope of climbing. All you have to do is command it to "climb" in elven and it will rise until it reaches the end or until you tell it to stop in elven.

Jair reached back up, jerked once on the dangling rope and said, "down" in elven. The rope gently fell to the floor where Jair gathered it up, winding it about his forearm. Once he had it gathered, he handed it to Tagor. "You might as well hang on to this. It will be lighter and stronger than the rope you carry now." Jair told him.

Tagor smiled brightly as he accepted the rope. He replaced the one he had in his pack. As he was doing that, Rakkon let out a yell and jerked around. He reacted quickly, swinging his axe. In a movement so fast they could barely see it, he sank his axe into the stone floor with a loud clang.

Jair jumped back from the sudden movement. The others turned to see what had happened. The four companions watched in horror as a large, bronze and gray serpent now lay writhing in two pieces upon the stone floor. The pieces slowly stopped moving, flopping onto the floor, and turning into to stone as they looked on. The stone cracked and several pieces broke off as it fell to the floor.

Tagor went over and examined the dead stone serpent, then said, "It must have been a guardian of some sort. We are lucky Rakkon has such quick reflexes, or it might have been one us now lying cold upon the floor."

"I would not have noticed it if it hadn't crawled across my foot." He told them. "I was moving more from reflex than anything else. We're lucky it didn't strike one of us." Rakkon said.

He picked up a piece of the serpent, stepped back over to the chest and glanced back into the bottom. He noticed something else in the bottom, so he reached down into it and pulled something. They all heard a small clicking sound, and then saw the wall behind the chest begin to slide away. It revealed another passage.

Tagor looked at Jair and shrugged, then stepped over the chest toward the opening. He motioned for the others to follow him as he set off down the new tunnel.

Rakkon retrieved his torch, which he had placed in an empty holder on the wall, and followed them in the rear. After taking a few steps on into the tunnel, Tagor stepped on a stone in the floor that sank slightly. They all heard another click and then a rumbling groan. From behind them came the sound of stone grating on stone as a giant slab fell into place, blocking the entrance to the tunnel. They were cut off.

Tagor turned and ran to the slab that now covered their only known way out. He examined it carefully and could find no means by which they could move it.

He turned toward the others and grimly stated, "Well, I guess we'll have to go on and hope we find another way out."

They headed on down the passage. Jair noticed that this tunnel was a lot smaller than the earlier ones. It also had a squared off roof that was supported by large wooden beams.

They followed the passage for a while until it ended at another large wooden door. This door was a lot older than the previous one and was in bad shape.

Tagor searched it carefully for traps and did not find any. He tried the latch and found that it was not locked, but would not open. Rust covered the metal of the door handle, the latch and it's old hinges.

Tagor tried several times to force it open, but could not make it budge. Kethok gently pushed him aside and handed him his club. He stepped up to the door and placed his two massive hands on it.

He then braced his feet firmly and set his mighty muscles in motion, pushing heavily upon the door. The old wood creaked and groaned loudly, but stayed put as the giant heaved with all his might.

The door must have been made of sturdy stuff because it held its ground. Kethok gave it one final massive shove and it finally burst inward, splintering into many pieces, crashing with a loud thud onto the floor of the chamber beyond.

Kethok stepped back and took his club from Tagor. Tagor moved forward with his torch in hand and peered into the room. This chamber was much smaller than the last one. Many racks and shelves covered the walls and freestanding shelves lined the middle of the room.

The racks were covered with an assortment of old weapons and armor. The shelves held what use to be food stores in many jars and boxes.

Jair shouldered his way past Tagor and went through the doorway. He began examining the contents of the room. He looked over at the others as he was exploring and said. "Remember to be careful. We don't know what kinds of traps the old wizard might have left behind."

At first, most of what they found was useless. The weapons were too rusted and what was in the jars had long ago spoiled. Jair sifted through the remains of some rations and other old supplies and found two small bottles that were filled with a thin, blue liquid.

He took them over to where Tagor was examining an old sword and asked him. "Tagor, what do you suppose these are?"

Tagor put down the old sword and took one of the bottles from Jair. He then examined it. He reached up to its lip and removed a cork stopper that had been sealed with wax. It let out a harsh, minty smell.

Tagor grinned at Jair and to everyone's surprise, turned the bottle up and took a long swallow of the strange blue liquid. He lowered the bottle and removed the bandage covering the wounds he had received earlier. As they all watched, the wounds began to close, sealing themselves up. After a few moments the wounds were completely gone, except for small pink scars.

"These are potions of healing. I've seen them before in the temple of Anu. Only the most skilled of wizards or clerics can make them. I suggest you put them in your satchel. They could come in handy." Tagor said.

Jair, Rakkon and Kethok each took a small drink from one of the potions before Jair placed them in his pack. They used up about half of one of the bottles. He put his satchel back over his shoulder and went over to where Rakkon was examining a shield.

The shield was a small round buckler that was finely crafted. The surface was slightly curved and it was painted red and black with the image of a winged black serpent. The outer edge was made of thick, banded steel. It had many small rivets along its outer edge. Rakkon had wiped away some of the dust so they could get a better look at it.

Jair frowned once he saw the creature that was painted on it. A small shiver ran down his spine. He had never been fond of serpents. Especially after their earlier encounter with the magical stone one.

Rakkon merely shrugged and dropped his own shield, replacing it with the new one. He weighed it comfortably on his left arm, then grinned satisfactorily and moved on.

Kethok motioned toward them from the far end of the chamber. He had found another exit. Tagor moved over to stand next to this door. He examined it carefully, then reached up and tried the handle.

This door was not locked either and opened easily. They looked through the opening and found another tunnel that was split, leading in two different directions. Tagor opted for the one to the right and led them down it.

This tunnel went on for several minutes until they finally came to another door. Tagor went up and quickly examined it, then listened for any sounds on the other side. He then motioned for Kethok to come over and for the others to be silent.

Kethok also listened through the door for a moment, shrugged, then reached up and pulled it open. It groaned loudly at first, and then crashed open. As the light from their torches spilled through the doorway, they saw many dark skinned humanoid creatures marching by in another corridor.

As the door was opened, the dark creatures yelled loudly, shying away from the light and covering their eyes. Tagor got a glimpse of what the creatures were and shouted, "Quick Kethok, close the door!" He moved forward to help shut it.

Several of the dark creatures responded quickly and leaped into their tunnel, attacking them. Rakkon moved to meet one of them while Kethok swung his club, catching another in its abdomen. His club collided with tremendous force, hurtling the creature back through the door and into the other hall. This knocked several more of the creatures off their feet.

Tagor swung the door shut with a bang. He slid a heavy metal bolt into place, locking it. Rakkon finished off the other creature he had intercepted. Jair did his best to fend off another that had gotten through the door before Tagor had closed it.

Jair grew pale when he realized what he was facing. The creature standing before him had dark gray skin, white hair and unmistakable elven features. Standing almost six feet tall, the dark elf moved swiftly, stabbing at Jair with a long, wicked looking curved sword.

Jair knocked aside its lunging blade with his satchel. He drew his dagger from his belt and threw it in a fluid motion. He did it just as Tagor and Rakkon had taught him.

His dagger struck the dark elf full in the chest, causing a small spark to fly as it penetrated the fine black, chain mail armor that he wore. The dagger sank in and pierced the creature's heart, killing it.

After the dark elf fell heavily to the floor, Jair reached down and retrieved his dagger. He wiped the blood on the dark elf's pants. He noticed how easily the dagger had cut through the mail. He examined his dagger a moment more, and then replaced it in the scabbard at his waist.

Loud banging started emanating from the door as Tagor motioned for the others to follow him back down the way they had come. They paused only briefly to throw open the other door to the storeroom, Tagor led them on down the other tunnel they had not yet explored.

They ran with everything they had. Tagor led the way up

through the winding and twisting corridors. After what seemed like a lifetime, the companions stumbled back into a chamber they had passed while descending earlier. It was the chamber that had the three tunnels leading away from it. They had come back up one of them.

Tagor found his mark on the far wall and called a halt so they could all catch their breaths. It was still a fair distance to the stairway and then up to the library.

Thinking as he ran, Jair wondered what dark elves were doing in a secret passage beneath the elven city. It had to be connected to the Dark Lord. It was part of the plot to overthrow the high elves and destroy their fair city.

As they rested, faint sounds emanated from one of the other tunnels. Something or someone was coming toward them. "Tagor, what are we going to do?" Jair asked in short, labored breaths. "It looked like an army was passing through that corridor and it sounds like they are coming this way." He said while pointing to the middle passage.

Tagor glanced down the tunnel and replied, "We have to reach the city and warn the elves. It looks like the dark elves are trying to make a night assault."

The others nodded their heads in agreement and they all set back off up the tunnel, toward the city. Jair dropped his torch and led the way using his infravision in order to help the other two humans to keep from stumbling onto anything. He also hoped they wouldn't come upon anything else.

Their time in the tunnel stretched on and on until Jair finally came to the bottom of the stairway that led back up to the library. They climbed as rapidly as they could. They eventually worked their way to the top landing where they burst back through the secret doorway.

The Ruby Helmet

They closed the door behind them. Kethok and Rakkon quickly started moving tables and shelves to block the door. A servant that was cleaning the room stared at them with shock and dismay.

Jair turned to the servant and yelled, "Go and find the city guards! The city is under attack by dark elves. They need to bring help fast!"

Jair paused for a few seconds seeing that the attendant hesitated. He drew his short sword and swung it over the man's head. "Go! Now!" He said forcefully, sending the servant sprawling toward the door.

Jair then looked at Tagor, who nodded his head in reassurance. While trying to figure out what to do next, he realized they were about to be in the middle of a bloody war.

Chapter 19

Jair set his satchel on the floor and retrieved the golden wand he had taken from the wizard's chamber. He held it aloft and checked it once, then prepared a few of his other spell components. At the same time Rakkon and Kethok rested in order to prepare themselves for the coming battle. Meanwhile, Tagor seemed to be just trying to catch his breath.

As Jair was preparing himself, he thought he heard the sounds of an alarm being raised and many people shouting far off in the distance. There also came the sound of many voices and feet shuffling from behind the bookcase that hid the secret tunnel.

He braced for what was to come. Everyone stepped away from the front of the bookcase and moved around behind tables they had turned over. Jair also heard the sound of many feet running toward them from inside the library, but wondered if help would come in time.

The bookcase started to smoke and hiss. Jair realized what was about to happen and yelled at the others to take cover as the bookcase exploded toward them. It showered the room with pieces of books, wood splinters and burning embers.

From the gaping hole that was now where the bookcase used to be, dark elves started pouring into the room.

Jair was ready for them as they charged through the opening. He aimed the golden wand at the first group that came through the smoldering door. He incanted the power of the wand and released a magical charge.

A huge sphere of white light burst from the wand's tip. It grew into a giant ball that sped toward the elves.

As the ball made it to them, the sphere turned into a giant red and yellow ball of fire. It exploded upon impact and gave off a great wave of heat. The fireball devastated the first group that had tried to enter through the door. It left only smoking, burnt bodies and scattered weapons strewn across the library floor.

After the smoke and the heat dissipated enough for them all to see, more dark figures moved toward the opening. Jair could hear strange words being spoken from across the smoke filled room. He realized a dark elf mage was working a spell.

Jair aimed the wand at the opening again to try and release another fireball. Before he could do so, Tagor had his bow up and had already loosed an arrow at the mage. It struck him in the shoulder and interrupted his spell. This gave Jair and the others time to act.

After being hit, the dark elf sorcerer stepped back to allow more dark warriors to charge into the room. Jair couldn't use his wand because they made it through the opening too fast and were too close to his friends. They quickly engaged Rakkon and Kethok, who had moved in to intercept them.

Rakkon used his axe with deadly accuracy. He cut the first few down as they entered the room. Tagor continued to fire his arrows randomly through the opening, being careful not to hit his friends.

At this point Jair paused in the confusion. He tried to decide what to do next and saw the other sorcerer coming back through the opening. Jair could see that blood was running down his shoulder and arm from Tagor's arrow.

The dark elf was speaking the same strange words as he came into the room and was able to finish casting another spell. The room went dark on Jair's side and became very cold. The wall and floor where Jair stood iced over. The cone of cold the dark elf had cast caught Jair's left arm and leg, practically freezing them. Pain shot through him as he tried to move away.

He dove to one side, barely avoiding being completely caught in the spell. He rolled back to his feet, and then charged at the dark elf mage. The cold spell slowed his movement somewhat, so Jair did not know if he could reach the wizard in time to stop him from casting another spell.

The dark elf sorcerer tried to dodge the cut Jair made toward his chest with his short sword. The dark elf hadn't expected Jair to be able to dodge out of the way of most of the cold spell.

Jair's sword shredded the right side of the mage's robes. The cut left a massive gash in the elf's ribcage, breaking several bones and cutting into his abdomen.

The mage screamed shrilly before he dropped to the floor just on the other side of the passage door. He writhed in pain as his life's blood poured out of him. Jair shoved the mage with one foot, rolling him over the top of the stairs. The falling body pushed back the troops that were on the stairway, knocking several down the stairs. Jair quickly turned to see what other enemies might still be in the room. After searching, he found himself free for the moment.

He quickly reached up and grabbed the shelf that was to the right of the passage opening. He pulled on it as hard as he could, toppling it over across the opening.

He then turned to check on his friends. He felt a stab of fear as he saw that they were about to be overrun by the dark elves that were still in the room. He picked up his satchel and headed toward the right hand doorway that led out of the chamber. He did this to block any dark elves from escaping and so he could come up with a plan to try and help his friends. As he made it to the doorway, city guards began pouring in through the opening.

He directed the guards toward his friends and the open passage that was about to be cleared by more dark elves, telling them, "The city is being invaded from below by dark elves. They are invading through that secret opening!"

A high elf captain nodded his head in understanding, and then started shouting orders. The high elven soldiers rushed forward to meet their most hated enemy in mortal combat. They quickly shouldered Rakkon and Kethok aside to get at them. Their rush pushed back the dark elves, putting them on the defensive. The passage by then had been cleared and more dark elves began pouring into the room.

As the ensuing melee took place, Jair stayed back and watched the elven forces meet in the middle of the small room. It was beginning to look like he and his friends had held the dark elves at bay in time for the high elves to keep them from invading the city. If Kethok had not discovered the secret passage, the dark elves would have been able to overrun the city from the inside.

Jair waited for only a moment more, then leapt forward to help Tagor who had been set upon by two dark elf fighters. He jumped into the mix; cutting at one of the dark elves' legs while Tagor shoved his sword point through the other one's throat.

Tagor stepped back and saluted Jair in thanks for his assistance. He then glanced around the room to check out the situation. He found Rakkon and Kethok had both pulled back, panting exhaustedly and sporting a few minor cuts and bruises.

Tagor motioned for them all to follow him and he led them out the exit and down the crowded hall into the main hall of the library. Troops still filed down the hallway along with what looked to be a wizard or two. They rushed past the companions to where the fighting was taking place.

When they made it across the main hall, they continued to follow Tagor as he strode out of the library's front doors. Once outside they found that the city had been thrown into utter turmoil.

Women and children rushed passed while clutching a few meager belongings. Soldiers jogged by on their way to their battle stations.

Jair looked about, wondering what all was going on. Tagor reached out to grab a passing elf and asked him, "What's going on?"

The elf saw the bloody sword still in Tagor's hand and shrank back in fear. Tagor backed off, indicating that he meant the elf no harm. The elf calmed down and replied, "The city is under attack. A large dark elf army with monsters is attacking us!"

Tagor thanked the elf and motioned for the others to follow him as he worked his way through the city toward the front gates. An attack from outside of the city explained the turmoil. No one in the city had had time to panic from the invasion coming from under the library.

A short while later they made it to the top of the battlements. They followed Tagor as he climbed the stone steps two at a time, until they reached the top. He strode quickly along the parapets, leading them to the left side tower, right over the gatehouse. In all of the confusion, no one questioned their presence. However Kethok garnered several hard looks.

Jair glanced over the wall and could see thousands of dark shapes moving in the moonlight across the open fields, just outside of the city. It was a mix of dark elves, dark dwarves, goblins, trolls and even more horrid beasts. The shapes were swarming around the outer walls. Hundreds of men shouted and screamed as they tried to repel the forces that were hurtling themselves against the city's massive stone fortifications.

Lightning and fire streaked across the sky, illuminating the area as the city's wizards battled the dark elf mages.

A full-scale attack had been engaged against the city while they had been exploring beneath it. It was an attack that had almost caught them unaware. The sneak attack from beneath had been narrowly avoided. Their actions were all that had saved the city from quickly being overrun from within. The outer assault had been well met by the city's well-prepared defenses. If the dark elves had been able to penetrate from within, the city would have quickly fallen.

It was evident that the dark forces had planned on an easy victory and had expected to have quickly breached the walls. By now they would have known that their attempt at invasion from within had failed. Passing conversations told Jair that the enemy had emerged from a large tunnel somewhere close to the city in the nearby hills. It was completely unexpected by the high elves.

As soon as they were at the top, Rakkon charged over to one of the walls. Dark dwarves had made it to the top by using a well-made siege tower and were coming over the wall. Rakkon chopped at one with his axe, sending it flying off the top with a guttural scream. Tagor dropped another with an arrow in its chest while Jair and Kethok ran up to a heavy ladder that was sticking up above the wall.

Jair cast a light spell right in the face of the next dwarf that was just reaching the top of the ladder, blinding it. Kethok came in around him and swung his mace straight down on top of its head. The dwarf's skull cracked inside his helmet and sank down into its shoulders, killing him. The force from the blow was so strong it sent him flying down the rungs of the ladder, splitting them and knocking all of the other dwarves off that were clambering up behind him.

Jair pulled out his wand and aimed it toward two of the catapults that were closest to their position. He used the wand, spewing several fireballs, one right after the other. They both hit their intended targets, obliterating the catapults along with their crews.

Before releasing a third fireball he noticed something moving among the throng below. He spotted a dark elf mage who was there with several assistants. It looked like they were about to do something nasty. They were moving some sort of device into place.

Jair pointed his wand toward them and his next fireball went straight down into the mass of milling troops. It engulfed the wizard along with his entire crew. A huge swath was cut through them, leaving charred and burning bodies. Molten armor glowed eerily in dark. Smoke billowed all around them. Whatever it was they were planning to do would never happen now. Their device was now ruined.

Kethok moved to the wall nearby and began sweeping elves and dwarves from atop it as they came over the top. His heavy weapon easily cleared them. Dwarves and elves screamed as he smashed into them. They had not expected to meet one such as he atop the wall. He threw them around as if they were rag dolls.

Tagor fired arrows until his quiver was empty. He then drew his sword and engaged the enemy as they came over the wall. He, Rakkon and Kethok worked together to keep their section of the wall clear and to give Jair time to use his magic.

Jair looked around and saw high elves running back and forth, trying to turn back the invaders. Nothing else was in range of his wand at the moment. He also did not know how many charges it had left in it. Large balls of fire and stone flew at them from the catapults that were still operating below. Occasionally they crashed into the walls or swiped defenders from the battlements. Arrows and spears fell among them regularly, clattering off of the stone. Rakkon held his shield up just in time to stop an arrow that came down at Jair. It bounced off his shield without leaving a scratch. The enemy had taken notice of his fireballs.

They all had minor cuts and abrasions from the intense fighting. Rakkon was covered with the blood of those he had vanquished with his mighty axe.

When there was a lull in the fighting, Tagor led their group away from that part of the wall. He located an officer and asked, "Who's in charge here?"

"General Illithian." The elven soldier said while pointing to a tall elf in silver armor that stood at the edge of the front wall.

Tagor walked over to the general and waited for him to notice that they were there. They followed Tagor, but stayed a little bit behind him. The general's aides eventually noticed them and one of the officers said something to the general, and then pointed in their direction.

The general glanced at Tagor, then back out over the wall. He had a serious expression on his face as he asked, "Who are you and what are you doing on my wall?"

"I am Tagor of the Barnook forest, and these are my friends Jair, Rakkon and Kethok." Tagor said pointing to the others. "King Galdath of Gallador sent us as emissaries on an important mission to your city's library." He said while handing him the letter of introduction the king had given them.

"We were searching a hidden passage that we stumbled upon in the library when we discovered the dark elves invading the city from below." Tagor continued as the general read the letter.

The general raised one eyebrow, and then nodded a couple of times while he listened to Tagor's story. He then handed him back the letter. He turned to one of his officers and spoke to him for a moment, then turned back to Tagor.

"Thank you for your assistance. My second tells me were it not for you and your friends, our city would have been overrun. You and your friends must have fought well. You held them off until our troops could arrive. The passage has been sealed, the tunnels cleared and the dark elves have been driven back from below."

"If you would like to rest and clean up, there is a place down in the guardhouse. When I get a chance I would like to speak to you at length. For now I must concentrate on strengthening our defenses and saving our city." The general said.

Tagor glanced over at his friend before responding to the general. On their way to the walls they had discussed their options and had all decided to fight on behalf of the elven people.

Rakkon had suggested that Jair use the power of the helmet, but Jair felt he was not ready to unleash the power of Estolorn just yet. He thought it would be better to wait until he had more practice with it. If the helmet were used now, Jair knew that the Dark Lord would know of it and possibly use it against them. He knew he wasn't ready.

Tagor looked back over at the general and said, "General, if it is all the same to you we would like to stay on the walls and lend a hand. We have as much at stake as all of you and we'd like to do what we can."

The general nodded his head in agreement and understanding the general said, "We are in your debt and are honored to have you."

He then gave several orders to one of his officers and turned his attention back to the siege that was taking place. The young officer quickly turned and walked over to where they stood waiting.

"I am lieutenant Gretto of the Blue Corps. The general has placed you under my command. If you will follow me I will take you so you can clean up and grab a bite to eat. It may be a while before any more action happens. We have pushed them back for the moment. After the general speaks with you I will find you a place on the battlements."

He turned and headed back down the stairs, leading them inside the main guardhouse. Once inside, he showed them where the water and rations were stored and told them to help themselves.

Tagor quickly pulled off his cap and doused his head with a pitcher of water. Rakkon found a bench and groaned as he seated himself, his body aching from exhaustion. Kethok moved over to the wall and seated himself on the cold stone floor after grabbing up an armful of rations from a cupboard. He quickly began stuffing food into his large, toothy mouth.

Jair reached into his satchel and withdrew one of the bottles of healing and handed it to Rakkon. "Drink," he told him. Rakkon took the potion and swallowed a large gulp. He handed it back to Jair. A small cut on his face disappeared and he looked more refreshed.

Tagor, Kethok and Jair did likewise, finishing off the first potion. Jair deposited the empty bottle in a waste barrel.

Feeling better, they cleansed themselves by using a barrel of water. They then ate some rations, not knowing when the next time would be before they would get to eat again.

The guardhouse they were in was fairly large and housed a full garrison. Cots lined both walls, all of which were now empty. Jair decided as long as they were waiting, he might as well try to get some rest so he lay down. Rakkon and Tagor stayed seated at the table and talked with Lt. Gretto, who had remained behind.

A short while passed and finally the sounds outside quieted. Evidently something else was happening. The attack so far had consisted mostly of heavy catapults and ballista firing upon the city, trying to soften them up. Soldiers being relieved from duty filed passed Jair and his companions. They headed for their own barracks or to the healers. Most of the ones coming down were wounded. There were a few that came in and lay on cots.

Jair jerked awake when the general and his first officer entered the guardhouse. The rest of the soldiers present snapped quickly to attention when they came in.

He waved the soldiers off with a salute, then walked over to the water barrel and dipped a cup in it. He then walked back over to the table and sat down.

Blood and sweat covered his armor. A tired expression was on his face as he turned to the four companions, motioning for them and his officers to gather around the table. He took a drink from his cup before speaking.

"The Dark Lord's forces have fallen back from the walls for now. Their initial onslaught was turned back successfully, but with heavy losses on both sides. Their attempt to breach the city from below has foiled them for the moment, so they will fall back and regroup. Once upon a time we would have easily been able to hold off an army of this size, but we do not yet know their full strength." The general said with a sigh.

"It would appear that the Dark Lord has more resources than we thought. My scouts have spotted several large bodies of armed men and monsters moving this way from out of the north. They also believe they spotted several dragons."

"Dragons!" Jair exclaimed. "There haven't been any dragons around for a hundred years."

"Not until now." The commander responded. "It was believed that most of the evil dragons were extinct, but evidently the Dark Lord has found a few that have answered his call."

"How many does he have?" Tagor asked.

"Our scouts spotted three, two reds and a black. But that's enough to cause some heavy damage to the city. We are not prepared for magical dragon attacks and their breath weapons."

"Our aerial defenses are mostly for smaller flying animals like giant bats, griffins and magic users. I have our top wizards working on a few things right now in the hopes of defeating the flying lizards."

"Once, long ago, Silvermist could have withstood a siege like this for many months if not for years. The walls were heavily fortified with warding spells when they were first built. We're not sure how strong those spells still are. None of our people have the skill to renew them. The Dark Lord has a large number of sorcerers and monsters at his command. More than I think we can handle without help."

"It looks like this army is mostly made up of dark elves and dark dwarves with a few hill giants and trolls mixed in from out of the nearby mountains. We have approximated them at fifty thousand. We hope it is the majority of what they have camped outside our walls."

"As far as the group that is coming to join them, our scouts say they are a blend of human mercenaries, orcs, ogres, trolls, giants, and a few other lesser human creatures. Our scouts estimated them to be somewhere in the neighborhood of twenty thousand. With a mob that big they must plan on attacking the wood elves next and then possibly the humans to the west."

"My advisors tell me we will not be able to hold out for very long. We have tried sending riders to the west and south for help, but don't know if they can make it through in time."

"This attack is something I have foreseen and feared. I tried to warn the city council that this might happen and tried to get them to boost our defenses. In their own foolish pride they believed no one could gather the force necessary to defeat our beloved city."

The general lowered his head as he finished speaking, resting it for a moment in his hands. Despair was written across his face.

Tagor looked over at the others, then stood and walked over to stand by the general with a thoughtful look on his face.

Tagor then asked, "General, have you thought of sending a rider to Fort Decadse to ask them for assistance? I'm sure that the commander there would be willing to send aid. Surely the other nations will also rally to this cause. If the Dark Lord is marching in such force, all of the nations will have to band together to defeat him."

The general raised his head and thought for a moment before answering. A look of hope gleamed in his eyes for a moment, then faded.

"Even if someone were to reach them in time, I do not believe the human forces would rally to our cause. Relations between the humans and the elves have been on better terms these last few years, but not well enough they would come to our aid. I fear that only when they see Silvermist fall and find the Dark Lord's army at their doorstep, will they try to do something. I only hope it will not be too late," the general said sadly.

"Our case seems to be a grim one, but my men are tough and well trained. We will sell our lives and our city for a high price!" He said with fierce determination as he stood. "We will show the Dark Lord and his minions that the cost of taking Silvermist will be high. One that will be paid in blood!"

"General, do you think the city has any chance at all?" Jair asked him.

He looked at Jair and replied, "At our present state I believe we will be able to hold out for a while. We have plenty of provisions and our forces are fresh and well trained, but the large amount of forces and magical capabilities the Dark Lord is bringing against us is overwhelming. It is my belief that Silvermist will fall within a fortnight."

Jair felt his heart sink at the general's words. He glanced over at the general's officers that were gathered about the table. He could see despair and sadness in their eyes at the grim words.

In all of the many hundreds of years Silvermist had existed, never once had an enemy breached its walls or set foot on its streets as a conqueror. It was obvious that the conquest of the world by the Dark Lord had begun, helmet or no helmet.

Chapter 20

Jair stood silently looking out over the city walls. The army's many campfires glittered below like stars. The army fanned out across the fields and farmland, spreading across them like a blanket. He could even see them in the woods far beyond.

As the sun rose slowly behind another thick veil of dark clouds, it dimly lit the bloody scene of death and carnage that the night's battle had left behind. Hundreds of dark, twisted bodies littered the ground below. Lightly clad bodies of the city's fallen were also scattered amongst them.

The dark elves and dwarves had attacked in the deep of the night, trying to use their stealthy underworld abilities to gain an advantage over the unsuspecting city.

Smoke curled slowly up into the sky as small fires continued to burn where ever a wizard's spells had struck or flaming arrows had hit, sending its victims up in flames.

The initial onslaught had been turned back, but with losses on both sides. The enemy had lost more than the defenders however. The dark elves and dwarves were fierce fighters, especially at night. This did not help them against the elves that could also see in the dark. The high elves were all well trained and had the advantage of defending from a heavily fortified city. Arrows littered the ground and bodies were strewn about before the city. It looked like some sort of strange grass in a field.

Ropes with grappling hooks dangled from the city's walls and broken ladders leaned against the wall's base, where the invaders had tried to scale its massive heights. Very few of the invaders had made it to the top of the wall. Those that had made it fought fiercely and took a terrible toll among the defenders. The catapults, ballista and dark elven archers had also taken a heavy toll.

Jair and his friends had been given a place to defend along the wall in Lt. Gretto's command, which was along the east side. His troops had fared better than most during the long night and had taken the least amount of casualties.

As the sun rose behind heavy clouds, Jair wondered what would happen next. The lieutenant had explained most of their basic defenses, but Jair didn't really understand a lot of it. He realized there was a lot more to defending a city than he would have thought.

Jair had used his magic to try to keep as many of the dark elf wizards out of the fight as possible. Even though Silvermist was supposed to have some of the finest sorcerers in the world, Jair had found out that in the last century, the study of the arcane arts had waned. Elven sorcery had given way to more profitable and more businesslike ventures. This had left the city shorthanded. They were going to have to rely on mostly mundane defenses.

Jair craned his neck to look for his friends along the wall. Rakkon and Kethok were placed farther east, to help repel the invaders in that section. Rakkon had his axe out and Kethok had prepared several large boulders that he was going to hurl at the enemy. While watching Kethok practice the night before, they had found that he could throw them with great accuracy.

Tagor had been placed at Jair's side, in order to use his bow and protect on of their few magic users. Jair felt more comfortable with his friend nearby. If the coming battle was to be anything like he thought, he felt more confident with Tagor close by.

During the night, the general had met with the city council and had argued about what needed to be done. They had discussed it until the first light of day. The general wanted the city to be evacuated immediately, but the stubborn city council thought they could hold out indefinitely.

He finally convinced them with all of the overwhelming

evidence they had and with what they were facing. The council finally started making plans for evacuating all of the civilians.

The council planned to use a series of escape tunnels and passageways. They had been dug hundreds of years ago when the city had first been built. These passageways had been all but forgotten until Jair and his companions had stumbled onto the old wizard's lair beneath the library. Further exploration beneath the library had revealed several other tunnels that led outside of the city.

Jair came out of his reverie and glanced around at the other soldiers upon the wall. Nervousness was coursing through the troops from movement that could be seen on the other side of the enemy camp.

Jair strained his eyes and picked out a long column of marching troops. He watched them as they broke through the ringing forest and began to merge with the other troops. He was able to pick out several different races. The Dark Lord had a wide range of creatures that served him.

The non-humanoid troops were sectioned off by themselves, as were the goblins, ogres, trolls, orcs and giants. They were kept away from the dark elves and dwarves. Even though they were all evil creatures under the influence of one leader, they still did not get along very well with each other for long periods time. Jair knew it was critical for the Dark Lord to keep his forces unified, and to keep them from killing each other before they accomplished their goals.

As Jair watched the new forces in silence, a terrible dread came over him. He glanced around to see if the other soldiers felt it too. As he did so, a large shadow passed over the wall. A cold chill to ran down his spine as it went by.

He heard several clangs as a couple of soldiers dropped their weapons and cried out in fear. A giant, bat-winged shape passed over. Jair heard a whispered "dragon!" from somewhere as he craned his head to see what it was that had made such a commotion among the well-trained soldiers.

He glanced up and spied a large red shape as it came out of the clouds and glided out over the sloping fields. It was a dragon and it was immense. It was over sixty feet in length from its scaly snout to its pointy tail.

Large, round scales covered it's bulbous body and sharp ivory teeth jutted out of its long, narrow maw. Smoke streamed from the creature's large, flaring nostrils as it flew over the massing army below.

As Jair watched the sky, two more floating shapes joined the first dragon. They soared casually above the gathering army of darkness. One of the other dragons was red like the first, but the second was as black as night. It looked like a giant, leathery bat that was winging its way across the early morning sky.

Jair let out a gasp when he realized he had been holding his breath. It was horrifying and fascinating at the same time, watching the giant, winged lizards flying above them. Fear and awe passed over him while he witnessed the dragons.

Jair looked at Tagor and gave him a questioning glance. In return, Tagor only set his jaw and shrugged his shoulders with a determined look of defiance.

As the army below grew, orders started being passed down among the elven officers. Preparations were being made for the impending attack. Jair and the other soldiers waited patiently throughout the day, watching in silence as their forces grew. Many of the elven troops tried to relax, but little rest was had by anyone. By the end of the day, the Dark Lord's troops all seemed to be gathered around the city. It was only a matter of time until they began to attack.

The Ruby Helmet

Several large groups of the enemy had entered the woods and began cutting trees to construct battering rams, siege towers, and catapults during. Jair could see the preparations that were being made as the people in the city waited.

The Dark Lord's army completely covered the fields around them. It was an impressive sight. They numbered more than eighty thousand. There were more than the general's scouts had first estimated. The Dark Lord's forces completely surrounded the elven city, cutting them off from the outside.

As the day drew to a close, Jair and his companions were relieved from their posts and allowed time to rest and get something to eat. Earlier that morning, before they had been taken to the walls, they had returned to the inn where the rest of their belongings had been.

While the others gathered their things, Tagor went to tell the innkeeper that they were leaving to fight on the walls. When Tagor had found him, the innkeeper was gathering his valuables and was preparing to flee the city.

The innkeeper waved to them a final farewell and wished them good luck. He then went back to rushing about, gathering as many of his belongings as he could before leaving. Having heard what the companions had done the previous night, he was nicer to them than he'd been when they had first met.

They worked their way back through the city to the walls. They made it to the barracks, where they had been given lockers for their things. Each of them had been given a cot, except for Kethok, who was too large to sleep on them. He'd had to sleep on the floor.

Jair laid down his satchel with the helmet. He had continued to carry it with him everywhere he went. Tagor, Rakkon and Kethok pulled up chairs around a table and sat. They ate a few of their iron rations while they relaxed.

They were allowed a few hours of rest, and then rose early the next morning so they could return to the walls. It was well before dawn when they got up. As they were getting ready to leave a messenger entered their barracks and came up to Tagor. "Sir Tagor, General Illithian has ordered you and your companions to meet with him in the war room, above the guardhouse. If you will follow me." The soldier said as he motioned with a sweep of his hand toward the door.

Tagor picked up his bow and motioned for the others to follow as the young man led them to the war room.

They climbed the stairway into the upper chamber of the guardhouse. The soldier led them to a large, wooden door. He knocked three times and waited until the door opened. Another soldier ushered them in.

Once inside, Jair could see that all of the top officers, the city council and General Illithian were present. The only person missing was the elven king. The general's armor had been cleaned and he looked as if he had bathed. The tired look still remained in his somber, gray eyes. The general motioned for them all to take a seat. Then he spoke. "Tagor, Jair, Rakkon & Kethok," the general said while pointing to each of them. "The king has asked you here for a very important mission. With the breaking of the dawn today we are expecting the enemy to attack. Before this happens we would like to have as many of our citizens as far away from the city as possible."

"As you know, the tunnels beneath the city have been collapsed or recaptured from the dark elf forces. The tunnels that were found lead to several places outside of the city. We believe that one of the tunnels comes out at the hills to the west of the city. They have not all been fully explored however. From studying ancient manuscripts and plans to the city, we believe these tunnels can lead our people to freedom. The king is currently overseeing the preparations."

The general's face grew very serious while he continued. "This is what we would like you to do."

"We know that it is a risk, but under the present circumstances, it would seem that we have no choice. By the end of the day today or possibly by tomorrow, the enemy will have attacked and start to overrun the city. It is our hope that you, as emissaries from the humans, will be able to get our people to safety and lobby the humans to help us fight." The general said while looking at each of the companions.

"If you will do this for us, we would be deeply grateful and in your debt. It would also mean your freedom from certain death if you remain in the city and save a lot of innocent lives." The general said.

Jair listened to the general and what he was asking them. He knew it was the most important thing he would ever do. More important that finding out about the helmet, or even finding out who his father had been.

Jair looked at Tagor, Rakkon and Kethok, and then looked back at the general and the other people in the room. The look on their faces was tired, worried and concerned. He came to a decision, and stood up and spoke.

"General, I can not speak for my friends, but I will help lead your people to safety."

Jair was amazed at the words coming out of his mouth. A year ago he would not have believed he would stand before Silvermist's high elven council. Nor would he have believed he would be asked to lead their people to safety.

After Jair spoke, he heard Tagor and Rakkon say that they too would help. Jair looked at Kethok who was nodding his head. He read the message of agreement and encouragement signed to him by his large friend.

The expression on the general's face turned to one of determination and relief at their response. The mood in the room changed from nervousness to tired relief.

"I and my people thank you all. Now if you will turn your attention to these maps, I will show you the most likely path," the general stated.

He then pointed to a series of small maps that were lying on the table. Several council members and officers gathered around with the rest of the group to listen and make suggestions.

They were to take a small patrol of the city's soldiers and lead the rest of the citizens through the tunnels. The general made an estimation that was based on the way the maps were drawn. He guessed they would emerge somewhere just southwest of the city, in a small hilly region in the nearby forest.

From there the companions were to lead the refugees through the forest and head for Fort Decadse. There they hoped the humans would help and protect them.

Jair looked up from the maps as he thought of a question. He asked the general, "Why don't we take the people into the southern forest and ask for the aid of the woodland elves?"

The general replied, "The wood elves have not been very friendly to us for the last few centuries. They keep mostly to themselves. Even if we were to lead the people into their part of the forest, it is unlikely we would find enough of them to help us. As far as we know, they do not have anywhere large enough to support our people. The wood elves live in the wilderness and in the trees. They would have no place to hide or protect us."

"The wood elves are a very strange people and tend to stay away from the rest of the world. The only way to bring them out is to enter their forest in large numbers, or to start destroying the trees.

I fear it will only be when the Dark Lord's minions enter their forest will they try to put up a defense." The general stated.

Jair nodded his head in understanding. He bent his head back to the maps. After going over what was to be required of them, he did not think it looked as if it was going to be all that difficult.

The general anticipated Jair's thoughts and said, "Making plans and seeing what is before you is two different things. The tunnels are mostly unexplored, so we do not know what might be in them. Nor do we know if they are even passable. It is also going to be slow work. It will be a large number of women, children, elderly and wounded. Do not get any ideas that this is going to be an easy trip." The general told Jair with a smile.

The general's words sank in. Jair considered his statement and realized this could be difficult indeed. He looked at Tagor and swallowing hard, then said, "Well general, when do we leave?"

"Hopefully within the hour," he replied. "The main tunnel led some of my men to a larger opening that is in the town square. It is from there that you will depart. Your squadron is ready and fully equipped with a weeks rations and supplies. I wish you all the best of luck."

Jair and his companions rose to leave. Many of the council members left in order to help organize the group of refugees. The general rose to depart for the walls.

Before the general left, Jair caught his attention and asked him, "General, after we are clear of the city, how are you and your men going to escape?"

"The people's safety is my main concern. If we can, we will try to retreat through the tunnels. Until that time comes, we will stay and fight to give you time to escape."

The general shook Jair's hand and added another, "Good

Luck." He then turned and left. Jair turned back toward his companions, who were waiting for him to one side of the chamber.

"Well Tagor, do you think we have a good chance of making it?" Jair asked him.

"I suppose," Tagor replied. "As good as any."

"We can handle anything that gets in our way." Rakkon stated in his deep voice. Failure was not an option for him. Jair didn't think he was afraid of anything.

Kethok placed a large hand on Jair's shoulder, nodding once at him to let him know he supported his decision to help.

Jair led the way out as they headed for the city square. The snow had melted quite a bit so they walked through a lot of muck. When they arrived at the square, the sun was just beginning to rise behind the clouds.

Jair and his companions saw that thousands of people had already gathered. There were even more people heading that way. At the center of the square there was a large fountain, with several statues of the city's founding fathers along its outer edge. The water had been turned off and the statues had been moved to one side. It revealed a large opening in the center of the square. A road sloped down into the opening. It was large enough to allow horses and small wagons.

As Jair and his companions worked their way through the crowd toward the opening, they could see that many people were already heading down into the tunnel. They all carried what few belongings they could.

Jair gently pushing his way past several of the older elves. They were waiting to enter the tunnel. He glanced back to make sure his friends were still following him. He heard a fearful gasp from several in the crowd as Kethok came into view. Everyone had not heard about Jair and his friends. The crowd parted quickly, making room for the giant.

Jair tried to calm their fears. He stopped and called out, "Do not be afraid, Kethok is our friend and has come to help us make our way through the tunnels."

Jair shouted as loud as he could, but the noise coming from the din of the crowd drowned him out. Fearing that the elven people might panic, Jair motioned for Rakkon and Tagor to help him try and calm them down.

The trio tried to gain the crowd's attention, but made no progress. A small group of armed soldiers then entered the crowd and surrounded Kethok with their weapons drawn.

Jair quickly ran to the aid of his friend, waving his hands to gain the soldiers attention. "Do not attack our friend, he means you no harm." Jair yelled to the soldiers.

The only officer with the group bared his sword and asked. "Who are you and why is there a hill giant in the city?"

"I am Jair of the Barnook forest and these our my friends. General Illithian has asked us to lead the people through the tunnels and to the safety of Fort Decadse." Jair replied.

Jair withdrew a piece of parchment with the city council's seal on it. He handed it to the officer and waited for him to read it. The letter had been given to Jair as he had left the council meeting. They had given it to him in case he met with any resistance.

After reading the letter, the soldier folded it and handed it back to Jair. He paused to salute him, and then put his sword back in its scabbard. He then turned to face his men and the people in the crowd, waving at them and shouting for them to be quiet.

He waited for the crowd to subside and said, "General Illithian has personally commanded that these men lead the escape from the city. The giant is a friend and has already proven his worth in combat in defense of our city. Now, if you will all cooperate we will continue entering the tunnel."

The soldier motioned for Jair to take the lead. He and most of his men followed them into the tunnel. They left a couple of soldiers to help make sure everyone made it down safely and they were to bring up the rear. When they arrived at the bottom, Jair found that the largest part of the refugees were already there. He had to squeeze by them in order to reach the other end, which took a while. There were tens of thousands of people in the large tunnel.

It was cold and damp in the tunnel, just like the ones they had been in two nights earlier. Torches lined the walls in various places or were held by refugees.

As he passed the long line of people, Jair could see their scared expressions. Fear and hope were on their faces. The crowd was made up of all types of people, most of whom were elven. Only a few were human, dwarf or halfling.

It was ironic that a half-elf, two humans and a hill giant should lead the majority of the high elven people to their freedom.

Once they came to the end of the group, Jair waited for the soldiers to catch up. Presently, the officer and several of his soldiers filed passed the crowd to stand beside him.

Jair thought he'd better introduce everyone. "Sergeant, this is Tagor, Rakkon and Kethok."

The sergeant replied dryly. "I am Sergeant El Kestolin of the 22nd Green Corps. My men and I are at your disposal."

Jair looked at Tagor and Rakkon after the sergeant's curt reply, Jair saw that they too had noticed the sergeants dislike of the situation. Jair thought about it a moment and realized that the young officer was sore at having to lead a band of refugees, while the rest of the army stayed behind to defend the city.

Feeling a little bit of empathy toward him, Jair let it pass and turned his attention to the work at hand.

"Well sergeant, I suggest you disperse the rest of your men in groups of twos along the line of refugees. Leave four with us in case we run into trouble ahead. You can take the rear in case we are followed or set upon from behind."

He saluted Jair, then turned and picked out four men to leave behind. He motioned for the rest of his men to follow him and set off back through the crowd.

Jair looked to Tagor for encouragement. He then set his shoulders and addressed the crowd. He raised his voice so as many people as possible could hear him. He then shouted; "Quiet please! Would everyone please be quiet?"

Jair waited for a moment to let the people settle down. He then spoke to them. "The High Council has asked us to lead you through the tunnels, to safety in the forest beyond and then on to Fort Decadse. During this time I must ask for your complete cooperation if we are going to make it safely through. Our greatest ally will be speed to reach the forest before the Dark Lord's forces enter the city and find that we have escaped." He said seriously.

"Please gather your belongings. We will leave in a few minutes. Pass the word."

Jair then turned back to face his friends. From behind him Jair heard some whispers that cut him like a knife. One voice said, "Who would of ever thought that the General and Council would put a half-elf in charge of us. Have our people sunk so low?"

He glanced over his shoulder and started to reply, but was cut off by another, softer voice that said, "How could you be so cruel to someone you do not know. We should judge a person by their actions, not by looks. It is through one's heart that honor is found."

Jair turned to see who it was that had come to his defense. A young lady elf stepped into the light of one of the nearby torches. Jair instantly recognized the lady as the one that had sung so wonderfully at the inn just a few nights before.

He waited for her to walk over. He blushed and stammered a little as he said, "Thank you for being so kind, but it is not necessary. I am use to it."

She looked up at him with tender blue eyes and replied, "No, it is not all right. We should judge a person for who they are, not what they look like."

Jair smiled at her and said, "I'm Jair."

"I am Shealandra." The girl replied with a smile. She then turned back to re-enter the throng. Jair gently caught her by the arm before she could leave and said, "If you need anything, just ask for me."

She smiled at him over her shoulder, and replied, "Thank you." Then she disappeared back into the crowd.

Tagor had a look of admiration and amusement on his face at how well Jair had taken up the role of leader. He also saw how uncomfortable Jair felt around the young lady.

"Well, it seems you have things under control for the moment. I hope they go as well along the way as they have at the beginning." Tagor told him while slapping him on the back in a friendly manner.

Jair looked into the crowd of fearful and expectant people, and then motioned for them to move out. There were a lot of lives depending on them. As they started moving down the tunnel, Jair hoped he would prove himself worthy of their trust.

Chapter 21

The sun cast a gloomy light as it rose above the infested land surrounding Silvermist. General Illithian stood atop the battlements, glaring down at the enemy.

With the rising of the sun the city had found the enemy set for battle. Their dark banners fluttered in the smoke and wind as they marched toward the city. Rows upon rows of tightly packed monsters set together in rugged formations crept toward the city's walls. They marched to the even beat of large, heavy drums. Within the enemy's ranks the general saw the many kinds of horrible men and monsters that were mixed together. It was hard to believe that the Dark Lord had been able to get that many different races to work together.

The majority of the army was made up of humanoids, like dark elves, dwarves and human mercenaries. There were also a large number of monsters. Goblins, orcs, and human made up the front line of infantry. Behind them came the dark elf archers and magic users. The dark dwarves manned the catapults, ballista and siege engines.

Scattered throughout were various monsters such as trolls, ogres, giants and bugbears. Their numbers were few, but their impact was great due to their size and ferocity.

Behind the elven archers and magic users were the heavy infantry. It consisted of five thousand fully armored human knights. Their leader was a giant figure in black plate mail armor. A gruesome helmet sat atop his head, completely covering his face.

As the enemy slowly marched toward the city, the three dragons lifted off the ground and soared into the sky. Two hundred harpies and a thousand giant bats followed the dragons into the air. The sky was quickly filled with them soaring around in varying formations.

General Illithian stared in awe and wonder at the sheer magnitude of the evil the Dark Lord had gathered. Within the city the general's forces were prepared for battle. The general hoped that Jair and his friends had led the city's people far away. The conflict that was about to begin was going to be terrible, and his major concern was the safety of the people.

Most of the bodies had been removed from the base of the walls. Many had been burned by the general's troops the day before. All available forces lined the parapets waiting for the main assault. The city's most powerful sorcerers were also scattered along the towers and walls with their spells prepared. They had a dozen griffins with wizards riding on them. They would fly up to meet the airborne enemy.

Archers, catapults and giant scorpions lay in wait among the city's defenders. They were all fully loaded with steel tipped arrows and heavy iron bolts. The missile weapons were to be used to help repel the invaders from the air. The city's sorcerers had also put spells on some of the magical bolts. They hoped to take out as many of the flying enemy as possible. A few of the archers even had magic arrows that were supposed to be able to penetrate a dragon's tough hide. The general had doubts as to whether or not the magic arrows would work. One of their wizards thought she could cast a spell to call for help from creatures in the surrounding forest. He hoped it worked.

The general looked about and reviewed his troops. He then stood back and waited for the assault to begin. If all went well they should hold the city for a day, maybe two. They would kill as many of the enemy as possible before withdrawing to the tunnels.

The primary concern was to hold the walls long enough to give the fugitives time to escape. However futile it may seem, the general still had hope that he and his men could hold the walls until help arrived or the people all escaped. He did not believe that the humans would help them. He knew the chances of that happening were very slim. They didn't even know if there was anyone out there that would help.

He stared down at the oncoming forces and waited patiently until they came to a spot, about a hundred yards from the front gate. The large warrior in black armor rode to the front of the long rows of evil minion. He stopped a few yards from the city's wall, a short distance from where General Illithian's position was above the gate.

The warrior removed his helmet after pausing for a few moments. General Illithian strained his eyes in the hazy morning gloom to try to make out his features.

The general noted that he was very large, probably standing over seven feet tall. His hair was long and black. He had it pulled back tight behind his head where it was tied into a long, wavy tail. It hung down to the middle of his back.

His features were dark and ominous, with thick black eyebrows drawn together above dirty gray eyes. His nose was broad and angular. It stuck out over a thick, black handlebar mustache that dangled down on each side of his angry mouth.

Several old scars crisscrossed his features, lending to the man's viscous countenance. He had on heavy black armor and wore a wicked looking broadsword at his hip.

The general looked at the sword and thought he recognized its markings. He'd seen drawings of it in old history books. It was a thing out of legend.

The large warrior looked up at the elven warriors that lined the city's walls and spoke. "I am General Deshtar, high commander of the army of the great Lord Telenok. It is Lord Telenok's wish that we grant you the opportunity to surrender this city in his name. If you do not choose to surrender, I will take it by force and we will give no quarter. What is your reply?"

General Illithian glared down at Deshtar. He was about to speak when someone placed a hand on his shoulder, stopping him. When he turned around he found the elven king. He was wearing his royal armor and carried the ancient sword of elven kings. It was a sword that had served their kings for many generations.

He looked proudly into the general's eyes and said, "If you don't mind general, I believe I will take it from here."

The general bowed and then backed away. He motioned for the elven king to step forward. The king did so and looked down upon the field, facing the enemy.

"I am Stelenost te Aranesh, king of Silvermist. Our response to your demand is that you can try and take our city, but you will pay the price in blood. We will cut you from our walls and crush you back into the ground from which you crawled!"

General Deshtar grinned evilly up at the elven king from atop his giant, black horse's back. He reached down and drew his weapon, raising it above his head. "So be it. By Kethelnard's might I will take great pleasure in killing you personally after we have leveled these walls and entered your precious city as conquerors. Prepare to die!"

Deshtar placed his helmet back atop his head and turned his mount around. He retreated to a position behind the front lines where he paused for a few moments to let the tension build. He watched his minions seethe with anxious energy, and generations of hate for the elves. He then gave the signal to begin the attack.

In a surging rush the Dark Lord's minions charged toward the city. Hate filled eyes glared evilly toward the waiting elves as the evil creatures charged in a surging mass. Hundred's fell to the high elf arrows that began to rain down upon them from atop the walls. They fired in ordered rounds as the General commanded.

The Ruby Helmet

When Deshtar had drawn his sword and said its name, Illithian had a cold chill run down his spine. The name was familiar to him because it was the name of the fabled magical sword Kethelnard, supposedly made by the first high wizard of the white robes.

This was not a good thing. That sword should not have been in the hands of someone evil like Deshtar. General Illithian drew his own long sword and prepared for battle. There must be powerful magic at work here for an evil person to be able to wield a good sword.

As the evil forces reached the walls, the General gave the order for their archers to begin firing at will into the horde below. Scores of orcs, goblins, humans and other vile creatures fell to the terrible onslaught.

Bodies toppled to the ground only to be trampled by their evil comrades, who hurried on in their evil frenzy for blood. Even with the constant downpour of arrows, the horde moved forward. They did not even seem to slow.

Once they arrived at the walls, they began raising ladders and releasing grapple hooks. Many raced to reach the top of the walls, where the defenders scurried to repel them. Catapults began hurtling large stones and flaming balls of fire.

After waiting for the ground forces to reach the walls, the aerial minions began their attack. The three huge dragons soared across the sky. They dropped down and skirted along the tops of the walls.

As they passed by, the red dragons let go with bursts of glowing orange and yellow spittle. Flames showered the elves along the walls, killing many instantly. As they flew by, spewing their fiery death, charred and burning elves toppled and rolled to the ground. Many were left screaming in agony.

The large black dragon followed the others and spit large

streams of acid. It seemed to burn through everything, including the elves armor.

Along with the dragons, the Dark Lord's harpies and giant bat swooped down upon the elves. They dove in, swiping at the heads and arms of the elves as they tried to defend against them. Many men fell from the walls to their death amidst the surging horde below the walls.

The elven archers also took a toll, striking down many harpies and bats. They pierced their flesh with their well-crafted, barbed arrows. The evil creatures continued to fall from the sky as the elves poured it on them.

As the evil forces attacked the walls, the defenders took a heavy toll among their ranks. Bodies stacked up into large piles at the base. This ironically gave the on-coming attackers a ramp with which to climb upon. The immense siege towers then moved forward. They reached for the walls so their evil forces could swarm over them.

The king fought valiantly along side of his solders, raising their spirits. The royal guard surrounded him as he fought. They did their best to protect him.

Throughout the morning the battle waged on with both sides taking terrible losses. Through the initial onslaught of the Dark Lord's forces, the elves cut a great swath through their ranks, but did not stop them. Wizards fighting on both sides lit the sky with spells. Fireballs and lightning, ice storms and magic missiles streaked everywhere, adding to the chaos.

Several of the elven wizards soared into the sky using magical spells or devises to lift them. The wizards on griffin back went after the dragons and tried to hold them at bay so that they could not wreak too much havoc among the troops along the walls. They were having enough trouble keeping the Dark Lord's forces from coming through the main gate.

Two of the siege towers were set on fire. The towers had been covered with thick animal hides and had been soaked with water to try to keep them from burning. Not much could stop wizard fire however.

Catapults continued to fling their projectiles toward the walls, sometimes taking out troops on both sides in the confusion.

By the end of the day, the Dark Lord's forces finally retreated. They withdrew as the sun went down. The clouds had broken slightly with the growing darkness, allowing just a little bit of sunlight to fall upon the fields and battlements. It was a grim scene that was revealed.

Illithian laid his sword down beside one of the large stone merlons that were on top of the city's walls. He rested for a moment as he watched the enemy withdraw.

He looked around him and took in the gruesome sight of the wreckage that the day's battle had left behind. Almost half of his men were dead with their bodies strewn all about. A third of his men were severely wounded, and most of his sorcerers had been killed. This only left a handful to try to fend off their attackers on the morrow.

Clerics and healers rushed about, trying to save as many lives as possible. Their task was a grim but determined one.

General Illithian gazed down upon the retreating horde and wondered at their persistence. Even though he and his men had taken a great toll, they still more than tripled his remaining forces. They had managed to kill one of the red dragons and wound the black one.

The Dark Lord must have very powerful magic indeed if he could gather this great of a horde of evil creatures that would unite and do his bidding. If the evil forces continued to grow, then it might be possible for the Dark Lord to conquer the world. That was of course unless the other kingdoms could unite to try and stop him. If that didn't happened, the general thought it would be impossible to stop him.

The general picked up his sword, then turned and started down the stone stairway that led into the guardhouse. He passed several officers and men, who all saluted. They were honored to be serving under him. The king was waiting for him as he entered the guardhouse. He had a terrible wound in his side that two clerics were attending to. The general had heard that the king had fought well.

"I am afraid you will have to take over for me general. These two tell me I will not be able to participate in the next round." The king said through clenched teeth as a cleric prodded his wound. Blood poured down his side as they removed his armor.

"It would be my honor my king. I live but to serve. I will do my best." The general replied.

The general then went over and took a seat at a nearby table, helping himself to something to drink and eat. He had slain more than a dozen invaders and had even killed an ogre single handedly. Only two of the Dark Lord's siege towers had made it to the walls. Two had almost been enough though. They had succeeded in taking two sections of the city's walls before the elves had thrown them back.

The siege engines had lumbered up to the walls, filled with assorted monsters. They were pulled by an assortment of trolls, ogres and giants. They dropped the heavy wooden door that also served as a bridge when the towers arrived at the walls. The enemy had rushed across the walkway and leapt amongst the elven defenders.

The defenders had used spears and pikes as well as they could. General Illithian had led an attack against one of the towers. His courage had helped the defenders to rally around him. He had fearlessly taken on a large ogre that had come out of the tower. His sword work had been so swift and skillful that the ogre hadn't been able to defend against it, even with its great size and strength. The general had cut him down.

The elves had battled heroically against the fearsome invaders as they poured out of the towers. They eventually turned them back, toppling the towers with a combination of magic and manpower.

They had lost a lot more men than the general had expected. He was sad and proud all at the same time. His elves had done more than he could have ever imagined possible.

As he sat thinking about the day, several elven officers came into the room. They bowed to the king, then came over and saluted the general. He motioned for them to be at ease and to take a seat. He then asked them to report.

One at a time the officers shared their information on the amount of damage and losses for the day. As the general had feared, more than half of their forces had been lost. All but a score of his sorcerers lay dead, and his clerics numbered but a handful. The archers had suffered the greatest loses due to their lighter armor and being primary targets. Most of his remaining troops were knights and foot soldiers.

The general gave some final orders then rested for a bit. His officers quickly left to carry out his orders. He tried to see to the needs of his men and made plans for a final stand. Hopefully they had bought his people enough time to reach their destination outside of the city.

The general's first officer, Chesier, came in and took a seat next to him. He reached for the water barrel and took a long drink from the dipper. He then poured water down his neck and over his face.

"Well General," Chesier said with exhaustion in his voice. "We've held out this long, what are your thoughts for the morrow?" He asked him.

The general looked at his first officer, then he smiled slightly as he responded. "Tomorrow we fight until we can fight no more. Every second we can delay the enemy from finding out about the tunnel is a second they are further away from here," The general replied.

"Tomorrow they will throw everything they have at us, and we will not be able to hold them back. The dragons have taken a terrible toll on our forces and we have no way to stop them. Most of our wizards are dead. Half our troops are gone. All we can do now is hold out a little longer. Then whoever is left will retreat," The general said.

Chesier nodded his head and took another drink of water from a glass he had filled. He looked at the general, refilled his cup, then held it up and said, "To Silvermist, may her walls shine as bright as the sun, and may her people live forever," He said in a toast.

The general raised his glass in return, and then drained it quickly. He set it down upon the table and rose. He motioned for Chesier to follow him as he walked back out into the chilly night to see to the last of their defenses.

As they walked, General Illithian thought to himself, it was going to be a grim day on the morrow. The Dark Lord's minions would probably be within the city's walls and the battle would be all but over. He hoped he had judged right in asking the young half-elf to lead his people to safety. There was something about the young man that the general trusted.

The Ruby Helmet

Epilogue

Jair and his friends, along with the elven soldiers, led the refugees at a brisk pace down the winding tunnel. The refugees slowly followed behind them. Throughout the first part of the morning they had not run into any trouble. So far the tunnel had been deserted, with only an occasional rodent to make any trouble.

Eventually the tunnel opened up into a larger chamber. Within the chamber were two more tunnels, each one leading in a different direction. Jair pulled out his map and examined it until he found the section he was looking for. He nodded to himself a few times, then refolded the map and placed it back in his satchel. He pointed at the tunnel on the right and said, "We go this way." Then started off down that tunnel.

So far the trip had been uneventful except for when they'd had to stop because an elderly woman had collapsed. Jair quickly had a litter built out of some spear poles and a couple of blankets. He then appointed a couple of elven boys to carry the woman.

As Jair led them down the dark, wet passageway, he thought he smelt something strange. He eventually held up a hand to alert the others that something was amiss and let them know to stop for the moment. Jair then motioned for his friends to come up to him.

Tagor and Rakkon reached Jair's side first, so he whispered to them, "Can you smell that?"

Tagor and Rakkon both paused for a moment while they sniffed at the air. They shook their heads negatively. Jair then looked to Kethok, who had also arrived. He took several large sniffs before he looked back at Jair and shook his head yes. He made several motions with his hands, signing to Jair that he smelt it too.

The four moved quietly into the tunnel, on the other side of the large chamber. Tagor and Rakkon both had their weapons drawn, just in case. Jair felt there was something wrong, but he couldn't put his finger on it.

The smell grew stronger the further down the tunnel they went. The smell grew so bad that after about two hundred yards, it was almost too much to bear. Jair reached into his satchel and removed a handkerchief that he tied over his face. Tagor and Rakkon both did likewise.

Jair looked at Kethok and noticed that he didn't bother to cover his nose. Evidently the smell didn't bother him as much as it did the others.

They continued on until the tunnel broadened into another larger chamber. Rakkon's torch barely lit the room. The four adventurers spread out to search the chamber.

It was probably two hundred feet across and a hundred and fifty feet wide. Its walls were straight and smooth, having been carved directly from the surrounding rock. Ten, huge, round columns rose up on either side to support the stone ceiling that rose up above them for around twenty feet.

At the far side, Jair could see that the tunnel continued on for a ways into the darkness. Between them and the tunnel exit was a large, round platform in the center of the room.

The platform was covered with large piles of old bones, clothing and an odd assortment of articles. Jair walked slowly over to it and reeled from the stench. He poked the end of his short sword into the pile. He raked them around and could see that there were many articles of clothing, jewelry, and a few rusted weapons in the pile. There were also many bones.

Most of the bones belong to small rodents and animals, but several were humanoid. Jair looked down at the refuse and could see that an odd ichor covered most of it. It seemed to be the source of the terrible stench they were experiencing.

"What do you make of this?" Jair asked the others in a low tone. Jair stepped closer to try and figure out what the substance was. His friends gathered around him.

"The bones look as if something digested them." Tagor said as he examined the remains. "They have been picked clean, not even leaving the marrow."

Rakkon finished looking at the remains, then stepped back and started looking around. "I think we had better get the people through here quickly. Whatever made this mess is probably going to be back, and we don't want to be here when it does." He said.

Jair nodded in agreement and turned and started to walk out of the chamber. As the others started to turn and follow him, Jair felt something touch his shoulder. He gasped with pain as he felt a burning sensation on his shoulder. He also felt a weight begin to settle on him from above.

Jair dropped to the floor and rolled to one side, then quickly came to his feet. The pain almost caused him to pass out. He glanced over to where he had just been standing and saw a huge green, slimy mass oozing onto the floor from the ceiling.

The green slime finished it's decent and settled to the floor. Jair took a few quick, deep breaths and glanced back over at his companions. They had stopped, just on the other side of the slime.

"Tagor, what is that?" Jair asked.

"I don't know. I've never seen anything like it," He replied.

As they spoke, the giant mass started quivering and then began oozing its way toward Jair. He backed up slowly and tried to think of a spell that might stop the moving mass of green slime. Nothing came to mind right away.

"Ahh, Tagor, do you guys think you could give me a hand here? It's got me cornered and I don't really care to be digested by a big green slime." Jair said.

Tagor didn't know what else to do so he charged forward, swinging his sword at the slime. He came to the back end of the creature and slashed downward, cutting into the mass. The force of his blow almost caused him to lose his balance. He almost fell into the slime when his sword passed right through it. His sword did not cause the creature any harm and struck the floor beneath it.

He jumped back just in time to avoid a pseudo pod of slime that had been snaking toward him. Tagor quickly backed away from the creature. Rakkon had an idea and thrust his torch toward the slime.

The creature was inching toward Jair again when Rakkon stuck the burning end of his torch into it. When the torch touched the rear of the creature, it shivered grotesquely and drew back the part that had been burned.

It sizzled loudly and gave off an even more terrible smell. The green slime hesitated in its movement toward Jair. This allowed him time to gather the components from his pouches to cast a spell.

Jair held out his hand and began to chant the mystic words. As he was casting, the air in the room began to grow colder. He said the final words, crumbled up the components that were in his hand and blew them at the creature.

From out of Jair's hand came the sound of a rushing wind and an icy cold blast struck the slime. It covered the entire creature for several moments.

After the ice blast struck the creature, it stopped moving altogether. Jair glanced at his friends before stepping forward to see if the creature was still alive.

He looked down at a frozen section of the slime and could see that it was quickly thawing out. As it thawed, the unfrozen section started to move, however slowly. Jair looked at his friends and asked, "Do either of you have a flask of oil in your pack?"

Rakkon nodded and removed his pack. He searched around in it for a moment and eventually found what he sought. He pulled his hand out of his pack, holding a small glass flask.

He threw the bottle to Jair who caught it deftly. Jair went back over to the quickly thawing creature. "My ice blast only slowed it down. If we hurry, I think we can burn it."

Jair pulled the cork out of the bottle with his teeth and started pouring oil all over the slime.

After he emptied the bottle, he motioned for Tagor to bring him his torch. Tagor walked toward the creature and motioned for Jair to get back as he neared it.

Tagor extended his torch and thrust it into the oil. Flames sprang up from the surface of the thawing slime. It had almost thawed out and was starting to move again. Heat and smoke quickly rose from the slime as the oil burst into flame and began to burn it.

It only took a few moments for the oil to catch and start burning the creature. The flames also helped thaw the creature out the rest of the way. Jair and his friends scrambled to safety at the other end of the chamber while the creature burned.

They watched from the other side of the room as the flames consumed the strange creature. Jair was fascinated at the site of the quivering, green mass that writhed upon the cavern floor. It did not take long for the creature to burn itself up. Jair waited until the last of the flames flickered out before going to investigate the remains.

He went over to the spot where the creature had been. Once there, he and the others could only find ashes and a dark oily substance. There was no other trace of the creature left. They then set off back up the tunnel to get the others and continue their journey.

Kethok eased up beside Jair and signed a question, asking about his injured shoulder. Jair reached up with one hand and felt the place where the creature had touched him. As he did so, searing pain lanced through his shoulder and down his arm again.

He peeled back his shirt that looked burned. He could see that the creature had exuded some sort of acid that had quickly eaten through his armor and into his shoulder.

When they got back to the awaiting refugees, many of them asked questions as to what had happened. Jair only waved them away. He then motioned for them all to continue down the tunnel.

As they moved on, Jair had Kethok remove the last bottle of healing from his pack. He handed it to Jair. As Jair drank, his shoulder stopped throbbing and when he checked, it was fully healed. The wound must have been fairly serious. Jair had to drink half of the potion to stop the spread of the acid and continuing burn.

Jair felt better and went to lead the refugees on down the tunnel. They went past where they had met the green slime. Everyone skirted the area where it had been burned.

They rested for a short time later that night. Jair estimated it was just getting to be dawn when he roused the people and started them all moving again.

He looked at the map and figured they should reach the end of the tunnel by mid-afternoon. He thought back on the day before and wondered how the general and his forces were holding up.

Thoughts of the Dark Lord's minions coming after them spurred Jair on. He tried to get a faster pace out of the refugees. Exhaustion set heavily on them as they tried to reach the light of day at the end of the tunnel.

A while later a commotion erupted from back in the tunnel, just as Jair thought they were getting close to the outside world.

Screams and other noises came from the refugees along the back of the line. Jair motioned for his friends to follow him and made his way back through the throng to see what was going on.

Once there they saw that several strange, moving shapes had separated the refugees. The shapes moved about in the darkness between the two groups.

One of the figures was huddled over a shape that was lying on the floor. The other one was walking slowly toward another figure that was also lying on the ground. To the far side of the tunnel another figure lay against the wall and several more were on the ground further down the tunnel. Jair ran over to get a closer look. He borrowed a torch from one of the human travelers that was mixed in with the crowd.

Jair drew back in fear when he got close enough to see what was happening. One of the creatures looked as if it used to be a human, the other was an elf. Both had a mottled gray skin that was covered with large holes and sores. The flesh dangled loosely from several places about their bodies, and their eyes were sunken or gone.

"These things are ghouls," Rakkon said as he stepped up beside Jair. "It looks like they have already some victims. We do not need to give them another."

Rakkon lifted his axe and started moving slowly forward to the left, trying to keep both of the creatures in front and to the side of him. Tagor eased his sword out of its sheath and moved around the same way.

Jair and Kethok both drew their weapons and started around to the right side of the ghouls. Both of the ghouls hissed loudly as the four tried to circle them. The one that was kneeling was eating the person it had killed, almost making Jair sick.

Jair gathered his courage and prepared himself to attack. Just as they were getting into position, the ghoul that was still standing rushed toward Rakkon. He cut at it, bringing his axe in low. The impact sent the creature reeling back. It then toppled forward in two pieces.

As the two pieces hit the floor, Jair could see they were both still moving. He watched the other ghoul out of the corner of his eye and saw Tagor step toward the first. He brought his holy symbol out from under his shirt. He then pressed it to the thrashing creature on the ground and uttered a few words of prayer. The symbol began to glow and smoke poured up from where it touched the ghoul.

After only a few seconds the creature burst into flames and after only a few minutes there was nothing left but ash. Meanwhile, the other ghoul felt the power of good emanating from the amulet and ceased its meal. It stood and lunged toward Tagor.

Kethok caught it. He swung his giant club, striking the ghoul in its stomach, throwing it back against the far wall. Tagor was quickly on it, pressing his holy symbol into its forehead.

As he pressed the symbol it glowed brightly again and burned into the creature's rotten flesh. Tagor said another prayer and stepped back. The second ghoul burst into flames and fell to the floor, leaving another heap of ashes.

Jair inspected the two figures on the ground and found that they were two of the guards sent to accompany them. Just as he was identifying the bodies, Sergeant El Kestolin came into view.

The sergeant took in the scene. "Ran into some undead?" He asked as he stepped over to the bodies. "Busleal and Herion. They were two of my best men," The sergeant said as he looked upon the mutilated bodies.

"There's nothing we can do for them now. They will have to be left behind," The sergeant said as he walked away.

Tagor stepped up to take his place. "He's wrong, there is something we can do. We must keep these dead from becoming like those others." He said nodding towards the ghoul's remains.

He pressed his holy symbol into each of the bodies' foreheads and uttered a prayer for each. He did this to keep them coming back to life as undead.

Jair had some of the others help him and set the bodies against the right wall. He then went back to the front of the group. He tried to reassure everyone along the way that everything was all right. They had lost five in all.

Jair set off once again, leading the refugees. They traveled on for the rest of the morning until they finally came to a small chamber. The other side was completely bricked up.

Jair went over and examined the wall. He then looked to Tagor and Rakkon for advice. Tagor and Rakkon both went over to also examine the wall.

Tagor placed one hand on the cold bricks and started running his hand along the surface. He stopped when he found something and put his face close to the wall's surface.

"Fresh air is coming in through these gaps." Tagor said as he stepped back and motioned for Kethok to come forward.

"Kethok, do you think you can put a hole in this with your club?" He asked him.

Kethok nodded, glad to finally having something else to do. He spread his legs and braced himself. The others backed away to give him some space.

Kethok raised his massive club and put both hands on it, then brought it back over his right shoulder. As he swung it toward the wall, it whistled as it flew through the air. He struck the wall sending large chunks of stone and mortar flying everywhere.

Through the hole Kethok made, sunlight filtered into the chamber along with fresh air. From behind him a cheer went up from the refugees that filled the room. Jair stepped through the opening and pushed aside vines that had grown over the wall and dangled down in front of the opening.

Once outside, Jair walked a little ways from the opening. When he stopped he could see that they had come out, just under a large oak tree on top of a small hill. Judging from the position of the sun that could barely be made out through the clouds, Jair determined that their position was somewhere just south and west of Silvermist.

Jair climbed up to the top of the hill and placed one hand over his eyes to shade them from the few beams of light that had peeked out through the clouds. He spotted something to the north and focused on it. He realized it was large columns of smoke drifting into the sky.

Jair heard someone come up behind him. He looked back to see that some of the elven people had made it out of the tunnel and were now filing out behind him. He pointed in the direction of Silvermist and a small cry of despair went out from many of the people.

"I think the city has fallen." Jair said to them as they watched the thick columns of black smoke rise into the late afternoon sky.

"We will have to keep moving if we are going to reach the fort ahead of them," Jair said sadly. "We cannot let their deaths be for nothing. We must warn the other nations and try to convince them of the Dark Lord's threat."

Anger and frustration built up inside of Jair as he looked at the smoke. He clenched his fists. From beside him he felt a small, soft hand touch one of his and force his fist to open so that it could clasp his.

Jair turned to see whom it was and looked into the sad, beautiful eyes of Shealandra. Tears flowed down her cheeks.

"Do not let your anger overcome you." She said to him. "You should rejoice that the people of Silvermist are alive and safe. As long as that holds true, there is always hope."

Jair smiled at her and tried to let his anger go. He soaked up the beauty of her smiling face. He glanced about and looked into some of the faces that were surrounding him.

He felt a renewed sense of hope and purpose. He led Shealandra, his friends and the remainder of the elven people down the hill and into the forest. They had made it safely out of the besieged city, but still had a long way to go before they were safe.

The only other comfort Jair had was the fact that he was carrying something in his old satchel that might be able to help defeat the Dark Lord. Only a few people knew what he carried and what it could do. They would have to be careful not to let anyone else find out about it.

Jair knew it would not take long for the Dark Lord's forces to discover they had been cheated. He also knew the Dark Lord would send his troops after them as fast as possible. The only edge they had was that the Dark Lord's forces would want to sack and pillage the city before moving on. Jair and the refugees had at least a full days head start. Moving that many people however was a slow process.

He hoped the general and most of the elven troops had

survived and found a way out of the city before being overrun. The refugees could really use their help in reaching their destination.

Jair realized that all of the things he had been through over the last year had really changed him. The once shy, timid young half-elf had come a long way. A lot had happened to him since he had run away from his cruel master. The young man that strode into the woods leading the large group of refugees was not the same one that had fled Bardor Keep. He was now an apprentice warrior and wizard and was confident in his own abilities.

With his courageous friends and the beautiful elven lady by his side, Jair led the refugees into the forest.

The End